ONE
CANDLE

Other Books by
GALE SEARS

The Silence of God

Belonging to Heaven

Letters in the Jade Dragon Box

Christmas for a Dollar

The Route

The Missing Christmas Treasure

The Autumn Sky trilogy
Autumn Sky
Until the Dawn
Upon the Mountains

ONE
CANDLE

a historical novel

GALE SEARS

**DESERET
BOOK**

Salt Lake City, Utah

Interior Images: keyplacement/Shutterstock.com and HN Works/Shutterstock.com

Visit us at DeseretBook.com

Library of Congress Cataloging-in-Publication Data

Names: Sears, Gale, author.
Title: One candle : a historical novel / Gale Sears.
Description: Salt Lake City, Utah : Deseret Book, [2018] | Includes bibliographical references.
Identifiers: LCCN 2017041040 | ISBN 9781629723945 (paperbound)
Subjects: LCSH: Waldenses—Fiction. | Mormon missionaries—Italy—Piedmont—Fiction. | Mormon converts—Italy—Piedmont—Fiction. | Piedmont (Italy), setting. | Eighteen forties, setting. | Eighteen fifties, setting. | LCGFT: Historical fiction.
Classification: LCC PS3619.E256 O54 2018 | DDC 813/.6—dc23
LC record available at https://lccn.loc.gov/2017041040

Printed in the United States of America
Edwards Brothers Malloy, Ann Arbor, MI

10   9   8   7   6   5   4   3   2   1

To George.
Hai reso il cammino una gioia.

To my forever family of Roma 3.
Vi voglio bene!

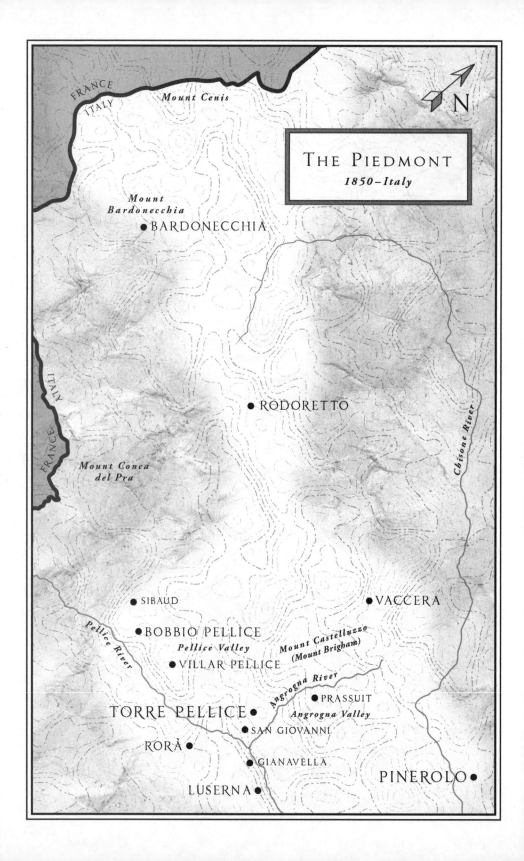

N

FRANCE
ITALY
Mount Cenis

THE PIEDMONT
1850–Italy

*Mount
Bardonecchia*
● BARDONECCHIA

FRANCE
ITALY

FRANCE
ITALY

● RODORETTO

*Mount Conca
del Pra*

Chisone River

● SIBAUD

● VACCERA

● BOBBIO PELLICE
Pellice Valley
*Mount Castelluzzo
(Mount Brigham)*

Pellice River

● VILLAR PELLICE

Angrogna River

● PRASSUIT

TORRE PELLICE ●
Angrogna Valley

● SAN GIOVANNI

RORÀ ●

● GIANAVELLA

PINEROLO ●

LUSERNA ●

PREFACE

In researching and writing books about pioneering individuals who have gone against their religious traditions or cultural norms, often stepping forward into unknown territory and its subsequent hardships, I have found myself challenged and uplifted. Such is the case with the characters living within the pages of *One Candle*: from the fearless Catholic reformer Peter Waldo, to the resolute missionaries of the fledgling Mormon Church, to the persecuted and visionary Waldenese of Northern Italy.

My journey began with an interest in the October 1849 call of Mormon Apostle Lorenzo Snow to preach the restored gospel of Jesus Christ to the people of Italy. He was accompanied by Joseph Toronto, a member of the Church originally from Sicily. Historical accounts of visions, miracles, and revelation surround their endeavors as they are led to an obscure Protestant enclave based in Northern Italy. These people were known as the Waldenese: followers of the Catholic reformer Peter Waldo (Valdo, Valdes, or Waldes). Although pockets of Waldensian faithful existed throughout Europe in the twelfth century, a large population found refuge from horrific persecution in the Alpine valleys of the Piedmont area of Northern Italy. (These people of faith were also called Vaudois or Albigenses.) Their founder, Peter Waldo, was a wealthy merchant of Lyon, France, who, in the twelfth century, gave away his possessions to live a life of poverty and commitment. He followed the example set by the apostles at the time of Christ. His followers became known as "The Poor Men of Lyon" and later as the Waldenese or Waldensians. Peter Waldo questioned many of the practices of the Catholic Church. He and his followers were later excommunicated from the Orthodox Church and treated as heretics because they became lay preachers (including women) who taught from the Bible and encouraged its reading by all. His break with the Catholic Church predated the reformation of Martin Luther by 300 years.

In the seventeen and eighteen hundreds, many followers of the Waldensian faith saw a departure from and diminishment of original dogma as taught by Peter Waldo, and were looking for a return to the doctrine and practices of the original Church of Jesus Christ. The 1850 arrival of Mormon missionaries onto Italy's shore, with claims of the restoration of the primitive Church of Christ, makes for an intriguing storyline.

CHAPTER ONE

Torre Pellice, The Piedmont, Italy

February 17, 1848

Perhaps he could chant a prayer to the Blessed Mother and she would warm the stone walls of his chamber and the ache in his hands would lessen. Perhaps the thin mattress on his bed would give some comfort and the stiffness in his back would drain away. Perhaps the kind sun would walk an unnatural course and slant through his window to dry the phlegm from his lungs. Perhaps. Or perhaps after eighty-one years of life, Father Andrew had learned not to expect.

The priest rolled onto his side, put his legs over the wood of the bed frame, and sat up. He opened his eyes, struggling to focus on something, anything: the wall with its crucifix, a rough-hewn chair and table, the nightstand with its tin cup and shallow food bowl. *Ah, my bowl.* He reached for it, fumbling at its edge a few times before his crooked fingers latched on. He drew it down beside his leg and banged it on the side of his bed. The sound echoed against the stone walls.

Andrew's mind went back seven decades to a voice and a place that would never leave his memory, to a name that hadn't belonged to him for a long time.

"Lucien Anton Guy! Put down those pots! They are for cooking, not noisemaking!"

"I am the Duke's lead man, Mama! I announce his coming!"

A slap on the side of his head.

"I will give you Duke Savoy. Give me those pots!"

"But Mama—"

Another slap, and an ear pull.

"Do you want supper or not?"

The pots are handed over.

"Now, go find your papa in the field and help him with the haying."

"May I take the mule?"

"You may take your legs . . . and a piece of bread."

"Really?"

"Yes. Go now, before I change my mind."

"Father Andrew?"

Did I close my eyes? He hadn't realized he'd closed his eyes. He opened them to look at the young priest in his dark cassock and smooth skin.

"I have emptied your chamber pot, and will now dress you and take you to morning prayers, honored one."

Father Andrew grunted. He was embarrassed by the young priest. What did he know, with his strong legs and perfect eyes? When Andrew was his age he had walked over the great mountains between France and the Duchy of Turin many times. He had written histories for the Duke of Venice. He had—

"Father?"

"Yes, yes, I heard you. It just takes time for my body to do what my mind is thinking."

The young priest chuckled. He finished latching the old priest's sandals, then grasped him around his upper arms and pulled him onto his feet. Andrew's nightdress bunched around his knees and he protested.

"Father Nathanael, the cloth! The cloth!"

The young priest untangled the fabric. "Better?"

"Tchet! That cloth is a demon."

Father Nathanael lifted the nightdress over Andrew's head. "A demon?"

"Yes, to hinder my progress."

"Nothing could hinder your progress, blessed one."

"Except an old body and an old mind."

"Your mind is a library."

"Full of dusty crumbling books."

With efficiency and respect, Father Nathanael dressed his superior, smoothing out the fabric of his cassock and placing the biretta on his head.

"Ready? The bells will be tolling soon."

Father Andrew nodded and inclined his body forward to begin the journey. The two men maneuvered the uneven stone floor, Father Nathanael matching Father Andrew's shuffling pace.

The bells will be tolling soon. It was a comfort. He loved the Offices of the Canonical Hours. They set a motion and an order to his life. When he was young, the held-to Breviary was not so dear; the bells only sounded in his ears. Now, his heart felt the thrum of devotion. Lauds, the first prayer of the day—the morning Office, was his favorite. He was fond of the evening prayers of Vespers—the lighting of the lamps, but the first gleam of dawn brought remembrance of Christ's Resurrection. Christ, the true light that comes to dispel spiritual darkness. The first thought of the day—God. The first act of the day—prayer.

"Tumble stone. Careful," Father Nathanael warned.

Father Andrew lifted his foot a little off the floor to avoid the hazard. He grunted. He had been down this hallway a thousand times . . . more. He did not need to be told how to keep his feet. Hadn't he crossed the daunting Alpine mountains? Hadn't he navigated the passes of Cenis, Conca del Prà, Bardoneccia—the high pass to his home in Lyon? Home to bury his father. Home again to bury his mother. Hadn't he traveled the valleys and challenged the mountains of the Piedmont from Torre Pellice to Vaccera and from there to

Rodoretto? His feet were the stones, his blood the rivers, his breath the very winds that blew through the thick pine forests.

Andrew stopped, placing his hand on the cold stone of the wall. *Those travels began sixty years ago. Sixty years.*

"Are you ailing, Father?"

"No, my son. I was walking."

"Walking?"

"In my mind—walking the mountainside."

"Ah."

They came to the chapel, and several of the priests, already in their places, nodded their heads in deference to Father Andrew.

He nodded back.

Father Pious stood and bowed low, placing his hand over his heart.

Father Andrew grunted and looked away as Father Nathanael led him to his place and covered his shoulders with his shawl. "Will you need help?" he whispered.

Andrew grinned. "Not today. Praise the Lord." The same question every morning, and the same answer.

The bells tolled and Andrew joined his voice to that of his brothers. "Praise ye the Lord. Praise ye the Lord from the heavens: praise him in the heights. Praise ye him, all his angels: praise ye him, all his hosts. Praise ye him, sun and moon; praise him, all ye stars of light."

Father Andrew had taken the thick spectacles from his eyes, laid down his pen, and abandoned the tall desk and stool for the comfortable chair by the library fire. The two younger priestly scribes had left hours before for prayers and other assignments, moving quietly past the sleeping legend so as not to disrupt his dreams. They wondered if his visions were of the Duke of Venice whom he had served or the thousands of pages of parchment that were inscribed with the perfection of his pen. If the two could have joined their mentor's mental wanderings they would have found him at his boyhood home, a simple farm on the outskirts of Lyon. Andrew smiled in his dreams. He liked to be home—home where he worked and played. Andrew saw himself sitting up high on a haystack, gazing intently at the distant mountains of the Savoy or Mont Blanc. He would dream of climbing those towering peaks to discover what was on the other side. His thoughts swirled to another scene as he watched his mother trap their prize white goose and pluck a tail feather. He saw his father laughingly take the quill and fashion it, removing the bottom fluff until only a flag of white remained at the top. His father winked at him as he took the knife and carefully trimmed and notched the quill tip. His father's large, weathered hands handed over the pen.

"Here, Lucien, a gift for your birthday."

His first pen. And his uncle Jacques from Paris had sent ink. It was on that day Lucien knew he would not share his father's life. He knew his younger brother, Tristan, would contentedly plow and harvest, but Lucien Anton Guy would live in words.

With the tolling of bells, his vision shifted to the city of Lyon. As a young man he stood inside the Cathédrale Saint Jean-Baptiste, watching the sunlight shimmer through the stained-glass windows. He wore the robes of a scholar, his hair long and tied back, his fingers permanently stained with ink. He was here to make a sacred decision, but . . . what was it? He could not think. His heart twisted in his chest and he felt a great weight on his shoulders. His knees buckled and he fell to the floor. The sound of bells drowned out thought and reason. He pressed his hands to his ears to block out the jangling in his head.

Father Andrew's mind lifted out of sleep. He frowned as his home and youth slid away. He opened his eyes and saw a blur of movement at the fireplace. He forced his eyes to focus and saw Father Nathanael placing a log onto the fire.

"What . . . what are those bells?" Andrew grumbled, struggling to sit straighter. "What time is it?"

"Four of the clock."

"It is not time for Vespers."

"No."

"Then why are our bells tolling?"

"They are not our bells. They are from the Waldensian temple."

"Why?"

Father Nathanael came to his side. "I do not know. But perhaps your visitors can tell you."

"Visitors?"

"Yes, I was just coming to wake you."

Andrew liked visitors. "Well, bring them in! Bring them in!"

Not as many important people came to see him now as used to come: the children of the Medici, bishops from far away, and men from the newly formed country of America. Now if he wanted to visit with his friends he must meet them in heaven.

"Uncle?" A lilting voice called.

Andrew squinted towards the doorway at the far end of the darkened library. All he saw were two small spots of light dancing in the gloom, then a halo of light illuminating an angel face. Andrew's heart jumped. "Mother?" The sound of tinkling laughter met his ear, and Andrew shook his head to clear his mind. "Ah, no! It is my Albertina! Albertina Marianella!" He saw his great-niece's face clearly now in the light of the fire.

Albertina set her candle on her great-uncle's work desk and took his wrinkled hands in hers. "I would need to be very old to be your mother." She laughed again and bent down to kiss both his cheeks.

"Ah! My old brain plays tricks sometimes." He turned his head as another young woman shyly approached. "And you have brought your friend Claire."

"Madeleine."

"Madeleine? Yes, yes, of course. How are you, Madeleine?"

Madeleine set her candle alongside Albertina's. "I am well, venerable father, thank you."

His brow furrowed as he thought—*My great-niece is fourteen . . .*

or is it fifteen? Her friend is close to that age. I have seen her before, but when? Where? Something to do with singing—

"Uncle?"

He looked up at his great-niece and saw Father Nathanael standing behind her. Andrew did not like the way the young priest was staring at him. "Stools! Bring some stools for the young ladies!"

"I've brought over the small ottomans. Will those do?" Father Nathanael said softly.

Father Andrew's bluster faded. "Yes. Good. Thank you." He looked at the girls. "Sit! Sit, sit!"

"You're like an old bear coming out of hibernation," Albertina said.

"Yes, true, true. But I will make it up to you with stories, and bread with currant jam." He looked at Father Nathanael, who nodded and left the room.

Albertina pulled her ottoman close so she could rest her hand on the arm of his chair.

Andrew looked at her fondly. *How could this delightful girl be the granddaughter of my brother, Tristan?* Tristan. He did not like his brother—a man of bitterness and unwarranted envy, who never embraced his life on the farm, or his wife, or his six children. Gratefully, Tristan's son Rene, the father of this beauty, was a source of redemption. As a young man Rene had left the farm at Lyon and walked over the great Alpine mountains to find his uncle.

"So what brings you to see me on this cold afternoon?" Father Andrew asked. "And how did you get here? There is deep snow on the ground."

"Madeleine's brother, Barthelemy, brought us in their work wagon." Albertina gave her great-uncle an encouraging look. "You remember. They are the children of Philippe Cardon, the stonemason, and he is the son of—"

"Of course!" Names and faces slid into place. "Of course! You are the granddaughter of my friend Jean Cardon! How foolish! Of course I know you. You and Albertina sang together in the district music competition at Pinerolo."

"That's right, Uncle!"

"And you won."

"Second place."

"Tchet! That other singer sounded like a screeching hinge."

The girls giggled behind their hands.

Ah, not completely women yet. "So where is your brother, Madeleine?"

Madeleine looked at her shoes, and Albertina answered. "Her brother does not . . . feel . . . comfortable in the monastery."

Father Andrew leaned forward and spoke softly to Madeleine. "You may not think I understand this, little daughter of the Waldenese, but I do. I know your stories. Your grandfather, Jean Cardon, came to me many years ago, and asked that I write down some of the memories of the people's lives and their persecution. He did not want the stories of the Waldenese to be lost to time or destroyed by enemies. He knew of my reputation and that my work would not be scrutinized. He trusted me with your history. That is how we became friends."

Her head came up, and she gave the old priest a narrow look. "But you are a Catholic priest."

"How old are you, Madeleine Cardon?"

"Fourteen."

He thought her brave for fourteen. "Yes, I am a Catholic priest, but before I became a priest I was a young man of the world. A scholar. A traveler. I learned languages and philosophy. I saw many acts of cowardice and bravery. I sank beneath the dark water of the world. Do you understand this?" Madeleine nodded. "And then I was lifted up, and I worked hard to discern truth from error and right from wrong." He gently took her hand. "And one of the many things I know is that the persecution suffered by your people is wrong, and has been wrong through all ages."

"See," Albertina said confidently, "I told you he would understand."

She turned to her uncle. "There is wonderful news, Uncle! Madeleine's grandfather wanted you to know, but was too feeble to come himself, so he sent us!"

Andrew sat back. "So, I am finally going to discover the reason for your visit?"

"Yes, Uncle! Yes! There is a great celebration going on in all the towns and villages of the Waldenese. Have you not heard the bells from their temple?"

"Yes. I hear them now."

"In all the valleys, high up into the heart of the alpine mountains, the people are singing and the bells are ringing!"

Andrew looked over at Madeleine. "And what is the cause for this celebrating?"

The young woman stood, her face shining in the light of the candles. "King Carlo Alberto has set down a constitution, and in it he recognizes the Waldenese as a free people—as citizens!" This last statement was said with a note of awe.

Father Andrew closed his eyes.

Albertina was instantly alert. "Are you well, Uncle?"

He patted her hand, but did not open his eyes. "Yes, my sweet Albertina. I am saying a prayer of gratitude for the brave action of the king of Piedmont-Sardinia."

"It *is* a brave action, isn't it? And it is right."

Andrew opened his eyes and smiled at his niece. "Yes, it is right." He looked at Madeleine. "You imagine that no one knows or cares about your people, but some of us do." He smiled at her. "King Carlo Alberto knows, and now your people will have more freedom—more freedom to come down out of the mountains, to live wherever you want."

"More freedom to speak out?" Madeleine asked.

Andrew nodded. "Yes, most assuredly. Freedom of conscience, freedom to worship."

"But not freedom to preach to others," Madeleine broke in.

Andrew hesitated. "No, probably not that, but still, a great oppression has been lifted from your people. Citizens! Just think of it! Freedom is a great thing." Tears jumped into Madeleine's eyes and she covered her face with her hands. "Here, here. Come here, little one. Come here."

Madeleine swiped the tears away with the palms of her hands and moved to the old priest. "And you are glad for us, even though you are . . . are a priest?"

"Yes. I am glad. No person of true faith would condone the history of injustice against your people. This edict from a Catholic king says much, does it not?"

Madeleine nodded.

Albertina put her arm around her friend's waist and beamed at her uncle. "Her grandfather said he would come to see you in a day or two for a lengthy discussion."

Father Andrew nodded. "Ah, good . . . good." He liked lengthy discussions with his friend.

The library door opened and Father Nathanael came in with a tray. He set it on one of the library's rustic wooden tables. "I've brought the bread, but I thought before eating, you may like to go out onto the balcony and see something."

"An interruption to our visit?" Andrew grumbled.

"You will like this interruption."

"Come on, old bear," Albertina said tenderly. "Let's go and see."

Father Nathanael helped him to stand, making sure he was steady, then placed a shawl around his shoulders. As the girls helped Father Andrew on either side, Father Nathanael preceded the three to the large carved doors that opened onto the balcony. He pushed against the accumulated snow, making room for the others to pass. A cacophony of joyous sound met their ears: cheers, shouts, singing. They stepped carefully through the few inches of snow to the stone railing.

The monastery sat on the mountainside, so their view was to the west where the winter sun was setting behind the distant Alpine peaks. The long shadows of night crept through the valleys, but where normally the hamlets and villages disappeared with the coming of dark, this night it seemed as though a thousand glowing stars winked through the pine trees.

"Ah!" the girls breathed out on a sigh.

Father Andrew squinted into the advancing dusk. "What? What is it?"

"A thousand torches, Uncle!"

"And many bonfires!" Madeleine added.

Andrew squinted again and saw glowing orbs flickering through the trees. And closer to them, in the streets of Torre Pellice, lights moving as people celebrated in the streets. "Ah! Beautiful!" he whispered.

"February 17. We will never forget this day," Madeleine said. "Never."

Father Andrew knew this was true. For generations, the children of the Waldenese would be joyous on this day of liberation. He breathed in the clean, cold winter air and adjusted the shawl around his shoulders. He saw the ink stains on his fingers, and smiled. *Nearly seven hundred years of oppression struck down by words.*

NOTES

The town of Torre Pellice, in the Piedmont area of Italy, was formally known as La Tour.

King Carlo Alberto was a member of the Savoy royal family and ruled the area of Piedmont-Sardinia from 1831 to 1849. He established a constitutional monarchy, and the 1848 constitution he set down was meant to be a standard for the eventual unifying of Italy, which, at the time, was a loosely woven group of city and papal states, the two kingdoms of Sicily, and areas ruled over by Austria. One of the things set down in the constitution was an allowance for greater freedom of worship for the Waldenese. King Carlo Alberto also declared them citizens of the state, thereby affording them recognition and security.

When Italy did unify in 1860, King Carlo Alberto's son Vittorio Emanuele II became its first king.

The 1848 constitution came only eighteen months prior to Brigham Young calling missionaries to labor in Italy.

Chapter Two

Torre Pellice

April 1848

Father Andrew lay prostrate on the cold stone floor of the un-adorned Beggar's Chapel. Christ on the cross seemed to look down on him with pity. Andrew had never understood or condoned the ancient works of self-flagellation, but perhaps the scourging of the flesh re-leased the poison of regret. Perhaps the penitent found relief from the revelations of personal depravity. Relief was what Andrew longed for. It was not the agony of personal depravity that haunted him; it was the ancient parchment in his hand, filled with words of evil and pain. Yet, he could not part from it; it was fused to his flesh as though branded there with a hot iron.

He had been in the library translating a work concerning Pope Innocent VIII when he'd come to the end of the parchment and real-ized that the final argument of the papal court was missing. There had to be another scroll. Instead of waiting for a fellow priest to help him, Andrew had made his way to the small back room where the oldest manuscripts of the monastery were kept. He was one of the few priestly scribes allowed to enter the room, and he was aware of and vigilant to the duty owed. He always wore his spectacles and handled the rare items with a deft touch. He was sitting on a short stool investigating books and parchments on the bottom shelf when he'd found it. He was at the back of the room, and the light from his lantern was hazy. He had just rubbed his eyes and moved aside two stiff leather tubes containing maps when his fingers brushed over the vellum sheath. Andrew's breath caught in his throat. There was no mistaking the feeling of well-prepared goat's skin. He'd lifted the old volume onto his lap and opened the cover. Inside were four unbound vellum parchments, each written in a different hand, each bearing marks of wear and age. He reached for one that had been partially burned. The archaic French spoke in voices that were three hundred years old. Andrew brought the document closer to his face to make out the faded writing.

> *I, Barba Revelli, pastor of the Waldenese, set forth the following account. It is made by my hand and I put my life in forfeit for so doing but I cannot be silent and face God.*
>
> *There is no town in Piedmont under a Waldensian pastor, where some of our brethren have not been cruelly persecuted or put to death.*
>
> *Hugo Chiamps of Finestrelle had his entrails torn from his living body at Turin. Peter Geymarali of Bobbio, in like manner.*
>
> *Maria Romano and Magdalen Foulano were buried alive at Rocco-patia.*
>
> *Susan Michelini was bound hand and foot, and left to perish of cold and hunger at Saracena.*

A band of pain and disgust tightened around Andrew's chest. He wanted the words to be false, but he knew they were not. He wanted to look away, but he could not. It was no wonder that the missive held evidence of burning. All such invectives that revealed the persecution of the Waldenese found their home in the fire.

> *Bartholomew Fache, gashed with sabers, had the wounds filled with quicklime and perished in agony.*
>
> *Daniel Michelini had his tongue torn out at Bobbio for having praised God.*

Paul Garnier was slowly sliced to pieces at Rorà for refusal on his part to abjure the gospel.

There were more names, more horrors, but Andrew could not endure the inhumanity. Sickened by the stench of evil, he had fled to the small chapel, brandishing the vellum parchment and sobbing out words of anger and recrimination. He cursed the knowing of letters and languages. He demanded understanding. He fought as the weight of disillusion pressed him to the ground. After an hour of anguish his strength was spent and he cried out for solace. Exhaustion brought quietude, and as Andrew struggled to his knees, simple words came into his mind. *Men are free to choose good or evil. Let not your heart be troubled, neither let it be afraid. In your midst are good men who call upon my name.*

Andrew felt a small sliver of pain leave his heart, and he sat back onto the floor with a groan of release. He had heard stories of the Waldensian torture from the mouth of his friend Jean Cardon. At Jean's request and dictation, he had written several accounts in his delicate penmanship. The stories had been brutal, but at that time he had detached himself as a scholar. Now he read the words of the parchment as a frail old man, and he was battered by the inhumanity of the world. He heard footfalls of soft-soled boots on the stones, but he was too weary to wonder at the wearer.

"Father Andrew! Father Andrew! Where have you . . . why . . ." Father Nathanael crouched down beside Andrew and put a comforting hand on his back. "Are you all right?"

Father Andrew tried to clear his thoughts.

"We have been looking for you. When I did not find you in the library, I . . . Here, let me help you up." With effort, the young priest lifted Andrew onto his feet. The old priest was unsteady and swayed precariously. Father Nathanael took his arm and reached for the crumpled parchment. "Here, let me take that."

"No!" Andrew barked. Then in a softer tone, "No. No, my son. I have it. I have it." He steadied himself.

"How long have you been here?" Father Nathanael questioned. He was watching Andrew with the eyes of a parent.

"I . . . I don't know."

"Why did you leave the library?"

"I needed to pray," Father Andrew said in a feeble voice.

Father Nathanael took his arm. "You are not well. Let me take you to your room."

Andrew only nodded. His thoughts were foggy and his body stiff from lying on the cold stone floor. He shuffled along, worried that he would fall, worried that he would cry. He must not cry. *Lord, I must believe that You spoke words of comfort to my heart. I must believe that there are good men in the church. I* know *that there are good men in the church. In my many years I have seen them: men who follow your ways, who care for the poor, who love thy word.*

"Steps," Father Nathanael warned. The two climbed slowly.

"Father Nathanael?" Andrew said when he'd recovered his breath.

"Yes."

"Why did you become a priest?"

Father Nathanael did not answer for such a long while that Andrew was about to excuse him the telling, but the young priest finally looked over at him and smiled.

"I grew up in Milan, in the shadow of the great cathedral. Many days when the other boys were playing their games and sports, I would wander the church, looking at the statues and paintings. I loved the stories of Christ feeding the five thousand, of walking on the water, and of raising people from the dead."

Andrew nodded. "The miracles."

"Yes. The miracles. But I was young. I thought of them like the fanciful stories my father told me of the Norsemen, or the gods of the Slavic countries."

"Yes, me too. Ghosts and witches."

"And then, when I was thirteen, my father died and my mother and I went to live with my grandmother."

Father Andrew stopped. "Am I tiring you?" Father Nathanael asked.

"No, no. The talking helps. It distracts me." He took a breath. "Now I'm ready." They started forward. "You were speaking about your grandmother."

"She was a formidable woman. It was her idea I join the clergy."

"Not God's idea?"

Father Nathanael gave a half grin. "Well, God's idea later, but her idea to begin. One did not get much past Grandmother. She wanted to control everyone's business, and she kept her eye on me. When I was sixteen she told my mother that I was definitely not suited to be a scholar or a merchant."

"And the military?"

"Not to my liking."

Andrew nodded. "Yes, I cannot imagine you on the battlefield."

Father Nathanael shook his head. "No." They neared Father Andrew's room. "When my grandmother mentioned the church as a possible place, I thought again of the statues and stories of the saints, and that is how my life's occupation was settled." The young priest opened the door and brought Andrew into the chamber.

Andrew looked anxiously into his face. "But what did you mean by 'God's idea later'?" Andrew put the parchment on the chair and laid his hat on top.

As Father Nathanael spoke he helped Andrew to undress. "At first it was an occupation like any other: Get up in the morning, learn what is expected, do what is expected, and go to bed." He helped Andrew with his robe and then had him sit on the side of the bed.

"But then?" Andrew asked.

"But then the words of the New Testament reached my heart." He removed Andrew's shoes, and helped him sit back against the pillow. "Christ was no longer just the Lord of miracles, but the preacher of truth to the woman at the well, the storyteller talking of lost sheep, candles on candlesticks, and lilies in the field." Father Nathanael placed a blanket over Andrew's legs.

"The Son of God praying for us in the garden," Andrew added.

"Yes."

Andrew felt the pressure of tears in his throat. *In your midst are good men who call upon my name.* He groaned.

"Father Andrew, are you in pain?"

He gave the young priest a kindly look. "I am old, Father Nathanael, so I am always in pain, but I have learned to accept my body's complaints." He shifted on the bed. "No, tonight it is my soul. Sometimes my soul is too much with the world." He took a deep breath. "Where there is hatred, let me sow love. Where there is . . . where there is—"

"Injury—pardon," Father Nathanael said softly.

Andrew nodded. "Where there is doubt—faith."

"The words of Saint Francis are a rock in turbulent waters," Father Nathanael said as he moved to the door. "Shall I bring you bread and soup?"

"Yes, thank you."

"Rest. I will return soon."

But before the young priest exited, Andrew called to him. "Father Nathanael?"

"Yes?"

Andrew looked over at the parchment on the chair. "What is the purpose of our calling?"

Father Nathanael hesitated, and then came back into the room and closed the door. He went to the chair and picked up the parchment and Andrew's cap.

"Do not read that!" Andrew croaked, his throat raw from his pleadings in the Beggar's Chapel.

"No. I will just move it to the table." When the items were deposited, Father Nathanael brought the chair closer to Andrew's bed and sat down. "This writing has brought you great sadness."

Andrew hesitated. "It was written by a Waldensian preacher—a Barba. It is a page of the Grand Inquisitor's inhumanity against the Waldensian people."

"Ah." Father Nathanael sat in silence, tapping his fingertips together. Andrew figured he was formulating his thoughts, reasoning out an excuse for the atrocities. Finally, the words came. "At one time, you were a worldly man, correct?"

Andrew was surprised by this candid question. "I . . . I was. Yes."

"You traveled to many places, met men of power and influence, studied philosophies, and analyzed systems of kingdoms and governments."

"I did."

"And were there flaws?"

Andrew thought of kings and princes who reveled in their tyranny; of men in government who, because of arrogance and avarice, twisted the law to their own benefit. *Were there flaws?* He looked at Father Nathanael straight on. "Yes, of course there were flaws."

"But were the flaws in the system, or because of the imperfection of the men that created them?"

Andrew took a breath. "In imperfect man."

Father Nathanael pressed his palms together and nodded. "Fallen man. It is my thinking that ever since we were sent out of the garden, we became men and women of the world. I like to say men and women of dirt."

"It is a good image," Andrew agreed.

"Subject to the devil. Subject to the flesh. And the devil makes us believe that the only way to get out of the mud is through power and money. And so, he beguiles the merchant, the soldier, the king, and even the priest."

Father Andrew stared at the young priest as if seeing him for the first time. He was taken aback by the argument and saw clarity in the thinking. "So, while the tenets of Christ's church were at first simple and sure, over time fallen man has changed them."

"Not only changed them," Father Nathanael attested, "but used the system to elevate his position and feed his avarice. That is the reason the princely priests could brook no dissension—because it threatened their power."

"All the way back to Arius at the Council of Nicaea," Andrew said.

"Yes, a good example. Arius was seen as a heretic for seeing Christ's relationship with his Father differently than the council. A heretic for questioning the fallen religious philosophies."

Father Andrew tapped his finger to his lips. "We sound like two heretics ourselves," he said wryly. "We'd better hope that Father Pious is not listening at the door."

Father Nathanael grinned. "We are never heretic against God. We are only heretic against falsehood and villainy."

Father Andrew sat higher against his pillow. "Well, that is one way to get around it."

Father Nathanael put his hand on Andrew's arm. "I think you and I long for the simple faith." Andrew nodded in agreement as Father Nathanael stood. "Perhaps it is why we both like the friar from Assisi."

"Yes, the simple faith."

"And now for soup and bread," Father Nathanael said, moving to the door.

"Thank you," Andrew said, his voice almost a whisper.

Father Nathanael turned back. "You asked me what I thought was the purpose of our calling. I will answer you in the words of Saint Francis. 'We have been called to heal wounds, to unite what has fallen apart, and to bring home those who have lost their way.'" He glanced at the parchment. "Perhaps if we put our feet on that path, we will undo some of the injustice."

"One would hope," Andrew answered.

Father Nathanael left, closing the door behind him. Father Andrew stared at the rough-hewn door for several minutes, chiding himself for his own arrogance. It was his arrogance that had kept him from knowing this companion who had served him for two years, arrogance that had kept him from knowing of the young priest's brilliant thoughts and tender heart. For all their time together, Andrew knew only bits and pieces of the man's life and educated musings. Andrew had walked the halls of the monastery receiving honor and accolades from his peers while the humble man next to him was laying up treasures in heaven.

More words from Saint Francis came into his mind. *Above all the grace and gifts that Christ gives to his loved ones is that of overcoming self.* He thought of his friends Jean Cardon and John Malan, of their bitter heritage. He had helped them with their history, and afterwards the three had fallen into an easy friendship. But why? After decades of sharing life's joys and vagaries, he still wondered why they had accepted him as a friend.

Father Andrew closed his eyes and saw the angel face of Madeleine Cardon in the glow of candlelight. He opened his eyes and leaned across to his side table, reaching, not for the parchment, but for his glasses and his Bible. He needed to find peace and a better path.

He had to laugh at himself. Eighty-one years old and still learning.

NOTES

The record of torture of the Waldenese comes from an actual ancient document written in the mid–fifteen-hundreds. It documents the torture and murder inflicted on the Waldensian faithful who refused to recant their faith in front of the Grand Inquisitor Michele Ghislier (later Pope Pius V).

In June 2015, Pope Francis traveled to a Waldensian temple in Turino to ask Waldensian Christians to forgive the Catholic Church for "the non-Christian and even inhuman attitudes and behavior that we showed you."

Saint Francis was born in either late 1181 or early 1182 in Assisi, Duchy of Spoleto, Holy Roman Empire, and died October 3, 1226, at the age of forty-four. He was the son of a wealthy silk merchant, and gave up the wealth and station of his youth after returning from a pilgrimage to Saint Peter's Basilica in Rome. He lived a life of poverty and service, gathering followers, and eventually establishing the Franciscan order of monks. Francis was a Catholic friar and preacher, but was never ordained to the Catholic priesthood. It is said that Saint Francis of Assisi was influenced by the teachings of Peter Waldo.

CHAPTER THREE

The Cardon Borgata, Angrogna Valley
September 1848

Dreams—Madeleine Cardon was used to dreams. They slid through her sleep like the rivers from the mountainsides, at times tumbled and hard to decipher, at other times quiet pools where Madeleine saw the reflections of the everyday: her father fixing the slate of the roof, her mother carding wool, her studies at the Waldensian school. Infrequently the nighttime images would bend into frightful pictures and her stomach would twist and her heart would beat against her ribs.

In this present terror she was struggling up a steep, narrow trail on the rugged mountainside, men's angry shouts echoing through the pine forest. Near. Very near. Her bare feet battered by the stones of the path. A flash of faces—women and children hiding in a cave, a fire lit at the entrance—smoke driving them into the swords and pikes of the soldiers. Snow. A winter path bloodied with small footprints. A shallow grave scraped into the hard dirt. A woman's scream. Her scream.

"Madeleine!"

Her sister Louise's voice. The grey blur of waking. Pressure on her shoulder. She opened her eyes onto darkness.

"Madeleine?"

A gulp of air. "Yes? Yes. I'm here. I'm fine."

"Well, you weren't fine. You were moaning and crying out in your sleep."

Madeleine sat up in the bed she shared with her sibling. "I'm sorry. Bad dream." She rubbed her face. "A bad dream about the torture of the Waldenese."

Louise grunted, lying down, and turning her back on her sister. "You and your dreams. Your apology will not put me back to sleep."

"Just because you never have bad dreams," Madeleine mumbled.

"I hardly ever dream at all," Louise answered, as though hers was the superior position.

"Would you like to hear what I—"

"No."

Madeleine looked to the window, but saw no sign of a lightening sky. "What time is it?"

"I don't know. Early. Papa isn't even up yet. Go back to sleep."

Madeleine lay down, afraid to close her eyes. She did not want to see the white snow and the small bloody footprints. She pondered the image. She did not remember being told a story of Waldensian children walking barefoot in the snow, though she was sure that within six hundred years of persecution, such an atrocity had played out many times.

Madeleine sighed and lay back against her pillow. Why had her people suffered hundreds of years of persecution for seeking the word of the Lord, for seeking the truth of Christ and His apostles? Why could a man or a woman not read the holy scriptures? Madeleine thought of the three-hundred-year-old family Bible hidden under her parents' bed, and the story of the Waldensian Barba who crossed the high mountains from France to bring her people the books of scripture. The great-hearted evangelist had been imprisoned for selling the Bibles to the Waldensian people, and later, when he would not recant his heretical preaching, burned at the stake. Whenever Madeleine read the flowing French words of the holy book, she said a prayer for the valiant Barba. Normally these preachers traveled in pairs, but this one had come alone; just himself, his horse, and the word of God.

I would do that, Madeleine thought. *I would cross mountains for the truth.*

Drowsiness began to tug at her reluctance and she snuggled under the covers and closed her eyes. She steeled herself against images of faces in a cave, of women and children being massacred, but those pictures did not come; instead she saw herself sitting in a beautiful meadow reading a small book of scriptures. Madeleine smiled. It was the vision from her youth, and her vision always brought a calm assurance of God's love. Surrounded by warmth, she drifted back to sleep.

"A little less flour," her mother instructed, and Madeleine immediately tempered the amount. Marthe Marie Tourn Cardon was known in the village for her cooking skill, and her barley bread was especially admired. They would do twelve rounds of bread today. As Madeleine kneaded the dough, she looked over to the corner of the kitchen at the hanging wooden rack. She was glad for the six loaves cooling there; only a few more hours and they'd be done with this task. A breeze blew the lace curtains in, and Madeleine caught a glimpse of the forested mountainside. How she would love to secure her knapsack and sneak off for a day of exploring.

"You are quiet today," her mother said, bringing a hot round to the cooling rack. She set the wooden paddle beside the table and came to her daughter's side. "Are you tired?"

"A little."

"Did you wake early?"

"No. I slept until I heard you putting wood in the bread oven."

"Well, then?" her mother pressed, scooping barley flour into the large bowl.

"I had a bad dream last night. A dream of the women and children in the cave." Marthe Cardon stared absently at the flour in the bowl as Madeleine continued. "And men were chasing me through the forest, and there was snow and blood." She stopped abruptly. "Because of the dream, I am doing a lot of thinking this morning."

Her mother put salt in the palm of her hand and tipped it into the flour. "I am sorry for such a bad dream. It seems the memory of persecution lives in our blood."

Madeleine nodded. "But then my vision came to me, and I felt calm and happy."

Her mother looked at her in surprise. "I haven't heard you speak of your vision for several years."

"That's because it usually comes to me in bits and pieces. But last night I saw the whole thing again."

"And it was the same as the first time?"

"Yes. I always remember every detail, even though I was only six the first time the images came to me."

"Only six," her mother said wistfully. She looked at Madeleine and smiled. "I would like to hear it again. Tell me."

"The vision?"

"Yes. Tell me."

Madeleine finished forming her bread round and set it aside to rise. She wiped her hands and sat down at the table. "I was upstairs in bed when this strange feeling came over me. I was only six, but it appeared that I was a young woman instead of a mere child. I thought I was in the meadow close to the vineyard, keeping father's milk cows away from the grapes. I was sitting on a small strip of grass reading a Sunday school book. I looked up and saw three strangers in front of me. As I looked into their faces, I dropped my eyes instantly, being very frightened. Suddenly the thought came to me that I must look at them—that I might remember them in the future. I raised my eyes and looked them straight in the face. One of them saw that I was afraid and said, 'Fear not, for we are servants of God and have come from afar to preach unto the world the everlasting gospel.'"

Marthe Cardon reached over and laid a floury hand on her daughter's. "It is the same story you told when you were little, only now you tell it in the words of a young woman."

"The images have not faded over the years."

"Remarkable," her mother said in a whisper. "So, go on."

"The man told me that the gospel had been restored to the earth in these last days, for the redemption of mankind—that God had spoken from the heavens and had revealed His everlasting gospel to a young boy."

"A young boy," her mother interrupted. "We still have no idea what that means."

Madeleine shook her head. "No idea. But I do remember the evangelist saying that the Lord's kingdom would be set up and that all the honest in heart would be gathered together."

Her mother nodded. "And that you would be the means of bringing your family into this great gathering."

"Yes. If those words seem strange to me now, just think of what I felt when I was six."

Her mother shook her head. "I cannot imagine." She poured warm milk into the flour and began mixing it with her hands. "There was more about our family."

"Yes. He said the day was not far off when we would leave our homes and cross the great ocean. We would travel across the wilderness and go to a place where we could serve God according to the dictates of our conscience." She took a deep breath. "When they had finished their message to me they said they would return soon and visit us. They took some small books from their pockets and gave them to me, saying, 'Read these and learn.' They disappeared instantly."

"Eight years ago," her mother said slowly. "Yes. I also remember the morning of the dream. I was cooking breakfast when you came stumbling down the stairs, clutching your clothes in your arms. You looked pale and sick."

"The dream frightened me so much that I could not speak."

"Of course. You were a little child. You didn't know what to make of such a thing."

Madeleine stood and dusted her hands with flour. She scooped up the sticky dough her mother had just dumped from the bowl and began kneading the mass. There was an ease to her voice when she spoke. "It frightened me then, but now when the pictures come to me, there is peace."

Her father came into the house at that moment carrying wood for the stove. "Not finished with the bread yet? I could have built a house in the same time."

Madeleine's mother grunted. "Huh! Empty boast."

Philippe Cardon stacked the wood. "Women. I suppose it has been all talk, talk, talk."

Madeleine threw flour onto the mound and continued working the dough. "Well, here is the thing; women can talk and work at the same time."

Her father turned slowly and gave his daughter an even look. "Well, I suppose since you are only speaking nonsense, it doesn't interfere."

Madeleine snorted with laughter and her mother scolded. "Shame on the two of you. Do not bring a foolish spirit into the house." She wagged her finger at both of them. "Besides, we were talking about important matters."

Philippe Cardon went to the bread rack and inhaled deeply. "Ah, yes?" He tore off a piece of a warm, crusty round and snuck it into his mouth.

Madeleine saw her mother press her lips together to hide a grin. "Yes, important matters."

He turned to them. "What then?"

"Madeleine's vision of the three evangelists."

Philippe looked over at his daughter. "You haven't spoken of that for many years."

"Last night the whole thing returned clearly to my mind." She set the formed dough on the sideboard to rise near the warm oven. "I wish I knew what the dream meant. Perhaps now that the king has given us some freedom, the Barbas will return to their traveling and preaching. Perhaps that is what it means."

"Perhaps," her father said, "but wasn't there something about our family gathering with these preachers and crossing an ocean?"

"Yes. I don't know what that means, or the part about the young boy."

Her mother measured out flour. "Yes. I don't know what that means either."

Philippe tore a larger chunk of bread. "Well, we could spend the day trying to figure this out, or we could get on with the work we need to do before the sun ages."

"Taskmaster," Madeleine said with a half grin. She moved to the bread rack and took off the top round.

Her father brightened. "Are you making me bread and cheese to take to the field?"

"No, I'm taking this to my friend Albertina. The guests at their inn will have a treat for dinner."

"The guests will have a treat, but what about your father?"

Madeleine took down the mangled round. "Oh, don't look so sad. I will cut you some slices."

"There's a good daughter," he said, continuing to stack wood.

Madeleine cut slices of bread and cheese, and wrapped them in a piece of cloth. "Of course you must have some bread. We want to make sure you have strength enough to work. Snow will be here soon and we must have wood to keep us warm until we move down to the valley for the winter months. A lot of wood. A *huge* pile of wood."

This comment came just as the last piece of wood made its way onto the stack. "Now who's the taskmaster?" he grumbled.

Madeleine held out the packet to him. "Man does not live by bread alone."

Philippe gave his wife a serious look. "Mother, you must teach our little daughter not to be so bossy. If she keeps on in this manner, no young man will want to court her."

"Ah, there is only a small problem with that, my dear Philippe."

"And what is that?"

"Haven't you noticed that she is no longer our *little* daughter? Womanhood has a hand on her shoulder."

Madeleine felt a rush of color in her cheeks as her father took the package of bread and smiled at her.

Later that day, when her chores were finished and she was making her way down the winding trail to her friend's home, Madeleine pondered the images of her dream. It was frustrating that while the images were clear, their meaning was not, and reflect as she might she could not grasp their full significance.

"Oh, stop being so serious," she chided herself. "And no matter what Mother says, you're only fourteen and you are far too serious for a young girl." Her inattention to the path caused her to stumble, nearly sending her into a thicket of gorse bushes. She righted herself. "See there! Keep your mind on the here and now." *Keep your mind on the here and now.* They were her mother's words, but in this instance, she didn't mind the counsel.

Madeleine adjusted her knapsack, deciding to pay attention to the footpath and the enchanting late summer afternoon. She would set aside the dream for another time—a time when the snow lay thick on the ground and the icy wind came howling down the mountain passes. Now a delightful breeze tousled her hair and the stream sang a playful song that captured her girlish fantasies. Swinging her arms broadly to encourage her nonchalance, she continued the journey to her friend's house.

NOTES

As a grown woman, Marie Madeline (Madeleine) Cardon Guild would include the dream of the evangelists in what she referred to as a brief sketch of her life. At the end of the telling she writes, "Now my dear children, I cannot doubt the faith and the principles which I have embraced; my whole soul is filled with joy and thankfulness to God for His regard for me and for you in thus manifesting to me the divinity of His great work in so remarkable a manner. How sincere is my prayer that you my children may realize how wonderful and yet how real and true is this, my life's testimony to you."

The Barba were itinerant Waldensian preachers, normally traveling in pairs. The word affectionately means "uncle." At Pra del Torno, in the Angrogna Valley, there are extant buildings known as "The School of the Barba."

The Waldensian faith was founded on the word of God, and they were the first people of Europe to obtain a translation of the holy scriptures. Hundreds of years before the Reformation, they possessed the Bible in their native tongue—French.

CHAPTER FOUR

Torre Pellice

May 1849

The three old friends sat on their favorite wooden bench, their backs and heads resting against the courtyard wall, eyes closed, faces tilted up towards the May sun. The priests who passed them on the garden path moderated their footfalls so as not to disturb the resting trio.

Andrew was with his uncle Jacques, wandering the halls of the Bibliothèque du Roi. He was eighteen again and he felt the power of his young body and the alertness of his mind. He saw the rows of books that rose above his head like the embellishments on the great Cathédrale de Notre Dame; he was breathing in the wondrous smell of parchment and leather, absently running his fingers over the spines of the books. Then came his uncle's voice.

"Lucien! Lucien Anton, pay attention! I am sorry, monsieur. I am afraid he is lost when he is among books."

"Much like myself."

He turned and saw his uncle conversing with a tall man—a man in foreign dress, but speaking French as though his tongue had known it from birth. Lucien liked the look of him. He went to stand beside his uncle, looking directly into the face of the unknown gentleman.

"Monsieur Jefferson, may I present my nephew Lucien Anton Guy.

Lucien, this is Monsieur Jefferson. Monsieur Thomas Jefferson, the statesman from the Americas. Do you know who—"

"Of course! Of course I know you!" Lucien said, putting out his hand. "I have read your declaration." He felt again his emotion as Monsieur Jefferson took his hand. He thought of this very hand holding the quill and penning inspired words that would change the world. His throat constricted. "I . . . I am honored, sir."

"So, you have read our Declaration of Independence?"

As Lucien stood mute, his uncle nodded. "Oh indeed, sir, Lucien read the entire declaration when he was ten. It had been translated into French, of course."

"Translated for all the world to read," Lucien said with reverence.

A bleating of sheep and Andrew jerked awake, blinking several times to focus his eyes.

"We are three old badgers lying in the sun," Jean Cardon said, laughing.

Andrew turned his head to see his friend rubbing his face into wakefulness.

"Sorry, old fathers!" the young shepherd called. He tapped the sheep into order on the narrow path.

Andrew understood the young man's diligence in keeping the sheep in line. Indeed, it would be a bad business if the noisy sheep trampled the tender plants of the monastery garden.

"I see you have the spring shearing done already," the third companion, John Malan, called out to the boy.

"Yes, sir, I am taking them into the mountains. Up into the beautiful Angrogna Valley."

Andrew glared at the wooden collars hanging around the neck of every sheep, each fixed with a clattering, gonging bell. "Well, hurry them along before you bring the dead from their graves."

Jean Cardon laughed loudly. "Someone does not wake up well."

Father Andrew sat forward, grumbling. "I was just having a nice dream."

"So was I," John Malan concurred. "I was shaking the hand of King Carlo Alberto. Thanking him for the freedoms to the Waldenese."

"And I was shaking the hand of Thomas Jefferson at the Bibliothèque du Roi," Andrew said.

Jean Cardon wagged his head. "Well, well, well. You two *are* among the high and mighty, aren't you?"

Andrew grunted. "Except mine is a remembrance, whereas his is purely a dream."

John laughed good-naturedly. "Yes, and when did that meeting of *yours* take place? A hundred years ago?"

"1785. When I was eighteen, in Paris with my uncle. Monsieur Jefferson was in France as a trade representative from the new country."

"And what? You just happened to bump into him at the bibliothèque?" Jean questioned.

John Malan spoke up. "It is not so impossible to imagine. Jefferson was a man of learning. Perhaps he liked to spend his time among books."

Andrew grunted. "Thank you, my friend."

Jean thumped Andrew on the shoulder. "Perhaps. Perhaps. But that was a long time ago. It is a wonder, old friend, that the memory has not slid from your brain."

"Oh, I remember the past things well. It is where I have left my spectacles now—that is my frustration."

The other two nodded their heads in agreement.

Quiet descended, and the three sat contentedly, surveying the landscape and listening to birdsong.

"Ah, it's nice to sit in the sun after the terrible winter," Jean Cardon said.

John Malan raised his fist in the air. "Bah! Bah to the winter of 1848, I say! I am glad it is 1849 and the spring has come again."

Father Andrew laughed at his friend, but had to agree. The winter had been long and bitter cold. He did not know how any of the Waldenese living in the high valleys had managed to survive. He decided to change the subject. "I was sorry to hear of the death of John Combe," he said in a sympathetic tone that brought them back to quietude. "He was your daughter-in-law's father, isn't that right, John?"

John Malan's head bobbed several times. "Yes. Yes. My daughter-in-law's father. But he went peacefully with prayers and the reading of the Bible."

"And tell Father Andrew about his prophecy," Jean Cardon said candidly, as though such things were to be expected.

"Prophecy?" Andrew questioned.

"Not long before he died, the man called his granddaughter Marie Catherine to his side. There were many of us holding vigil with him, but he must have seen the girl because she was standing near, or perhaps it was because—"

Jean cut across him. "Do not wander, my friend. Stick to the point."

"Oh! Sorry. Sorry," John said without offense. "You are right, his words are the meaningful thing. So, anyway, he called to her. He told her that she must heed his words and remember them. He said that the old may not, but the young and rising generation would see the day when the gospel would be restored in its purity and powers." The storyteller's eyes grew misty. "Then he patted his granddaughter's hand and said, 'In that day, remember me. Remember me.' It was not long after that he died."

Father Andrew sat pondering for several moments. "In that day, remember me," he quoted back. "What did he mean by that?"

"I don't know," John answered. "But he seemed clear of mind at the time, and very insistent."

"The gospel restored in its purity and powers?" Father Andrew grinned at his companions. "Do we not believe that *we* are already the stewards of the gospel? You from the tendrils of the primitive church, us from Peter?"

Jean Cardon pointed his finger at Andrew. "Ah, you are not going to get us into a religious discussion today, old friend. The grass is too green and the breeze is too pleasant."

Andrew winked and sat back against the warm wall. He sighed contentedly. "So, another spring has come."

"Yes, and my son Philippe will begin to fix the slate roofs damaged by the snow," Jean Cardon said.

John Malan yawned. "And my son John will go back into the mountains to run the cows and start up the dairy."

"It is good your families can come down out of the high valleys when the merciless winter comes," Father Andrew said.

"Oh, yes. Yes, indeed," Jean Cardon said.

"My heart aches for those who are too poor to come down," John Malan said, shaking his head. He glanced up to the high mountain peaks still covered in snow. "I am just grateful that my son John and his family can be here with me in the winter."

Father Andrew leaned forward, looking around Jean Cardon to his other friend. "You are not very imaginative when it comes to picking names, are you?"

"What do you mean by that?"

"You are John Malan, your son is John Malan, your grandson is John Malan, and your father is John Malan."

"If it is a good name, why change it?" John answered with a shrug.

Father Andrew laughed. "If it's a good name, why change it!" he said, sputtering. He sobered abruptly when he noticed Father Pious coming into the garden.

The priest in his shiny black cassock passed by the three men. He carried a Bible and a look of contempt for the men of the mountains.

Jean Cardon waved at him. "He therefore that despiseth, despiseth not man, but God, who hath also given unto us his Holy Spirit."

The priest lifted his chin and moved quickly around the corner of the garden wall, while Father Andrew stifled a laugh.

Jean raised his eyebrows. "First Thessalonians 4:8. What? He thinks we don't study the word of God?"

Father Andrew laughed outright. "Father Pious is new to the

monastery from Verona. I am sure he has no idea of the learning of the Waldensian people."

"From a young age it is school and Bible reading," John Malan interjected. "School, school, school! Learning, learning, learning. I am sure the 'critical one' has no idea that the shepherd boy who passed earlier can quote entire passages from the holy word. Entire passages! It is our lifeblood."

Jean Cardon nodded. "And my granddaughter Madeleine speaks beautiful French and Italian, as well as the dialects of the mountain people."

Father Andrew noted that he said it simply and without presumption. "I know your granddaughter," he said. "She is friends with my Albertina."

"Ah yes, the two little songbirds," Jean answered. He pulled his hat forward to block some of the late afternoon sun. "Madeleine says that Albertina is very respectful of our people."

Father Andrew smiled. "My nephew Rene has taught his son and daughter the lesson of respect for others."

John Malan snorted. "Are you sure his little boy Joseph is learning? What? He is only three or four?"

Father Andrew gave his friend a reproachful look. "Joseph is very bright for his age. Very bright. Besides, it is never too early to teach good lessons."

"Indeed," Jean stated. "And I am sure Rene received some of that schooling from you, my friend. You have seen much in your life."

Andrew was silent. He closed his eyes and passed through events in his life that had blessed him with temperance of judgment. As a young man, he had been vain and arrogant. At twenty his blood had boiled with the fever of France's revolution, and he'd mingled with the writers who stirred up thought and discontent. During those years of terror and anarchy, he had known Jean-Paul Marat and Georges Jacques Danton. Indeed, had he not been in the square when King Louis XVI was introduced to the guillotine? Did he not hear the colossal and coarse Danton yell out, "The kings of Europe would dare challenge us? We throw them the head of a king!" Andrew's conscience berated. Arrogance. A few years later, Danton would lose his own head to the sharp blade. To the compassionless crowd he yelled bitter words against Robespierre and the chaos that would ensue without his—Danton's— masterful presence. But the final words of the man that most often came to Andrew's memory were not the words of pomp and power, but words of regret. "Ah, better to be a poor fisherman than to meddle with the government of men."

Danton had gone back to his faith, his thoughts not on the crowd, or honor, or glory, but on Peter, the Lord's fisherman. A small but pow- erful lesson was on display that day, but it was a lesson that twenty- five-year-old Lucien Anton Guy did not learn. He had turned from the macabre spectacle of the chopping block to pursue the temptations of the world. He had flaunted his brilliance, and, for a time, his brilliance served him well. He craved the accolades of accomplishment and the praise of men. Women found him attractive, and princes paid him handsomely for his writing and translating skills. He ate, and drank, and gambled to excess. His path was in the wilderness, and slowly his soul began to wither in the cruel sun of sophistry. It was here the Lord found him. Broken and miserable, Lucien Anton Guy had climbed the steps to the Cathédrale Saint-Jean-Baptiste de Lyon. The glow of the stained-glass window bathed him in rose-colored light as he pros- trated himself in the Chapel of the Cross and poured out his sin and sorrow to God. And God heard him. He gave Lucien a new life and a new name—Andrew. God had also given him new eyes to discern the struggles of men, and a new heart of compassion to serve. Andrew would still use his gifts, but now the world would diminish, and the sacred cross would dictate his usefulness.

Andrew slowly opened his eyes and looked across the meadow- land spreading out behind the monastery garden, the colors of a few wildflowers winking from the greening grass. He squinted to make out the clump of chestnut trees at the foot of the mountain, their pale new leaves quivering in the slight breeze. *New life.* The words of Saint Francis floated into his mind. *Dear Mother Earth, who day by day unfoldest blessings on our way.* He had written out the saint's words many times over the years. Words of beauty and peace. Words of life.

Next to him Jean Cardon was struggling to his feet. "Ah! Ah! I have been sitting too long. My legs are charlatans!"

"Be careful, old friend," John Malan warned. "I will help you."

"You help me? Tchet! We would fall down together."

Father Andrew looked with fondness at his old friends as they steadied themselves and reached to secure their canes.

"Are you going in now?" Jean asked.

"Soon. I will wait for Father Nathanael to shepherd me."

"Well, you *are* the oldest of us," John Malan said, grinning. "I suppose it is only right for you to have a young one to hold you up."

"Ha!" Andrew bellowed. "I have walked over these mountains more times than both of you put together!" His two friends laughed raucously. "Oh, off with you now! At your pace it will take you hours to get home and you will miss your supper."

"Perhaps we will see you tomorrow," Jean Cardon called back, as the two made their way along the path.

"Yes! We can sit on our bench and watch the grass grow," John Malan added with a laugh.

Father Andrew shook his head, and watched them go. He thought of the wisdom of his friends, of the sheep heading for the mountain valleys, and of the faces of the two young girls, the two songbirds. But mostly in his ears he heard the resonating words of prophecy from a dying man. *"The gospel will be restored in its purity and powers. In that day, remember me."*

NOTES

Thomas Jefferson served as an ambassador to France from 1784 to 1789. He was a trade representative appointed by the Continental Congress to replace the aging statesman Benjamin Franklin. Thomas Jefferson was thirty-three years old when he wrote the Declaration of Independence.

Owning and reading the Bible showed the commitment of the Waldenese to follow the pattern of Jesus Christ and His followers in studying the gospel. During the time of the Waldenese and other religious reformers, the Catholic Church forbade these practices and severe punishments were meted out to those disobeying.

The deep regard held by the Waldenese for the scriptures is apparent in the education of their youth. While attention was given by the pastors to branches of general learning, the Bible was made the chief study. The young committed to memory the Gospels of Matthew and John along with many of the epistles. The youth were also employed in copying the scriptures.

The deathbed prophecy of John Combe, father of Pauline Combe and father-in-law of John Malan, was an actual occurrence written down by several family members who were present at the time.

The French Revolution began in 1789 and continued through the late 1790s, subsiding with the ascent of Napoleon Bonaparte. During these years of turmoil the French citizens revolted and restructured the political landscape, attacking the monarchy and feudal system while pressing for a more representative form of government.

Chapter Five

Salt Lake City

October 6, 1849

Eliza R. Snow broke away from the group of women with whom she'd been conversing about the church conference and crossed the courtyard to intercept her brother. "Elder Snow."

He turned to her. "Sister Smith."

She gave him an inclusive smile. "I will take a 'dear sister' from you, little brother, and be glad of it."

He tipped his hat. "Dear sister."

She gave him a hug. "So—called to be an apostle of the Lord eight months ago and now called to a mission."

He nodded. "Both daunting assignments."

"As they should be. It will keep you humble." She considered his face. "Another mission for you across the great ocean."

"It would seem."

"Now that you are no longer a bachelor, I thought they would give you time to be with your wives and children."

"Hmm." He looked about. "Where is that family of mine, anyway?"

"They have abandoned you for the warm cabin. Charlotte told me to tell you. She also said that you are not to linger too long discussing things with the brethren."

"She knows me well."

Eliza put on her gloves and took her brother's arm. "And I have been invited to your home for supper, so you may walk me."

At that moment, several people came over to congratulate Elder Snow on his call and to wish him well. The last to approach was Joseph Toronto. He smiled broadly and shook Lorenzo's hand with vigor. "I am blessed. So blessed. Going back to my home country to be a missionary. And to be working with such a good man. A smart man."

"I will lean on you for the language, Brother Toronto."

"Yes, I teach you. Italian is not so hard. And you help me with everything else." He gave a little bow to Eliza. "*Buonasera, Sorella* Snow. Your brother, they keep him busy, no?"

"Yes, Brother Toronto, as you. There is no use for drones in the Lord's kingdom."

Brother Toronto's eyes narrowed. "This word, *drone*. What means it?"

"A lazy bee."

"Ah! The lazy bee. Oh, no, no, no! No lazy bees in Deseret."

The three laughed, and Lorenzo patted Brother Toronto on the back. "I will see you tomorrow at the meeting."

"Yes. Yes, of course. I am no drone."

Lorenzo smiled. "No, you are not." He and Eliza waved as Brother Toronto moved off. "A drone," Lorenzo scoffed. "That man is one of the hardest workers I've ever encountered."

Eliza looked up at her brother. "He came across with the first wagon train west, didn't he?"

"He did. Thirty years old, and President Young called him to be the herdsman over all the cattle moving west."

"You two are quite a pair," Eliza said as they left the crowded street near the center and wended their way towards Lorenzo's house.

"How do you mean?"

"You, tall and slender. He, short and solid. You, calm and thoughtful. He, full of energy and action. You, an American man of Pilgrim heritage. He, a man from the shores of Sicily. I think you will complement each other."

He smiled at her. "At least we are near the same age—me thirty-five, and he thirty-three. And both with strong testimonies of the restored gospel."

"That will be helpful," Eliza said. "Wasn't he a sailor in his young life?"

"He was. He traveled the world."

"What a joy to gather all that knowledge and experience."

"And a fair amount of money."

"How did he come to the Church?"

"He heard the word preached when he was in port in Boston. He jumped ship and followed the Saints to Nauvoo."

"That took faith," Eliza said.

Lorenzo nodded. "Indeed. It was Nauvoo where I first met him. When he arrived in the city he came to the building committee and gave all his money for the building of the Nauvoo Temple."

Eliza looked over in surprise. "Really?"

"Brother Toronto did not want it known."

"Remarkable," Eliza said as she waved to a friend. "The gospel net is drawing in the pure in heart from the world."

"Speaking of the gospel and the world, what did you think of the congregation's reaction to President Young's announcement about the perpetual emigration fund?"

"I think it took their breath away."

"Pure revelation."

"Pure."

A cool wind blew down from the canyon and Eliza stopped to secure more buttons on her coat. She looked over to the west, across the Great Salt Lake, where the sun was setting in orange streaks through billowing gray clouds. It had rained off and on during the day, and now that night was coming, the saturated air was chill. She took her brother's arm again, continuing their conversation as though no pause had been made.

"Think how many of those without funds, those who have longed to gather with the Saints here in Zion, will now be able to come."

Lorenzo nodded. "The gathering is a miracle."

"What I find a miracle is that after only two years in the valley, we are sending missionaries out to the world."

"Proselyting has never ceased since the restoration, Eliza. The Prophet Joseph sent out missionaries even in the darkest times."

At the mention of her deceased husband's name, Eliza stiffened. Lorenzo patted her hand. "I'm sorry. The pain is still great."

"I miss him every day, Lorenzo. Every day."

"Yes, there's a hole in the fabric of our society that will not mend." They walked in silence for a time. Finally Lorenzo spoke. "He would have loved being here with the Saints."

Eliza nodded. "He would. Think of him helping to build the great city."

"Or planting crops," Lorenzo added.

"Or trying to get crops to grow in a desert with little water." The two shared a brief laugh, and then Eliza sobered. "Oh, to have him here, receiving revelation and guiding us as he did at Nauvoo."

"Yes. He was one of the earth's great men. He and his brother Hyrum. 'In life they were not divided, and in death they were not separated,'" Lorenzo quoted. He cleared his throat. "How blessed we were to know them. How very blessed."

They walked for a time without speaking, then Eliza turned to her brother. "Do you remember when we first met Joseph?" she asked.

"Yes. Ohio. Our home in Mantua. I only met him briefly before leaving for Oberlin College."

"That's right. Well, Leonora and I thought him a common thing—a country bumpkin with little education."

"Yes, the highly educated and accomplished Snow family condescending to listen to what the lowly yokel had to preach."

A tear ran down Eliza's cheek and she brushed it away. "Mother and Father were open to all thoughts and opinions, but Leonora and

I held ourselves aloof." Another tear. "Such arrogance. We had been searching for the primitive Church of Christ for years, and when it came pure to our ears, we were reluctant because of the preacher."

"As I recall, you and Leonora were not reluctant for long."

"Once I softened my prideful heart."

Lorenzo chuckled. "Well, you were an intellect—a well-known poetess."

"Oh, fiddle," Eliza said. "*He* was a prophet of God."

"He was," Lorenzo said, the spirit of testimony in his voice. "Remember how I came from Oberlin College to Kirtland to visit you?"

"I do. You'd been studying Hebrew."

"With a noted professor," Lorenzo said, giving her a half grin. "And when I discovered that Hebrew was being studied by Joseph and others of the apostles of the Church at Kirtland, I decided to join them."

Eliza grinned. "To show them up, if I remember correctly."

"It didn't take me long to come to know the spiritual brilliance of the Prophet," Lorenzo said, shaking his head. "To think of all he accomplished in his brief life: ancient scripture translated, priesthood restored, thousands of converts gathered . . ."

"The building of the beautiful and ordered city of Nauvoo," Eliza added.

Lorenzo nodded. "The beautiful city of Nauvoo crowned with a temple to the Most High God."

"The power of eternal sealing," Eliza said. She took a deep breath, and looked around at the hundreds of Saints wending their ways to their homes. "And the mobs thought by killing Joseph Smith that Mormonism would be crushed into oblivion."

"Yet here we are," Lorenzo countered.

"Yet here we are." She looked up at her brother, taking him into her confidence. "Joseph often said to me that he knew the Church would go on—that even if something were to happen to him . . ." She took another breath, "That even if something were to happen to him, all would be well. If the keys were in place the Church would go on."

"And expand into many parts of the world," Lorenzo said.

She gave his arm a squeeze. "Italy is a long way away."

Lorenzo nodded. As they turned onto a side road off the wide avenue, he could see the lights of his cabin home, and his heart ached. "It would be impossible to leave my family without the firm knowledge that I am doing the Lord's work. To go to a country of such spiritual superstition without the testimony that I'm bringing them the light of the restored gospel? Impossible. But I know there are people waiting for the truth—praying for the truth." He stopped and faced his sister. "Please look after my family for me, Eliza. I will not be here for the births that will come just months after I am gone, and . . ." His voice faltered.

Eliza took his hands. "You know, of course, that it is my calling to be Auntie Eliza? I will make sure that all your babies are protected and spoiled, and I will write you detailed descriptions of their beautiful faces and charming dispositions. Letters will be our lifeline." She squeezed his hands. "As your older sister, I tell you to be at peace. The Lord is over all. Now, go and greet your wives with a smiling face and show them the trust you have of His infinite care."

"I will take your counsel because you are *so* much older than me," Lorenzo teased. Eliza began to protest, but he cut across her response. "And . . . and because trust in the Lord is the principle on which you live your life."

"A much better reason."

Lorenzo opened the door for his sister and followed her into the warmth and embrace of his family.

NOTES

Lorenzo and his older sister Eliza were the offspring of solid Puritan stock. Their first paternal ancestor to reach America was Richard Snow, who settled in Woburn, Massachusetts, within two decades after the Pilgrim landing.

Eliza Snow was ten years Lorenzo's senior. She joined the Church in 1835 and proved to be a strength and asset to it from the onset. She was a poetess of the highest caliber who penned more than 500 poems during her lifetime. Many of these poems became favorite hymns of the Latter-day Saints.

In the October 1849 general conference of the Church, President Young called three apostles to open missions abroad: John Taylor in France, Erastus Snow in Scandinavia, and Lorenzo Snow in Italy. Elder Franklin D. Richards was called to preside over the already established European Mission.

CHAPTER SIX

Torre Pellice

December 24, 1849

Father Andrew stood facing his adversary, his walking stick raised to strike. The glow from the fire was the library's only light, and it cast the two combatants in grotesque image.

"These . . . these statements are blasphemous!" Father Pious spluttered, holding out the parchments in a clenched fist.

"Hand those to me, or I will crack your skull!"

Father Pious retreated a step. "Why would you have these in your room? I thought you were someone to admire, but I've watched you. You think yourself above the rules—above the rest of us."

Andrew swung the stick, but Father Pious sidestepped. Andrew glared at the insolent priest and steadied himself. "It is none of your concern, you toad! Why were you in my room?"

"I was ordered there to replace the straw in your mattress. That's where I found these hidden away. Hidden instead of destroyed."

"You have no say over them."

"And neither do you. I came to deliver them to the fire where they belong." He made a move for the fireplace and Father Andrew blocked him with his stick.

"Those are ancient parchments!"

"Which are heretical! There is no excuse you can give me," Father Pious hissed, pushing past Andrew and hurrying forward to the fire.

"Stop!" Father Nathanael's voice demanded as he came into the room. "What is this about?"

Father Nathanael's abrupt command had momentarily stayed Father Pious's hand, but now he scowled at Father Andrew, opened his fingers, and dropped the parchment into the flame.

"No!" Father Andrew bellowed as he stumbled forward.

Father Nathanael rushed past him, grabbed a corner of the vellum, and flipped it onto the hearthstone. He tapped out the flame with his sandaled foot.

"Carefully!" Father Andrew called to him. "Carefully."

Father Pious glared at the two priests, but dared not go against Father Nathanael simply because he was cowed by his physical strength. "I will be reporting this to the Abbot," he said, his voice strangled with anger.

The three turned abruptly to the library door as the Abbot and his assistant entered. The Abbot's lined face was void of expression, but his stride into the room spoke purpose. Father Andrew glanced at his foe and saw a look of triumph light his face. Father Pious moved forward to intercept his superior, but the Abbot held up his hand.

"Never fear, Father Pious, I will get to the bottom of this." He went to Father Andrew. "Report came to me of angry words being spoken in the library. Of course, I found this difficult to believe, as ours is an order where civility is expected." His look flicked from the parchment on the hearthstone to the faces of the three priests. "Now I surmise that there may be a basis for the concern."

"Your Holiness—" Father Pious began, but the Abbot again held up his hand to stop him. He turned. "Father Andrew?"

Though the Abbot was twenty years his junior, Andrew knew the deference owed his superior. He looked at him squarely. "Father Pious removed some ancient parchments from my room."

"Heretical parchments," Father Pious interjected.

The Abbot ignored him and motioned for Andrew to continue.

"I was here in the library when Father Pious came in to burn them."

The Abbot frowned. "Burn them?"

"Yes. Three-hundred-year-old parchments."

Father Pious stepped forward. "But they were—"

Andrew cut him off. "I merely tried to stop him."

The Abbot looked at the partially burned parchments and then to Father Pious. "I do not know what the policy was in Verona, Father Pious, but in our monastery, we do not burn parchments. We are stewards for the care of historical and sacred records."

"But these are not sacred records, your Holiness. And I found them hidden under his mattress."

The Abbot paused, and then turned to Father Andrew. "Explain this."

"They are historical records of the Waldenese. I found them in the records room and wished to analyze the vellum and the archaic writing."

Father Pious inched forward. "But why hidden? Perhaps he means to give them to his Waldensian friends."

The Abbot held up his hand for the third time. "I believe I've received from you all the information I need, Father Pious. You are dismissed."

"But—"

"You are dismissed."

Father Pious took a last withering look at Father Andrew, bowed low to the Abbot, and exited.

The Abbot turned to his assistant. "Bring them to me."

The priest moved immediately to retrieve the scorched manuscript.

Father Andrew watched as flecks of ash fell from the parchment as it was lifted. He closed his eyes in resignation. He saw himself sitting at his kitchen table in Lyon, writing out his letters with the white quill pen.

"I can teach you, Mama. I can teach you your letters."

"What need I with those?"

"But everything is in letters, Mama. Everything."

"Will it help me make a better pot of soup?"

"Father Andrew, I find much here which troubles me."

Father Andrew opened his eyes to see the Abbot reading the parchment. Before thinking he said, "Yes, it troubles me also."

The Abbot straightened. "The past is the past, Father Andrew. We live here in the valleys of the Waldenese. We live with them in peace." He picked up the parchment. "None of this matters now." He handed the scorched parchment to his assistant, and more of the writing fell away in ash.

Father Andrew groaned, but did not speak.

The Abbot brushed off his hands. "I will keep these safely secured in my private rooms, and if you find any others, you will bring them to me. Is that understood?" There was no reply. "Father Andrew?"

"Yes, your Excellency."

The Abbot left the library, his assistant trailing behind.

Tears leaked from Father Andrew's eyes, and Father Nathanael was beside him. "Shall we be off, then?"

"What?"

"You remember—I was coming to get you for the outing."

Father Andrew shook his head. "Outing?"

"To hear the Christmas music."

Andrew wiped away a few tears. "Ah, yes," he said slowly. "I remember. My Albertina is singing with the Waldensian choir."

"She is, and I'm afraid we may be late now."

Father Andrew growled, "Stupid toad!"

Father Nathanael took Andrew's arm. "Shall we go listen to beautiful music and forget all this?"

They started forward.

Andrew glanced back at the fire. "I would like to forget, but I fear Father Pious will not be satisfied until those pages are cinders."

"The Abbot is a careful and sensible steward. He will protect them. Besides," Father Nathanael said lightly as he opened the library door, "can we not be assured that Father Pious's intentions and actions will be recorded in heaven?"

"Yes," Andrew said, a slight smile touching the corner of his mouth. "Yes. Thank you for that, Father Nathanael. We will leave it in His hands."

"There! See there? It is my friend. He is waving to us. I think he has a place for me."

"Your eyes are better than mine tonight," Father Nathanael replied to his anxious charge.

Andrew pointed. "There, by the water trough—my friend John Malan."

"Ah, yes. I see." Father Nathanael said. "The one waving his hat. Careful now. The snow has been packed down."

They advanced slowly through the crowd of people, many stepping back to ease the way for the old priest, others giving the two men in their black cassocks and dark coats a wary look. Of either of these occurrences Andrew was unaware; his sight was fixed on his friend and a place to sit.

As they neared, Andrew heard the gentle splash of artesian water as it came naturally through a wooden spigot and into the trough. Pure water. The trough was simply a large log hollowed out and set in place, the spigot pouring water in one side, and a channel cut in the wood allowing runoff on the other side. Father Andrew thought about all the fountains he'd seen in his younger days: the ornate fountains of Paris, the small courtyard fonts in Venice, the marvelous waterworks of Tivoli, and the fountains of Rome adorned by magnificent statuary. Yet Andrew loved this little trough more than the rest. He had drunk its refreshing water the first day he'd come into Torre Pellice fifty years ago. He smiled at the memory.

"There you are!" John Malan said brightly. "The joy of the Savior's birth!"

Andrew sat down next to his friend, grateful for the place to rest. "The joy of the Savior's birth to you!" he returned to John. He looked up at Father Nathanael. "I am settled, Father Nathanael. Thank you for your help." The young priest went to stand by the trough, leaving the friends to their visit.

John put his hat on his head and sat down. "There are clouds tonight. I hope it doesn't snow."

Andrew looked up at the sky. "No, I don't think it will."

"You were almost late," John scolded. "The music will begin soon."

Andrew frowned. "There was some trouble at the monastery."

"Trouble?"

Andrew flicked his hand dismissively. "Ah, it's over now. Besides, any more it takes me some time to get from place to place."

John nodded. "Yes. I know this well myself."

"And where is Jean?" Andrew asked, suddenly aware that his other friend was absent.

"Oh, he is over on the other side of the courtyard with his family."

"And where is *your* family?"

John chuckled. "Scattered about. We Waldenese are all related in one way or another, so when there's a gathering of any sort we like to do our visiting. And where are your nephew Rene and his family?"

"Close to the front, I would imagine. They wish to give Albertina encouragement."

"As if she needs such a thing," John scoffed. "She has the voice of an angel."

Andrew smiled. "As does Jean's granddaughter Madeleine."

"Do we know what they're singing?"

"Albertina said two songs with the choir, and then she and Madeleine will sing 'To the Choir of Angels.'"

John brightened. "Ah! A beautiful Christmas song. And we will get to sing along?"

"Yes."

"And will Albertina sing a solo?"

Father Andrew nodded. "Yes. Yes, I believe so."

"And what will it be?"

"That I don't know. No one will tell me. It is supposed to be a surprise."

Soft strains of music issued from the small orchestra as the choir members filed into their places on the raised steps. Behind and to the side of their position, the Waldensian temple's pale yellow facade seemed to glow in the fading light. The audience settled itself on makeshift wooden benches arranged for the occasion.

Father Andrew squinted, finally catching sight of his great-niece on the front row with Madeleine Cardon right beside her.

"Do you see your Albertina?" John asked.

"Yes. Front row. And Madeleine is beside her."

The conductor came to the front and motioned to the two girls, who stepped forward.

"Ah! Look at that!" John Malan whispered excitedly. "They begin the program! It is a great honor."

Andrew grinned, but kept his excitement in dignified silence.

The music started and the girls sang:

> *To the choir of angels*
> *Descending from the heavens*
> *Let us add our praises*
> *And sing Noel!*
> *Let us add our praises*
> *And sing Noel!*

Andrew and John joined their voices with the other congregants in singing the final part of the chorus:

> *Noel! Noel! Let us all sing Noel!*

After the girls' song, there was the dancing of the children, and everyone clapped and encouraged the youngest set, whose clumsy antics showed it to be their premiere performance.

The choir then sang several carols, among them one of Andrew's favorites, *Adeste Fideles*. In his mind, he translated the Latin. "*Oh, come, all ye faithful, joyful and triumphant. Oh, come ye, oh, come ye to Bethlehem.*" Bethlehem. He had been to that sacred place. The long journey to the Holy Land had been one of his pilgrimages. At the town of the Lord's birth he had bowed through the low arch of the church door and crawled to the steps that led to the underground grotto. He had seen the star on the floor, the urns of incense, the many candles. He had prayed for the heat of devotion to pierce his heart, but it did not come. Instead, when he emerged from the church, he felt a longing for the simple place, the shepherds' field, the dark sky with a thousand stars.

A heavenly voice brought him back to the courtyard and the chilly night. Albertina stood in front of the choir, her pale face glowing amidst the gathering dark, her voice alone bringing the sacred words and joyous melody to the ears of the captivated audience. Tears pressed at the back of Andrew's throat. This was his favorite carol. This was his surprise. He felt the pain and anger of the library diminish, and he smiled.

> *Angels from the realms of glory,*
> *Wing your flight o'er all the earth;*
> *Ye who sang creation's story*
> *Now proclaim Messiah's birth!*

Her voice was thrilling, and Andrew knew that other hearts were beating faster just like his. He looked over at John Malan and found him staring at the singer as though an angel had just stepped from heaven.

> *Shepherds in the fields abiding*
> *Watching o'er your flocks by night*
> *God with man is now residing*
> *Yonder shines the Infant Light.*

"*He is the way, the truth, and the light,*" Andrew recited silently. He cupped his hand behind his ear to better catch the words of the next verse. It was his favorite.

> *Sages, leave your contemplations*
> *Brighter visions beam afar;*
> *Seek the great desire of nations*
> *Ye have seen his natal star.*

Emotion flooded his aged frame as Andrew thought back to that day in the Cathédrale de Saint-Jean-Baptiste when he had repented the hollow wisdom of the world and given his life to God. "*Sages leave your contemplations—brighter visions beam afar.*" His great-niece's voice gained strength and emotion as she shared the final verse. To Andrew it seemed as though she called out to the listeners—calling them to prepare for the Lord's coming.

> *Saints before the altar bending*
> *Watching long in hope and fear*
> *Suddenly the Lord descending*
> *In His temple shall appear.*

Andrew saw John Malan look quickly at the Waldensian church. The Waldenese called their churches temples, and perhaps his friend was startled by the thought of the Lord Jesus coming to teach in their temple as he had in the synagogue at Capernaum, or the temple at Jerusalem.

> *Come and worship*
> *Come and worship*
> *Worship Christ, the newborn King!*

The pure voice beckoned to the faithful followers, and without hesitation their voices joined in the offering.

Come and worship
Come and worship
Worship Christ, the newborn King!

The joy of the celebration filled every heart as the final note of the carol faded into the Christmas night. John Malan turned to Father Andrew, blinking back tears.

"She is a gift from God."

Andrew nodded several times. "Yes. Yes, she is."

Father Nathanael came forward as people stood, some milling about and talking, some heading off for the warmth of home. "Are you ready to leave?" he asked quietly.

"Yes. Help me up, please; my bones are beginning to freeze."

Just as Father Nathanael had the old priest on his feet, Albertina rushed to his side. She threw her arms around him. "So? So? How did you like your surprise?" Andrew staggered back and Father Nathanael steadied him. "Oh, sorry, Uncle! I am just so glad to see you here. I didn't know if you would try with the threat of snow."

"Ha! I remember going over the steep heights of Mount Cenis on snowshoes. It was January and the snow was twenty feet deep." Albertina gave him a glowing look. "Besides," he continued, "could a little snow keep me from hearing your perfect voice?"

Albertina blushed. "Oh, Uncle, don't tease me."

John Malan stepped forward. "He is not teasing you, my dear. It is a perfect voice."

Albertina nodded her head in recognition of the compliment, but then adroitly moved the subject away from herself. "Were you glad that I sang your favorite?"

"Delighted."

"And we also liked the song you and Madeleine Cardon sang," John said.

"Thank you, sir."

Andrew looked about. "Where is she, by the way? I wanted to congratulate her."

"She is with her family."

"And I must go and find my family," John said, moving off. "The peace of Christmas be with you!" he called.

Andrew waved. "And with you, old friend! Be careful on the snow!"

At that moment, Andrew's nephew, Rene, his wife, Francesca, and their son, Joseph, arrived. Joseph sat like a little king as his father pulled him along on one of the family's wooden sledges. The thick wooden runners slid easily over the packed snow, which made for an exciting ride for the little one. Joseph's cheeks were red from the chilly wind, and his blue eyes shone with the wonder of Christmas.

At the sight of the boy, all sadness left Father Andrew's heart. "Well, there he is! There he is!" he boomed. "The little soldier. The little man who just had his birthday!"

Joseph scrambled off the sledge and ran to grab the hand of his great-uncle. "I am three now!" he babbled. "Three, three, three!"

"You *are* three, and getting to be such a big boy." Joseph looked up into the face of his great-uncle and grinned. Father Andrew winked at him. "Did you like the concert?"

Joseph hopped up and down. "Yes, yes, yes!" he said on every hop.

"And what did you like the best?"

Joseph looked at his sister and pointed at her. "I liked Albi." The family laughed as Albertina stooped down to hug her brother.

"Yes, so did I," Andrew concurred.

"The dancing, too!" Joseph added. "I liked the dancing!"

"Oh, yes? Well, in a few years you will be dancing with them," Andrew promised.

Joseph skipped around for a few moments performing his imitation of the dancers, until his feet slipped on the hard-packed snow, and he fell. The assembled group gasped as Albertina rushed to help him.

"Are you all right, dear one?" She looked quickly to her mother's face and saw unmasked alarm. "He's all right, Mother. He's fine. Just a little bump."

"I fell down," he said meekly as Albertina helped him stand. His lower lip began to quiver.

Andrew reached out his hand to the boy. "There, now. Come to your uncle, brave boy. Come on. Should I tell you how many times I have fallen on the snow and ice?"

Joseph moved forward and took his great-uncle's hand. "How many?"

"More than you can count on all your fingers and all your toes," Father Andrew said in a triumphant voice as though proud of the accomplishment. Joseph giggled. "There's a boy. There's a brave boy," Andrew said lovingly.

A soft snow swirled among the group, and for a moment they were quiet—captivated by the magic of the unexpected snowfall. Finally, Francesca Guy moved to Andrew's side. "Christmas joy," she said softly.

"Christmas joy," Andrew returned.

"Come along, little one," she said to Joseph. "It is long past your bedtime."

"But I want to stay with Uncle."

Andrew took Father Nathanael's proffered arm. "I would love to stay with you, my dear Joseph, but it is past my bedtime, too."

The boy gave him a puzzled look and then smiled. "Because you are old."

Andrew stifled a laugh. "Yes, because I am old."

Albertina came to give him a kiss. "Good night, old bear. Christmas joy."

"Christmas joy, my angel. Thank you for my song."

Rene picked up Joseph and set him on the sledge. "Good night, Uncle. Francesca and I may see you at the midnight Mass."

"If Father Nathanael can keep me awake."

As the snow thickened, they parted ways, Andrew carefully

navigating the uneven cobbles of the street and the patches of snow. He was grateful for Father Nathanael's steady arm, and told him so.

Father Nathanael was taken aback, but said only, "Christmas joy, honored one."

"I am just an old priest," Father Andrew returned. "The true Honored One is the baby in the manger." *The one who saved my life*, Andrew reflected to himself.

A snowflake fell on his nose and he brushed it away. Another year ending, he thought, and soon another year beginning. A new decade. Perhaps life would go on as usual, or perhaps he would see new things. Another year. In all likelihood, he would be in heaven with his mother and father and his uncle Jacques. That would be nice. "Life eternal," he said out loud without realizing.

"What's that?" Father Nathanael asked.

"Life eternal," Andrew said again. "Think how many gifts came with the babe of Bethlehem."

"The greatest gifts," Father Nathanael answered simply. "The greatest gifts."

NOTE

The Waldensian temple (church) in Torre Pellice was the work of Colonel Beckwith, an English missionary and philanthropist who collected the necessary money for its building from his friends in England. He also made preparations for the project and guided its building. The temple was completed in June of 1852. I place its completion at an earlier date in the book, because of the significance to the Waldensian faithful and the impression made on the early LDS missionaries.

CHAPTER SEVEN

Salt Lake City

December 24, 1849

Eliza settled her sister-in-law Charlotte in the small bed, plumped her pillow, and placed a blanket over the coverlet.

"I don't know that an extra blanket is necessary," Charlotte said.

"Let me pamper you," Eliza returned. "I know you are as healthy as an ox, but you just had your baby ten days ago, and Lorenzo would be incensed if I didn't fuss a bit."

Charlotte smiled. "Oh, well then, fuss away."

They spoke quietly as the makeshift bed for the newborn occupied the same small room as her mother's. Eliza checked on Roxcy Armatha to make sure she was covered. The crude log cabin in which the Snow family lived had its share of unplugged chinks through which the winter wind found passage. Eliza discovered one of these cracks not far from the baby's bed, and put her hand over it.

"Draft?" Charlotte asked.

"A rather large one."

"Plug in one of the braid pieces."

Eliza went to a basket in the corner of the room and rummaged through strips of braided fabric until she found one the right length. "These are ingenious, you know," she remarked as she moved to the chink and shoved in the colorful braid. "You could probably sell these at the mercantile for all the drafty cabins we have in the valley."

"As if I need anything more to keep me busy."

Eliza looked over at the young woman and smiled. She liked her. Charlotte Squires was a woman of faith, kindness, and intellect. She had been tested in the fire of adversity, and had held to her covenants. Eliza was a keen judge of character and she found the twenty-five-year-old Charlotte faithful and wise beyond her years.

Shortly after she and Lorenzo had married in the Nauvoo Temple in Illinois, mobs had driven them from their home into the harsh wilderness across the Mississippi. At Pisgah, Iowa, Charlotte and Lorenzo had buried their first child—five-month-old Leonora Charlotte, and then, without vindictive accusation of God, husband, or church, the young woman had turned her face to the West and crossed the thousand miles of untested territory only to finish the journey in the arid desolation of Salt Lake.

Even now, coping with a new daughter, an absent husband, and a drafty house, Charlotte maintained an equanimity that touched Eliza's heart. She moved over and put her hand on Charlotte's shoulder.

"Is there anything else you need before I leave you?"

"Yes. Would you mind sitting with me for a time? The quiet nights are the most difficult."

"Of course." Eliza sat down in the rocker next to the bed. "I admire you, Charlotte."

"Me?"

"Yes. And don't look so surprised. You were strong tonight when you read us Lorenzo's letter."

"Well, it wasn't easy." A slight grin touched the corner of Charlotte's mouth. "Especially when he shared the story of the Indian attack."

Eliza placed a hand over her heart. "Goodness sakes, what was he thinking? That scared the wits out of us."

"But then came the miracle that saved them," Charlotte offered quickly.

"Yes, but we didn't know that until after the telling of the tale! It was one time I wished my brother did not have such a command of the language."

The two women chuckled, and the baby stirred. Eliza looked over anxiously.

"Don't worry," Charlotte said. "Once she's asleep only hunger or a stampede will wake her." She reached over to the side table and laid her hand on the letter. "And what did he write about the Indian attack? That it was a *thrilling* scene?"

"Huh!" Eliza scoffed. "From here on I will be grateful for civilized encounters and calm seas, thank you!"

"Amen," Charlotte concurred. "But the miracles do testify that the Lord's watchful eye is on them."

Eliza reached over and patted her hand. "That is a comfort."

Charlotte changed subjects. "Elder Toronto seems to be a great help with the language and teaching about the Catholic faith."

"I know Lorenzo will find both useful when they reach Italy."

Charlotte nodded and yawned. "Where do you think they are now?"

"Perhaps near to setting sail in New York," Eliza said.

"First to England for several months."

"Yes, and then to Italy."

Charlotte sighed. "Each ship taking him farther and farther from home."

"You know he would not take one step from your side unless the Lord asked it."

"I *do* know that," Charlotte said with a sad smile. "And I'm not complaining . . . just missing him."

"Of course."

"After he was called to Italy, he spent many hours on his knees. He told me he would leave his family and cross the ocean for even one convert." Her voice became thick with emotion. "But he wondered if there would be one person willing to hear his words. He kept praying and pleading, and before he left, he was filled with feelings of love and compassion for the Italian people. He knew he was called to take them the light of the gospel, no matter the sacrifice."

Eliza nodded and wiped away a tear. A stiff wind blew through another crack between the logs, and she went to stuff a braid piece in the chink.

"Did you ever think you would find the light of truth, Eliza?"

"I hoped."

Charlotte leaned forward. "Yes. I hoped too. My entire family was searching. We went out to all the revival meetings. We found some truth here and some truth there, but we never could get back to the primitive church. We never felt like we were sitting on the seaside as the Lord taught the apostles, or fed the five thousand, or healed the sick. Where was the purity and the priesthood?"

Eliza sat back down in the rocker. "Our family was searching for the same."

Charlotte laid back. "And then we met the Smith family, and we were given a Book of Mormon." She rubbed her eyes. "Everything changed. Everything. We gave up position, and kin, and security. We faced mobs and were forced time and time again from our homes into a barren wilderness. I wondered what would break our faith, but—"

"But nothing could," Eliza finished.

"No, nothing could." They were both silent. Charlotte closed her eyes again.

"Charlotte?"

"Hmm?"

"You're tired. I think it's time for me to go."

Charlotte opened her eyes. "I'm sorry. I've kept you too long."

Eliza stood. "Not at all. It was a joy talking about someone we love."

"And bringing him near for Christmas."

Eliza went over to admire the sleeping child. "Is there anything else before I go?"

"No, dear sister. Little Roxcy and I are tucked in for the night."

Eliza smiled. "How kind of you to give her one of my names."

"It is fitting," Charlotte said. "I only hope she will grow up to possess half your remarkable qualities."

"I'm just a worker in the kingdom," Eliza said, running a finger along the baby's cheek. She took a deep breath and turned. "I will be here tomorrow around noon with squash pie, cornbread, and a chicken to roast." She went to put on her coat. "Oh, and of course, a few small presents for the children."

"That is so generous."

"Nonsense. My mother taught me to never attend to an invitation empty-handed. Besides, your family is doing the largest portion."

"As is fitting."

Eliza leaned over and kissed her sister-in-law on the cheek. "Merry Christmas."

"Merry Christmas, Eliza."

"Get as much rest as you can."

"I will. We have a lot of helping hands here in Lorenzo Snow's family."

Eliza smiled. "He would be proud of you." She walked to the door and opened it onto a dark house. As she glanced back, Eliza saw Charlotte reaching to blow out the candle. Her heart ached, knowing the feelings of loneliness and separation Charlotte was experiencing—feelings she carried with her from the loss of her husband at Nauvoo. She moved quietly through the main room to the front door, and out into the night. She paused and lifted her face to the stars twinkling in the cold night sky. "Merry Christmas, dear brother. May the Lord keep you safe, wherever you are."

NOTE

The letter to which Eliza and Charlotte refer is actual correspondence written by Lorenzo to his family. The event of divine protection during an Indian attack was an actual occurrence encountered by the brethren as they crossed the plains.

CHAPTER EIGHT

Torre Pellice

April 1850

The snap of the crisp linens in the spring air made Albertina smile. As she hung the last of the inn's pillowcases, she sighed with contentment. She loved hanging laundry: one, because it meant the washing was finished; two, because she loved the look and sound of the sheets flapping in the sunshine; and three, because it meant her little brother would soon be creeping out to play "catch the goose." It was Joseph's favorite sport; every Monday, secreted away behind a tree or stone wall, he would watch until the last clothespin was secured, and then he would run for his hiding place among the sheets. He would growl in his wild fox voice and chase his sister up and down the rows. Albertina was an engaging goose, honking madly, and running just out of reach of the fox's claws.

Albertina gazed at the shimmery tunnel created by the white fabric, and saw in her mind's eye her sister, Pauline. Pauline, the creator of the game, Pauline the trickster. There was the crooked grin and the patched dress as she stood with her hands on her knees, waiting expectantly for the fox to strike. The girl who was the best at games and playful mischief. The girl whom little Joseph loved more than any other member of the family. Albertina took a deep breath to stop her emotions. They had lost her last year to fever, a loss that had laid a permanent sorrow on her mother's heart. Albertina shoved another clothespin onto the pillowcase. *They had lost her to fever.* Why had her mind conjured *those* words? She hated it when people used those words about someone who had died. It was like the family had gone on a hike into the mountains and one of them had simply taken another path, never to come home. After Pauline's death, their mother had become fretful and overly cautious about the well-being of her remaining two children, especially Joseph. Albertina brought her mind to the clothespin. Now where was that cunning fox? She expected to hear his growl at any moment, but instead she heard someone calling her name.

"Albertina!"

It was her friend Madeleine! Albertina ducked around the side of the sheet and waved. "Here I am! What are you doing in town?"

Madeleine held up her satchel. "I've brought bread for your guests!"

Albertina knew the bringing of bread was more of an excuse for the two of them to visit than it was concern for the guests at the inn. Madeleine came puffing to her side.

"There's only one problem with your charity," Albertina informed her.

"What's that?"

"We don't have any guests at the moment."

Madeleine frowned. "Not one?"

"Not one."

"Well, what am I to do with this big round of bread?" She looked disconsolate, and then she brightened. "Would your family like it?"

Albertina picked up the laundry basket. "I'm afraid not. Mother just went to the bakery."

"Oh." The two girls walked together to the house. "What are you looking for, Albertina?" Madeleine asked after a time.

"What do you mean?"

"You keep looking around. Are you expecting someone?"

Albertina smiled. "Yes, my little brother. Every wash day we play this game while I'm hanging the laundry, and today he didn't come."

Madeleine shrugged. "Maybe he found another game."

As they rounded the corner of the house the reason for Joseph's absence became evident. He sat up on one of the Guy family's work horses while his father led him carefully around the yard. As soon as Joseph saw his sister he called out.

"Look! Look at me, Albi! I'm riding!"

Albertina looked quickly around to find her mother. She was standing by the front door, a taut expression on her face and in her body. Albertina went to her. "Are you all right with this?"

Francesca Guy pressed her lips together and then said, "He will be fine. His father promised." She turned to Madeleine. "A good day to you, Miss Cardon."

"Good day, Mrs. Guy."

"So your family has moved back up into the high valley?"

"Yes, we've been there a month now."

"Of course. That's why we haven't seen much of you."

"There is always so much to do when we move back up."

"And the weather has been good? Not too much rain?"

"No."

"Too much rain and I would worry about mudslides."

"Mother," Albertina interrupted, "you don't need to borrow trouble."

Mrs. Guy gave her daughter a dismissive look. "All I'm saying is that the mountains are dangerous. Is that not true, Miss Cardon?"

"Yes, that's true. But I guess our people have lived there so long we don't think about it. We see the mountains as a fortress."

Mrs. Guy nodded. "You have walked far for a visit."

"I have. And I brought bread for your guests, but Albertina tells me you don't have any guests."

"No, not today." She stepped forward as Rene urged the old horse to a faster pace. "Rene, not so fast."

"Fast?" Rene called back. "This horse is moving so slowly he's almost going backwards."

Albertina's mother gave a huff of frustration and stepped back. She broke her gaze from the horse and its rider and focused on the two girls. "Why don't you take the bread to Rene's uncle at the monastery? I've made soup for supper and you can take him some of that, too. He likes my soup."

"That's a good idea!" Albertina said happily. "I haven't seen the old bear in weeks."

"But I'm sure this bread will be too country for him," Madeleine said with concern.

Mrs. Guy opened the door and stepped inside the house. "He likes heavy country bread. He can dip it in his soup." She led the way into the kitchen and the girls followed.

Father Andrew sat on the stone bench, watching the reaction of his two supper companions as their table was set on the library's balcony. He observed their wide-eyed stares as the table was placed in the sunshine, covered in a linen tablecloth, and laden with an array of plates, glasses, and silverware. The serving plates held cheese, early pears, orange melon, prosciutto, dark olives, pickled cucumber, French pastries, and Madeleine's country bread. And in the center of all the glory was a china tureen filled with Mrs. Guy's vegetable soup. When the preparations were finished, and the workers on their way back to the kitchen, Father Andrew barked at the girls.

"Come on, you two! Stop standing there with your mouths open and help me up." The girls rushed to his side, giggling. He put a hand on each of their shoulders and pushed himself to his feet. "No sense letting a good meal go uneaten."

"The old bear needs his supper," Albertina said, helping her great-uncle to sit. "Would you like me to serve you?"

He smiled at her. "First you bring supper and now you want to serve?"

"Well, we didn't bring all of this!" Madeleine broke in, gazing at the banquet in front of her. "The least we can do is serve." Moving to the table, she picked up the knife and began slicing the bread.

"If I weren't so old, I would be serving you. You have brought light to my dreary day. Just look at those shining faces."

Albertina patted his face. "Aw, you're a tenderhearted old bear, aren't you? Now, what would you like to eat?"

"A little bit of everything!"

After the girls had served him and made their own selections, the three companions sat eating and talking in the early evening gloaming. The talk was mostly of everyday events and activities: the work in the high valley, the pruning of the vineyard at the inn, Joseph riding the horse for the first time. The girls asked about Father Andrew's work— was he copying old boring records or translating something interesting for a king? His niece teased him about his ink-stained fingers and his love of words. Andrew's mind went to the vellum parchment with its words of torture and death. He looked at the little Waldensian daughter and grief tightened his breathing.

"Uncle! Are you all right?" Albertina asked in alarm.

Andrew focused on her. "What?"

"Are you all right?"

He took a breath and nodded. "Yes . . . yes, of course. Why do you ask?"

"Your face went very white. Are you having a hard time breathing?"

Andrew sat back in his chair and forced another breath. "No, no. I'm fine. I think I just had a few too many pastries."

"You see, that is why gluttony is one of the seven deadly sins."

"There are far worse things," Andrew mumbled.

"What was that, Uncle?" Albertina asked, leaning forward.

Instead of answering her, he looked over at Madeleine. "Life has been difficult for your people in their high mountain valleys, hasn't it—a prison of sorts for hundreds of years?" From the look on her face and ensuing silence, Andrew could tell she was surprised by the change of topic and the unexpected question. "I am being genuine in my question, Miss Cardon. I want to know your feelings."

"But you and my grandfather are friends. You've talked about our people—about our stories."

"Yes, but I want to know more of *your* life. I want to know if the stories have been passed down. The Glorious Return. The Easter Massacre."

Madeleine looked down at her empty plate. "Perhaps we should just forget those things, Father."

His mind conjured a vision of the ancient parchment in the fire. "No," he said gently. "No. I think they should be remembered. Not for sorrow or for vengeance, but to correct us on our path."

Madeleine looked at him. "The Easter Massacre was two hundred years ago."

"Yes. 1655," Andrew said.

"So long ago," Madeleine answered.

"Yes, but you know the story, right?" She nodded. "Go on then," he prompted. "It begins with the Duke of Savoy, Charles Emmanuel."

"Uncle, she doesn't want to."

Andrew looked at his niece. "There is a reason for my asking, sweet Albertina. There is a reason." He turned to Madeleine. "Please, Miss Cardon. Tell us."

Madeleine took a breath. "My grandfather says that Duke Charles Emmanuel was a zealot for the Church, and he saw us as evil heretics because we went against its authority."

"Your presence here in these beautiful valleys offended him."

"Yes. The Waldenese in the old days had to be careful about their worship. They hid their Bibles. They held their meetings in caves. But after joining with the other Protestants they started to pray and preach openly. The duke didn't like it." It took Madeleine time to get out the next words. "He gave orders to exterminate them."

"Exterminate?" Albertina questioned.

Madeleine nodded. "Yes. The Duke of Savoy said the Waldensian people must either convert and attend Catholic Mass or be driven into the high mountain villages. It would become their prison. It was January, but even with the snow and cold, most of the people left their homes and lands in the lower valley and traveled to the upper valleys. They would not give up their faith."

Andrew looked over to see how Albertina was accepting the information, and found her still and watchful. He figured she had talked with her friend about her beliefs, but supposed she knew little if anything of the persecutions they had endured. She needed to understand. "So by April, the duke was tired of waiting for the other Waldenese to follow his order," he said.

Madeleine nodded. "He sent his troops into the valley to slaughter the people. And they . . . and they were . . ." her voice trailed away. "The soldiers were like animals. They killed people in the cruelest way. Women and children torn to pieces." Albertina sat up abruptly as though burnt by fire, but Madeleine was unaware of her. She looked up towards Mount Castelluzzo as she continued. "People thrown alive from the cliffs. Tongues cut out. Families burned in their homes. Young girls buried alive." She was crying now, as was Albertina. The anguish in her young voice made Andrew cover his face. "Thousands of people . . . my people." There was a long hesitation before Madeleine's voice came again. "Why? Why would you want me to tell you this story?"

Father Andrew dropped his hands. His voice was thick with emotion when he answered. "Because I want Albertina to know what your people went through for their faith, and I need to be reminded of the same."

Madeleine wiped her face with her napkin and quieted her emotion. "But you are a priest."

"Yes. Even more the reason."

"I don't understand."

"I am not long for this world, child, and—"

"Uncle!"

Andrew turned to look at his great-niece. "How long do you want me to live, my sweet Albertina?"

"Forever."

"One can only live forever in heaven." He reached over and patted her hand. "Don't worry, I am not going today." He looked back to Madeleine. "But when I do go, little daughter of the Waldenese, I would like to go to heaven." He leaned forward. "And even though you and I are far from that cruelty, I would like to ask your forgiveness."

"Mine?"

"Yes. For I would like to go to heaven with a heart filled with compassion and peace. Do you understand this?" Madeleine nodded. "Good." He smiled at them. "Good."

Madeleine stood and moved to the balcony's railing.

Albertina watched her for a moment, and then turned back to her uncle. "Why would the church condone such a terrible action?"

"Fear."

"Fear?"

"Those in power would not have their power threatened."

"By the simple Waldenese?"

"By anyone whose preaching would draw people away from the church."

"That makes me sad," Albertina said.

"Yes, because you have a good heart." Andrew glanced over at Madeleine. "I think it is enough for today." He called out. "Now, I think we need singing! First from Madeleine, then from Albertina, and then from the two of you together."

Madeleine turned. "If I can." She wiped the last of the tears from her cheeks and moved to stand beside her friend. "What would you like me to sing, Father?"

"I want the one your grandfather often sings—the one about the strength of the hills."

"It is one of my favorites," Madeleine returned.

"As it should be," Andrew said, as he sat back and tried to get comfortable.

Madeleine hummed a little to get the melody and then began:

For the strength of the hills we bless thee,
Our God, our fathers' God!
Thou hast made thy children mighty
By the touch of the mountain sod.
Thou hast fixed our ark, our refuge
Where the spoilers foot ne'er trod;
For the strength of the hills we bless thee,
Our God, our father's God!

As the song continued, Andrew closed his eyes and saw images of the Waldenese holding fast to their faith in spite of bitter persecution, of teaching God's word in dark caverns, of finding strength in the very cliffs surrounding them. He let the words wash his soul. Truth was to be honored whatever its source. He knew Father Pious would be alarmed by this broad thinking. Father Andrew smiled. All the more reason to hold to it.

NOTES

The Easter Massacre occurred in April 1655 in the valleys of the Piedmont. Between 1,800 and 2,000 Waldenese were slaughtered, and thousands more displaced. The incident caused such outrage in Europe that the English prime minister, Oliver Cromwell, Lord Protector of Britain, threatened the Duke of Savoy with military action. He also encouraged the English people to pray and fast for the Waldenese and raise money for their financial support. John Milton, one of England's great poets, wrote a moving poem entitled "On the Late Massacre in Piedmont."

The House of Savoy was established in the eleventh century. It controlled an area known as the County or Duchy of Savoy, which straddled the Cottian Alps. It included the Savoy land of eastern France and the Piedmont land of northwestern Italy.

CHAPTER NINE

Genoa, Italy

June 28, 1850

"Ah, brethren, it is Italy! Do you feel the gentle kiss of the air? Do you smell the lavender and the salt of the sea? And look! Look there, that beautiful old villa with the statues and fountains."

Elder Snow shared a look of amusement with Elder Stenhouse, and then turned back to watch Brother Toronto striding exuberantly down the Via di Porta Soprana, pointing out first a remarkable vista and next the smell of bread from a bakery tucked away on a narrow side street. Lorenzo had to agree, it was a *bella vista*—a lovely land of enchantment. He looked out over the port of Genoa where lay fishing boats, schooners, war frigates, steamers, and ships of many nations. The harbor was embraced by the arms of the gentle rolling landscape, which rose to higher hills, and then, hazy in the distance, the Apennines mountains. Scattered within the hilly province they were traversing, Lorenzo noted palaces, churches, simple stone houses, ancient buildings, promenades, and parks. He breathed in the smell of lavender and felt a sudden pang of melancholy. His wife Charlotte sometimes brushed a light scent of lavender into her hair. The longing for family and home tugged at his heart, so Lorenzo turned his attention to a conversation with the man next to him to allay the gloomy feelings.

"It seems as though Brother Toronto is glad to be back in his native country."

Thomas Stenhouse grinned. "Hmm. Whatever gave you that idea?" Elder Stenhouse's Scottish manner and articulation added to the humor of the comment, and both men laughed. "'Tis a wonder of a place, no mistaking. In Scotland and England it's likely we'd still be having fog and cold rain."

"And in Salt Lake, we'd be having heat and dry wind."

"Well, as the saying goes, 'One must thrive where one is planted.'"

Lorenzo sobered. "I am very grateful you accepted the Lord's call, Brother Stenhouse. Only being in England those few weeks, I did not anticipate calling other missionaries to assist in this field of labor."

"I'm just glad I was living in England at the time of your arrival. And about anticipating the call, I often find it near impossible for us puny mortals to figure out the mind of God. Isn't that truth?"

"Indeed. And here you are, only twenty-four—"

"Twenty-five, actually," Elder Stenhouse corrected.

Lorenzo smiled. "Twenty-five, as old as that? Twenty-five, and asked to leave a new wife and home."

"Ah, to be sure. The beguiling Fanny Warn." Elder Stenhouse tried to keep his demeanor light, but his voice thickened with emotion. "She's a fair one, to be sure. The light of my life."

Lorenzo put his hand on the man's arm. "And I witnessed how difficult it was for you to leave her, Thomas."

"No more so than you, Elder Snow. No more so than you when *you* left *your* family. If the people of Italy only knew the sacrifices we have made for their sakes, they would have no heart to reject us." He gave Lorenzo a steady look. "Here's the thing. I believe you to be an apostle of God, set apart to do the work the Lord has called you to do. If that is my testimony, then who am I to say no when my name is called out?"

"Thank you for that, my friend."

Brother Toronto came back from his wanderings to join them.

"I am sorry, my brothers, to leave you behind. I am going off in a trance. My heart cannot stop bringing everything to it." He made a sweeping motion with his arms as though bringing all of Genoa to him.

Brother Stenhouse thumped him on the back. "Perfectly understandable, Brother Toronto. The air of Italy is in your lungs."

"Yes! Yes, that is it, right? I have not been feeling so well, but now my blood is gaining the energy."

"Yes. We can hardly keep up with you," Elder Snow said.

Brother Toronto stood straighter and placed his hand over his heart. "So now I will be a good missionary and stay nearby. You tell me where you want to go. We can go to the docks, to the house of Christopher Columbus, or perhaps to the Cathedral di San Lorenzo. It is beautiful. Not too far." Brother Toronto stopped talking and looked expectantly at Elder Snow.

"The library," Lorenzo said.

"The library? You have been in Italy three days and you wish to go to the library?" Brother Toronto studied his leader with skepticism.

"Do not worry, Brother Toronto. I have not lost my wits. There is purpose in my request." Four Catholic priests in black robes and three-cornered hats passed them at that moment and Lorenzo nodded to them. After they passed, Lorenzo continued his explanation. "When President Young was calling out the fields of missionary service at the general conference, I had the calm impression that I would be among the names called. What I did not expect and what unsettled my spirit was the *place* to which I was called. I know that the men and women of Italy are my brothers and sisters. I know that God loves them tenderly as He does all His children, but how to reach them with the gospel message is our dilemma."

"Considering the government will not let us preach openly," Brother Stenhouse said.

Lorenzo nodded. "And the people live under a shroud of religious superstition and tradition."

"This I know well," Brother Toronto said. "It makes it hard for the ears to hear new things," he added, pointing to his ears.

"Yes," Lorenzo agreed. "It is something I have been contemplating with deep solicitude. How are we to proceed? Where does the Lord wish us to go?"

"We have been praying for guidance also," Brother Stenhouse said.

"For that, brethren, I am grateful. The Lord knows our hearts and hears our prayers. Of this I am sure. And I believe there may be a glimmer of light hidden away in the valleys of the Piedmont."

The two companions were silent at this pronouncement. Finally, Brother Stenhouse said, "Have . . . have you received revelation, then, Elder Snow?"

Lorenzo smiled. "Well . . . guidance, Brother Stenhouse. Guidance. Last evening, on returning from one of my solitary walks, I met with a teacher from England who is in Italy doing research. In the course of our conversation he inquired as to my business, and I told him I was a missionary for The Church of Jesus Christ of Latter-day Saints. He was of no particular faith, but felt for the difficulty of our situation in the towns and cities of Italy. He then inquired whether I had heard of the Waldenese people."

"Waldenese?" Brother Stenhouse questioned.

"Yes. A group of Protestant believers living in the Alpine mountains of the Piedmont." Lorenzo turned to Brother Toronto. "Have you ever heard of them, brother?"

"I have not, Elder Snow. I have never heard this name."

"I tell you, brethren, when I heard it, a flood of light seemed to burst upon my mind, and I determined to learn more about them."

"Hence our trip to the library," Brother Stenhouse said with a smile.

"Yes." Lorenzo laid his hand on Brother Toronto's shoulder and looked between the two men. "I didn't share this news with either of you last night because I needed time to contemplate."

Brother Toronto chuckled. "Of course—you are the apostle. I

am not going to question what you do." He tipped his hat. "So even though I cannot read, I know what *I* am going to do."

Lorenzo gave him an amused look. "And what is that, Elder Toronto?"

"*I* am going to take *you* to the library!"

Lorenzo had never been in a library housed in what had been a palace. The marble floors of the ballroom were covered with exquisitely woven area rugs and furnished with leather couches and armchairs. These heavy furnishings sat in contrast to the pastel-painted ceiling and sparkling chandeliers. Lorenzo brought his gaze back to the thousands of books that lined the walls. They sat on dozens of tall, ornately carved bookshelves, each flanked by spiral malachite pillars. Ten impressive world globes stood in a row down the middle of the room. He and Eliza had always loved libraries, and he couldn't wait to write her a letter describing this marvel. He turned to the desk as the librarian approached. As his companions had deserted him for the intrigue of the books, Lorenzo steadied himself to attempt a bit of Italian.

"Good day, sir."

"Good day."

"I . . . I am desiring a book on the Piedmont. On the Waldenese people. Do you have anything?"

"The Waldenese? Yes, we do. But I am sorry. A lady has just taken it."

"Just taken it?"

"Yes, just a couple of hours ago. I am sorry. Maybe you can come back next week?"

"All right. Thank you." Lorenzo turned from the desk, a twinge of disappointment blunting his enthusiasm, and the urgency for information still troubling his spirit. He passed by a female patron in his search for his companions, but before he'd taken five more steps, the voice of the librarian called out to him.

"Sir! Sir! Here is the lady! The lady with the book!"

Lorenzo turned, feeling the warmth of the Spirit enfold him. He walked back to the desk just as the woman was handing the book to the astonished librarian.

"Oh, this *is* a remarkable circumstance," he said. "This gentleman has just called for that book."

"Oh, yes?" the woman asked. "Well, I went to the park to read, but found the content too heavy for a summer's day. Do you understand this?"

Lorenzo smiled. "Oh, yes, I understand many things."

She spoke nonchalantly as she retied the ribbon of her hat. "I was going to return it tomorrow, but then felt as though I did not wish to carry it around. So I brought it back. I am glad if it serves you."

"Yes. Thank you very much," Lorenzo said with a slight bow.

"Good day, sir," the woman said to the open-mouthed librarian.

"Ah . . . ah, good day, madam." As the woman turned and left, the librarian's gaze slid over to Lorenzo. "Well, what good fortune!" he said with a shake of his head. "What good fortune." He handed Lorenzo the book. "Would you like to take it with you?"

"No, thank you. I would love to read it here in this beautiful place."

The librarian beamed. "Yes. Yes, of course. There are many comfortable places."

Lorenzo nodded and went off to find his friends. They were settled on a couch at the back of the room with a large atlas opened across their laps. Elder Stenhouse looked up from turning pages. "Did you find what you were looking for?"

"I did."

The men sat staring as Lorenzo related the improbable story of the book's return.

"Really, ought we be surprised?" Elder Stenhouse said with a grin when Lorenzo finished. "It never ceases to amaze me what the Lord can orchestrate."

"Nor I," Lorenzo agreed. He leaned forward in his chair to peruse what his companions were studying. "Maps?"

"Maps of northern Italy. I cannot read the words, but I am looking at the pictures," Brother Toronto said with a wink. "We are trying to find one that gives details of the Alpine region of the Piedmont."

"Wonderful idea!" Lorenzo answered. "I will sit here and read, and you two will be geography experts."

For the next two hours the three Mormon missionaries sat in the splendid library in Genoa studying about a place and a people that, prior to this, had been unknown to them. While Brothers Stenhouse and Toronto found maps of the Waldenese homeland and made several rather exquisite renderings of the area, Lorenzo read of the beginnings of their doctrinal desires, their longing for the primitive faith, and their fortitude against hundreds of years of torture and oppression. His spirit recognized a kinship—a brotherhood of truth seekers.

After deep contemplation, Lorenzo looked up from the book, his face filled with reverence. "Brethren," he said quietly, "I am convinced that these people are worthy to receive the first proclamation of the gospel in Italy."

NOTE

The incident at the library in Genoa concerning the serendipitous return of the book is actual. Lorenzo wrote about it in his journal.

CHAPTER TEN

Genoa, Italy

July 20, 1850

To Franklin D. Richards

My dear Franklin,

Having safely reached the land of my mission, I take the earliest opportunity to inform you of my location and prospects. The ancient city of Genoa where I now reside contains about one hundred and forty thousand inhabitants, and though the lovely turquoise waters of the Mediterranean embrace its shore, and a perpetual blue sky reigns overhead, the minds of the people are shrouded with spiritual folly and superstition.

The city is filled with armed men; so, in fact, is almost every seaport and city through which we have passed since leaving England. There has been revolution in Paris and Vienna, and rebellion in Venice. Indeed, in Italy, the call has come to leave the rule of the city-states and the oppression of intrusion from other countries and to become a united and independent country. The entire region seems to be in turmoil. Little money is circulating, and commerce languishes on every side. The country is not yet sufficiently settled to induce the enterprise of the capitalist. Since the revolution, the working classes have suffered severely from the depression of business. Wages are, of course, very low; upon an average, not more than twenty cents for a day's work for a laborer, which is commonly made to consist of about sixteen hours.

Many of the customs, laws, and institutions are very singular. Priests are seen in great numbers on every side. I meet them on every street. From the peculiarity of their dress, there is no mistaking their profession. Those of the superior order are clothed in black, and their heads display the accompaniment of a three-cornered hat. Those of another class present a shorn crown to the evening breeze and the noonday sun, and the meanness of their garments is intended to represent their vows of austere indigence. A coarse woolen dress is attached to the body by a rope loosely tied around the waist, from which hang their rosary beads and a small crucifix. Their feet are shod with a species of sandal. They are generally seen two together, and are very unlike the wealthy ecclesiastics, who mingle freely with the best society.

The other day, as I was returning from a walk, I fell into the following reflections: I am alone and a stranger in this great city, eight thousand miles from my beloved family, surrounded by a people with whose manners and peculiarities I am unacquainted. I have come to enlighten their minds and instruct them in principles of righteousness, but I see no possible means of accomplishing this object. All is darkness in the prospect. Are they prepared to receive the voice from on high? "Behold, the Bridegroom cometh; go ye out to meet Him!"

The Lord knows that I bade a heart-trying farewell to the loved and tried partners of my bosom to obey His call. Does He not have some chosen ones among this people to whom I have been sent? My prayer is that He will lead me unto such and I shall give Him all the glory.

After I wrote the foregoing, I received a letter from Elders Stenhouse and Toronto. On the first of July, I sent them off to the Alpine region of northern Italy, and since that time I have felt an intense desire to know the state of that province to which

I had given them an appointment. I felt assured it would be the field of our mission. Now, with a heart full of gratitude, I find an opening is presented in the valleys of Piedmont, when all other parts of Italy are closed against our efforts. I believe that the Lord has there hidden up a people amid the Alpine mountains, and it is the voice of the Spirit that I shall commence something of importance in that part of the nation.

Prudence and caution prompt me to request that you will not, at present, give publicity to my communications. I will leave off now so I may get this letter to the post. Barring any impediment, I plan to organize my affairs and depart for the Piedmont in two or three days.

Your brother in the Gospel, affectionately,

Lorenzo Snow

NOTE

With a few minor changes, this was a letter written by Lorenzo Snow to Franklin D. Richards, who presided over the European Mission.

Chapter Eleven

Torre Pellice

July 25, 1850

All he saw was ash—wood, wool, and flesh charred to disintegration. Hot ash, picked up by the wind and whirled into stinging red eyes, forced into nostrils and mouths, smudging the air gray. Andrew watched as Duke Charles Emmanuel picked up a charred branch and pressed the toe of his boot into the ash. "So, what am I stepping on?" he called out. "A Waldensian pig or a Waldensian woman? No difference. It serves the heretics right for going against God's choice. For thinking themselves above the church—above me!" A shaft of morning sunlight breached the hill and the powerful Duke of Savoy squinted and cursed. "Vexing nonbelievers— can they not just recant their sins, and leave me to mate and eat my meals in peace?" He threw the blackened stick at a scavenging rat. "Any flesh you find today will be well-done, master rodent. I have seen to the cooking."

Andrew heard a woman's mewling whimper behind him and turned to see a young female moving towards the duke with a blade in her hand.

"Stop her!" the duke ordered.

Andrew reached out and grabbed the woman's burnt arm. The knife fell.

"I know you!" the woman screamed, her eyes fixed on the duke's face. "I have known you through all time. I was there on the mountainside

when you nailed His feet to the cross; I was there five hundred years ago when the great reformer Peter Waldo brought the word of God forward."

Andrew watched in terror as the duke raised his sword, but he did not release his grip on the woman's arm.

"Do not speak the name of the blasphemer, witch, or my sword will find your throat," the duke growled.

"I have always known your face. I have always seen the blood upon your hands. You were there in the service of the power-hungry leaders of the holy church, who were more soldier than disciple."

Andrew dropped her arm and stepped back, waiting for the blow that would cut her throat.

"You place your feet in the lake of damnation to speak against the power of the church," the duke hissed.

"I set my feet on the straight path when I stand against darkness. I have no quarrel with the humble priest or the simple monk who live their lives in the service Christ taught." Andrew was held in place by her words. "I vilify those who think themselves above the laws of Christ, who refuse to let the words of the Bible go out to the people, who have changed the nature of God."

"These falsehoods will be your death!"

"Truth! I speak the truth! That which was spoken from the mouth of Christ to His apostles, from the mouth of Paul to the seven churches. I speak the truth of the primitive church."

The duke grabbed her around the throat, and she looked straight into his eyes. "Remember, I know you. Through all time I have known you. All of you who have drowned, and gutted, and burned my people. I know you. And one day you will stand before the judgment bar of God and you will see my face."

Andrew could not breathe. There was a great weight on his chest. Her words burned into his ears.

"I do not fear death, for I know the place I am going. I would have gladly died with my family, but I needed to look into the eyes of my *murderer and tell him the fate that awaits him for his butchery—a place of wailing and gnashing of teeth. A place without light."*

"Enough!" *the duke screamed, shoving her away from him. He looked directly at Andrew.* "You!" *He threw his dagger at Andrew's feet.* "Cut out her tongue." *Andrew saw terror in the woman's eyes.* "Yes, witch. The world has heard the last of your evil rantings. Try quoting scripture or praising the great reformer now." *He pointed at Andrew.* "Do it! You are my lead man. Cut out her tongue!"

"No!" Andrew forced himself awake, forced himself to breathe. The weight was still heavy on his chest, and he struggled to sit. He pressed his bedding against his face, crying to relieve the pain. "Oh, Father. Oh, my Father. Please! Why do these images haunt me? What am I supposed to do? What am I supposed to learn? That we are men of dirt? Yes, yes. I know this. We are men of dirt."

The trill of a morning thrush came floating in through his opened window, and Andrew stopped his lament. He focused on the song, and worked to steady his breathing and stop the tears. After a time, he lay back against his pillow, looking up at his small patch of sky. "I am just an old man, Lord. What is it you want from me?"

CHAPTER TWELVE

Torre Pellice

July 26, 1850

"Where are you from?"

The young boy spoke French, but in a dialect that was nearly impossible for Lorenzo to understand. "Excuse me?"

The boy folded his arms across his chest and gave the stranger a surly look. "Where are you from?"

"Ah! Where did I come from? I came from Genoa."

"No, no, no!" The boy moved forward and cocked his leg back as if to kick.

"Joseph! Stop!" Rene Guy had just come around the side of the inn in time to see the aggressive actions of his youngest child. He ran forward and took Joseph by the arm. "What are you doing?"

"He's trying to come into our yard," Joseph said in a gruff voice.

"Many people come into our yard. We run an inn, you little Bonaparte! Besides, he may be the man we have been waiting for." Rene gave his son's arm a little shake as his eyes moved from the boy to the stranger. "Perhaps you are the friend of Monsieurs Stenhouse and Toronto?"

"I am that man," Lorenzo said, smiling. He extended his hand and Rene took it.

"Welcome! Welcome, Monsieur Snow. I apologize for my son, sir.

He thinks *he* is the proprietor. Here, let me get your bags." He picked them up.

"Ah, that is not necessary."

Rene went on as if not hearing. "And Joseph can carry that little bag to make up for being rude to you. Joseph, say you are sorry, and pick up the bag."

Joseph gave Lorenzo an impish grin and picked up his bag. "I am very strong."

"I can see that," Lorenzo said.

"And the apology," Rene insisted. "Do not try to get around it."

"I am sorry," Joseph called back as he dragged Lorenzo's bag across the rocky courtyard.

Rene let out an exasperated bark and hurried after his son. "Ah, Joseph! Pick it up! Pick it up!"

"Yes, Papa!" Joseph said, wobbling as he attempted to lift the satchel higher into his arms.

Lorenzo smiled at the retreating pair, loving the little boy's transformation. Joseph's dirty face and disheveled hair were charming, and Lorenzo's heart took a sudden lurch. He had been away from his family for nine months and he missed the chatter and joyous chaos. He also knew he had missed births and milestones of growing. What child was walking, and who was speaking in sentences? Did any of them call his name?

Lorenzo squared his shoulders and followed Rene and his boy towards the picturesque stone inn—the Pension de l'Ours. Chestnut trees sheltered the southern wall from the sun and giant peony bushes covered in pale pink flowers softened the lower facade. As Lorenzo was admiring the outbuildings and the small vineyard, the door of the inn opened and Elders Stenhouse and Toronto came eagerly into the cobbled courtyard.

"We thought you might arrive today!" Elder Toronto boomed, coming close and giving Lorenzo's hand a firm shake. "My eyes are happy to see you, dear brother!"

Elder Stenhouse thumped Lorenzo on the back. "A bit dusty from travel, but none the worse for wear. Welcome to a land just a slight bit east of paradise!"

Lorenzo shook their hands heartily. He was glad to see them. Their shared faith was reassuring, and their optimism lifted his spirit. The inn sat on a rise and Lorenzo turned to take in the verdant landscape. "It is exquisite, isn't it?"

"It is," Elder Stenhouse said. "And wait until you taste Madame Guy's cooking. That is exquisite as well. Today she is making lamb stew."

"Sounds wonderful, but I would like to walk the town before nightfall. We have much to discuss," Lorenzo said.

The two companions laughed, and Elder Stenhouse took Lorenzo's arm, steering him towards the inn. "Yes, yes. We will have time for walking and talking, but first don't you think it wise to take a wee bit of a rest and have a bite of food?"

"And clean some of the dust from your hands and face?" Elder Toronto added with a chuckle. "We knew you would put us to work when you arrived, but not the very moment."

Lorenzo laughed at himself. "I guess the work is always before me."

"As it should be," Elder Stenhouse said, opening the door of the inn. "But even the apostles of old took time to eat some bread and fish."

Elder Toronto followed the two into the cool interior of the inn. "Or, in our case, lamb stew."

"*Lux Lucet in Tenebris*," Lorenzo said in a low voice. He stood in the center aisle of the Waldensian church, looking up to the front alcove with its frescoed wall and raised pulpit. He was studying the painted wooden plaque that fronted the podium. The patina of the wood and muted color of the paint indicated age, but Lorenzo was captivated by how the masterful carving still held the form of the symbolic images. On an ancient book of scripture sat a single candle on a candlestick. Rays of light emanated from the candle's flame, and this was haloed by seven stars. Curving around the perimeter of the plaque were the Latin words *Lux Lucet in Tenebris*.

"Is it Latin?" Elder Stenhouse asked, coming to Lorenzo's side.

"It is," Lorenzo answered. "'The light which shines in darkness.'"

"Beautiful."

Lorenzo nodded, looking around at the church's simple interior: a worn wooden floor supporting rows of simple wooden benches, a cast-iron stove for winter warmth, and pale yellow walls absent of ornate paintings or statuary. The only adornments were the wooden plaque and the fresco on the wall behind the pulpit. The painting, done in soft colors, was of an open Bible with words in French that Lorenzo easily translated as, "Thou shalt love thy neighbor as thyself." Matthew 22—the words and sentiment simple to understand. Not like the capricious language of the valley people, which, his companions assured him, would both amuse and frustrate him. French was generally used, but many spoke it with a mixture of provincialism and Italian. Italian was understood by a considerable number, but wasn't used extensively. Often it was like hearing three languages spoken simultaneously. In fact, their landlord, Monsieur Guy, had told them that there were at least five distinct dialects spoken by different classes in the small region of the Piedmont.

"Thou shalt love thy neighbor as thyself," Lorenzo said quietly. He sighed with contentment as the glow of sunset poured in through the western windows, creating a soft cocoon of solitude. It had been a long time since he'd felt this kind of peace, and he offered a silent prayer of gratitude. He also felt assurance that here in the mountain valleys of the Piedmont was the place to preach the gospel—and he was eager to begin the work. Lorenzo thought about where they would preach, how they could contact those who were interested, and which pamphlets would need translating. His mind was busy with these strategies when a whispering came distinctly to his mind. *Be still and wait.*

Wait? Patience was not a usual product of his personality. *Wait?* What would be the point of waiting? The prompting came again to move slowly, and Lorenzo grumbled to himself even as he submitted to the guidance of the Spirit.

"Are you all right, Elder Snow?" Elder Toronto asked.

Lorenzo opened his eyes and looked over at the man. "Did I grumble out loud?"

Elder Toronto smiled. "You did."

Lorenzo smiled back. "I suppose I was grumbling at my own persistent imperfections." He appraised his two companions. "Shall we walk out into the evening coolness? There are things we need to discuss concerning the mission."

Elders Stenhouse and Toronto moved to the church doors and out into the night. They waited on the porch for their leader to join them, and then the three men walked together towards the town center of Torre Pellice. For a time they walked in silence, enjoying the cool breeze from the mountains, the smell of cooking fires, and the trill of birdsong. When Lorenzo spoke, his voice carried the calmness of the surroundings.

"Brethren, I feel assured that we have come to the place where the Lord wishes us to serve." The two men voiced agreement and waited for further counsel from their leader. "But the prompting has also come that we should wait for a time before we begin our labors."

"Wait?" Elder Stenhouse asked.

Lorenzo smiled at him. "Yes. Wait. We are to lay a foundation for the work. We are to silently prepare the minds of the people for the reception of the gospel by cultivating friendly feelings in their hearts."

"I like that. It feels right to me," Elder Stenhouse said.

"For how long?" Elder Toronto asked.

"Until we are prompted to do otherwise," Lorenzo answered, stopping to look at a shop display featuring a variety of writing paper and ink pens. "And," he said slowly, "I think I shall write a treatise on the Church to be translated into French."

"But we have already told the Guy family that we are preachers," Elder Toronto interrupted. "I don't think that will remain a secret."

"That doesn't trouble me," Lorenzo answered. "I think it appropriate to introduce ourselves as preachers, but we can also inform the people that we wish to better understand the language and the culture before we set up our church."

"This is a grand inspiration!" Elder Stenhouse exclaimed. "I have been wanting to get out among the people, to hike the narrow trails up into the mountains, and see life in the villages and hamlets. I think this will give us a better understanding of their faith."

"I agree," Lorenzo said. "From what I've read there is much we share with the Waldensian faithful in their longing for the primitive gospel of Christ."

"And in persecutions suffered for the truth," Elder Stenhouse added.

Lorenzo nodded and turned to Elder Toronto. "What do you think, Elder Toronto?"

"Yes. Yes. It is a good idea," Elder Toronto answered with forced enthusiasm.

The man's words spoke of support, but his look was somber. Lorenzo moved to him, placing his hand on his shoulder. "What's troubling you, my friend?"

It took Elder Toronto time to answer. "I meant to wait a week or two before bothering you with this, Elder Snow. I know you've been worried about where to settle the mission, and I did not want to add to your burden."

"It is fine, Brother Toronto," Lorenzo said. "Your thoughts and feelings are important to me."

The troubled look on Elder Toronto's face eased. "Thank you. Thank you for that." He looked to Elder Stenhouse and back to Lorenzo. "Since my health has returned to me, I have been feeling a strong desire to travel to Sicily and meet with my family there. When I joined the Church in Boston, I had been away from home for many years—an adventurous sailor, out to see the world." He shook his head. "But now, back in my country, I find that I miss my family and the friends of my youth. I want to return home and see if I can turn their hearts to the gospel. Perhaps they will find an interest in what I believe." He looked steadfastly at Lorenzo. "Does this make sense to you?"

"Perfect sense," Lorenzo said. "It is a desire filled with charity."

Brother Stenhouse stepped forward. "It is Lehi standing by the Tree of Life and longing for his family to come and partake of the fruit."

A few tears leaked from the corners of Brother Toronto's eyes. "Thank you, brothers. I have been worried that I was abandoning my mission."

"Not at all," Lorenzo assured. "I think you will do a good work among your family, Elder Toronto. A good work."

"But what of all the work to do here in these valleys? It will be difficult for two, especially with the language."

"The Lord will provide, Brother Toronto. If He has prompted you south to your family, then He will give guidance on how we are to proceed. In fact, on my journey here from Genoa, I had the feeling to call another missionary from England to join us."

Elder Toronto's eyes widened. "Really? You are not just saying that to make me feel better?"

Lorenzo chuckled. "Well, I'm glad if it makes you feel better, but that's not the reason for the prompting. I think the work here will take many interesting paths and we must be ready to serve where we are called."

"Any ideas on the new missionary?" Elder Stenhouse asked.

Lorenzo grinned over at him. "Not at the moment, but we will counsel together and see if a name presents itself."

"I may have a few suggestions," Elder Stenhouse answered with a confident nod.

"Excellent!" Lorenzo said. "You see, Elder Toronto, all is well. We will send you off on the first of August and a new missionary will join us here sometime in September." Lorenzo looked to the darkening sky. "I feel assured, brethren, that the Lord has directed us to a branch of the house of Israel." He looked over at his two companions. "I also feel that we will find many good people with the same mind and heart as those Saints we know in the valleys of the West and the green isles of Britain."

"Amen to that," Elder Stenhouse said.

"So, to home and to bed," Lorenzo said, turning immediately and heading in the direction of the inn. Elders Stenhouse and Toronto hurried to catch up as their leader continued talking. "Tomorrow I will buy paper and ink and begin writing the publication about the Church; Elder Toronto, you will prepare for your journey south; and Elder Stenhouse, you will take a hike up into the valley to gain acquaintance with the people of the mountains."

Elder Stenhouse heartily concurred with his assignment, and then began singing:

> *Praise to the man who communed with Jehovah!*
> *Jesus anointed "that Prophet and Seer"—*
> *Blessed to open the last dispensation;*
> *Kings shall extol him, and nations revere.*

His lilting brogue fit well with the lovely Scottish melody, inspiring his companions to join in.

> *Hail to the Prophet, ascended to heaven!*
> *Traitors and tyrants now fight him in vain.*
> *Mingling with Gods, he can plan for his brethren;*
> *Death cannot conquer the hero again.*

Lorenzo felt the press of tears at the back of his eyes, and was amazed to find that they were tears of awe, not anguish. Only six years prior, their beloved Prophet Joseph had been murdered by a cruel mob in Carthage, Illinois. The surrounding secular world believed it to be the end of the odd sect with its claims of angelic visitations and new scripture, and for a time, the heart of the Mormon people could scarce imagine a future in which the Prophet Joseph was not present. But the core of the faith held firm through sorrow, persecution, extermination orders, and expulsion, while thousands of converts from Europe and Scandinavia bolstered the beleaguered group of Saints moving west.

Lorenzo strode down the pathway, singing in a voice filled with wonder, resolve, and gratitude, for although he missed his family terribly, he was grateful to be a part of the magnificent work of the restoration.

Sacrifice brings forth the blessings of heaven!
Earth must atone for the blood of that man.
Wake up the world for the conflict of justice!
Millions shall know Brother Joseph again.

NOTES

The Guys' inn, Pension de l'Ours, was most likely located in the center part of Torre Pellice, but I placed it in a more rural locale simply for a more picturesque setting.

The single candle haloed by seven stars with the words "The Light Which Shines in Darkness" is an important symbol for the Waldensian people, and plaques and pictures of this representation can be found in every Waldensian temple or meeting place.

CHAPTER THIRTEEN

Torre Pellice

August 11, 1850

"Mama wants potatoes and cabbages," Joseph said, pulling up carrots from the monastery garden.

Father Andrew shrugged. "Well, those are carrots, not potatoes, but you are welcome to a few of those, too." Andrew sat on a stool near the middle of the garden, enjoying the company of his great-nephew and -niece and the afternoon sun.

Albertina moved over and took the carrots out of her little brother's hand. "I told you to wait for me to tell you what to pull up." She laid the carrots in her basket alongside a huge cabbage.

"Sorry. Sorry, Albi," Joseph said contritely. "But I thinked they was potatoes." He brightened. "We like carrots, too!"

Father Andrew laughed out loud, and Albertina scowled at him. "Don't encourage him. He'd probably pull up the entire garden if given half a chance." She turned her scowl on Joseph. "We have carrots in our own garden."

Joseph's mouth worked back and forth as he thought. "But *these* are *holy* carrots!"

Now both Andrew and Albertina laughed. Joseph hopped up and ran to his sister. "You're not mad at me now?"

She leaned down and brushed dirt from his trousers. "How can I be mad at you? You're a little treasure."

Joseph pushed her hand away when she tried to clean dirt off his face. He ran to his great-uncle and climbed onto his lap.

"Joseph!" Albertina scolded. "You're too big to climb up on Uncle's lap." He immediately began to slide down, but Andrew caught him.

"He's fine. He's just fine. I can hold him for a little while."

Joseph made himself comfortable. "See, he wants to hold me 'cause I'm a treasure."

Albertina shook her head. "Oh, for heaven's sake. He thinks he's the king of Piedmont-Sardinia." She walked off toward the potato plants.

Father Andrew leaned over and whispered in Joseph's ear. "You are *better* than the king." The little boy giggled, and Andrew gave him a squeeze. "But you must not make me love you so much."

"I can't help it."

Andrew's voice became gruff. "I am actually angry with you."

Joseph turned to look into his great-uncle's stern face. "Why?"

"Because you haven't come to visit me in a long time."

Joseph sighed dramatically. "We have been very busy, you see."

"Oh, yes?"

"Yes. We have men at the inn." He held up three fingers. "There was this many." He put one of his fingers down. "But now there are this many."

"What happened to the other man?"

Joseph shrugged. "I don't know. He went away." He slid off his uncle's lap. "Oh, I know! Papa said he went home to Sicily." He brushed dirt off Andrew's cassock. "Maybe he missed his mama."

Andrew gave the boy an affectionate grin and ruffled his hair. "Maybe he did. Maybe he did."

"I am not going to leave home," Joseph said.

"What's that about leaving home?" Albertina asked as she approached.

"We are not going to," Joseph declared. "We won't, will we, Uncle?"

"Never," Andrew said.

Albertina set down her heavy basket. "Never?"

Joseph frowned at her. "No. We won't." He took ahold of her skirt. "You won't leave home, will you, Sister?"

"Well, of course. When I marry, I'll move into a different house."

"No, you won't."

She noted the troubled look on her brother's face. "Yes, I will, dear one. I will have a big new house with my husband, but . . ." she paused for dramatic effect, ". . . I will make sure we build our house right next door to the inn."

"Next door?"

"Yes. And every day you can come and see me." He hugged her legs and she patted his back. "And if you're very good we will make a playroom just for you."

Joseph's face filled with wonder. "A playroom?"

Andrew raised his eyebrows. "Now who's treating him like he's the king?"

"Can I help it?" Albertina replied. "Look at that face."

"My face?" Joseph asked.

"Yes, your face, dirt and all. Come here. Let me clean it."

"No!" Joseph squealed. He ran across the rows of vegetables, treading on green leaves as he went.

Andrew laughed, but Albertina was horrified. "Joseph Guy, stop!"

At that moment, Madeleine Cardon appeared around the garden wall. She stopped in her tracks, watching with delight as her friend jumped vegetable rows in pursuit of her brother. "Run, Joseph! Run!" Madeleine called.

Albertina grunted. "Don't encourage him!"

Joseph made a dash for Madeleine, but Albertina caught him just before he made it to the safety of her skirts. There was giggling and laughing all around as the girls tried to secure the wriggling boy.

"No! No! Don't wash my face! Don't do it!"

"Oh, goodness! All this fuss over a clean face?" Albertina scolded. "You scrub too hard."

"Do you want Mother to do it?"

Joseph's eyes widened and he stopped squirming. "No."

"Then come with me to the trough, and I promise to be gentle."

"All right," he said slowly. He took her hand and Madeleine's. "You can swing me!"

The girls swung him over to the hollowed log at the edge of the garden into which poured clear artesian water. It was near the place where Father Andrew was sitting, so he had a grand view of the washing-up scene. Soon hands and face were clean, and Madeleine sacrificed her apron for the drying. After the bath, Joseph ran into the arms of his great-uncle.

"You're warm," he sighed.

"One of the advantages of a black cassock on a sunny day," Andrew said, holding him close. "You look lovely." He patted Joseph's back. "My lovely, lovely boy."

Joseph smiled up at him.

Albertina and Madeleine came over then, talking, laughing, and trying to fix their disheveled appearance.

"Someone would think you were in charge of five boys, not one," Andrew commented.

"Well, perhaps we should give you the task next time," Albertina said pointedly.

"Uncle could take care of me," Joseph said defiantly. "He would let me have a dirty face."

Andrew laughed. "Well, aren't you a smart boy? You have everything figured out, don't you?"

Albertina narrowed her eyes at her brother. "Sometimes he is too smart for his own good."

Father Andrew changed the subject. "Good afternoon, Mademoiselle Cardon. What brings you down from the mountain?"

"I'm here to pick up your great-niece. She's coming to spend a few days with me."

A look of longing flickered across the old priest's face. "Ah, heavenly. The high valleys are beautiful in the summer—the pine and the sycamore, the narrow mountain trails, and the waterfalls tumbling from the rocky heights. What glory." He gave Joseph another hug. "I wish I could go with you, dear niece."

Albertina laid her hand on his shoulder. "I wish you could come too, old bear, but then it would ruin our surprise."

"What surprise?"

Albertina glanced over at Madeleine, who nodded approval. "We are beginning to practice our song for the music competition in Pinerolo."

"Are you? How wonderful! And you want to sing among the pine trees where no one will hear you."

"Exactly."

"And what will you be singing?"

"Oh no, old bear. That is the surprise. We don't want anyone to know."

"Not even your kind old uncle?"

"No. And don't try to trick us into telling you." She picked up the basket of vegetables.

"But I would not tell a soul."

"No, no. Anyway, we are safe from your questioning because I see Father Nathanael coming to take you in for your afternoon nap." She pointed toward the monastery.

"I would rather stay in the sunshine with you," Andrew grumbled.

"I would like that too," Albertina said tenderly, "but I must get ready for the mountain, and Mother needs these vegetables for dinner. Our lodgers are very fond of her cooking."

"They have been with you awhile."

"One for six weeks. The other for two weeks."

"And their business?"

"They are ministers of some sort, but I've never heard them preach. Most of the time the one is off hiking up in the valleys and the other is writing."

"Writing? Writing what?" Andrew asked with real interest.

"I don't know. I am not one to nose into other people's business. You should come sometime and meet them." She leaned down and kissed his cheek. "Now, stop trying to delay us. I have a busy afternoon."

"And so does your uncle," Father Nathanael said, coming to stand beside the old priest. "Good day, Mademoiselle Guy, are you well?"

"I am, Father Nathanael. Thank you."

"Now, now, what's that you said?" Andrew questioned. "*I* have a busy afternoon?"

"Yes. The king of Piedmont-Sardinia needs some papers written out."

Andrew looked delighted, but spoke as if perturbed. "Oh, does he? And what of my afternoon nap? Does he not care anything about that?"

Father Nathanael gently helped the aged priest to his feet.

Albertina laughed. "Oh, stop growling, old bear, and get to your work," She went to him and gave him a tender hug. Joseph copied her actions.

Andrew gave Albertina a wink. "Take breaths of mountain air for me, will you?"

"Of course."

"And you, young man," he said to Joseph. "Stay clean for five minutes and your sister won't have to wash you."

"Yes, Uncle."

Albertina took her brother's hand. "Come on, time to go." The three waved good-bye and moved out of the garden and onto the wagon track.

Andrew watched them, and then turned with a sigh to take Father

Nathanael's arm. "Do you know what I want to do when I die? I mean after I die?"

"What, dear Father Andrew?"

"I want to climb to the top of Mount Boucie and look down on the world. I want to look down on the mountains covered in snow, and the greening chestnut trees in the spring, and I want to watch my little Joseph as he grows."

"That sounds like a piece of heaven," Father Nathanael said as they started towards the monastery.

A piece of heaven, Andrew thought. *Surely the Lord God will grant me that kindness.*

Chapter Fourteen

Torre Pellice

September 6, 1850

"I have been to Luserna and San Giovanni just east of Torre Pellice, and then Villar Pellice, Bobbio Pellice, and Sibaud up into the Pellice Valley." As Elder Stenhouse recounted the names of the towns to which he'd hiked, Lorenzo traced the route and the locations on the map. It was the same map Elders Toronto and Stenhouse had rendered during their visit to the library at Genoa, and Lorenzo's thoughts flew back for a moment to that good day—the splendid library and the smell of lavender. He tried to capture an image of Charlotte baking bread, teaching one of the children, or brushing out her long hair. A year away from home weighed on his heart. The precious pictures blurred and vanished.

"Bobbio Pellice is the larger of the towns up the valley," Elder Stenhouse said, unaware that Elder Snow's mind had wandered.

Lorenzo brought his thoughts to the present. He sat with Elder Stenhouse at a rustic wooden table outside the inn, where they were eating breakfast and discussing the objectives of the day. "And are there villages farther up into the mountains?" he asked.

"Well, these are the major towns and villages," Elder Stenhouse said, pointing. "The higher you go into the narrow valleys, the communities become small; some are only a cluster of stone houses. It's remarkable how they scratch out an existence up there. Often the mountainsides are steep. In one valley, I could have shot an arrow from one side of the canyon to the other."

"Remarkable," Lorenzo said. "And how are the people?"

"Simple and hardworking. Their lives are one long round of unremitting toil. And that goes for men and women alike. They have these large baskets fashioned with shoulder straps in which they carry everything from manure to wood to huge loads of hay. And these are carried not just by strong young men, but by elderly women with gray hair." Elder Stenhouse shook his head. "Up and down on those rugged mountain paths. I don't know how they do it."

"And what of their demeanor?"

"Quite open. Of course, at first they are curious about my solitary wanderings, but when introductions have been made, with me using my modicum of French and Italian, they are quite solicitous. And I was never denied food, even though their stores were meager."

Lorenzo nodded, running his hand across the paper. "And when we begin to preach, do you think they'll be accepting of our message?"

Elder Stenhouse took a bite of bread and cheese and chewed while he thought. After swallowing and taking a drink of water, he made his observation. "I think some will hear the truth of the restored Church and embrace it, some will cling to the traditions of their fathers, and some will be too busy keeping alive in their harsh circumstances to care much."

Lorenzo gave him a half grin. "Perhaps we can entice them to come gather with the Saints in the blessed ease of the Great Salt Lake Valley."

Elder Stenhouse laughed. "Oh, yes! Travel thousands of miles over a roiling ocean, and then trudge another thousand miles—"

"—A bit over a thousand," Lorenzo said.

"Ah! A bit over a thousand! Trudge *more* than a thousand miles across a country to settle in a barren wilderness of dirt, sagebrush, and very little water, where you'll have to fight harsh summers, harsh winters, and crickets! A life of ease, I'm telling you. They'll be signing up by the thousands!"

Lorenzo laughed with him, and then sobered. "It truly is a miracle, Thomas, how conversion carries people. I have watched people leave everything for the truth."

"Your own life a testament," Elder Stenhouse said.

"And yours."

The two men sat quietly, taking in the stillness of the morning. Finally, Lorenzo spoke. "Now that I've finished writing and compiling *The Voice of Joseph* to help with our work here, I feel I have time to make a few travels with you."

Elder Stenhouse sat straighter and smiled. "'Twould be a wonder. Where would you like to go?"

Lorenzo evaluated the map. "Let's go up this small valley to the village of Rorà."

Elder Stenhouse stood. "Done! *When* would you like to go?"

"Today. As soon as we've packed our knapsacks."

"Ah! A man of action and vision. And the gospel will roll forth to fill the whole world!"

Lorenzo chuckled at the man's enthusiasm. "Well, let's just try to fill the valleys of the Piedmont, shall we?"

At that moment, the landlord's daughter came out of the inn, carrying a large basket of laundry. Lorenzo stood and moved to intercept her.

"Here, Mademoiselle Guy. Let me carry that for you." She relinquished the basket without speaking or smiling, which was very uncharacteristic of the normally cheerful girl. He also noted dark circles under her eyes and a drawn expression. "Are you well, Albertina?"

She moved on in silence while the two missionaries shared a look of concern. They reached the clothesline and Elder Stenhouse stepped in front of the stoic girl. "Albertina, please let us take over this task. You look nigh unto the end of your strength."

A flood of emotion came with the offered kindness, and Albertina covered her face with her hands and turned away.

"Is there anything we can do?" Lorenzo asked softly.

"My . . . my brother Joseph." The men waited as emotion stifled her words. "My little brother Joseph is ill . . . very ill."

"Oh, no," Lorenzo whispered. He now understood the unique arrangement of breakfast on the outside table and the absence of Madame Guy fussing over them as was her wont. Lorenzo's heart ached. In the past month of interaction with the Guy family he had grown to admire Rene and Francesca's competent industry in working their small farm and running the inn, Albertina's quiet confidence and beautiful singing voice, and young Joseph's likable jauntiness. His own girls Rosetta and Eliza were near Joseph's age and Lorenzo often found solace from his loneliness in a game of hide-and-seek with the little trickster, or walking the near trails around the property and answering a hundred questions posed by the precocious boy, who was smart beyond his years.

"What can we do?" Elder Stenhouse asked.

"Prayers," Albertina answered, hanging a sheet on the line. "I don't know what else can be done. Poor Mother is grieving—Father too." She pinned another sheet to the line. "My younger sister, Pauline, died a little over a year ago. I don't know what the loss of another child would do to them."

"I'm so sorry," Lorenzo said. "My wife Charlotte and I lost a child. I know what it feels like." Albertina nodded, unable to speak, as Lorenzo stepped closer. "Perhaps there *is* something more we can do for your family." He looked to Elder Stenhouse and back to Albertina. "May we go and see your brother?"

Albertina hesitated. "I . . . I suppose so. But perhaps you should speak with my father."

"Yes, of course," Lorenzo said. He turned to the inn and Elder Stenhouse followed.

"Are you planning to bless the boy?" Elder Stenhouse asked when they were out of Albertina's hearing.

"If the parents give their consent and the Spirit directs," Lorenzo answered, increasing his pace. "I have been praying earnestly, Thomas, for the Lord to assist us in our efforts. I now feel fully awake to a sense of our position." He hesitated with his hand on the door latch. "Should we not show forth the power of the priesthood restored to the earth?" He opened the door and moved through to the back of the inn. He knocked softly on the door that led into the Guy family's private living area. He heard the sound of chair legs being scooted across stone flooring and then approaching footsteps. The door opened a crack and Rene's face appeared there—a pale mask of exhaustion.

"Ah, Monsieur Snow. Monsieur Stenhouse. Can your question wait? Our . . . our little Joseph is not well."

"We know," Lorenzo said softly. "Albertina told us. We have come to offer help."

"Help? Are you doctors?" Rene asked without rancor.

"No," Lorenzo answered with a sigh. "But we want to offer you something from the Lord that may give you and Madame Guy hope. Please, may we come in to see the boy?"

Slowly the door opened. "He is in the small bedroom up the stairs," Rene said as Lorenzo and Thomas moved past. They climbed the steps with Rene following closely. "He is beyond speaking to anyone. He . . . he does not respond or move." The anguish in Rene's voice made Lorenzo falter. He sent a prayer heavenward for strength and inspiration. The three men moved quietly into the room, and Francesca stood up quickly from the bedside.

"Rene? Now is not the time . . ."

"They wanted to see Joseph," Rene answered feebly. "They said they might be able to help him."

Francesca stood staring. "Help him?"

Lorenzo stepped forward. The room was so small that a few strides took him to the side of Madame Guy. He looked down at the once-healthy little mischief-maker, reaching down and picking up his hand. "I didn't realize he was so ill. I am so sorry," Lorenzo said, working to keep alarm from his voice. Joseph's lifeless visage shocked him, and it seemed the child's end was near. Lorenzo looked directly at Francesca, well understanding her distress.

"What can you do?" she pleaded. "What?"

Lorenzo held her gaze. "Do you believe in the Lord Jesus Christ?"

Puzzlement washed her face. "We . . . we do, yes."

"And that while He was on the earth, the Lord and His apostles performed miracles of healing?"

Francesca hesitated, then answered warily, "Yes."

Lorenzo looked over at Elder Stenhouse. "This gentleman and myself are ministers of the restored gospel, and we hold the same holy priesthood as the apostles of old." He turned back to the grieving mother. "We have the power to bless and heal."

Rene's shaky voice broke the ensuing silence. "You can heal him?"

"If it is the Lord's will, we can."

"Then please, please, keep him from death!" Francesca begged.

Lorenzo took her hands. "We need time to pray and prepare ourselves."

"But he is dying now!"

A stillness came into Lorenzo's voice. "The Lord will keep him through the night, Madame Guy, and tomorrow Joseph will receive the blessing meant for him."

"But—"

"Pray, and have faith," he said softly. He knew it was much to ask as he noted the pale marble hue of the child's skin, indicative of dissolution, and the cold perspiration of death covering him. As he and Elder Stenhouse left the room, Lorenzo's spirit chilled at the sound of Madame Guy's desperate sobs.

The next morning, the two Mormon missionaries stood on the outcropping of rock near the top of Mount Castelluzzo, catching their breath and surveying the beautiful Lucerne Valley below. Lorenzo marveled at the patchwork harvest of man's handiwork coupled with God's creation of trees, rivers, and surrounding mountains. It was the perfect place of beauty and solitude to have their prayer.

They had come fasting, knowing the nearness of death for the young child and the need they had for the Lord's intervention. The priesthood was merely a conduit through which the power of the Lord moved, and humility was the foundation for the requisite faith.

"I am glad we decided to come here for prayer," Elder Stenhouse said. "My spirit has been quite unsettled since seeing the little tyke yesterday." He shaded his eyes and gazed down into the valley. "This is a tonic."

Lorenzo nodded. "God's power and love made manifest."

After a long silence, Elder Stenhouse cleared his throat. "Do . . . do you have any feeling about the outcome?"

"Since yesterday I have called upon the Lord to assist us. I laid before Him the course we wish to pursue concerning the Waldenese people and the claims that we will be making concerning the restoration of power and authority from on high." He began weeping. "The work we do here, my brother, will be of vast importance, and the sparing of the life of this child will be a manifestation of the restored truth." The passion in Lorenzo's voice deepened. "I know not of any sacrifice I can possibly make that I am not willing to offer that the Lord might grant our request." The force of the apostle's pronouncement hit Elder Stenhouse like a thunderbolt, and he stepped back, awed by the power and unremitting love inherent in the words. Lorenzo placed his hand on the shoulder of his companion. "And now, brother, shall we kneel in prayer and ask the Lord to spare the life of our little Joseph?"

At three o'clock in the afternoon, Elder Snow and Elder Stenhouse stood in the small bedroom of the Guy home surrounded by weeping family members and an old priest who had apparently come to give the child last rites. The palpable feeling of hopelessness in the room was worsened by Joseph's father repeating the tortured words, "He dies, he dies."

Lorenzo too saw that death was apparent, so he did not take time for talk or introductions. He moved quickly to the side of the bed, drawing a vial of consecrated oil from his pocket and speaking gently to Joseph's mother. "Madame Guy, I will need you to step back for a moment so Thomas and I may place our hands upon Joseph's head."

Madame Guy gave him a blank look, but when Lorenzo undid her grip on Joseph's lifeless hand, she pressed her lips together and stepped back. "It is too late, Monsieur Snow. Too late."

Lorenzo poured the consecrated oil onto his hands and laid them on the head of the child. Elder Stenhouse joined him, and through the power of the Melchizedek Priesthood, the apostle pronounced a blessing of healing and restoration. As he prayed, the dark aura in the room seemed to dissolve until the gloom was replaced with a spirit of tranquility. At the conclusion of the prayer, Lorenzo took a deep breath and slowly opened his eyes. When he looked up he noted that Francesca and Albertina had stopped crying, and that Rene was kneeling at the foot of the bed. The old priest took a few tottering steps forward, staring in wonder at the child in the bed.

"*Mieux*," he said in a choked voice. "*Mieux*. Better."

Joseph's eyeballs were no longer turned upward, and a blush of color marked his cheeks. Madame Guy rushed over and slumped at the bedside. "How? How is this possible?" She took her son's hand. "You have worked a miracle!"

Lorenzo gathered his Italian words and spoke slowly, "*Il Dio di cielo ha fatto questa per voi.*"—"The God of heaven has done this for you." He moved to the door, followed by Elder Stenhouse. He turned and looked tenderly at the family. "You should be able to get some rest now."

The elders left the room and exited the inn into the late afternoon sunshine. A young priest turned to watch them as they moved across the courtyard. Lorenzo noted an air of sadness about the young man, and presumed it was related to the ill health of the little boy. Lorenzo altered his course and approached the priest, giving a slight bow of his head, and holding out his hand.

"Hello, Father. I am Lorenzo Snow, and this is my friend Thomas Stenhouse. We are lodgers at the inn."

Father Nathanael shook his hand. "Yes. Rene has told us of you. You are ministers from America."

Lorenzo smiled. "Well, I am from America. Mr. Stenhouse is from Scotland, but yes, we are ministers of the same church."

Elder Stenhouse shook the priest's hand. "Pleased to meet you, Father—"

"Nathanael. I am Father Nathanael. I attend Father Andrew. I brought him this morning to be with his family."

"His family?" Lorenzo questioned.

"Yes. Father Andrew is a great-uncle to little Joseph."

"Ah, I see. That would explain his distress at the boy's illness," Lorenzo replied solemnly. He had not had enough conversation with the members of the Guy family to know much about their friends or extended family members.

"Have you come from seeing the boy?" Father Nathanael asked.

"We have," Lorenzo replied.

"It is so very sad. I think his death will be a great blow to Father Andrew. His heart holds a special place for the lad."

Lorenzo hesitated. "I think that Joseph will live."

Father Nathanael frowned at him. When his words came they were slow and deliberate. "How . . . how can you think that? I saw him. The signs of death were evident."

Lorenzo nodded. "Perhaps. Perhaps you are right. But perhaps the Lord will watch over him. We will continue to pray and see what to-morrow brings." He spoke without rancor or pretention, causing Father

Nathanael's look to change from disbelief to puzzlement. Before he had a chance to respond, Rene came to the doorway of the inn and called out to him.

"Father Nathanael, come quickly! Father Andrew wishes to see you."

The young priest turned and ran to the inn. He and Rene withdrew into the building, and Elder Stenhouse took off his cap and fanned his face.

"I suppose I shouldn't wonder at the Lord's grace and power, Elder Snow, but I tell you truly, it near takes my breath away."

"He loves His children."

"Aye, 'tis a fact," Elder Stenhouse replied with a grin. He replaced his cap and stretched his back. "And I'm thinking after this we may have a few inquiries as to the doctrine we're preaching."

Lorenzo smiled. "I think you're right. I think it's time to commence our public duties."

Elder Stenhouse grimaced. "Just one small question before we commence?"

"What's that?"

"Can we have a bite to eat first? I'm nigh on keeling over with hunger."

Lorenzo laughed. "A young lad like you?" Elder Stenhouse gave him a pitiful look. "Oh, all right. Let's go to the eatery in town and I'll treat you to supper."

Elder Stenhouse brightened. "Oh, now, that would be grand!"

The two men set off for the center of Torre Pellice, the one singing a Scottish hymn, the other sending silent prayers of gratitude heavenward.

NOTE

The miraculous healing of Joseph Guy is a true story, as noted in Elder Snow's journal. He also wrote the exact words he spoke to Madame Guy when she realized the life of her son had been saved: *Il Dio di cielo ha fatto questa per voi.* "The God of heaven has done this for you."

Chapter Fifteen

Torre Pellice

September 18, 1850

"He's here! He's here!" Joseph Guy called out excitedly, running to the door of the inn and hollering inside. "Monsieur Snow, Monsieur Snow, I see him!"

Elder Stenhouse came around the corner of the inn, wiping his brow, and setting the ax against the side of the building. "What's all this ruckus, young master Guy?" he asked good-naturedly.

"The man you are waiting for! I think he is there!" Joseph said, pointing off into the distance. "See him?"

Elder Stenhouse came to Joseph's side. "That little speck? How can you tell if that's a man or a cow?"

Joseph laughed. "A cow? That is not a cow. A cow standing up?" He looked to the door of the inn. "Why is Elder Snow not coming?"

"He went into town this morning."

"He did? He did not tell me."

Elder Stenhouse covered a grin. "Well, I think he left before you were awake."

"Oh," Joseph answered, kicking at the dirt.

"Don't worry. He should be home soon."

"And you did not go to town?"

I see why his father nicknamed him Little Bonaparte, Elder Stenhouse thought. He laid his hand on Joseph's head to stop his kicking. "If you must know, I have been chopping wood."

Joseph scowled at him. "Oh, no."

"What do you mean, oh, no? The inn will need lots of wood for the winter."

"Yes, but then *I* have to work."

Elder Stenhouse shook his head. *This little boy is more like a forty-year-old than just being shy of four*, he mused. He addressed Joseph with mock solemnity. "Yes, that's right, Joseph. Your job is to stack the wood, and I am sorry, but we all must do our work." He expected some sort of reply, but when he looked down, he found the boy staring down the track.

"Is that the man? He's closer now. Can you see him?"

Elder Stenhouse squinted at the approaching figure. "Yes, Joseph. I believe that is the man. I believe that Brother Jabez Woodard has come from far-off England to do the work of the Lord." He turned abruptly and strode quickly in the opposite direction.

"Where are you going?" Joseph called after him.

"To get my suit coat. I do not want to meet such a great man in my shirtsleeves."

Joseph stood staring for a moment, then turned and ran towards the inn. He ran past Elder Snow, who had just come into the courtyard.

"Joseph? Where are you off to in such a hurry?"

"To get my Sunday coat. The great man is coming!"

"The great man?" Lorenzo turned and looked down the road. He took a deep breath when he recognized the traveler. "So, you have answered the call." His heart felt light as he moved off down the path to meet the new missionary.

The next morning, Jabez Woodard sat at the inn's dining table, eating scones and currant jelly and conversing with the Guy family as though he were a native son of the Piedmont valleys. The twenty-nine-year-old teacher was appealing in manner and appearance, and held his audience captive with his engaging wit and easygoing character. It was not the custom for the inn's proprietor or his family to intrude on their guests' meals, but one by one, beginning with Joseph, they had lingered by the table, intrigued by Elder Woodard's interesting tales of his journey from England. The missionaries had insisted that the family sit and join them, which made for a merry morning.

Eventually Albertina gathered the courage to speak. "You speak French very well, Monsieur Woodard. Did you learn in school?"

"Mostly from my own studying."

"The man speaks six or seven languages, if I remember correctly," Elder Stenhouse remarked.

"That *is* impressive," Rene said.

Elder Woodard smiled. "For my part, it's more of a fascination. I find languages captivating—especially French. It is a beautiful language."

"And I can understand everything you say," Joseph chimed in. "Not like them." He pointed his finger at Elder Snow and Elder Stenhouse, who burst out laughing at the indictment.

"Joseph Guy!" his mother exclaimed in dismay. "That is not a nice thing to say."

"Why not? Do *you* understand everything they say?"

Francesca sat with her mouth open, but no words were forthcoming. When everyone laughed at her silent admission, her face softened and she laughed with them. She gently pulled one of Joseph's earlobes. "Oh! What am I going to do with you, little man?"

"Keep me," Joseph said, playfully batting her hand away and rubbing his ear.

"Yes, we will keep you," Francesca said tenderly. "Because of these men, we will surely keep you."

"And let me go with them on their hike!" Joseph ventured. "I can be their guide!"

"I am sure they know where they are going without your help," Rene said. "They do not need you tagging along asking a million questions."

"Besides," Francesca added, "you're just trying to get out of your chores." She stood, and the men stood with her. "Come along, family. We have kept these gentlemen from their activities long enough." She turned to Lorenzo. "Elder Snow, did you get the food from the kitchen? The food for your hike?"

"I did, Madame Guy. Albertina made sure we had it. Very kind, thank you."

Francesca looked at her children. "Joseph, off to your dusting, and Albertina, we will be canning plums today."

"Yes, ma'am."

The family departed for their activities and Lorenzo looked after them with an expression of fondness. "They are good people."

"Indeed," Elder Stenhouse confirmed.

Lorenzo picked up his knapsack, checking inside for his scriptures, paper, pen, ink, food, and canteen. "Today, brethren, we will not just be going for a hike into the mountains, but we will dedicate this land for the preaching of the gospel." The announcement stunned his two companions into silence. Lorenzo smiled at them. "I know you have just arrived, Elder Woodard, but the urgency of the work is upon me."

"That I understand completely, Elder Snow, and I am awake to the resolve, and fit for the walking, but . . ." he looked sheepishly between his two companions. "It is just that I have overindulged myself with scones and currant jelly, which puts me in a questionable spiritual frame of mind."

Lorenzo laughed. "We have eaten as well, Brother Woodard, but it is a long hike to the top of Mount Castelluzzo, and trust me, breakfast will have worn thin."

"Ah, good! Then let's be on our way!" Brother Woodard answered, picking up his backpack, and heading for the front door. His voice came back to his companions as he went. "'How beautiful upon the mountains are the feet of him that bringeth good tidings, that publisheth peace; that bringeth good tidings of good, that publisheth salvation; that saith unto Zion, Thy God reigneth!'"

"A linguist *and* a man of the scriptures," Elder Stenhouse said in an uplifted voice. "I think this mission will make good use of your talents, Brother Woodard."

Elder Snow heartily agreed.

Although it was nearing the first day of autumn, the temperature on the face of the mountain spoke more of summer, affecting the climbers with shortness of breath and frequent stops for water. When they finally reached the rocky pinnacle near Mount Castelluzzo's summit, the three missionaries sought what limited shade was available, and freed themselves from their knapsacks.

"Whew!" Elder Stenhouse breathed out after pouring a bit of water on his head. "I thought since I had done this once or twice before, this time would be easier." He looked over at Elder Woodward sitting in the shade of a nearby tree, wiping his face with a handkerchief. "Are you well, Brother Woodard? Do you require assistance? I mean, you are a bit older, so . . ."

Elder Woodard gave him a half grin. "Only a few years older than you, Brother Stenhouse." He took a deep breath, and shook his head. "It's not the age, it's the altitude. Like you, I'm a lad from sea level."

Elder Stenhouse motioned with his head. "Aye, but look there. There's the oldest of us all, standing on the precipice and looking out over the valley as though he'd just taken a stroll through a meadow."

Elder Woodard sobered. "I think his mission carries him."

"To be sure," Elder Stenhouse agreed. "When he was writing out the tract about the Church, he'd go for days on just a few hours of sleep."

"A new tract about the Church? I'd like to read it," Elder Woodard said.

"*The Voice of Joseph*," Elder Stenhouse said, standing and stretching his back. "Elder Snow has the original. He sent a copy to Orson Hyde in England for translation."

"Elder Hyde is doing the translation?" Elder Woodard questioned.

"Elder Hyde? Oh, no. *He's* not doing it. He has an acquaintance, a professor from the University of Paris, who agreed to do the work."

Elder Woodard sat up. "That's impressive. Academics tend to take a deleterious view of religion."

"Too smart to contemplate salvation," Elder Stenhouse scoffed.

Elder Woodard smiled. "Exactly."

At that moment, Elder Snow approached. "Are we sufficiently rested, brethren, that we can begin?"

Elder Woodard stood. "Yes, Elder Snow."

Elder Stenhouse nodded.

"I've found a flat area where we can kneel. And a comfortable place for you to sit, Elder Woodard, if I can impose upon you to be our scribe?"

"Of course."

"First, let us sing a few of the hymns. I think it will bring the Spirit of the Lord into our efforts; after which I will proclaim the dedication for this remarkable land."

A cooling breeze whispered through the branches of the pine trees as the missionaries for The Church of Jesus Christ of Latter-day Saints sang praises to the God of Heaven and readied themselves for the prayer of dedication. Elder Snow made sure his scribe was ready, bowed his head, and waited for the words of inspiration. In a slow and deliberate voice, he began.

> We, Thy servants, Holy Father, come before Thee upon this mountain, and ask Thee to look upon us in an especial manner, and regard our petitions as one friend regards the peculiar

requests of another. Forgive all our sins and transgressions, and let them no more be remembered.

Look, O Lord, upon our many sacrifices in leaving our wives, our children, and country, to obey Thy voice in offering salvation to this people. Receive our gratitude in having preserved us from destruction amid the cold wintry blasts, and from the hostile savages of the deserts of America—in having led us by the Holy Ghost to these valleys of Piedmont. Thou hast hid up a portion of the house of Israel.

In Thy name, we this day lift into view before this people and this nation the ensign of Thy martyred Prophet and Patriarch, Joseph and Hyrum Smith, the ensign of the fulness of the gospel—the ensign of Thy kingdom once more to be established among men. O Lord, God of our fathers, protect Thou this banner. Lend us Thine almighty aid in maintaining it before the view of these dark and benighted nations. May it wave triumphantly from this time forth, till all Israel shall have heard and received the fulness of Thy gospel, and have been delivered from their bondage. May their bands be broken and the scales of darkness fall from their eyes.

From the lifting up of this ensign may a voice go forth among the people of these mountains and valleys, and throughout the length and breadth of this land, and may it go forth and be unto thine elect as the voice of the Lord, that the Holy Spirit may fall upon them, imparting knowledge in dreams and visions concerning this hour of their redemption. As the report of us, Thy servants, shall spread abroad, may it awaken feelings of anxiety with the honest to learn of Thy doings, and to seek speedily the path of knowledge.

Whosoever among this people shall employ his influence, riches, or learning to promote the establishment of Thy gospel in these nations, may he be crowned with honors in this world and in the world to come crowned with eternal life. Whosoever shall use his influence or power to hinder the establishment of Thy gospel in this country, may he become, in a surprising manner, before the eyes of all these nations, a monument of weakness, folly, shame, and disgrace.

Suffer us not to be overcome by our enemies in the accomplishment of this mission upon which we have been sent. Let messengers be prepared and sent forth from heaven to help us in our weakness, and to take the oversight of this work, and lead it to a glorious consummation.

Remember our families. Preserve our lives and hearts from all evil, that when we shall have finished our missions we may return safely to the bosom of our families. Bless Elder Toronto in Sicily, and give him influence and power to lead to salvation many of his father's house and kindred. Bless President Young and his council, the Quorum of the Twelve Apostles, and Thy Saints universally; and to the Father, and to the Son, and to the Holy Ghost, shall be the praise, honor, and glory, now and forever, amen.

After a long while of stillness, Lorenzo opened his eyes and lifted his head. He found Elder Stenhouse with his head still bowed and Elder Woodard writing out the final words of the prayer. Lorenzo rose to his feet and went to sit by his scribe. "Were you able to apprehend most of it?"

"I was, Elder Snow. We may have to go over a few things."

"Of course."

Elder Woodard swiped his coat sleeve across his eyes to dry the tears. "That was powerful, Elder Snow. A powerful manifestation of the Spirit."

"God loves His children, Brother Woodard."

Jabez Woodard nodded. "This I know truly, Elder Snow."

"And those of us called to this work have sacrificed our wills for His. I have said before and I say again, I do not know of any sacrifice I would not make to have this work move forward in this remarkable country."

"Amen."

Lorenzo laid his hand on Brother Woodard's shoulder. "I believe the Lord takes note of our offerings, Elder. It has been noted in heaven that you have left your wife and two small children in London, your home, your teaching position—"

"You have left much also, Elder Snow," Elder Woodard interrupted.

Lorenzo took a breath to stanch the emotion, as images of Charlotte, Sarah Ann, and the children came unbidden into his mind. He thought of Charlotte's positive character and her sweet, endearing smile. He took another breath and gently pushed the image to the side. "Yes, I . . . I have left behind those dearest to my heart, we have all done that, because we know that God's children must be offered the light of the gospel. And because we willingly sacrifice, He trusts us with His most sacred errands."

"Even though one is hardly proficient to take on the task?" Elder Woodard questioned, wiping the ink from the metal tip of his pen, and putting the cork in the ink bottle.

"I hardly think you lack proficiency, Jabez. You speak the languages of the area fluently, you are a natural teacher, and you have a deep love for the Lord and His gospel."

"Yes, a gospel with which I've been acquainted for just over a year—not much time to get a deep understanding of the doctrine."

"You do not need a deep understanding of the doctrine to share the gospel with others, Elder. You only need a testimony that Christ is our Redeemer, that Joseph Smith was His prophet and received the keys of the priesthood, and that the truths of the gospel have the power to exalt us."

Elder Woodard guffawed. "Oh, just that? Well, that shouldn't test my spiritual ability in the least now, should it?"

Elder Stenhouse came to stand beside them. "What are you two laughing about?"

Elder Woodard moderated his conduct. "Oh! I am sorry, Brother Stenhouse. Our light manner has intruded upon your prayer."

"Not at all, brother. I was finished. Besides, my knees were getting tired."

Elder Snow thumped Elder Woodard on the back. "You see? The Lord will work with us, weak knees and all!" He stood and Brother Woodard stood with him. "Now, we have some business to transact as far as organizing the Church here in Italy, after which I would like to hear prophecy from each of you concerning the work."

The color drained from Elder Woodard's face. "Prophecy?"

"A testimony guided fully by the Spirit," Elder Snow reassured. He shaded his eyes and looked up to the summit of Mount Castelluzzo. "But first, I feel prompted that we should rename this mountain, and also this prominence of rock on which we stand."

"Can we do that?" Elder Stenhouse questioned.

Elder Snow smiled over at him. "The designations will not change on the maps, but among the people of God they will be known by different names. Mount Castelluzzo will be called Mount Brigham, and this area where we stand will be known as the Rock of Prophecy."

"The Rock of Prophecy. May the new name give me inspiration," Elder Woodard mumbled, and his two companions laughed.

Elder Snow clapped his hands together. "So, organization, prophecy, a hymn or two, and then food. What do you say to that, brethren?"

"Amen and amen!" Elder Stenhouse responded, while Elder Woodard nodded silently in agreement.

NOTE

With minor changes, this is the dedicatory prayer for Italy, given by Elder Lorenzo Snow on the 19th of September, 1850, and later transcribed into his journal.

CHAPTER SIXTEEN

Salt Lake City

September 25, 1850

Eliza R. Snow, widow of the martyred prophet Joseph Smith, wife of President Brigham Young, poetess of the Church, secretary of the Nauvoo Relief Society, and in years not a young woman, was running—running down one of the main streets of Salt Lake City without bonnet or shawl. The few people she passed on the street were so surprised by this odd sight that they gave her no greeting or comment. They barely heard the frantic words she mumbled as she raced by. "Not possible. Not possible. It is *not* possible."

A chill entered Eliza's body that had nothing to do with the late September breeze that descended from the mountain heights, and she clenched and unclenched her hands in an attempt to get blood to her fingertips. She turned up the road leading to her brother's cabin, and saw warm light coming through the windows. *See, everything is fine,* she told herself. *Charlotte is in the kitchen making supper. She is in the kitchen laughing with the other wives and taking care of little Roxcy.* Eliza forced herself to slow her pace and still her tumbling thoughts and ragged breathing. She wanted to bring serenity to whatever lay on the other side of the door.

She knocked.

Immediately the door was thrown open and Sarah Ann flew into her arms. "Oh, Auntie Eliza! It's not possible. It's not possible!"

Eliza's heart twisted as she heard her own words of distress echoed by Lorenzo's second wife. She held the young woman tightly. "Calm yourself, Sarah Ann. Calm yourself." She stepped back and held the girl at arm's length. "Let's see what we can do, shall we?"

Sarah Ann's bowed head wagged back and forth. "There's nothing. The doctor said there is nothing we can do."

Eliza gently nudged Sarah Ann into the house and shut the door behind her. She hurriedly greeted the other members of the family. Their absent stares spoke of shock and disbelief. "Is the doctor with her?"

"He is," Sarah Ann answered dully. "But he says there is nothing we can do."

"I don't understand. I saw her just the other day. She was well. She was healthy," Eliza said. "What happened?"

Sarah Ann's crying increased. "We don't know."

"You sleep in the same room, Sarah Ann. Was she complaining of any illness last night?"

"No. And then today she said she felt a little dizzy, and then . . . and then she collapsed."

Charlotte's daughter Roxcy began crying for attention, and Sarah Ann stumbled over to pick her up. Eliza turned and walked to the bedroom, opening the door quietly and stepping inside. An older gentleman with wispy hair and wire spectacles looked up from monitoring Charlotte's pulse. He studied Eliza's face for a moment and then shook his head.

"I'm sorry, Sister Snow. Truly sorry. What with Elder Snow so far away."

Eliza's gaze was fixed on Charlotte's face. There was no imprint of pain, or telltale signs of fever. In fact, her sister-in-law seemed only to be sleeping—deeply sleeping. Her skin color was chalky, but her beautiful face was composed, her body relaxed. Eliza shook her head, attempting to bring reality to the situation. "I don't understand, Doctor Prescott. What is the diagnosis? What is wrong with her?"

The doctor laid his patient's hand gently on the bed. "I am not sure. It may be a stroke, or something to do with her heart. She has not regained consciousness, so I have not been able to ask her questions."

"But she's only twenty-six, and she's always been healthy." A coil of frustration wound itself around Eliza's heart. "How can she be dying? She walked across the country!"

"I know, my dear. Sometimes there are no answers."

Eliza was impatient with that response. "There has to be something we can do."

"Pray," the doctor said simply.

She was impatient with that answer also, but moderated her reply. "Do you mind if I spend a few minutes alone with her?"

"Not at all. I must go out and speak with the family. Arrangements must be made."

Eliza felt a jab of pain in her heart.

Doctor Prescott moved to the door and hesitated. "Alert me if there's any change."

Eliza nodded and the door closed. She slumped down by the side of the bed, bowing her head and praying fervently for a miracle. She had seen many miracles during her life in the Church and knew that faith could intervene, even in death. Eliza poured out her heart to the Lord, seeking reassurance, seeking answers, pleading that Charlotte's life might be saved. In mid-thought, her words stopped, replaced by other words. *Be at peace. She is fulfilling a covenant.* Eliza felt movement and looked up to see Charlotte's eyes opening a slit. She moved quickly to sit on the bed and take her sister-in-law's hand. "Charlotte?"

"They tell me that all will be well," came the whispered words.

"They?"

"All will be well."

"Oh, Charlotte."

"Tell . . . my . . . Lorenzo."

"Tell Lorenzo? What do you want me to tell him?" Eliza waited for more words, but they did not come. A draft of air tickled the hair on her neck, and Eliza turned to stare at the chink where nearly a year before she had placed one of Charlotte's braided plugs. On the logs were water marks where the rain had dripped. Her sight slid to the floor where Charlotte's worn boots lay, then to the dresser, to her hairbrush and small bottle of lavender cologne. Charlotte's lavender cologne. Slowly Eliza released Charlotte's hand. How would she ever tell her brother of this sad occurrence? She had been given the gift of words, but Eliza knew of no combination of words that would make sense of this for her brother or lessen his pain. This was his dear one, as beautiful in death as she had been in life. Charlotte loved others with a sweet sincerity and so she was truly loved by all. The pain in Eliza's chest increased, pouring from her body as tears and pitiful moaning. She moved numbly to the door and opened it.

"She's gone. Our Charlotte is gone."

NOTE

In Eliza Snow's book *Biography and Family Record of Lorenzo Snow*, she relates added insight concerning Charlotte's death. "On the mountain in Italy . . . on the same memorable day in which The Church of Jesus Christ of Latter-day Saints was there organized, Lorenzo, in the force of his spirit . . . and probably without realizing the weight of his covenant, told the Lord that he knew of no sacrifice he could possibly make he was not willing to offer, that the Lord might grant a request concerning the mission before him. When I received a copy of the report of the proceedings of the day, in which the above was included, I was deeply struck with the coincidence. Just at this time, as nearly as I could calculate by comparing dates and distances, the Lord removed, by the hand of death, from my brother's family circle, one of the loveliest of women" (p. 233).

Chapter Seventeen

The Angrogna Valley
September 28, 1850

The orange, red, and yellow leaves of autumn adorned the mountainsides of the Piedmont with wonder, and though the harvesters of grain and the gatherers of fruit were diligent in their labor, it was not uncommon for industry to be momentarily forgotten for a drifting look at the enchanting vistas.

Madeleine Cardon lay on her stomach under a walnut tree at the edge of the meadow, tending the family's cows and reading a small book of scripture. She glanced up periodically to make sure the cows were not invading her father's vineyard and also to take in the beauty of her surroundings. This was her favorite time of year. She loved the cutting of the grain and the gathering of pears, apples, walnuts, and chestnuts. She loved the storing of potatoes and cabbages in the cold cellar, along with the rounds of cheese. She loved the chill in the night air that incited the glorious colors of the leaves.

Madeleine turned over and sat up. She hummed the song that she and Albertina were preparing to sing at the festival. She looked around when she heard the gonging of a cowbell at a close distance, laughing to see the silly antics of their best milk cow as the beast scratched her head on a tree stump. "Too bad you don't have fingers!" she called to the cow. Madeleine looked out across the meadow to make sure their other animals were not wandering off, and caught sight of three men walking up the mountain path. She paid them little attention, as it was a common occurrence for people to be on the path, but when the three left the track and headed in her direction, she became concerned. She squinted to ascertain their identity, only to discover that they were strangers. Strangers? What were they doing on the mountain? Were they coming to speak to her? They drew closer and Madeleine lowered her head. Perhaps if she didn't look at them, they would go away.

When she could hear their footfalls on the ground in front of her she stood and took a quick look at their faces. A calmness washed over her. She *knew* these faces.

"Don't be frightened," one of the men said in perfect French. "We are ministers of God and have come to preach His gospel."

Madeleine looked directly at them and burst into tears. "Yes. Yes, I know you. I have seen you before."

The three men looked startled at this pronouncement, each standing mute before the young Waldensian woman, trying to discern the meaning of her words. Finally, Elder Woodard spoke. "Have you seen us in the town, then?"

Madeleine swiped at the tears on her cheeks. "No, I haven't. I haven't been to town for many weeks." She took a deep breath. "You see, I had a dream when I was six years old, and you three were in the dream." She figured they would take her for a fool, so was surprised when they met her odd statement with acceptance and even reverence. "You don't question my story?"

"No." Elder Woodard said, looking at his companions, then back. "May we ask your name?" he said politely.

Madeleine nodded. "It is Madeleine Cardon. I am the daughter of Philippe Cardon and Marthe Marie Cardon."

"We are honored to meet you, Madeleine. I am Monsieur Woodard, and this is Monsieur Stenhouse, and Monsieur Snow." Madeleine curtsied and the men bowed. "Yes, indeed, we are very glad to meet you, and we do not question your story in the least, Madeleine. We believe the ancient gospel of Christ has been restored to the earth, and that personal revelation is one of its gifts."

"And that all the honest in heart will be gathered into the kingdom," Madeleine said.

"Yes. Yes, my dear girl," Lorenzo said struggling to keep his voice steady.

"And where are you from?" she questioned.

"I am from England," Elder Woodard answered. "Monsieur Stenhouse is from Scotland, and Monsieur Snow is from America."

Madeleine's eyes widened. "America? That is very far away. I was told that you would come from far away to preach the gospel to the world."

"Remarkable," Elder Woodard said laying his hand over his heart. "Remarkable."

"And is there a young boy in your story?" Madeleine asked. "In my dream you told me that God had spoken from Heaven to a young boy." No longer able to contain his emotion, Elder Snow put his hands over his face and wept. Madeleine was alarmed. "I'm sorry, Monsieur! Did I say something wrong?"

Elder Snow looked at her, smiling through his emotion. "No, my dear. No. It's just that I feel the confirmation of the Spirit . . . that we have come to the right place."

"The right place?"

"Yes. That here in these mountains are a people prepared to receive the restored gospel."

Madeleine beamed at them. "I think you should come to our home and speak to my father and mother and then to our neighbors. I think there will be many people who will want to hear you preach."

"We would be honored," Lorenzo said, regaining his composure. "Might you point the way?"

"I will take you!" Madeleine said without hesitation.

"But what of your cows?" Elder Woodard questioned.

"Oh, they will not wander far. They are lazy, you see. I will probably find them exactly where I left them." She headed off towards the path. "Follow me, then. My father is working, but we will be able to find him."

The three Mormon missionaries shared a look of wonder and followed the young Waldensian girl towards the village.

Philippe Cardon and his son Barthelemy laid down a piece of slate on the roof of their neighbor's house, stopping afterwards to rest and feel the cooling breeze against their faces. Philippe gazed to a nearby hillside where a bush in a blaze of orange stood flamboyant against a stand of dark green pines.

"The colors are bright this year," Philippe Cardon said, pulling his attention back to the slate and squeezing his eyes shut.

"We've had more rain than usual this summer," Barthelemy answered. He glanced over at his father, whose eyes were still closed. "Are you all right? You look tired."

Philippe opened his eyes and rubbed his face. "I am tired. I did not sleep well last night. A dream."

"A dream? A troubling dream?"

Philippe pulled another piece of slate into position. "Not troubling . . . just . . . unusual. Two men kept trying to give me a book."

His son laughed. "Oh, now! That would have kept me awake. That would keep anyone awake. I know I could not sleep if someone tried to give me a book."

Philippe growled. "Very funny. Get back to work."

"Maybe we should stop work. I think that book dream has robbed you of your strength."

"Stop laughing or you're going to fall off the roof," Philippe warned, moving a stone into place for the chimney. "Come on now, we need to finish."

"Stones ready!" a workman called from below, and Barthelemy, still chuckling, went to hoist up the basket. Philippe went to help. He put his hand on the rope and began to pull. After only two or three pulls, he dropped the rope and stepped back. He turned and moved to the ladder.

"Hey! Where are you going?" his son grunted. "Aren't you going to help me?"

"I need to go home," Philippe answered, starting down the ladder.

Barthelemy dragged the basket onto the roof. "Home?" he panted. "You said we had to finish. Is it the dream? Are you going home for a nap?"

"No, I just need to go home."

Barthelemy moved to the edge of the roof to watch his father descend. "And what are we supposed to do?"

"Keep working."

"And when will you be back?"

"I don't know." Philippe reached the ground and started off immediately in the direction of his home. "Keep working until dusk. I need to put on my Sunday clothes and go into Torre Pellice."

"Your Sunday clothes? Why? What are you talking about?" Barthelemy called after him.

"I can't explain!" Philippe yelled back over his shoulder. And indeed he could not explain, even to himself. He just knew that a distinct thought had come to him to go home, put on his Sunday suit, and walk down into Torre Pellice. He knew when he got to the house, his wife would pose the same questions as to his odd behavior, and he would only be able to give her the same vague answer. He didn't understand the persistent urging. Perhaps there were two strangers he needed to meet. Two strangers with a book.

A short time later Philippe Cardon was dressed and on his way to the town, and even though his head did not know a logical reason for the journey, his emotions were enthusiastically engaged. *Perhaps the book in my dream is a ledger,* he thought, *and the two men have a new business opportunity for me. Perhaps Colonel Beckwith has a new school for me to build. That would certainly explain the book in the dream.* Philippe was so busy pondering the options that he nearly knocked into his daughter as he rounded a grove of trees.

"Papa!"

"Madeleine! What? Why aren't you with the cows?" he stammered. He glanced up from his daughter's face and noticed the three men stopping on the path behind her. "And . . . and who are these gentlemen?"

"They are the evangelists, Papa! The ones from my dream!"

"Your dream?"

"Yes, the evangelists I dreamed about when I was six. You remember."

Although Philippe knew well his daughter's dream, and could see the joy of surety on her face, he was confused by the array of circumstances. It was one thing to have a dream, another to have it standing in front of you in the light of day. Without thinking, he thrust forward his hand. "Excuse me, where are my manners? I am just . . . just surprised at seeing you. I am Philippe Cardon."

Lorenzo moved forward and took the proffered hand. "I am Lorenzo Snow." He brought the other missionaries forward. "And this is Thomas Stenhouse, and this is Jabez Woodard." The men shook hands as Lorenzo continued talking. "We are ministers from The Church of Jesus Christ of Latter-day Saints and have come to preach the everlasting gospel." Though Lorenzo struggled with the French, the power of his testimony was tangible.

"See? The everlasting gospel! See, Papa? The three evangelists come to preach the everlasting gospel. It is the same as my dream."

Philippe was in a fog. "Yes, yes. Amazing."

"We were just coming to find you," Madeleine said, giving her father a perplexed look. "And where were you going in your Sunday suit?"

"I . . . I was going into Torre Pellice," Philippe answered.

"Why?"

He looked directly at her. "I had a dream last night that two men were trying to give me a book, and today while I was working, the thought came to my mind that I should put on my Sunday suit and go into the town."

"Another dream?" Madeleine said with a giggle. She turned to the missionaries. "Do you think we were supposed to meet you?"

Elder Woodard smiled. "I believe so."

"And *do* you have a book for my father?"

Elder Woodard shared a look with his companions, and then back to the father and daughter. "We do have a book, Madeleine. A very special book."

"Wonderful!" Madeleine exclaimed. She smiled at her father. "Perhaps, Papa, we should invite them to our house to tell us more about their church?" She giggled. "Especially since you are already dressed for company."

With that remark, Philippe Cardon came to himself and took on a more assured bearing. He nodded to the missionaries. "Yes. Yes, gentlemen. We would be honored if you would come to our home and share your message. And of course, you must stay for supper."

"And you can sleep in our barn if the hour gets late," Madeleine offered.

"You are very kind," Lorenzo said. "We are the ones honored by the invitation. Thank you."

"We should go, then!" Madeleine said as she started off towards the Cardon Borgata. The others followed.

Lorenzo walked beside the girl. "And we will want to hear all about your dream," he said in a soft tone.

"Of course," Madeleine answered simply. "I want to share it with you. I think it is your story, after all."

Lorenzo's spirit lifted. How good was the God of Creation to love each of his children personally? To be aware of a young girl living in a small stone house on a mountainside in northern Italy. To send her a dream in the night that would make her feel comfortable with the message and messengers of the gospel. Lorenzo's heart swelled with gratitude and love, and as he walked the grassy path of the Angrogna Valley, he reaffirmed that he would serve the Lord all his days.

NOTE

Philippe Cardon's dream of the men offering him the book and his prompting to put on his Sunday suit and go into town were actual occurrences written in several Cardon journals.

CHAPTER EIGHTEEN

Torre Pellice

October 10, 1850

Avenge, O Lord, thy slaughter'd saints, whose bones
Lie scatter'd on the Alpine mountains cold,
Ev'n them who kept thy truth so pure of old,
When all our fathers worshipp'd stocks and stones;
Forget not: in thy book record their groans
Who were thy sheep and in their ancient fold
Slain by the bloody Piedmontese that roll'd
Mother with infant down the rocks. Their moans
The vales redoubl'd to the hills, and they
To Heav'n. Their martyr'd blood and ashes sow
O'er all th' Italian fields where still doth sway
The triple tyrant; that from these may grow
A hundred-fold, who having learnt thy way
Early may fly the Babylonian woe.

John Malan, the poem's orator, stood in front of his friends, hat over his heart, and walking stick thrust high into the air. Without its support, the old man swayed precariously, and both his friends called out to him in alarm.

"Hey! Watch it! Careful!"

"Put your stick down, you old fool!" Father Andrew commanded. "You're going to fall on your head!"

John steadied himself and glared at his companions. "What? No applause for my moving recitation of Milton's sonnet?"

Jean Cardon blew out a puff of air. "Bah! Vanity, my friend. Vanity."

Father Andrew gave John a measured look and smiled. "Well, I suppose since I was the one who asked for the poem, I should applaud its offering." He began clapping and Jean Cardon joined him.

John Malan leaned on his walking stick and bowed. "It is but a small gift I give. A small gift to the country peasants."

Andrew stopped clapping. "Enough of that now, you peacock. Come here and sit before you fall down."

John flourished his hat, plopped it on his head, and shuffled forward to the bench. His chortling laugh accompanied him. "And I remembered every word," he said proudly.

Jean helped him to sit. "You did, my friend. It was a miracle."

"What? What's that?" John barked. "My mind is as clear as it was twenty years ago!"

"Thou shalt not bear false witness," Andrew instructed.

The three friends laughed together. Slowly the calm of the autumn afternoon returned, and the men sat contentedly in the sun, listening to birdsong and watching the young priests as they harvested the last of the monastery garden. After a time, Andrew spoke.

"It is a powerful poem."

"It is," John said. "But why do you like it so much, my friend? It is a poem for the Waldenese. A poem for their suffering."

"Can I not have compassion for their suffering? You are my friends. It is your heritage. I admire what Cromwell did in your defense; I admire what Milton wrote." He turned to them. "I wonder at times that we are friends. I'd think your anger would exclude me."

Jean Cardon gently tapped his cane on the hard dirt. "Should I live in the cemetery of my martyred race? Should my life be defined by something that happened two hundred years ago?"

"But the persecutions—"

Jean Cardon interrupted. "No, my friend. My soul would wither if I kept going back to that dark time."

John Malan leaned forward. "That's not to say that we're not grateful to Cromwell. We would not be sitting here today if he had not stood up to the butcher of Savoy. Our people would have been exterminated. Jean and I would never have been born."

"And that would have been a great pity," Andrew said sincerely. "I would have missed your company."

"Think how we would have felt," John scoffed.

"Well, actually we would not have felt anything," Jean quipped. "Because we wouldn't have been born."

"Oh, now *you're* the entertainer," John returned. "Perhaps *you* should have recited the poem today."

"No, no," Jean said quickly. "I know my limitations. I am not meant for the stage. I will leave that for others."

"Such as your granddaughter Madeleine," Father Andrew said.

"Yes, my sweet granddaughter," Jean replied, his voice tender. "She loves to perform for people." He turned to Andrew. "As does your great-niece Albertina."

Andrew smiled. "The two songbirds."

"The Pinerolo festival will be here soon," Jean said.

"Yes," Andrew answered. "A little over a month. Do you know what they're singing?"

Jean shook his head. "No, Madeleine won't tell me."

Andrew growled. "Albertina won't tell me either."

John Malan chuckled. "Ah! The two *secretive* songbirds."

At that moment one of the gardeners approached the trio. "We have found these thistles at the edge of the garden," he said, holding out the prickly plants to the Waldensian men. "We will give a quantity to our apothecaries, but I wondered if you would like some for your winter store?"

"Ah! The plague killers!" John Malan said excitedly. "Yes, yes! Of course we would like some." He looked at his friend. "Jean?"

"Yes. I would love some, thank you," Jean answered.

John reached out and touched the purple fluff at the top of one of the plants. "They are delicious for food, too, not just medicine," he instructed the young priest. "You should cook some up."

"I'm sure the cooks and the apothecaries will make good use of them," the priest said, smiling. "We will gather yours into sacks and leave them by the edge of the garden." He turned and headed back to join his fellows.

"Thank you!" John called after him. "Not too heavy! I can't carry much weight anymore." He looked about and sighed deeply. "It is getting on towards the late of day, isn't it? It will chill when the sun goes down. I guess I should be going." He stood and looked up at the mountains. "It is hard to think of winter coming soon."

"Then do not think about it," Jean said, standing.

"Six or seven months of snow in the high mountains," John replied. "My heart weeps for those who must battle the harsh conditions: not enough wood for the fire, sleeping in the shed with the animals for warmth at night, eating the last of the turnips."

"There, there, old friend, you must let go of your sadness," Jean said. "The Waldenese have survived their mountain ghetto for hundreds of years. God is aware of the suffering we have endured to keep the primitive church alive." He patted his friend on the back. "Besides, warm weather has held on for a few extra weeks—perhaps we will have a mild winter." He turned to Andrew. "Good-bye, old friend. We will see you tomorrow."

"Thank you for the conversation and the poem," Andrew answered.

Jean laughed. "Conversation? John and I would bore a tree stump— weather, crops, life in the mountains, our aches and pains. Pshaw! You are very kind, my friend, to put up with *us*. You, who have traveled Europe and dined with princes."

Andrew took his friend's gnarled hand. "I used to like conversation with clever men, now I like conversation with good men."

Jean's head nodded several times. "Well, *I* may be good, but I don't know about John Malan."

"What? What's that?" John questioned, being too far away to hear the subdued exchange.

"Nothing, nothing. Andrew was just saying how much he enjoyed your poem."

John beamed. "Well then, tomorrow I shall come with another."

"Delightful!" Andrew said. "I will be glad to hear it."

The two men waved and trudged off to get their sacks of thistles. As they made their way onto the path to town, they passed by a man who nodded to them and stopped to talk. Andrew could not hear what they were saying, but it seemed likely the man had asked for directions, because he saw both his friends point to the monastery. The man gave them a little bow, and then headed towards the garden to speak to one of the young priests. Andrew leaned forward. He thought he recognized the man, but couldn't be sure. He squinted, and saw Father Pious pointing at him. *What is all this about?* Andrew wondered. As the man drew near he recognized the minister who had blessed his great-nephew. It was evident that the man was seeking him out and he wondered at his intent. Father Andrew smiled at the man as he neared and he smiled back.

"Good day, Father Andrew," Lorenzo said, holding out his hand. "I am Lorenzo Snow, and I was wondering if I might speak with you? I'm staying at your nephew's inn."

"Yes, yes. I know you. Please, sit down. You were at the bedside of my little Joseph."

"Yes."

"And you are a minister from America?

"Yes."

"And you wish to speak with me about your faith."

"Actually, no."

"No?"

"Well, I mean, if you were to ask me questions, I would certainly answer, but I'm more interested in asking you questions."

Andrew gave him a smile. "Well, that is unusual. A preacher who does not want to preach."

"It's just that I am unsure of my French and Italian; I don't think they would be sufficient for someone like you."

"Tchet! Someone like me? What do you mean?"

"Rene and his family have told me stories about your life."

"Ah! Exaggerated. Highly exaggerated, I am sure, Monsieur Snow! That would be the way of it."

"Well, if even half of what they say is true . . ." Lorenzo said.

"That was another lifetime. Another lifetime," Andrew deflected. "And what's this about you having trouble with the language? Not so. I have heard you speak both the languages now, and you are not bad. A little halting, but it is to be expected."

"Thank you for that. Your little Joseph says he can hardly understand me at all."

Andrew laughed loudly. "That boy is a pestilence!"

"Perhaps," Lorenzo said. "But a funny pestilence."

"Oh, indeed," Andrew affirmed. "The boy makes me laugh." He wiped his eyes and looked over at Lorenzo. "And you are a minister from America?"

"I am."

"I know your America well, Monsieur Snow. I admire your founding documents—the Constitution, the Declaration of Independence. I have translated them several times." The old priest looked down at his ink-stained fingers. "We, the people . . . in order to form a more perfect union." He recited the words softly as his mind wandered to another time and place. He rubbed his hands together and cleared his throat. "I have even met your Thomas Jefferson, you know," he said in a stronger voice.

"What?"

Andrew beamed over at Lorenzo. "Ah, *that* my family did not tell you?" Lorenzo shook his head. "Yes, I met him when I was eighteen," Andrew continued. "In a library in Paris."

"How . . . what . . . what was he like?" Lorenzo stammered.

"Magnificent. He was quite tall. I remember wondering if the vibrant air of America made men taller. And he was bright. So bright, so learned—yet he was not pompous. He carried himself with great dignity. The French did not know what to do with him."

"What do you mean?" Lorenzo asked.

"Well, your Monsieur Jefferson did not go for women, excessive drinking, or gambling. What were they to make of that? The favorite pastimes of the French did not tempt him? How odd. Indeed, the court of King Louis and Marie-Antoinette considered him very odd. Your Monsieur Jefferson would rather be off buying books."

"But others admired him?"

"Of course, the intellectuals and those wishing for a different kind of government. We looked to him—to America—as our guide."

"France did negotiate a constitution," Lorenzo said.

Andrew sighed. "True, but it lacked the wisdom and inspiration of the American document. We did not take the time to study things out as did your founders. We were too heated by the fire of revolution." Father Andrew fell silent.

"Amazing," Lorenzo said, attempting to envision the events the priest was describing.

Andrew roused himself. "Ah, Monsieur Snow! I am sorry. It has been wonderful to speak to you about America, but you have come to see me for a purpose, and here I am wasting your time with my meanderings."

"Far from wasting my time, Father Andrew."

"So, why have you come to see me, Reverend Snow?"

"Actually, ministers of The Church of Jesus Christ of Latter-day Saints are called elders."

"Elders?"

"Yes. But please, you must call me Lorenzo."

Father Andrew nodded. "For respect, I think I will call you Elder Snow." He chuckled. "But the name of your church is long, Elder Snow."

"It is," Lorenzo answered.

"Say it one more time for me."

"The Church of Jesus Christ of Latter-day Saints."

"Well, the Church of Jesus Christ is clear, but what is the meaning of Latter-day Saints?"

"We believe under the direction of Jesus Christ, the primitive church of the Lord has been restored."

"Restored?"

"Yes. And attaching "Latter-day Saints" is a way to distinguish the Saints of today from those two thousand years ago."

Andrew nodded. "That is sensible . . . sensible." He clapped his hands together. "But again! I am keeping you from your errand, Elder Snow. Why have you come?"

"Several reasons, Father Andrew. If you don't mind me taking up your time?"

"Of course not; I have an abundance of time."

Lorenzo reached into his coat pocket and pulled out a small soft-cover booklet. He stared down at it as he spoke. "We have just received these from the printer in Torino. It is a treatise I wrote explaining our beliefs." He handed it to Father Andrew.

"For me? Thank you, Monsieur. Something you wrote?"

"Yes."

Andrew fished a pair of glasses from his pocket. *The Voice of Joseph,*" he read from the cover.

"It was translated into French by a professor from the University of Paris."

"Very good. And you would like me to read it?"

"Yes, but more than that I would like you to peruse it: correct anything you see wrong, or question something that isn't clear. Your suggestions will be helpful if I need to rewrite it." Lorenzo hesitated. "If it wouldn't be too much trouble."

Father Andrew took his glasses off and looked straight into Lorenzo's eyes. "After what you did for my great-nephew, Elder Snow? I would be glad to take on many projects for you. This will be no trouble at all." Andrew's gaze slid over to the burnished hillsides. After a time, he spoke—his voice a whisper. "It is as though you stood on the edge of the great lake of death and called the child back to you. How did you do that?"

"The Lord was the power of the blessing."

"Yes, of course. But it was your voice to which He listened. Your voice that brought the miracle."

At that moment Father Pious approached. He gave Lorenzo a distrustful look before bowing to Andrew. "Honored one, Father Nathanael told me to come and fetch you when I was done with the gardening."

"Fetch me? Did he actually say you were to *fetch* me?" Father Andrew barked.

Father Pious stiffened, and Lorenzo could see that he was incensed by his superior's tone and embarrassed by the rebuke, especially since it was in front of a stranger. "I . . . I . . . no, he did not say *fetch*."

"I would hope not. What do you think me, the family dog?"

"I am sorry, your grace."

"And how dare you interrupt me when I'm having a fine conversation with this gentleman."

Father Pious's eyes narrowed and he turned to speak to Father Andrew as though Lorenzo were not present. "Your grace, we have heard word of this man and his companions."

"Oh yes?"

"Yes. They have been going about the countryside preaching heresy to the people. It is probably best that you send him away."

"Really? Send him away?"

"Yes. You do not want to give the wrong impression."

Father Andrew leaned forward. "And what impression is that?"

Father Pious's eyes flicked over to Lorenzo's face. "Well, that you are listening to his false teachings. It would not be good for our congregants to see you associating with him. I mean, what would they think?"

"Yes. What would they think, indeed?" Andrew closed his eyes and turned his face heavenward. "Brother Pious?"

"Yes, Father Andrew?"

"Would you do me a favor?"

"Of course," came the stiff reply.

"Would you go in and find Father Nathanael? Tell him that I want to stay outdoors for a few more minutes speaking with the false preacher who brought my nephew back from the grave."

Father Pious pressed his lips together. After a chill hesitation, he managed the words, "Of course."

Father Andrew opened his eyes and gave the man an even look. "And then say that I would like for *him* to come and *fetch* me."

Father Pious flinched at the unmistakable reprimand. "You do not wish me to return and—"

"No."

Father Pious stood straighter, gave Lorenzo one last scornful look, and moved off quickly to the monastery.

"I am sorry to have caused trouble," Lorenzo said as he watched Father Pious retreat into the building.

"Do not be silly, Elder Snow. I am sorry to have lost my temper, but I find it difficult when Father Pious does not live up to his name." He smiled over at Lorenzo. "Now, you said there were *several* things for which you needed to speak to me. What are the others?"

"Just one more thing," Lorenzo said, standing, "and then I will leave you in peace."

"Do not worry, my friend. We have a few minutes before Father Nathanael arrives."

"I have a book that I would like translated into Italian. Do you know of anyone competent for the task?"

Father Andrew gave him an amused look. "A book? An entire book? Well, I am immensely competent, but at my age I am afraid I could only help you translate a letter."

Lorenzo was mortified. "Oh no, Father Andrew! I did not mean for *you* to undertake the work. I just thought you might know of someone."

"Yes, yes. I know a few men, but I am afraid you will need to take the book to one of the major cities: Paris, Rome, or perhaps London."

"I thought that might be the case."

"I know several men in London. With a letter of introduction from me, I think they might be persuaded to help you."

"That is very gracious of you," Lorenzo said. "More than I could have asked."

Andrew suddenly raised his hand into the air and waved. "Ah, see there? My keeper is coming to *fetch* me." There was an unmistakable note of mischief in his voice as he spoke the word *fetch*.

Lorenzo turned to watch as another young priest came striding from the monastery. "Then I will be on my way, Father Andrew. Thank you for the wonderful conversation, and thank you for reading the booklet."

"Yes. I will be interested to see what it says," Andrew answered. He fixed Lorenzo with an evaluating stare. "May I give you a bit of advice, Elder Snow?"

"Of course."

"You have a family in America?"

"Yes."

"A family you have left to come here to preach?"

"Yes."

"And I can see the hardship of that sacrifice in your face."

"It is the Lord's work."

"And the Lord's guidance?" Andrew asked. Lorenzo nodded. "And he has put your feet on a path into these obscure Alpine valleys?"

Lorenzo cleared his throat. "Yes. I believe we are to bring the message of the restored gospel to the Waldenese."

"Then that is what you must do, Elder Snow. You must preach to the Waldenese. They are a remarkable people and these valleys have always been a special place where faith is obvious. It is as if faith is engraved into the very soil." Lorenzo thought this a singular thing for a Catholic priest to say, but from the tales told by the Guy family about their uncle, Father Andrew was a singular priest. His next words proved the assumption. "And I would like you and your companions to come and have supper with me sometime soon—would you do that?"

"Of course."

"You can tell me all about your American church." Father Nathanael arrived at Andrew's side. "And here is Father Nathanael come to *fetch* me. Father Nathanael, this is Elder Lorenzo Snow from America. Elder Snow, this is my helper, Father Nathanael."

"Yes, we've met," both men said together, and Andrew laughed.

"Have you?"

"Yes," Nathanael confirmed. "When Joseph was sick. Good afternoon, Monsieur Snow."

"Good afternoon, Father Nathanael."

"Wonderful!" Andrew said, as he stood with Father Nathanael's help. "And we will plan for you to come for supper."

"Supper?" Father Nathanael questioned, offering Andrew his arm.

"Yes, I have invited Elder Snow and his friends to supper sometime. Is there a problem with my invitation?"

"No, of course not," Father Nathanael replied. "I just thought we may want to find out what they like to eat."

Father Andrew laughed loudly. "Ah! Ah!" he spluttered. "You see, you see here? Here is one who knows the Savior's name."

Father Nathanael gave Andrew a puzzled look as he patted him on the back. "Calm down, old one, or I shall be taking you to the infirmary instead of to prayers."

Andrew took several deep breaths, and wiped his eyes. "Oh, this *has* been a good day." He stood a little straighter. "Thank you, Elder Snow, for your visit. Come on Friday for dinner. Friday is good. We will have fresh trout." He patted Father Nathanael's hand. "Father Nathanael will go to the Pellice River and catch it for us."

Father Nathanael encouraged his charge towards the monastery. "You are full of ideas today, aren't you?" As they moved off, Father Nathanael turned back. "Yes, come on Friday, Elder Snow. How many will there be?"

"Three. Just three of us," Lorenzo said, hoping their presence would not be a burden on the monastery.

As he watched the two holy men move slowly off towards their prayers, a scripture came to his remembrance, and he spoke the words aloud. "'Ye are the light of the world. A city that is set on a hill cannot be hid.'" He turned back towards the inn. "'Neither do men light a candle, and put it under a bushel, but on a candlestick; and it giveth light unto all that are in the house. Let your light so shine before men, that they may see your good works, and glorify your Father which is in heaven.'" Lorenzo shook his head as he thought of Father Andrew's remarkable life—certainly not a life hidden under a bushel basket.

NOTES

The French Revolution, from 1789 to the late 1790s, was a period of radical social and political upheaval in France that profoundly affected not only France but much of modern history and government, marking the decline of powerful monarchies and churches and the rise of democratic republics.

In his journal, Lorenzo Snow writes about meeting a Catholic priest and being invited to dine with him.

CHAPTER NINETEEN

Rorà

October 26, 1850

"Brethren! Brethren! Please do not stop on my account," Colonel Beckwith called out as he approached the three men pausing on the steep trail. One was slumped against a tree, the second was tapping a rock out of his boot, and the third was bent over, hands on his knees, attempting to catch his breath.

Elder Woodard gave the colonel a half smile as he stood. "I think we are pausing for *our* benefit, Colonel. You, indeed, are doing splendidly for a man thirty years my senior."

"Posh," the colonel said as he came to stand beside the men. "I just have these mountain heights in my blood, that's all, and my wooden leg has been navigating these trails for over twenty years." He thumped Elder Woodard on the shoulder. "You youngsters just need a tad more practice."

Lorenzo laughed inwardly as he watched Elder Woodard wincing from the blow. He put on his boot and tested its condition.

Colonel Beckwith walked over to Elder Stenhouse, who was laboring to catch his breath. "What say you, Stenhouse? You are the youngest among us. Shall we onward to conquer this mountain?"

"Yes sir, Colonel!" Elder Stenhouse replied, attempting to stand straight and to speak without gasping.

"That's the spirit!" Colonel Beckwith said. "Good man you've got there, Brother Snow. In truth, you are all good men."

"High praise coming from you," Lorenzo said. He watched as the colonel unstopped his canteen and took a drink. What a blessing to have met the man, Lorenzo thought. And now to be counted among his associates was an honor. Lorenzo knew American patriots who had fought fierce battles in the Revolutionary War, hearing from them acts of courage and brave deeds in battle, but Colonel Beckwith had fought in the battle of Waterloo, having had four horses shot out from under him before taking a bullet that would cost him his leg. The three missionaries had met the colonel the night they went to the monastery to dine with Father Andrew. Lorenzo remembered the night with fondness: a delicious dinner of trout, leeks and potatoes, bread, cheese, and melon; interesting conversation; a viewing of the library and the chapel; and a chance to preach the gospel. Father Andrew and Colonel Beckwith had listened with great attention and posed many interesting questions. It was evident to Lorenzo that Father Andrew had a deep respect for the soldier turned philanthropist and missionary. Beckwith had given up a life of privilege and honor in London to build schools in the Piedmont and bolster the worldly circumstances and spiritual strength of the Waldenese. It had been a grand evening, at the end of which Father Andrew had presented him a book of Italian grammar in which he'd inscribed his name.

"Nellie!" Colonel Beckwith called, bringing Lorenzo's attention back to the group. "Come on, boy, high to!" The colonel's scruffy gray Cairn terrier came leaping over undergrowth and rocks to his master's side.

Elder Stenhouse laughed. "I find it odd that you named your male dog Nellie."

The colonel gave a one-note whistle, and the dog jumped into his arms. "Actually, I named him after a man I greatly admired—Lord Nelson."

"I see," Elder Stenhouse replied. "'Tis a very noble name, then."

"Indeed, but I could not very well go around all day calling the lowly cur Lord Nelson. He would have acquired a much too grand opinion of himself."

The company laughed and Nellie barked as though he knew they were talking about him. Beckwith set the dog on the ground.

"Get on with you then, you mangy mongrel." Nellie took off up the path as though given the command to be the guide. "Should we follow on then? Less than an hour more to Rorà," Beckwith encouraged. The men started, all except Elder Stenhouse, who was taking one last drink from his canteen. "High on, Stenhouse!" the colonel called back. "You wouldn't want a wee dog to show you up now, would you?"

Elder Stenhouse gulped down his mouthful of water and hurried to catch up with his companions.

The cluster of thirty stone houses that made up the village of Rorà clung to the mountainside, mimicking the rock outcroppings surrounding it. The four men trudged along the switchback trail, pushing ever forward to the heart of the town. Their destination was the recently built Waldensian church where they had been invited to preach. As they managed another switchback and headed in the direction of the village, Lorenzo could clearly see the temple with its bell tower and pale yellow walls. The light facade of the building stood in stark contrast to the rustic stone houses and barns.

Lorenzo took a deep breath of the crisp mountain air and noted the quietude and beauty of the surrounding countryside. Where grassland escaped the dominion of trees, terraces were etched into the hillside, creating flat areas for grapevines and vegetables. The trees were near the end of their vibrant fall colors, and the last of the dead leaves on the grapevines twitched in the cold autumn breeze.

In the distance, Lorenzo could hear Nellie's bark. He smiled. It seemed the dog was announcing the imminent arrival of the colonel and his companions to the villagers. Shortly thereafter the bell in the church tower began ringing, and people could be seen emerging from their dwellings into the lanes and streets. As he and his companions navigated the final switchback and drew nearer the village, Lorenzo was intrigued by the vision of the villagers dressed in their Sabbath costumes: the men in rough woven suits with vests and white shirts, the women in dark dresses with plum, green, or brown aprons, white shawls, and white bonnets.

The foursome walked up the main dirt road and the people came running, surrounding the colonel with warm and robust greetings. Nellie cavorted and barked as though he was the center of attention, and, in actuality, received his share of accolades. Lorenzo and his companions were approached with a respectful but measured greeting. The villagers did not know these foreign preachers, but afforded them hospitality because of the great love they carried for Colonel Beckwith.

"My friends! My friends!" Colonel Beckwith called. "How happy I am to be with you! It has been much too long."

An older gentleman stepped closer. "See, we have been taking good care of the church you built for us."

"Ah, I was just a part . . . just a part of the work," the colonel deflected. "Do not forget the many English Protestants who sent funds to raise your temples and your schools."

"No, no! We do not forget. We will never forget them. They are always in our prayers of thanks," the old man replied quickly.

Beckwith nodded. "And you are always in their prayers of fellowship." He turned toward the temple, laying his hand on the man's shoulder. "It is beautiful. A place of truth and worship."

"And warmth," the man added, his head bobbing up and down. "Better than the cave where my grandfather's family went to read their Bible."

"Indeed," Beckwith said. "Indeed." His voice lifted to the group. "Shall we in, then?" He moved up the steps to the door, the group following with murmured conversation and cheerful faces.

When they entered the temple, they encountered men and women already seated on the wooden pews, a few others standing along the walls and talking. Lorenzo surmised by the number of walking sticks and cloaks that these had come from places other than Rorà to hear the preaching of the foreign evangelists.

Elder Woodard came to Lorenzo's side, speaking in a lowered voice. "I believe the word is out that the colonel has listened to our preaching."

Lorenzo nodded. "And has taken no thought to dismiss it."

Elder Stenhouse stood near and overheard. "I hope that means the people of the mountains are curious about the message," he added. His voice shook with nervousness, and he tried to hide it with a cough.

"There are Waldensian pastors here," Lorenzo added. "Those who invited us and others who did not."

"That is unsettling," Elder Stenhouse said, looking about.

"Do not be troubled, Elder Stenhouse," Elder Woodard assured, leaning near to him. "We will leave the preaching to the apostle among us."

Elder Stenhouse smiled broadly, the look of fear dropping from his face. "I agree. It's only right that the apostle should be the mouth-piece."

Colonel Beckwith led the Mormon missionaries to chairs at the front of the congregation and as they sat, a hush settled on the gathering. The pastor of the Rorà parishioners came forward to greet them and to receive introductions. He then went to stand at the heavy wooden table at the front of the hall on which lay an ancient opened Bible. It seemed to Lorenzo that the rural preacher was intimidated by the large gathering and the presence of Colonel Beckwith. He took a breath and laid his hand on the Bible.

"God be with all of you this day. Many of you have come from Torre Pellice, Gianavella, Bobbio Pellice, and some from the Angrogna Valley. It is good to be together in faith. We are honored to have Colonel Beckwith with us, and with him the evangelist from The

Church of Jesus Christ of Latter-day Saints." He turned to Elder Snow. "Is the name correct?"

"Yes, exactly correct," Lorenzo answered.

The pastor turned back to his congregation. "These gentlemen have been preaching in homes in the valleys for several weeks now, and questions have begun to arise. The leaders of the synod felt it appropriate that they be given a chance to preach their doctrine in front of several pastors who will then ask questions."

Lorenzo saw Elder Stenhouse sit straighter in his chair and heard him clear his throat.

"I have been informed that Elder Snow will give the address, and then we may ask questions." The pastor stepped aside. "Elder Snow."

Lorenzo stood and walked to the table, laying his hand on the Bible and saying a silent prayer for inspiration.

"My friends, we thank you for your willingness to listen with open hearts to the message we bring to your mountains. I hope that you will accept my halting attempt at Italian. Perhaps in a little while we can invite Elder Woodard to speak to you in lovely French." He turned to smile at Elder Woodard, and then back to the congregation. "The gospel we preach is that of the Lord Jesus Christ—the primitive church restored by revelation to a prophet." Audible gasps were heard throughout the gathering. "I will tell you of this restoration, which came by divine manifestations and heavenly visions. I will tell you of the restoration of priesthood keys—the authority to bind on earth and in heaven. I will tell you of a people who love the holy word of God and preach from its pages. I will tell you of ancient scripture brought forth out of the ground and translated by the gift and power of God." Lorenzo paused and looked out into the faces of the Waldensian faithful. "You are well acquainted with persecution. For hundreds of years you have been persecuted for your faith as taught by God to His prophets, and as taught by Christ to His apostles. Persecution has also been the lot of the Mormon people. I will tell you of the persecution we have faced in bringing forth the restoration of the Lord's primitive church. I will tell you of a modern-day prophet slain by his countrymen for daring to speak the truth. I will tell you of an exodus of people driven from their homes by bloodthirsty mobs whose hearts were hardened against this truth. I will witness these things to you as one who was there; as one who walked with the Prophet, as one who heard revelations from his mouth, as one who journeyed thousands of miles across a continent to escape persecution." He paused. "I will speak to you as an apostle of the Lord Jesus Christ."

There was immediate loud dissent from several men, and people in the congregation began speaking to each other in uplifted voices. Several of the pastors stood and began questioning Lorenzo directly, their voices raised to be heard above the tumult.

"You know nothing of persecution!" one yelled. "Over six hundred years we Waldenese have suffered!"

"And how dare you usurp the holy calling of apostle?" another challenged.

Elder Snow held up a hand. "Please, let me—"

But the contention rolled over him. "We honor Christ and His apostles and the words they taught!"

Suddenly one of the pastors slammed a book onto the table; the sharp sound brought instantaneous silence. He was a large man with an intimidating bearing. He glared at Lorenzo. "There in front of you is the only word of God, Monsieur. We have been preaching from its pages for hundreds of years. In candlelit caves, defying retribution, suffering torture and death."

The pastor from Rorà moved to the man. "Pastor Monastier, perhaps we should—"

But the man only stepped closer to Lorenzo. "Do not think you can come here with your puny religion and abuse our faith."

Agitated voices rose again from the congregation.

Colonel Beckwith rose slowly from his chair and patiently waited for the room to quiet. "My friends, we must hear their words. If these gentlemen say anything contrary to the Bible we may feel free to dismiss their testimony, but we must first listen, wouldn't you agree?"

Several heads nodded, and several of those standing took their seats grudgingly, but Pastor Monastier did not move. "No, Colonel Beckwith. No. I honor and respect you, sir, but I will not remain silent when there is a wolf among the flock. And I will not stay to hear blasphemy preached." He went to gather his cloak and walking stick, turning at the door and fixing the Mormon missionaries with a reproachful stare. "Mark my words, gentlemen. You do not have a friend in me." He strode out of the church, snapping the door shut behind him. An ominous silence hung in the room until Colonel Beckwith spoke, quoting from the book of John.

"Do not treat prophecies with contempt, but test them all; hold on to what is good." He looked out steadfastly at the congregation, letting the words of the scripture sink into their hearts. "Shall we hear the words?" There being no objection, he turned to Lorenzo. "Please, Monsieur Snow, continue."

Lorenzo prayed for enlightenment from the Spirit and the gift of tongues as he slowly turned the pages of the ancient Bible. He stopped at a verse and began reading. "If any of you lack wisdom, let him ask of God, that giveth to all men liberally, and upbraideth not; and it shall be given him." He looked up into the watchful faces. "On a beautiful spring morning in the year 1820, a young man by the name of Joseph Smith knelt in the grove of trees near his home, to ask God a question that had been troubling him . . ."

Three hours later the Mormon missionaries stood in front of the Waldensian temple speaking with a few stragglers and handing out the last of their *The Voice of Joseph* pamphlets. A young couple approached Elder Woodard, taking a booklet and turning to leave with only a word of thanks.

Elder Woodard called after them. "Excuse me." The couple stopped and turned back as Elder Woodard walked to them. He held out his hand and the man took it. "We are glad you came today. I am Jabez Woodard."

"I am Antoine Gaydou and this is my wife, Mary Malan Gaydou." He smiled over at her. "We are glad we came today also."

"Are you from Rorà?" Elder Woodard asked.

"No, we live in Torre Pellice. I am a tailor. I have a small shop. We came because we have heard rumors about the doctrine you preach."

Elder Woodard chuckled. "Well, do not believe all the gossip you hear."

Antoine smiled. "Yes, there are many strange tales. That is why we decided to come today, so we could find out for ourselves."

"Thank you for that," Elder Woodard said. He tapped the pamphlet Antoine was holding. "I think you will find many answers here."

"Yes, we will read it," Antoine said, reaching out to shake Elder Woodard's hand again. "Thank you."

"Thank you," Mary added.

Elder Woodard watched the two with a light heart as they headed off down the path towards Torre Pellice. He was so engrossed with the spirit that surrounded the brief meeting that he did not notice Elder Snow and Elder Stenhouse approach. He started when Elder Stenhouse spoke.

"Elder Woodard, we want to introduce Monsieur Jean Antoine Bose. He speaks Italian but seems to be most comfortable with French. We thought you might speak with him." He brought the man forward. "Monsieur Bose, this is Elder Woodard."

Elder Woodard evaluated the man and found him to be neither grand nor ordinary. His clothes were homespun, but his bearing spoke of intellect and quiet confidence. "Good day, Monsieur Bose. It is good to meet you."

"It is very good to meet you, Monsieur, and I wanted to tell you and your friends that I thought it was a significant meeting."

"Thank you, Monsieur. I am afraid some did not share your view."

"Well, no, but that is because they were listening with their brains alone. One must hear spiritual things with the spirit inside them, no? My ears and my head heard words, but my spirit heard the truth."

Elder Woodard was set back by the straightforward declaration. "That . . . that is wonderful, Monsieur. Wonderful!"

"I believe you are servants of God, and I would like to be counted among your flock."

Elder Woodard stared at him. He opened his mouth several times to speak, but no words were forthcoming.

"I am sorry, Monsieur Woodard. Did you not understand what I said?"

Elder Woodard nodded. "I did, yes. I . . . I am just astonished by what you said." He turned to Lorenzo. "I am not exactly sure, Elder Snow, but I think Monsieur Bose has just applied for baptism."

"Really?" Lorenzo asked excitedly. "Ask him again. Find out where he lives. Ask if he has any family."

Elder Woodard shared his leader's questions with the man, who answered each with a calm assurance. "He wishes to be baptized!" Elder Woodard reported. "He lives in Gianavella—the small town near Torre Pellice."

"Yes, I know it," Lorenzo acknowledged. "And family?"

"He does have family, but he is the first to hear the words of the gospel."

Lorenzo came forward and extended his hand. Jean Bose took it. "We are so glad you have felt the truth in our words, Monsieur Bose. When would you like to be baptized?" Even though Lorenzo was speaking Italian, it was evident the man understood him, for at the word "baptized" a wide smile planted itself on the man's face.

"Tomorrow, in the Pellice River," he answered. "Is it possible?"

"Tomorrow?" Lorenzo said, stepping back.

"It is not possible?"

"Yes, it's possible," Lorenzo answered. "But we have many other things we need to teach you."

"Are you going back to Torre Pellice now?" Monsieur Bose asked.

"We are."

"Then I will walk with you, and Monsieur Woodard can tell me everything I must know."

Colonel Beckwith joined the group at that moment. His eyes narrowed when he noticed Elder Woodard's stunned expression. "Are you feeling all right, Elder Woodard? It looks like you have been struck by lightning."

"Indeed, Colonel. Yes, indeed, for that is just the way it feels."

"Monsieur Bose has just applied for baptism," Lorenzo said by way of explanation.

Colonel Beckwith shook hands with Monsieur Bose. "Truth will out, I always say! The best to you, sir."

"Thank you, Colonel Beckwith. It is an honor to shake your hand."

"It is an honor to shake the hand of a man who will stand against the odds when he finds truth." He turned to the group. "Are we off then? I am ready for supper and bed." The others heartily agreed. "Nellie!" the colonel called. "High to, you irascible mutt!" The terrier came running around the side of a house with a bone in his mouth. "What's that you have there, devil dog? How dare you start supper without me!"

The company laughed as they headed down the mountain, Nellie and Colonel Beckwith at the front, and Monsieur Bose and Elder Jabez Woodard at the back, already in conversation.

NOTES

John Charles Beckwith was born in Halifax, Nova Scotia, in 1789. He left Halifax to join the British army at age fourteen. After losing his leg in the Battle of Waterloo in 1814, he stayed on in military service until 1820. In 1827 while in a library in London, he picked up a book by Dr. William Gilly about the history of the Protestant Waldenese. Inspired by their struggles, Colonel Beckwith consecrated the rest of his life to serving the Waldenese by living among them and building schools and churches in the valleys of the Piedmont.

In a letter from Lorenzo Snow to Brigham Young dated November 1, 1850, Lorenzo relates having met Colonel Beckwith and having several interesting interviews with him. After one such meeting Lorenzo quotes Colonel Beckwith as saying, "You shall receive no opposition on my part; and if you preach the gospel as faithfully to all in these valleys as to me, you need fear no reproach in the day of judgment." Colonel Beckwith died in 1862 in Torre Pellice.

Jean Antoine Bose was the first LDS baptism in Italy. He was baptized October 27, 1850.

CHAPTER TWENTY

Torre Pellice

October 27, 1850

In the early morning hours of sleep, Lorenzo had experienced strange dreams. And now, as he sat on the bank of the Pellice River, waiting for the arrival of Jean Antoine Bose, his mind wandered among the disjointed pictures of his nighttime imaginings. The one scene that was most complete included a lake, a boat, and fish.

"Are you tired this morning?" Elder Woodard asked, sitting down next to Lorenzo.

"No. Just thinking."

"It is a good day for thinking. An eventful day."

"Yes. The first baptism in Italy," Lorenzo said.

Elder Woodard shook his head. "Monsieur Bose's conversion is a wonder to me."

"But *you* are a convert."

"Yes, but it took me a month to enter the waters of baptism. For Monsieur Bose it was one day!"

Lorenzo nodded. "Ah, I see what you mean." He slowly tossed a few pebbles into the swirling water. "I liked what he said about hearing the words with our ears, but feeling the truth with our spirits. He obviously felt the Spirit." He gave Elder Woodard a half grin. "I have to admit that I was one of those intellectuals who spent a long time evaluating the words."

"Yet, here you are, sacrificing your life to preach the gospel."

Lorenzo pulled his mind away from home. "Yes, here I am." He yawned and stretched his arms above his head.

"You *are* tired," Elder Woodard insisted.

"A little. I had many dreams last night."

"Any of importance?"

"I do think one odd little dream carried significance."

"We have time before Elder Stenhouse arrives with Brother Bose. Will you share it with me?"

The only other people with whom Lorenzo had shared his dreams were his sister Eliza and his sweet wife Charlotte, but since they were thousands of miles away and unable to help him puzzle out the meaning, he figured he would rely on the friend at his side. He threw a few more stones into the water as he gathered his thoughts.

"I seemed to be in the company of friends descending a gentle slope of beautiful green. We came to the bank of a large body of water and found two boats at its edge. I climbed into one while my friends followed in the other. We moved slowly over this ever-widening bay, without wind or any exertion on our part."

"The boats just moving along on their own?" Elder Woodard interrupted.

"Just on their own."

"Interesting how unusual things can happen in dreams that we just accept as everyday."

"It is interesting," Lorenzo concurred. "For example, in the dream I somehow knew that we were on a fishing excursion, and then, to my delight, I saw all these large and beautiful fish on the surface of the water—hundreds of fish all around, to a great distance."

"Fascinating!" Elder Woodard said, obviously enjoying the story.

"I saw many persons spreading their nets and lines, but they all seemed to be stationary, whereas we were in continual motion. While passing by, I discovered that a fish had got upon my line. When my boat reached the shore, I drew in the line, and was surprised and mortified at the smallness of my prize. It was very strange that among such a multitude of noble, superior looking fish, that I should have made so small a haul."

"At least you caught a fish," Elder Woodard cajoled.

"That's true," Lorenzo returned. "And all my disappointment vanished when I discovered that its qualities were of a very extraordinary character."

"And that is the whole of the dream?"

"It is. As I said, an odd little dream."

"Yes, but I think it meaningful," Elder Woodard returned. "I think it is a vision of our work here in Italy. All around us are lofty and important people who will not be caught in the gospel net, and yet here in the Piedmont, we find simple men and women of extraordinary quality who are being drawn to the truth."

Lorenzo smiled. "Yes, I was thinking in that direction also."

"Elder Snow!" came an unexpected voice behind them.

The men stood and turned toward the approaching pair. Lorenzo shaded his eyes from the sun and raised his hand. "Mademoiselle Cardon! Mademoiselle Guy! Hello!" He turned to Elder Woodard. "Did you mention where we'd be holding the baptism?"

"I did not," Elder Woodard said simply.

"Nor I," Lorenzo returned. "Perhaps it is just coincidence."

The girls drew close, each dressed against the autumn chill and carrying a woven basket. "I thought it was you," Albertina said as they came to the missionaries' side. "Madeleine didn't think so, but I knew it was."

"Yes. You guessed right," Lorenzo said, smiling.

"What brings you out?" Elder Woodard questioned.

Albertina held up her basket. "We're going to pick the last of the wild berries." She pointed upriver. "There by the bridge."

"Is your mother going to make a cobbler?" Lorenzo asked with anticipation.

Albertina laughed. "No. I'm sorry, Elder Snow, she's not. If we find any berries today we're taking them to my great-uncle. We hope it will cheer him."

"Is he unwell?"

Albertina nodded. "For the past several days."

"I am sorry to hear that."

"I think he's just tired. He's very old, you know." The two missionaries held back chuckles as she continued. "He'll be up and about in a few days, growling at everyone."

"And are you two off on another hike into the valleys?" Madeleine broke in.

"No, we're waiting here for Elder Stenhouse and Monsieur Bose to arrive."

"Monsieur Bose?" Madeleine asked.

"Yes. He wishes to be baptized."

"Into *your* church?" Albertina blurted out.

Now the missionaries actually did laugh.

"Yes, Mademoiselle Guy, into our strange and wonderful church," Elder Woodard said.

Albertina's face reddened. "Oh! I didn't mean anything by it."

"I know," Elder Woodard returned. "I am just teasing you."

"Is he the first baptism, then?" Madeleine asked.

Elder Snow smiled. "He is, Madeleine. The very first."

"Heigh-ho!" came Elder Stenhouse's voice from a distance. The girls and the two missionaries looked over to where the men approached.

Elder Woodard patted Elder Snow on the shoulder. "Well, we have a simple and extraordinary man to bring into the waters of baptism."

"With satisfaction, I attend to this ordinance," Lorenzo said, his voice growing husky. "And I rejoice that the Lord has blessed our efforts. What an astounding occurrence."

"Yes, indeed. Who thought it possible to open the door of the kingdom in Italy?" Elder Woodard added.

"Amen."

Lorenzo felt a tug on his coat sleeve.

"Monsieur Snow, would it be all right if Albertina and I stayed to watch?"

"Perfectly all right, Mademoiselle Cardon."

The four waited in silence for Elder Stenhouse and Monsieur Bose to arrive. The sun was shining and the sky was a brilliant blue with wisps of white clouds. In shade or shadow, the grip of autumn was evident, but with the sun on his face, Lorenzo could feel the last vestiges of summer. He pondered the miracle of the moment. A man had found the truth of gospel restoration, and this he had found even though the Church's presence in Italy was just tolerated and not recognized as any lawful right. This man had sorted through the slander and poisonous lies that were already circulating about the Church, beginning with its rise to the death of Joseph. He had heard the truth of the gospel even though many of the Waldenese considered the Mormons' preaching to be an attempt to drag them from the banner of their martyred ancestry. In this last obstacle, Lorenzo could understand the people's reticence. Though the underpinnings of their dogma had undergone transformation when they integrated with other Protestant faiths, many of the Waldenese still felt themselves the firstfruits of reformation. Many still saw themselves as the keepers of the original faith.

"Good morning, brothers!" Elder Stenhouse said heartily as he and Monsieur Bose arrived in company. "'Tis a fine day for a baptism, I'm thinking!" He noticed Madeleine and Albertina. "And who do we have here? Two more candidates?"

"Ah, no, Elder Stenhouse!" Madeleine spluttered. "We just came here by accident. Elder Snow said we could watch."

"Accident, eh? I'm thinkin' there be no accidents."

"But I—"

"Are you sure you don't want to be gettin' your feet wet, Miss

Cardon?" She laughed when she realized he was teasing her. "All right. All right," he said with a shrug. "I'm not counting you out for another day." He winked at them. "Even you, Miss Guy."

Albertina leaned close to Madeleine and whispered. "Imagine what my family would say to that."

Elder Woodard stepped forward, extending his hand to Monsieur Bose. "How are you doing this morning, Jean?"

"I am doing well, Elder Woodard. I have prayed for peace concerning my decision."

Lorenzo was next to shake his hand. "And how are you feeling?"

"I am calm, Elder Snow. All night I pondered the words Elder Woodard shared with me, and I found nothing amiss. My desire is still strong to join with you."

Lorenzo smiled. "Then let's take you into the water and prepare you to become a member of the Lord's Church."

The two men removed their shoes, socks, and suit coats and walked out into the cold waters of the Pellice River. Lorenzo thought of the Savior standing with John in the waters of Jordan, of Joseph Smith and Oliver Cowdery baptizing each other in the Susquehanna River, having just received their priesthood commissions from that same John. He thought of himself in Kirtland, Ohio, being immersed by Elder Boynton, an apostle of God. And now he, as an apostle, took the hand of Jean Antoine Bose, and while his two companions stood as witnesses and the two young women looked on, Lorenzo spoke the words in the soft sounds of Italian that would open a door that no man could shut.

NOTE

The dream of the boat and the fish was an actual dream experienced by Elder Snow and recorded in his writings.

CHAPTER TWENTY-ONE

Torre Pellice

November 1, 1850

"Another log on the fire! This cold is cracking my bones!"

Albertina laid down the book and went to fulfill her great-uncle's command. "Stop growling. You nearly made my friend jump out of her chair."

Father Andrew turned to Madeleine Cardon. "Please forgive me, Mademoiselle Cardon. The cold makes me grumpy."

"Don't worry, Father Andrew. I've become used to your grumbling."

Albertina laughed. "See there? *There* is someone who will stand up to you."

"Well, it's not difficult to stand up to an old dog without sharp teeth."

The fire blazed in the grate and tendrils of warmth drifted into the library. Father Andrew sighed. There were still a few pleasant things about the world: a warm room, a cherished face, and prayers at eventide.

"Uncle?"

"Yes, my dear one?"

"Do you think you will be able to come to the singing competition in Pinerolo?"

"Singing competition? What singing competition?"

"The singing competition at . . . Oh! You are teasing me!" Andrew chuckled at his great-niece's pique. "That is not funny, Uncle! I should stop reading to you for that."

"Oh, no!" Andrew protested. "We were just at the eventful part where the mad priest is going to tell Dantes about the hidden treasure!"

Albertina sat down and closed the book. "You know this story from end to end anyway."

"But *I* don't know it," Madeleine said.

"See, your friend wants to know what will happen to the mistreated Dantes. What kind of friend are you to keep it from her?"

"All right, you trickster. I'll read, but first you have to answer my question about the singing competition."

Andrew gazed at her fondly. "I would not miss it for anything. I will make it to Pinerolo even if they have to drag me along on Joseph's little sledge."

"Well, *that* would be an amusing sight," Albertina said, opening the book.

"And you will not give me the slightest hint as to what you're singing?"

"No."

Andrew looked crestfallen, and Madeleine giggled.

"Oh, all right," Albertina said with a sigh. "It is a song . . . by . . . a . . . very great composer."

"Pshaw!" Andrew grunted. "Now who is teasing?"

"Enough of this," Albertina said, stifling her laughter. "If you want to hear about the hidden treasure, then we must get to it before Madeleine and I have to leave."

"Leave? Where are you going? I thought you might stay for the midday meal. After all, you did bring your mother's stew."

"Sorry, Uncle, but Madeleine is helping the Mormon missionaries this afternoon at one of their 're-unions.'"

Andrew turned to the girl. "Helping?"

"Yes. The missionaries are preaching today to a group of Waldenese who have come down from the high mountains. One of the missionaries speaks French and Italian very well, but is unfamiliar with this mountain dialect."

"And so you will translate for them."

"Yes."

"Your family is listening to their message, little daughter of the Waldenese?"

Madeleine nodded. "And many of our neighbors also."

Andrew put his hands together and leaned forward. "I bet that is causing a stir in the churches."

Madeleine nodded again. "More than a stir. Many of the ministers are upset."

Andrew eyebrows raised. "I'm sure." He gave the girls a half grin. "I have heard their preaching, you know, these Mormons."

"Really?" Madeleine said, her eyes widening. "Won't you be in trouble for that?"

A gentle smile covered Andrew's face as he sat back in his chair. "Me? What could they do to me?"

"Put you in a dungeon? Toss you out into the snow?" There was genuine concern in her voice.

"Toss me out into the snow?" Andrew laughed. "Well, I am quite sure Father Pious would like to see that, but actually I think I'm safe from retribution." He glanced to the fire and back. "How could I not listen to their words? Albertina and I both saw a miracle at their hands."

"Oh, yes, of course," Madeleine replied. "The healing of your little Joseph."

"Yes. And Albertina has shared with me the story of your dream when you were six."

Madeleine looked quickly over at her friend. "She did?"

"Don't look so surprised," Albertina said. "I knew he would be fascinated by it."

"And so I was. I find it all fascinating."

Madeleine looked at Father Andrew straight on. "Still, you are taking a chance."

Father Andrew grinned at her and nodded. "I guess we are both taking a chance."

"And I am taking a chance too," Albertina said quickly.

"How is that?" Andrew asked, looking to her.

Albertina hesitated. "I have been attending several of the re-unions with Madeleine."

Andrew frowned at her. "I see. Do your mother and father know?"

"Yes, of course."

"And?"

"They . . . they allow me to go because of their gratitude to the missionaries for Joseph's life, but . . ."

"But?"

"We are Catholic. Our family has always been Catholic." Tears came into her voice. "And we honor you." She came and knelt by his chair. "I wouldn't do anything to make you unhappy. You are a priest."

Father Andrew put his hand gently on her head. "Ah, but haven't you heard? I am a different kind of priest." Albertina laid her head on the arm of the chair and cried. Andrew patted her. "This has been bothering you, hasn't it?"

Madeleine stood quickly. "I'm afraid it's my fault," she said. "I invited her to a meeting, and during the meeting Elder Woodard asked her to read from the Bible. She liked reading from the Bible. Then the other day we watched as Elder Snow baptized a man. It was like Jesus' baptism, and—"

"But we are Catholic," Albertina blubbered.

"Look at me," Andrew said. Albertina did not respond. "Look at me, little sparrow." She looked up. "I think you are brave. And if you are brave you must seek for knowledge; if you are brave you will ask questions and not be fearful of the answers." He wiped the tears from her cheeks. "One can find truth in many places. You can take the little bit of knowledge the Mormons have to offer and put it with the truth you already know. It doesn't mean you have to change anything."

Albertina sat back and stared at her great-uncle. "That's right. I don't have to change anything." She hugged him. "I have already been baptized."

"Exactly. You can listen to their words and read from their Bible, but nothing has to change." Albertina took a deep breath, and he wiped the tears from her cheeks. "So—enough of this worry and sadness, yes?"

"Yes, Uncle."

"Now, you two should be on your way." He gave them each a serious look. "It seems you are abandoning me and poor Dantes." The girls began to protest, but he waved them off. "No, no, no! It seems you will just have to come another time for more of the story. Now, off with you. You have work to do."

Albertina stood and kissed his cheek. "Old bear." She stepped back and Madeleine joined her. "Is there anything we can do before we go, Uncle?"

"One more log for the fire?"

The girls grinned as each went to secure a log. "There, that should keep you," Albertina said, brushing off her hands. She handed him the book and picked up her coat.

"Yes, I think I will survive. Now, off with you! You do not want the missionaries to worry."

"I think they would manage without me," Madeleine answered, putting on her coat. "Thank you for the exciting book, Father Andrew."

"Promise you will come again to read more."

"Of course! We must find out what happens."

Andrew watched the girls as they moved into the shadowed expanse of the library. *Not girls anymore*, he thought with a twinge of sadness. At seventeen they were nearing womanhood, which meant different interests—interests that would probably not include spending time with a doddering old priest. Andrew chided himself for such melancholy thoughts.

"We do not know the end of the story," he said out loud. "We must wait and see what happens."

He heard the library door close, and turned his face to the fire.

"Where are those wolves in sheep's clothing?"

"Let's bring them out!"

"Drag them out!"

"Where is the young lady who is helping them?"

Madeleine closed her Bible and looked over at Elder Woodard, for whom she'd been translating. Elder Snow and Elder Stenhouse stood from the congregation and Elder Snow moved quickly towards the door as the shrieks and yelling outside the house continued.

"Wait! Wait, Elder Snow!" Madeleine yelled. "Let me go!" She strode to his side. "Let me go out!"

"I can't let you do that!" Lorenzo said firmly.

"But I know one of the voices. He is my pastor, Pastor Monastier. He will not harm me." Madeleine reached for the latch, but Lorenzo pressed his hand against the door.

"This is a mob. I have seen mobs, Madeleine, and you do not know what men can do when their feelings are overtaken."

Albertina now stood at her friend's side. "Listen to him, Madeleine. It is dangerous."

"I am a daughter of the Waldenese, Elder Snow. I know what men can do; I have heard the stories all my life, but I know the Lord will be with me. Let me go out."

The fervor of her commitment forced Lorenzo to the side. Madeleine opened her Bible and stepped out to face the gathering of angry men. They were quiet for a moment, surprised by the appearance of the slight girl, but then the jeering and ridicule began anew.

"Here is one whose spirit is black!"

"Helper of the wolves in sheep's clothing!"

"She carries a false bible written by the Mormon elders to deceive the people!"

Madeleine walked directly to her pastor and laid the Bible in his hands. "You confirmed me when I was fifteen. Here is the same Bible I studied from at that time—the holy Bible used by the Mormon elders to preach the words of Christ!" Her voice was strong and calm. It carried such power that the cacophony diminished.

Pastor Monastier scowled at her. "You are disloyal! You have violated your oath to the church!"

"I am loyal to the truth!" she called out, laying her hand on the open Bible. "I believe in this Bible, but now I understand it better than before." She looked intently into the eyes of her pastor. "You taught me that it was the duty of all of God's children to learn and walk in the true way of salvation. That is what I am doing."

"Blasphemer," he hissed. He raised his voice. "They have stolen her soul!"

The yells of the mob burst forth.

"Bring out those wolves!"

"Make them pay for their treachery!"

The men surged forward, but Madeleine held her ground. She grabbed her Bible from the pastor's hands and thrust it into the air.

"You will leave this place! The elders are under my protection and you will not harm one hair on their heads!"

The mob stopped as if they'd run into a wall, the Satanic oaths strangling in their throats. Madeleine knew that God was with her, filling her with calm as she looked at the strong, ferocious body of men standing helpless before a weak, trembling—yet fearless—girl. The combat was on. The spirit of Satan had struck the first blow, but now the Spirit of God assumed control.

Pastor Monastier stared at her, then turned and instructed the mob to depart. Some dispersed with sullen faces, some in fear and shame, some broken in pride and remorseful in spirit. The pastor waited until he was alone with the girl.

"I am sorry for you and your family, Madeleine. You are being led away by deceivers. I will pray that you will be guided back to the truth. If not, may God have mercy on your soul." He turned to go.

"Pastor Monastier," Madeleine called softly after him. He turned back. "I pray also that you may find the truth." Her voice was soft and sincere, and for a moment the stern resolve on the man's face flickered. He lowered his head, turned, and walked away.

As the door to the house slowly opened, Madeleine fell to her knees. Albertina was immediately by her side.

"Madeleine! Are you all right? Did they hurt you?"

"No."

Elder Snow knelt down and took Madeleine by the arms, glancing over his shoulder as the last of the retreating men disappeared over the slope of the hill. "Sister Cardon, what have you done?"

Madeleine looked up into his face and gave him a weak smile. "God placed words in my mouth," she said meekly.

"And, it would seem, the sword of truth in your hand," Elder Stenhouse added, looking down at the young woman with admiration.

Elder Woodard helped Elder Snow lift Madeleine onto her feet. He leaned close. "We can close the meeting now, Sister Cardon, unless you desire to tell these anxious people the story of your encounter."

Madeleine looked over at the members of the gathering, noting their worried expressions. She stood straighter, holding the Bible against her chest. "I think I should like to stand as a witness, Elder Woodard, if you wouldn't mind."

Elder Woodard shared a look with his leader. "What say you, Elder Snow? Would we mind if Sister Cardon stands as a witness?"

"I think it would be fitting."

With Madeleine Cardon in front, the Mormon missionaries led their small flock back into the house to finish the meeting.

NOTE

The story of this mob attack at the re-union was recorded in Madeleine Cardon's journal (*Reminiscences*). Many of the words are exactly as she wrote them.

CHAPTER TWENTY-TWO

Torre Pellice

November 24, 1850

Madame Guy stood at the doorway of the inn, calling after her child. "Run! Run quickly, Albertina! They won't be far up the road. Run and catch them!"

Albertina waved the letter in the air and called back. "I will!"

Joseph pushed past his mother into the cold autumn morning. He wore his coat and a pair of mittens. "I want to go with her, Mother."

Francesca laid her hand over her heart. "Oh! Well, I don't think you can catch her, little rabbit."

"I can catch her! I can! Let me go."

"All right then, run fast!"

Joseph ran. "Sister! Sister, wait! Don't leave me behind."

Albertina heard his small voice and slowed so he could catch up. "What are you doing here?"

Joseph panted. "I wanted to go too. Mother said I could carry the letter."

"Oh, she did?" Albertina smiled, knowing her little brother's propensity for big stories. "And I suppose she said that we should go to the bakery after we deliver the letter and get a scone."

Joseph's eyes widened. "No, she didn't say that, but . . . could we?"

"Yes, if you can keep up."

"I will!" he said, breathing hard. "I want a scone."

The two moved around the side of the barn and immediately saw the three missionaries hiking along the track.

"Wait!" Joseph yelled. "Wait! Monsieur Snow! A letter!" His small voice went unheard, so he began running.

Albertina followed. She soon outpaced him, quickly narrowing the gap between herself and the missionaries. "Monsieur Snow!" Lorenzo stopped and turned. When he saw who had called his name, he smiled and waved. Albertina came panting to his side. "My brother . . . my brother has a letter for you, Monsieur."

Lorenzo brightened. "A letter?" He looked down the path, watching with delight as Joseph's wobbly run brought him closer and closer. "He is serious about his duty, isn't he?"

"He is, Monsieur."

At the final distance, Joseph waved the letter in the air. He arrived at Lorenzo's side red-faced and gulping for air. He held out the letter. "A . . . a . . . a—"

"A letter for me?" Lorenzo asked.

Joseph nodded. "Mama says it's from . . . America."

Lorenzo took the envelope. "And so it is! From my sister Eliza." He reached into his pocket and gave Joseph a coin.

"What is this?"

Lorenzo chuckled at the look of wonder on Joseph's face. "It's a coin."

"Why?"

"Because you brought me this special letter. I have not heard from home for many, many months."

Happiness showed on Joseph's face. "Now I can buy my own scone!"

"Say thank you," Albertina prompted.

"Thank you, Monsieur."

"You are welcome. Enjoy your scone."

"I will, Monsieur!"

Albertina put her hand on her brother's shoulder and the two turned back toward town as the missionaries continued their journey on the path up the mountain. Lorenzo was so intent on studying his sister's handwriting on the envelope that he stumbled several times.

On the third time, Elder Woodard laughed. "Elder Snow, I think we can afford to stop for a few minutes and let you read your letter."

Lorenzo looked over. "You wouldn't mind?"

"Of course not."

"The mountain isn't going anywhere," Elder Stenhouse added.

"There," Elder Woodard said, pointing. "You can sit on that stone wall over there, while Elder Stenhouse and I leave you in peace. We will search for mushrooms for Madame Guy's larder."

"She will be thrilled," Lorenzo said.

The men moved off in different directions—Lorenzo to his solitude, his companions to the woods. Lorenzo took off his knapsack, sat down on the stacked-stone wall, and drew in a deep breath of the autumn air. His spirit was full of serenity and gratitude for the work of the Lord accomplished in the weeks prior: they had talked openly to many concerning the tenets of the Church, passed out the *Voice of Joseph* pamphlet to several interested Waldenese, and preached the restoration to a large group of ministers and members of the mountain faith. After the re-union, one man, feeling the power of their words, had come forward for baptism.

The screech of an eagle caught Lorenzo's attention and he looked up to follow its path through the sky. It was true that they had met with some resistance and harsh questioning, but when had that ever been different in the preaching of the gospel of Christ? Lorenzo said a prayer of thanks for those truth-seeking Waldenese who showed genuine interest in the message.

Joyful at the prospect of news from home, Lorenzo undid the flap on the envelope and withdrew the letter. He noted the date, September 28, and marveled that the missive had made the trip in only eight weeks. He ran his finger over his sister's penmanship and began silently reading.

> *My dearest brother Lorenzo, September 28, 1850*
>
> *In many of life's encounters I have put my pen to paper to relate the details of a scene or tell of its effect, but now my heart and hand tremble with such trepidation that I fear to drop the ink onto the page. Because of my great love for you and confidence in your unwavering faith in the Lord Jesus Christ, and the power of temple covenants, I will relate the news that hesitates in my fingertips.*
>
> *Three days ago your dear companion Charlotte departed this fragile world.*

Lorenzo's heart stopped beating. He stared at the words as if they had no meaning. Silently, he read them again. *Three days ago your dear companion Charlotte departed this fragile world.*

Lorenzo slumped to the ground, a howl of misery pouring from him. "Charlotte, Charlotte," he moaned. He squeezed his eyes shut against the pain as his grieving mind conjured pictures of worn boots, a dusty skirt, a faded bonnet, and a smiling face. He smelled lavender cologne and his heart again split open. *Why? Why? Why?* The word pulled at his brain, muddling his reason. It couldn't be true. Charlotte was in the little log house in Salt Lake. She was taking care of their daughter and hanging the laundry. She was reading her scriptures and brushing her hair. *You wouldn't do this to me, Lord. You wouldn't take my Charlotte.* Lorenzo crumpled into himself. He couldn't breathe. Why couldn't he breathe? He felt hands on his back and heard the distant calling of his name.

"Lorenzo! Lorenzo! What has happened?" Elder Woodard pleaded, dropping all sense of protocol at the sight of his suffering friend. "Lorenzo," he said softly. "What can we do?"

Lorenzo took a shuddering breath and sat back against the wall. The uneven stones dug into his back and he welcomed the physical discomfort. He was only thirty-six, but he felt old. There was a weight pressing his body into the boggy ground. His mind began to slide sideways into madness so he forced his eyes open. Through the slit he saw frost-covered grass, his companions kneeling by his side, and the letter crumpled in his fist. He held it out to them. Elder Woodard slowly took it.

"Are there words here that have caused you pain?"

Lorenzo nodded.

"What can we do?"

Tears coursed down Lorenzo's face. "I . . . I can't finish it, but . . . I must know the rest. I must. Will you please . . . read it to me?"

Elder Woodard started. "Oh, my friend! Are you sure? I do not wish to cause you more grief."

"I need to know all of what my sister has written. I know she will give me words of solace. She must." He sat a bit straighter and wiped his face with his coat sleeve. "Please. Begin with 'three days ago.'" Tears came again, and his two friends sat down beside him.

Elder Woodard silently read over the first part of the letter until he came to the significant words. He began reading. *"Three days ago your dear companion Charlotte departed this fragile world."*

"No!" Elder Stenhouse exclaimed, darting to his feet. "No! How is that possible?" He began pacing and muttering. "It's not possible. It's not possible. We're on the Lord's errand. Will He not protect those we've left behind, since we are on His errand?" He pressed his fists to his temples. "Oh, Brother Snow, how can you endure it?"

"Elder Stenhouse, mind what you say!" Elder Woodard chided.

Elder Stenhouse continued pacing. "I'm sorry. I'm sorry. But I do not think I could endure it if anything should happen to my wife." His voice was ragged with emotion.

"Then you must leave us if you cannot be a support."

The young missionary stopped abruptly. "I . . . yes, of course, you're right." He folded his arms tightly across his chest. "You're right. I'm sorry. Please, go on. I will just stand here."

Elder Woodard gave him a withering look, and then found his place in the letter. "Her passing was unexpected and startling in its quickness. Dr. Prescott is still unsure of the cruel illness that stole her from our midst. She went within a day, without pain or suffering, and with your name tenderly upon her lips." It was nearly a minute before Elder Woodard could contain his emotion enough to continue. "Oh, my dear brother, I wish I could gather my sisterly love and fly to you as quickly as the lightning divides the sky. I would sit quietly by your side, listening to you weep her name. I would cry with you and testify that a great soul was welcomed into heaven."

Silence descended again, and Elder Stenhouse turned to look out over the spreading valley, its harvested fields obscured by cold, swirling mist. A pale sun climbed partway up the eastern sky and a flock of sparrows flitted overhead.

"She didn't suffer," Lorenzo whispered.

"No."

"Continue reading, Brother Woodard."

"Are you sure?"

"I must hear to the end."

Elder Woodard found his place and began. "Just after you left on your mission, Sarah Ann moved her small cot into Charlotte's room for comfort and companionship, and was completely content in the arrangement. But after Charlotte's death she felt such a sad loneliness that, even with all the control of feeling she could exercise, a shuddering sensation came over her at the thought of sleeping in that desolate room. It required all the bravery she could command to enter it in the daytime, and so, for several nights she had made her bed in an adjoining room. Then, last night, a circumstance occurred that she related to me. I will share it with you, dear brother, knowing it will bring peace to your sorrowing soul."

Lorenzo sat forward.

"Sarah Ann told me that last night, a vision commenced, and she could not tell whether she was awake or asleep at the time, but it seemed as though it was midday. The family were all seated in their dining room, when a very bright light, above the brightness of the sun, burst into the room, and in the midst of that light Charlotte entered, sat down, and took her little daughter Roxy Armatha on her lap—at that time, the extra light in which she came disappeared. Charlotte said she was happy, which her calm, settled expression verified. She said, 'I dwell in a beautiful place.'"

Elder Woodard paused in his reading and looked over at Lorenzo, an expression of wonder in his eyes. "Well, this is a miracle I've not yet experienced in the Church."

Some of the strain left Lorenzo's face, though tears still flowed freely. "Words of solace. A verification of eternity."

Elder Stenhouse took a step towards his companions. "Aye, 'tis indeed. Read on then, Elder Woodard."

"The brilliant light returned after a short time, and Charlotte went as she came, in the midst of the light. At this time Sarah Ann was fully awake, and although no moon was shining at the time, her room was sufficiently lighted that (as she describes it) 'one could see to pick up a pin.' The singular manifestation so completely revolutionized her feelings that today, with the greatest pleasure, she is replacing her bed in the deserted room, from whence all gloom and loneliness has departed.

"This encounter bears witness to me, dearest brother, that the Lord is aware of us. How tenderly He holds us in His hand. My heart knows the anguish you are feeling and we all deliver mighty prayers for you in far-off Italy to find strength for the weight of this affliction.

"Please write when you can. I know you are thoroughly engaged in the work, yet it would settle my heart to know how you are and that this news has not overwhelmed your commitment. Know that your little Roxy Armatha is being well tended by the family. She is a darling girl and carries her mother in her features.

"May the Lord bless you, dear brother.

"Your loving sister, Eliza"

Far off, the bells of the Catholic monastery were calling the priests to prayers, their soft pealing tone an elegant supplication in itself. Elder Stenhouse turned back to look over the peaceful valley, rubbing the tears off his cheeks with the palms of his hands. The three missionaries did not speak, but listened to the bells, the call of an eagle, and the bleating of sheep from a nearby farm, each man enveloped in an unanticipated spirit of calm and constancy.

Finally, Lorenzo pushed himself away from the wall and struggled to his feet. Elder Woodard stood with him, carefully folding the letter and handing it to his companion. Lorenzo took it and placed it back into its envelope. He put the missive in the inside pocket of his suit coat and picked up his knapsack.

"Where are we going, then?" Elder Stenhouse questioned.

"Up the mountain," Lorenzo said simply. "There is work that must be done and therefore prayers needed for its accomplishment." He set off for the forested trail, leaving his companions to stare in amazement. It was not the answer or action the two men had anticipated. They quickly gathered their wits and their knapsacks and followed their leader.

NOTES

Sarah Ann's vision of Charlotte returning to speak to the family was related by Eliza Snow in her book *Biography and Family Record of Lorenzo Snow.*

In a letter to Elder Orson Hyde, Lorenzo related the Church work accomplished on Mount Brigham, November 24, 1850: "Amid the sublime display of the Creator's works, we sang the praises of His eternal name, and implored those gifts which our circumstances required. I then ordained Elder Woodard a High Priest, and asked our Heavenly Father to give him wisdom and strength to watch over the church in Italy . . . I also ordained Elder Stenhouse a High Priest, and prayed that his way might be opened in Switzerland for carrying forth the work of the Lord in that interesting country."

CHAPTER TWENTY-THREE

Torre Pellice

December 1, 1850

Several inches of snow fell during the night, but the morning came with intense blue skies and the promise of bearable temperatures. As Lorenzo walked the path into town with his companions, his thoughts were not on the snow or the shops of Torre Pellice, but on a small log cabin in Salt Lake City—a room, a quilt, a straw hat with blue cornflowers circling the brim. He saw slender fingers managing yarn and knitting needles. Swirled with the scene he heard a sweet laugh and the voices of children, then, unbidden, Charlotte's face. Lorenzo's heart chilled and he pulled his mind to the snow-dusted path at his feet. He heard someone call his name and a dog barking.

"It's the colonel!" Elder Stenhouse said, waving his hat.

"And his crazy dog," Elder Woodard added.

"Oh, now, don't let him hear ye calling his dog names," Elder Stenhouse warned. "He might just throw you into the stocks."

The colonel approached with Nellie leading the way. Lorenzo admired the way the man navigated the snowy path without hindrance, his wooden leg finding purchase on the rutted ground.

"Good morning, gentlemen!" the colonel called to them. "I was just on my way to the inn to search you out."

"Well met, then," Elder Woodard replied, bending down to pat Nellie.

Colonel Beckwith turned to Lorenzo, laying a hand on his shoulder. "Brother Snow, I was coming to you with deepest sorrow for the loss of your wife Charlotte."

Lorenzo set his jaw against emotion. Since the Guy family had been told of Charlotte's death, Lorenzo knew it was only a matter of time before the news spread. This, though, was the first time he had to acknowledge the loss to someone. He took a breath. "Thank you, Colonel."

Fortunately, Colonel Beckwith was an astute judge of the pathos surrounding the loss, so he moved the conversation on to other subjects. "I have heard that two of you are set to travel soon."

"Yes," Lorenzo said. "I have assigned Elder Stenhouse to undertake the mission in Switzerland. He will leave this month. And I will be going to London in January to oversee the translation of the Book of Mormon into Italian."

"The work calls, it seems," the colonel said.

"It does."

"But I keep you from your errand. Would it impose if I walked with you to town?"

"Not at all," Lorenzo said starting off. "We would be glad for your company."

The colonel walked with him, calling out to Nellie. "High to, you mutt! Leave the rabbits for another day!"

Elders Stenhouse and Woodard laughed to see the short-legged terrier racing across the snowy ground.

"He knows his master, that's for sure," Elder Stenhouse said, admiring the dog's obedience.

"He knows who feeds him, more like," Colonel Beckwith said with an unconvincing reprimand in his tone. He playfully nudged Nellie with his walking stick and the dog fell into cadence at his side.

"Military training," Elder Woodard said to Elder Stenhouse, who grinned and nodded. They both turned their attention to the colonel as he addressed them.

"I thought I might share a bit of advice concerning your ventures, if I may?"

"With all your knowledge of these mountains? We would be grateful," Lorenzo said.

"So what I've heard is true? You plan to go up over the Alps?"

"That was our thinking."

"And there is no way you can postpone till next summer?"

"I'm afraid not," Lorenzo replied. "As you said, the work calls."

"Well, the snow is already falling thick in the mountains. Next month there could be five to six feet in the high passes—and fifteen to twenty by January."

Lorenzo frowned over. "Will the passes close?"

"Most will, except for the main track over Mount Cenis."

"Yes, that's the route we were planning to take—from Torino up over Mount Cenis."

Colonel Beckwith shook his head. "It is an arduous crossing. At times the teamsters will hitch up twenty horses to the sledge to make the climb. They usually get you over, but be prepared to use snowshoes. You might want to practice ahead of time."

"Good advice," Lorenzo acknowledged. He tried to sound confident, but his youthful bravado was waning. Perhaps a winter crossing was too dangerous. It was the shortest route to Geneva, Switzerland, but perhaps they should wait until summer. As soon as the thought flickered through his mind, the Spirit set his resolve to hold to their plans. His mind left the deep snow of the mountains and returned to the colonel's narrative.

"The guides are expert at watching and listening for avalanches, but you will want to send out mighty prayers for safety."

"Indeed," Elder Stenhouse murmured.

"And how are you fit for rugged clothing?" Colonel Beckwith continued.

"We're on our way to the tailor's to have flannel lining secured in our wool coats," Lorenzo said.

"That will work well," the colonel concurred. "And trousers?"

Lorenzo hesitated. "Well, we . . ."

"I have a couple pair of wool trousers that would probably work for the two of you. The tailor will have to size them."

"That is very generous of you, Colonel."

"Not at all. We can't have you freezing on the heights."

They came to the edge of the town and Colonel Beckwith hesitated. "You on to the tailor's, and I shall go home to secure the trousers. I take it you're going to Monsieur Gaydou's?"

"Yes, Antoine Gaydou."

"Good, good. He is the best. Tell him to take measurements for trousers and I will bring them shortly." Without waiting for a reply, the colonel turned in the direction of his home. "High to, dog!"

The missionaries watched them go and then headed for the tailor shop. The bell over the door jangled when the three entered, and Antoine Gaydou looked away from the man to whom he was speaking to welcome possible customers. When he recognized the men entering, his face lit up with delight.

"Elders! What a surprise!" He moved from behind the counter to shake their hands. "I do not know if you remember me, Elder Woodard, but . . ."

"Of course I remember you. You and your wife were at the meeting in Rorà."

"Yes, yes. That's right. That was us." At that moment, Mary emerged from the back room. "Ah, here is my wife now. Look, Mary, it's the Mormon missionaries."

Mary approached timidly. "Good morning, gentlemen. It is very nice to see you."

"Yes, yes it is," Antoine agreed. "And you have come at a good time. My wife's brother and father are here, and I am sure they would like to meet you."

Lorenzo took note of the man to whom Antoine had been speaking and the young man who stood behind Mary. The shop was small, so Mary moved to the side and brought her brother forward.

"Elder Woodard, this is my brother Stephen and my father, John Malan."

Elder Woodard held out his hand to each in turn. "A great pleasure to meet you," he said. "And may I introduce Elder Thomas Stenhouse and Apostle Lorenzo Snow?"

"Snow?" John Malan said, stepping forward. "You are the one who wrote *The Voice of Joseph*?"

"I am."

"Ah yes," Antoine interjected. "My father-in-law has read that tract many times. He found it in the shop the day after Mary and I returned from Rorà and he absconded with it. So we have yet to read it."

Elder Woodard pulled a pamphlet from his pocket. "Here is your own copy, Monsieur Gaydou."

Antoine held the pamphlet high in the air. "See here, Father Malan? My own copy! You may keep the other one for as long as you like."

"Or until it falls apart," Stephen added.

Antoine laughed. "Yes, yes, or until it falls apart!"

"You find the words of the tract interesting, Monsieur Malan?" Lorenzo asked.

"More than interesting, Monsieur Snow. I am drawn to the message and I have many questions."

"We are fond of questions," Lorenzo answered.

"Excuse me, Elder Snow," Stephen interrupted. "Did Elder Woodard introduce you as an apostle?"

"He did."

"An apostle of Christ?"

"Yes."

"As the apostles of old?"

"Yes." He smiled at the gawking boy. "We believe that the Church of Christ has been restored, Stephen, with all the keys and priesthood power as found in the primitive church."

"But an apostle. That is a wonder."

"We have a tender feeling for the apostles, Monsieur Woodard," Mary said. "You see, when our mother was fifteen years old she had a vision of twelve apostles."

"I beg your pardon?" Elder Woodard questioned.

"Yes, she saw them and sang with them," Mary affirmed. "It is a marvelous story, but I think it best that she tell you."

John Malan spoke up. "Yes. We would love you to come to our home for a re-union. Would that be possible? It is less than a two-hour walk from here."

"We would be honored, Monsieur Malan. Elder Stenhouse is on his way to Switzerland in a few days and we are preparing, but Elder Woodard and I would love to share the gospel with you and your family."

"And perhaps a few of our neighbors?"

"Of course," Lorenzo said. He felt the Spirit of the Lord fill the room, and, as he looked into John Malan's eyes, he knew that he and his family would be essential to the gospel work in the Piedmont. He reached to shake John's hand. "May we plan for a week from today?"

"Yes, that will be good."

Mary moved to stand beside her father. "Perhaps this is what you've been waiting for, Father," she said softly. She turned to the missionaries. "Several months ago my father was called by the synod to be an elder in the Waldensian church, but he refused the honor."

"Mary," John gently reprimanded.

Lorenzo noted that Mary's fragile confidence wavered, but he could also see that there was more she intended to say. She took her father's hand and stood straighter. "I just find it interesting that as much as you love the Waldensian faith, you have always felt that something was missing."

He patted her hand. "Well, that is true." He looked at the

missionaries. "It will be interesting to see if your doctrine can clarify my questions."

Lorenzo smiled. "We will do our best."

"Good," John said. "Now, you have business, it seems, with my son-in-law—and Stephen and I have work. Come along, son." He turned towards the door and Stephen followed. The young man stopped to shake hands with Lorenzo. "It was good to meet you, Apostle Snow." His voice faltered, so he looked over quickly to Elders Stenhouse and Woodard. "Good to meet all of you."

"Thank you," Lorenzo returned. "We will be honored to preach to your family."

Stephen grinned. "I'm afraid there might be a crowd."

"That would be gratifying. I believe it is why the Lord sent us here, Stephen."

"Yes, Monsieur. I think so too."

"Give the man his hand back, son," John Malan instructed.

Embarrassed, Stephen let go of Lorenzo's hand and joined his father at the door. John gave him a gentle look of chastisement, and then addressed the elders. "Have a safe journey to Switzerland, Elder Stenhouse. We will see the two of you in a week."

"Without fail," Lorenzo said.

"Mary and Antoine will bring you," John said. With that, he and Stephen moved out into the bright day.

Before the jangle of the doorbell faded, Antoine turned a proprietor's eye to the missionaries. "Now, elders, how may I help you?"

NOTE

Elder Woodard's meeting with Stephen and John Malan in the tailor shop of John's son-in-law was an actual occurrence. Elder Snow is not mentioned as having been in attendance (he may have already left for London) but I felt it important for the story to have him involved in this first meeting and in teaching at the re-union.

CHAPTER TWENTY-FOUR

Torre Pellice

December 10, 1850

*The fighting men emerged from the fog, heads bleeding, arms slashed, their long-barreled muskets slung across their backs and their sharp farm machetes—*beidanas*—dragging along the ground. Journey's end.*

Father Andrew walked among the exhausted troops, searching for their captain, Pastor Henri Arnaud. As he walked past a jumbled group of men laid out like corpses on the ground, a young one reached out a bloody hand and caught the hem of his tunic.

"Have pity, priest. Do not take my life before I have seen the river by my house, the beautiful falls tumbling over the rocky cliff."

Father Andrew tried to pull away. "Take your life? No, no. I welcome you back to the Piedmont—back to your valleys."

Another soldier cursed and spat upon the ground as he glared at the priest. "Yea, though I walk through the valley of the shadow of death, I will fear no evil."

Father Andrew broke free and moved up the hill beyond the accusing stare of the skeletal man. His lungs burned with the effort of climbing. Where was his strength? He'd hiked these mountains a hundred times. He forced his feet to move. Suddenly, on the path ahead, he saw Albertina, her face smudged with dirt and tears. Impossible. Why was she here? She was in danger. She must stay safe at home. He called to her. She glanced back furtively and then hastened her pace away from him. "Wait! Come back! Where are you going? Come back!" But she did not come back, and as soon as she disappeared into the fog, a boy with blood on his face hissed at him from the shadows of the forest and pelted him with stones.

"Go away, priest!"

"Stop! Stop!" Father Andrew called out, a note of desperation in his voice. "I am looking for Henri Arnaud!"

Several men brandished their menacing farm implements and moved to surround him. Andrew felt panic drop into his chest. He turned to escape down the narrow trail, but the uneven ground was treacherous and a precipice fell away on either side. He heard footfalls close behind him and guttural yells from men intent on butchery.

"Wait! Wait! I will go back! I will go back!" Andrew screamed. His old legs tried to run, but he could not run. Where was his Albertina? Had she escaped into the fog? He heard the whoosh *of a beidana near his ear. "Wait! Wait! I am just an old man. I mean no harm! Let me go back!"*

The fog encased him.

"I will go back!"

"Father Andrew?"

"Let me go back!" He opened his eyes onto weak morning sunlight slanting its way through his small window. Andrew squinted. "Where am I? Who is that?"

"It's Father Nathanael. Are you all right?"

Father Andrew became aware of his rapidly beating heart and sweat-covered body. "No. No, I am not all right." He rubbed his face and struggled to sit up. Father Nathanael helped him. "These cruel dreams," he grumbled. "Will they not leave me alone?"

Father Nathanael went to the cupboard. "What was this one?"

Father Andrew put his legs over the side of the bed. "All I was trying to do was find Henri Arnaud and welcome him back to the valleys."

Father Nathanael brought out Father Andrew's clothes. "The Glorious Return? Well, that dream took you back in time. You must have heard stories yesterday when you were visiting with your Waldensian friends."

"Tchet! Those Waldensian men in my dream—you would have thought I was one of the king's soldiers come to kill them or chase them back to Geneva." He squeezed his eyes shut, thinking there was something about Albertina in the dream, but the images were fading, and he could not be sure. He shivered as the bitter cold from the stone floor crept into his feet and made his ancient bones ache. "I need my slippers."

Father Nathanael fetched them and knelt to put them on Father Andrew's feet. "Can you stand?"

Andrew grunted. "Of course I can stand." But the saying and the doing were two different things. His legs shook and he clutched Father Nathanael's arm. "My legs are traitors."

"Take your time."

"I am afraid I don't have much of that left." He wobbled and Father Nathanael steadied him.

"Shall we forgo the trip to Pinerolo?"

"What?"

"The monastery is letting us borrow the sleigh."

"To go to Pinerolo?"

"Today is the music contest in Pinerolo," Father Nathanael reminded Father Andrew, placing a shawl over his shoulders.

Andrew brightened. "Yes, yes. I know this. I know this." He stood straighter. "I have been looking forward to it."

"You have. So I was thinking that perhaps you forgo prayers this morning, and go for a nice warm bath."

Forgo prayers? The morning prayers were his favorite meditation. But soaking his old bones in a warm tub sounded like a heavenly proposition, and might just exorcise the bothersome dream. "Bath," he said decisively. "But on judgment day you will need to step forward and say it was your idea."

Father Nathanael chuckled. "I do not suppose the Lord will think too badly of me."

The two started forward, Andrew with more momentum than his legs had strength.

"Slowly," Father Nathanael encouraged. "You do not want to arrive at the concert with a bump on your head."

She had won! Albertina and her friend Madeleine—the two songbirds—had won the music competition. Andrew stood clapping with the rest of the audience, as proud of his great-niece as any father would be of a daughter. What a glorious afternoon. His mind went back to the delightful sleigh ride from Torre Pellice—his body covered in warm furs, his heart light with anticipation, Father Nathanael escorting him into the city music hall and to his seat with Rene, Francesca, and Joseph. He had listened to the other musicians and singers with half a heart until the announcement of his Albertina and her friend. He felt as though heaven was present as they sang Handel's duet "Sing unto God." In simple country dress, without accompaniment or false pride, their pure voices filled the music hall with precious hope. Andrew's heart was taken back to his boyhood in Lyon—running in the fields, the stone farmhouse, his mother's face. He wondered if others in the concert hall were experiencing the same transport of emotion. It seemed so, for as the song ended, there was a shared sigh, a breathless pause, and then enthusiastic applause. And now, as the songbirds were presented as the winners, the clapping and cheers broke out in earnest.

The family had seats close to the stage, so Andrew could see the girls well. They each carried a mingled look of surprise and elation as they moved forward from the group to accept their flowers, a laurel wreath, and a small wooden box containing their winnings. As Albertina took the box, her hand trembled, and Andrew noted a look of sadness behind the smile, and when Madeleine reached over and hugged her, she burst into tears.

"Poor little sparrow," Andrew said to Rene. "She is just over-wrought with all the noise and attention."

"Perhaps so," Rene answered.

Andrew thought his nephew's voice sounded convinced, but noted that his face was one of fatherly concern. "She will be better when she returns to the quiet mountains."

The concert over, the audience members slowly dispersed, and the participants came down the marble steps to mingle with family and friends.

Joseph ran to his sister and flung his arms around her. "You sang beautiful!"

Albertina knelt down, hugged him to her, and cried on his shoulder. After a moment, Joseph pushed away from her. "Don't be sad, Albi. Look! They gave you flowers!"

"And well deserved," Father Andrew said, laying his hand on her shoulder. "It was perfection."

She took a deep breath and stood. "Only God is capable of perfection, Uncle. You know that. But thank you. We tried our best."

He smiled at her. "I would say you did more than try."

"You winned!" Joseph piped in, running around her. "You winned! You winned!"

Albertina laughed weakly at his antics as she went to hug her mother and father. But then the tears began again.

Rene held her at arm's length. "What is it, daughter?"

She shook her head several times, brushing distractedly at the tears on her cheeks.

"Albertina, what is all this about?" he insisted.

"I . . . It's just the excitement," she whispered. "Too much excitement."

"I told you," Andrew said, patting her back. "She is a quiet girl from the mountains."

"But Madeleine Cardon is also a quiet girl from the mountains, and she is not weeping," Rene said, motioning with his head to where Madeleine stood with her family.

Andrew looked over and caught Madeleine's eye. She smiled broadly and waved at him. "Well, maybe she is a mountain rock and Albertina is a mountain flower."

Albertina laughed outright at that. She shook her head and wiped her face with a handkerchief her mother had given her. "Oh, Uncle! Thank you." She took his hand. "You are right. I am being too fragile, and not giving much thanks to God for this good day."

"God is over all," Andrew said.

Joseph stopped running and looked up to see if God was hovering above his head. The family laughed and Andrew saw the last of the sadness leave Albertina's face.

As he dozed in the sleigh ride back to the monastery, Andrew saw again Albertina's trembling hand as she reached for the box, the hidden sadness in her eyes, the tears. "She was just overwrought with all the noise and attention," he mumbled. He tried to convince himself that that was the only truth, but his heart knew something different—his heart knew that his great-niece was hiding a painful secret.

NOTE

In 1686, the Duke of Savoy, Victor Amadeus II, issued an edict that decreed the destruction of all the Waldensian churches, and maintained that all the inhabitants of the valleys must denounce their heretical faith. The far-outnumbered Waldensian soldiers put up a brave resistance, but were soon overwhelmed by the duke's superior forces. To avoid extinction, the remaining Waldenese chose exile from their beloved homeland, with most settling in Geneva, Switzerland. In 1689, pastor and soldier Henri Arnaud led more than 1,000 exiles back over the Alpine mountains. After many battles and miraculous interventions on behalf of the Waldenese, they were allowed to return home. This event became known as the "Glorious Return."

CHAPTER TWENTY-FIVE

Prassuit

December 15, 1850

Stephen Malan had not exaggerated when he said that a fair number of neighbors might fill the Malan home to hear the preaching of the Mormon missionaries. The Malan family alone had nine members, and with fifteen others, the house was crowded. Everyone was affable, and Lorenzo was grateful for each soul willing to hear the message of the gospel and weigh its soundness. He knew if the people would open their hearts even a pinprick, the light of truth could penetrate.

As people found places to sit or stand, John Malan welcomed his neighbors and gave a short testimonial of the unique message contained in *The Voice of Joseph*. He told of their meeting with the elders in his son-in-law's tailor shop, and having invited them to preach. He then introduced the elders and gave them permission and protection to preach their doctrine in his home. Lorenzo stood, positioning himself so he could see most everyone in attendance. He would speak to them in Italian and hope they would understand his words concerning the first principles of the gospel. He knew his command of the language was ragged, but he prayed for guidance. He opened his mouth to speak, but the Spirit restrained him. He stood silent, noting the looks of puzzlement on the attendant faces. He took a breath and prayed for the right words and that his heart would be open when those words came. He tried again.

"In my youth, I heard stories of Italy: the Renaissance, the art and the poetry, the charming landscapes. I was captivated by the passion of Christopher Columbus to find a new world, and by the bravery of Galileo to find new truths. It is hard to tell of all the greatness that breathes in the stories of Italy's past." He felt a stillness of spirit as he continued. "And now I am here, and I stand in awe of the grandeur of the towering Alpine peaks, the noble forests, and the verdant valleys laden with golden grain, orange trees, olives, and grapes. It is an enchanting realm."

Smiles softened the rough weathered faces as Lorenzo continued.

"But under the flowered meadow and dust of the fields are laid low the poets who sang the praise of nations, the princes who wielded the scepter of power, and the warriors who reigned in tyranny." The vivid words flowed from his mouth as though he were a native speaker, and Lorenzo knew they held meaning for the people. "Mighty works and deeds have disappeared into antiquity. I look around and wonder if there is something here except the tomb of the past? Has an eternal winter flooded the summer of your fame, frosted the flowers of your genius, or clouded the sunbeams of your glory?" His voice became thick with emotion. "Oh, Italy! I tell you that the future of your story will outshine your past and your children will yet be more renowned than the ages of old. The sure working of the gospel will weave for you a fairer wreath—a brighter crown." Lorenzo felt the Spirit carrying the message to its listeners and their hearts accepting. He saw John Malan look with wonder at his wife, Pauline.

"I see around me many an eye that, with delight, will see eternal truth, and many a face that will adorn the assemblies of the living God." He looked at the Malan children. "There is the blood of heaven's nobility in the hearts of many of your sons and daughters. I tell you these things as an apostle of the Lord Jesus Christ." Lorenzo stopped talking, for that was all the Spirit prompted. There was hardly a motion or sound as people sat mesmerized by the message and the messenger. Finally, Pauline Malan spoke.

"Thank you for those well-spoken words, Elder Snow. They have touched our hearts." She looked over at her children. "May I share with you a story about my father, John Combe?"

"Of course."

"He died only three years ago, and on his deathbed, he spoke words of prophecy. He said that the old may not, but the young and rising generation would see the day when the gospel would be restored in its purity and powers." She leaned forward and fixed Lorenzo with a steady gaze. "At the end of that, he said, 'In that day, remember me.' In that day, remember me," she restated. "Can you attach a meaning to those words, Elder Snow?"

Lorenzo felt a jolt as the Spirit moved from the top of his head to his feet. It was a moment before he could gather himself to speak. "Yes. I can tell you exactly what those words mean. We will find them together in the book of Malachi." He wanted to go on and tell her about the temple in Nauvoo, of the eternal sealing ordinances of the holy priesthood, but he knew that milk came before meat, and that the principle of eternal sealing would have to wait for another day. "Soon you will know the joy of that doctrine, but first I would like Elder Woodard to tell you of the vision of the Prophet Joseph Smith and the restoration of the Lord's primitive church. He, like myself, has been commissioned to preach the gospel in the same manner as Christ's apostles. I pray that you will open your hearts to the message." Lorenzo stepped to the side and Elder Woodard stood to address the roomful of attentive listeners.

Later that day, John and Pauline Malan walked with Elder Snow into the afternoon gloaming. They were going down to see the Malans' oil-press operation. When Lorenzo heard of the walnuts, hazelnuts, and hemp seed pressed for cooking oil and home use, he had a feeling that this type of enterprise might be of interest to President Brigham Young. Besides, Lorenzo was anxious to get out in the open. At the conclusion of Elder Woodard's preaching and testimony, the press of the people's interest and questions had begun to overwhelm his still-sorrowing sensibilities.

Now, as he walked in the chill mountain air, some of the melancholy lifted. The sky was pale blue and a soft pink crown lay atop the snow-covered western peaks. It had snowed in the morning, and as the sun moved towards the western horizon, the fresh covering of white sparkled on the ground and the branches of the pine trees. Lorenzo missed having Elder Woodard with them, but he had gone, at the request of one of those attending the Malan re-union, to preach at another meeting. Lorenzo walked in comfortable silence with his two companions, each content with their own meditation. Eventually John Malan spoke.

"Do you know if Elder Stenhouse has reached his destination in Switzerland?"

Lorenzo shook his head. "I do not. I suppose it's too early to have heard anything."

"He seemed like a good man."

"Yes."

"And Elder Woodard is a wonder. He speaks like a son of the mountains."

"Yes. I feel very confident in his ability to watch over the mission while I am away."

"Do you know how long you'll be in London?"

"It depends on how long the translation takes, and what the Lord desires."

Pauline stopped to secure her scarf more snugly around her neck. "It is a great blessing to be taught about revelation and priesthood power—to have the holy scriptures opened to a deeper understanding. For many years I have felt that a time of refreshing was coming."

John looked over at Lorenzo. "And to think that the Lord guided you to us, this small handful of Christian believers hidden in these valleys for hundreds of years."

"Never hidden to the Lord," Lorenzo said. His thoughts went back to the great revival in America, a time when his family, along with thousands of others, were looking for the original Church of Christ. "Many people in the towns and villages of America wondered of God's observance. Had He forgotten His children? Many wondered if the pattern of the Lord's church would ever be manifested."

"That has been our concern," John said. "The Waldensian faith is woven in antiquity, and yet many of the doctrines have changed or been lost through the centuries. Where was the power to act in God's name?"

Lorenzo nodded. "That was my dilemma. Where was the pattern of the ancient church?"

Pauline started walking and the two men attended. "My vision of the twelve apostles has much more meaning now," she said.

"I think perhaps it is time for me to hear of this remarkable vision," Lorenzo said. "Will you share it with me?"

"I would be honored," Pauline said. She placed her hands into the warmth of her coat pockets. "Just like Joseph Smith, my vision came in the spring of 1820, just before my fifteenth birthday." Lorenzo looked surprised and Pauline smiled. "Do I think the Lord is aware of things from the beginning to the end, Elder Snow?" She paused. "Yes, I do. Miracles are all around. We just need to have the eyes to see them."

"True words," Lorenzo replied.

Pauline nodded and continued. "My father and I had gone down to the plains of the Piedmont to take charge of silkworms on a large silkworm farm. There was the cocoonery and a hall where each of the workers had a cot for resting and sleeping. About a week before we left to go home, I was alone in my area. Night was falling and I was reading the scriptures. I was reading about the life of Christ and His apostles, and pondering the gospel as taught by them. I was wishing

I could have lived in those days. The large hall became light as noon, and I sat up. I felt a heavenly influence in the room and I began singing a sacred hymn. Twelve personages dressed in white robes appeared and formed a half-circle around my cot. They began singing with me. At the end of the song they and the light vanished." She stopped, having come to their destination and the end of her story.

"Remarkable," Lorenzo said. "And you have never doubted the vision or its source?"

"No," Pauline returned. "Nor has one image of it faded in all these years."

"Remarkable," Lorenzo said again. "And what did your parents think?"

"They believed me. They had no reason to question the story because I'd always been a child of truth."

"Again, like Joseph Smith," Lorenzo remarked.

"When I told my mother the story, she opened our Bible and read Acts 2:17—'And it shall come to pass in the last days, saith God, I will pour out of my Spirit upon all flesh: and your sons and your daughters shall prophesy, and your young men shall see visions, and your old men shall dream dreams.'"

John moved forward to stand beside his wife. "And we are in the last days, are we not, Elder Snow?"

"The last dispensation of the fulness of time, Brother Malan."

John Malan grinned. "I like the thought of us being brothers." He sobered. "Your words ring with truth, Elder Snow, and we want you and Elder Woodard to return to our home and preach again."

"Of course," Lorenzo said. "If I'm away to London, then Elder Woodard will join with you and continue what we have started."

John Malan took a large key from his coat pocket. "The Book of Mormon in Italian. I will be interested to read it." He inserted the key into the lock and opened the old wooden door. "I'll light a lantern," John said, entering. "Please, please, Elder Snow, come in."

As Lorenzo walked into the old stone building, he breathed in the pleasant smells of nuts and rich oils. He thought of five lamps filled with oil—five lamps burning brightly in a dark night, awaiting the advent of the Bridegroom. He thought of the Cardon family, the Malan family, Jean Bose, and Albertina Guy. This was why he had come. This was why he was willing to sacrifice so much for the work of the Lord. *Oh, Charlotte. My dear, dear Charlotte.* He heard the peaceful trill of a lark, and somehow the lingering melancholy that had held his heart throughout the day released and drifted away with its song.

NOTES

It is unknown whether Lorenzo Snow was in attendance at this gathering at the Malan home, but for the sake of continuity I have him attending and speaking.

Many of the words of Elder Snow's talk are taken word for word from his writings.

Pauline Combe Malan's vision of the twelve apostles was included in her writings and confirmed in several family histories.

CHAPTER TWENTY-SIX

Torre Pellice

January 23, 1851

"Wait! Wait! I know this part. Let me tell this part!" Joseph jabbered as he jumped from the bed.

"Shush!" Albertina scolded. "You were supposed to be asleep half an hour ago, Joseph Guy. Now, get back into bed. It's freezing."

"No, I won't! I won't unless you let *me* tell the story."

"Shush! All right. All right. Anything to keep Mother from taking the stick to the both of us." Albertina had come to her brother's small upper bedroom to sing him to sleep, but instead she'd been coerced into reading from the book of the Catholic martyrs, replete with gruesome pictures.

"Promise?" came Joseph's skeptical reply. "Promise I can tell this part?"

"Yes. Now get into bed, you tyrant."

Joseph giggled and hopped back into bed. "Mother would never take the stick to us," he said matter-of-factly as he snuggled back against his pillow and pulled the covers to his chin.

"And why is that?" Albertina questioned.

"Because you're too grown up and I'm too precious."

Albertina burst out laughing, and immediately covered her mouth to stop the sound. Joseph laughed too, immensely pleased with himself for having wrecked his sister's scolding.

"What shall I do with you?" she said in a whisper.

"Let me tell the story!"

"All right. Yes. But this is the last of the stories about martyrs."

"But—"

"No, I mean it." She opened the book to the story of Saint Lawrence. "I don't know how you can sleep after this." The old wood-block picture showed the saint being burned alive on a metal grill as the wicked Prefect of Rome looked on. "Ugh," Albertina said, turning her face from the picture. "Disgusting."

"No, it's not," Joseph protested. "Saint Lawrence was so full of God's love that the fire didn't even hurt him."

"So goes the story," Albertina returned.

"Yes. And I like what he said to the mean old Roman officer," Joseph said, sitting up straighter in bed. "'Turn me over, please. I think I'm done on this side.'" He collapsed into a fit of giggles. "I think I'm done on this side!"

"Oh, mercy," Albertina said. "I'll never get you to sleep now."

Just then a loud crack sounded on the inn's front door, and the two involuntarily cried out in alarm.

"What in the world?" Albertina gasped.

The sound came again and again, and then the sound of the door being wrenched open, and the din of angry voices.

Albertina leapt out of bed. "Stay here!" she commanded. She was fully dressed, but in her stocking feet.

"Wait!" Joseph shrieked. "I want to go with you!"

"No! Stay here!" Albertina ran out of the room and down the stairs. She stopped abruptly at the open doorway that led from their living quarters into the guest sitting area. A group of four men were pushing past her father and moving towards Elder Woodard's room. Her father and mother were both protesting as the men shoved them out of the way. Suddenly, Jabez Woodard stepped into the room; he wore trousers and an untucked shirt and his feet were bare, which gave him the look of vulnerability, yet the strength of his bearing momentarily stopped the gang of men in their pursuit. The leader of the mob glared at him, moving forward to grab his arm.

"Leave him!" Rene bellowed. "He is under my protection in this house!"

"Then we will take him outside," the man said, yanking Jabez forward.

Elder Woodard pulled back, but the big man's grasp did not release. Another man stepped forward and clamped his hand on the back of the missionary's neck. The two pressed him towards the door as Elder Woodard struggled and Rene tried to intercede. Rene was shoved against the wall by one of the other brutes as Francesca's arms were pinned behind her back by the fourth.

Albertina came out of her stupor. She raced across the room, lunging at the man holding her mother. "Stop! Stop it!" she screamed. "Leave her alone! Let her go!" She was vaguely aware of the sound of Joseph weeping from the doorway.

"Get away, girl," the man growled, turning his back to her to deflect the blows from her small fists. "We don't mean you harm—just the Mormon."

"He is under our care!" Albertina yelled, frustrated tears coursing down her cheeks. She saw that the leader of the group was at the threshold of the main door. "Wait! You can't take him out. He'll catch his death!"

"That's what we're hoping," the man said over his shoulder as he and his companion dragged Jabez out into the frigid night.

The cold poured into the house, overtaking the pitiful warmth from the dying fire.

"Stop!" Albertina yelled, running to intercept them.

The man guarding her father caught her around the waist, pulling her to him and wrenching back one of her arms.

"Albi!" Joseph cried, running into the room.

"If you don't stay out of it," the man hissed at Rene. "I'll break her arm."

Joseph ran to the man and began kicking him.

"I mean it!" the man bellowed.

"Joseph! Joseph, stop," Rene said. "Come here to me. Come here, you brave boy."

Reluctantly Joseph left off the attack and went to his father, who picked him up and hugged him.

"Why are you doing this?" Albertina pled. "You are Waldensian. You know what persecution feels like. You're assaulting a man of faith."

"Albertina, be quiet," her mother said.

The man tightened his grip and Albertina cried out.

Rene stepped forward. "Please—please don't hurt her."

"Then she must learn to keep her mouth shut. Just like that Mormon blasphemer must learn." He leaned over and whispered menacingly in Albertina's ear. "He is no man of faith. He is the devil and you would do better to turn from his lies." He glared at Rene. "We have seen her going to their re-unions. Giving up her own faith for the words of a devil. We will beat the heresy out of him. We will—"

The man's words were cut short by sounds from outside of men shouting and a dog barking. The two brutes, fearing their companions in trouble, let go of the women and charged out the door.

The Guy family stood frozen in place, listening to a deep male voice issuing threats, the sound of blows, more threats, and then the sound of footfalls retreating into the distance.

Rene set Joseph down. "Stay here," he instructed, grabbing his coat and moving out into the dark night. Joseph ran to his mother as Albertina went to look out at the door.

"Shut the door!" her mother said. "We'll all catch our deaths."

"No," Albertina replied. "I see them coming. I see Colonel Beckwith!"

Within moments, Colonel Beckwith and her father entered the inn, dragging Elder Woodard along.

"Bring him over here," Rene gasped, hauling the young missionary to a chair near the fire.

The rest of the family stood staring at their guest's gruesome visage; a gash slit the top of his forehead, producing a stream of blood down one side of his face. The other cheek looked as though he'd been dragged across the icy courtyard cobblestones, showing scrape marks and the beginnings of a massive purple bruise.

Joseph hid behind his mother's skirts and Albertina started crying.

"Joseph, shut the door," Rene barked. "Francesca, bring warm water and towels. Albertina, more wood for the fire."

The commands gave purpose and the three went immediately to their tasks.

Joseph picked up Colonel Beckwith's dog and brought him inside. "It's all right, Nellie. You're safe now." He shut the door and struggled to secure the bolt. The dog ran to sit on the hearth rug, alert to his master's presence and command. "Hey! Come here, you!" Joseph said, hurrying to Colonel Beckwith's side. "Guess he just wanted to be with you, sir. Sorry."

"Better for me to keep an eye on him," the colonel said in a low tone.

Joseph nodded. His attention was diverted by the sight of Elder Woodard brushing absently at the blood on his face.

"I . . . I'm sorry, Rene," he mumbled. "Sorry for this."

Colonel Beckwith gently pushed his arm down. "Hold on, son, we'll get that cleaned."

Rene laid a hand on his shoulder. "And there is nothing for you to be sorry about. Those brutes should be arrested."

"Oh, I'll see that justice falls heavy on their heads," the colonel answered.

Albertina came in with the logs and placed several on the fire. "How did you ever make them stop, Colonel Beckwith?"

"They know my influence. They do indeed. Plus, I had this," he said, holding up his sturdy walking stick. "And . . . that." He pointed the stick at Nellie, who barked his allegiance.

Joseph laughed, then sobered as he looked at the missionary's face. "I'm sorry they hurt you," he said, stepping forward and placing his hand cautiously on Elder Woodard's arm.

"Step aside, now," Francesca ordered as she brought in the towels and pan of warm water.

Joseph went to Albertina, taking her hand, and watching wide-eyed as his mother began gently washing Elder Woodard's mangled face. Albertina saw her brother wince several times and thought perhaps the book of martyrs might not come off the shelf as often as before.

"What brought you to us this time of night, Colonel?" Rene inquired.

"Intercession, it would seem," the colonel answered. "I had a question for Elder Woodard that I was planning to discuss in the morning, but something told me I should come tonight."

"It was fortunate you did. Things might have been much worse."

"I don't understand how they could do this," Albertina said suddenly. "The Waldenese know injustice—they know cruelty. It's in their history."

Colonel Beckwith leaned over and rubbed Nellie's head. "A few are afraid of this Mormon teaching, Mademoiselle Guy. And a few actually believe it is the doctrine of the devil."

"But it's not. I have heard them preach, and we have seen a miracle at their hands."

"This I know," Colonel Beckwith said, winking at Joseph. "But some people do not like their truth threatened. Do you understand this?"

"Yes, I do."

Francesca cleared her throat. "Yes, threatened. And when people feel threatened they can do despicable things." She glanced over at

Albertina, then back to her work. "I think it is too dangerous for you to be attending any more meetings," she said in an even tone.

Albertina stared at her. "What?"

Francesca stood and applied a clean cloth to the gash in Elder Woodard's head. "No more meetings. It is too dangerous."

"But I am learning. I am—"

"We will not discuss it tonight," Rene broke in.

"But Papa, I—"

"Albertina," Elder Woodard interrupted, his voice tired and shaky. "I have to agree with your mother. These are no longer idle threats."

"But my friend Madeleine will still be attending meetings."

"Yes, she probably will. But she will have her family with her, her brothers and parents to protect her."

"And I have no one."

Francesca turned to her in shock. "Albertina!"

"Your parents love you, Albertina, and they *are* protecting you. You must obey their wishes."

"Thank you for that, Monsieur." Francesca said, turning her back on her daughter and wrapping a long strip of gauze around the missionary's head to secure the bandage.

"No more tonight," Rene insisted. "Albertina, please take Joseph up to bed and this time be sure he gets to sleep."

"Yes, sir." She took Joseph's hand, and turned to Colonel Beckwith. "Good night, Colonel. I'm very glad you were here to save our Elder Woodard."

"Always up for a bit of adventure," he returned, and Nellie gave several barks.

Joseph giggled. "He likes adventures too!"

"Ah, he does. He does, indeed," Colonel Beckwith said, ruffling Joseph's hair.

Albertina paused in front of the missionary. "Good night, Elder Woodard," she said timidly. "I will say prayers for you."

"Thank you, Albertina." Then, softer, "Do not lose heart."

Albertina gave him a small nod and tugged her brother closer to her side. "Come on, enough excitement for you tonight." She noted that he was uncharacteristically quiet as they climbed the stairs and entered the dark bedroom.

"Albi?" he said as he climbed into bed.

"Yes?"

"Why were those men so angry with Elder? He is a nice man."

Albertina sat on the edge of the bed. "He *is* a nice man."

"So?"

"So, I think what Colonel Beckwith said is true—they're afraid."

"They didn't look afraid."

"Sometimes when you're afraid you act tough to cover it up."

Joseph's eyes widened. "I do that!"

Albertina bit her bottom lip to keep from smiling. "Yes, I think we all do that. Now it's time for sleep."

"Albi?"

"Yes?"

"Will you hum me to sleep?"

"I will if you stop talking."

"I won't talk anymore."

"You just did."

"Only to tell you that I wouldn't."

Albertina put her fingers on his lips and began humming his favorite lullaby.

Joseph yawned and closed his eyes. "Albi?"

"Shhh."

"I'm sorry you can't go to the meetings anymore. I was going to go with you when I got bigger."

"Go to sleep."

Joseph yawned again and rolled onto his side.

Albertina pulled her shawl close and continued humming. Her thoughts drifted out into the dark, cold night. She thought of being absent from Madeleine's side as Elder Woodard preached. She thought of missing the feeling of peace when scriptures were read and prayers were said. The blanket slid off Joseph's shoulder and she covered him again. *I will wait a few days,* she thought. *I will wait until the scare of the attack is less, and then I will tell them that I must be allowed to attend. I am not a child anymore, and the meetings are important. Surely Elder Woodard will change his mind and help me in convincing them.*

An owl hooted outside the bedroom window and she jumped. "Silly," she whispered to the dark room. "Just an owl. Nothing to fear. Nothing."

CHAPTER TWENTY-SEVEN

Torre Pellice

January 26, 1851

Father Nathanael found the old priest standing out in the frozen garden, out among the frosted clumps of dirt and the skeletal cornstalks. His face was towards the sky and he was mumbling. The young priest moved quickly to his side.

"Father Andrew! How did you get out here?"

Andrew raised his walking stick. "Go away! Leave me alone!"

"But you can't stay out here."

"Go away!"

Father Nathanael stepped back, outside the range of the walking stick. "Father Pious saw you here, and—"

"Meddling toad," Andrew growled. "Can he not keep out of my business?"

"Your business of standing out in the cold garden?"

"Leave me be."

"Come in and we can talk about what has upset you," Father Nathanael coaxed.

Andrew turned to glower at him. "Go away!"

Father Nathanael stood still and clasped his hands together. "I am afraid I cannot do that."

Father Andrew lost his balance as he turned to swipe at the young priest with his walking stick, and Father Nathanael moved quickly to catch him before he fell.

"Can I not have a moment's solitude?" Andrew bellowed.

"It is too cold out here, honored one," Father Nathanael said as he righted his charge.

Andrew slapped his hands away. "Too cold for solitude? Solitude *is* cold. Solitude is the black tunnel—the fearful loneliness." He looked again at the sky filled with swirls of dark storm clouds.

Father Nathanael stepped away again, and stood quietly as Father Andrew mumbled his prayers to heaven. It was only when Andrew leaned forward on his walking stick, groaning from the cold, that the young priest intervened. "Shall we go in now?" he asked softly.

Andrew nodded. "There are no answers here. No answers."

Father Nathanael put his arm around Andrew's back. "Come, my friend. Perhaps you can find answers by the warmth of the fire."

Andrew began weeping as he walked. "Lord, grant me the strength to accept the things I cannot change."

"Wise words from our favorite saint."

"But Saint Francis did not have an errant great-niece," Andrew said gruffly—his petulance overruling some of the sadness.

Father Nathanael was silent. Earlier in the day he had taken Rene Guy to the library to visit with Father Andrew. He recalled now that Rene had looked tired and anxious, and when he had left the monastery it seemed as though sorrow was added to his load of cares. Had they discussed Albertina Guy? Was she the source of the sadness? Father Andrew had used the word *errant* in connection with her name, but Father Nathanael could not imagine that a possibility; the girl was dutiful and kind, and she sang with the voice of an angel.

As they came into the courtyard, a slivered shaft of sunlight broke through the clouds and illuminated the stone fountain at its center.

"A simple sunbeam is enough to drive away many shadows," Father Nathanael quoted.

"I do not think Saint Francis has the words today to calm my soul," Andrew answered.

Father Nathanael unlatched the monastery door and guided Andrew inside. It was a side door into the larder, and Andrew was nearly overwhelmed by the smells of dried herbs, apples, and root vegetables, as well as dirt and hay. It was a smell from his boyhood and he longed for the hayfield and his father's hand on the scythe.

The two priests stood still, allowing their eyes to adjust to the dimness, and then they moved to the end of the larder, climbing carefully up a set of stairs and through another door into the kitchen. Andrew blinked as they stepped into the room, assaulted by the light and the bustle. People hurried from here to there, pots bubbled on the central stove, and a brace of rabbits roasted on spits over an open flame. The warm air caressed his old body and Andrew sighed.

"It feels good," he said absently.

"Of course it does," Father Nathanael answered, moving him along. "You nearly froze yourself out in that garden. I don't know what you were thinking. We'll get you settled by the fire in the library, and I'll bring you a cup of broth."

"Why do you put up with me?" Andrew asked as they moved out into the chill of the hallway.

"My brother's keeper, I suppose," Father Nathanael said flatly, and Andrew laughed.

"You are a young man of sense, Father Nathanael. Why can't all young people have sense?"

Father Nathanael gave him a curious look. "Such as yourself? Running around during the French Revolution with the likes of Danton? Imbibing in the luxuries of princes?"

"Now, now! Don't bring up my infamous past! I will grant you, I am not a good example. Besides, that was a thousand years ago."

Father Nathanael smiled. "I suppose each of God's children must find their way through the forest."

"Tchet! Do not give me such a wise answer."

"My apologies."

They reached the library and Father Andrew began to shiver. "The cold has leached into my bones," he moaned.

"Here, sit down, and I will put more logs on the fire."

As Andrew sat and Father Nathanael went to the wood bin to get the logs, the library door opened and Father Pious came in, followed by a man Andrew could not quite make out. As they neared, his anger rose.

"I do not want to see you," he said, pointing at Father Pious. "And I definitely do not want to see you!" He glared at the second man and waved him away.

"Where are your manners, Father Andrew?" Father Pious said, looking shocked. "That is no way to speak to your visitor. I thought you were fond of the Mormon missionaries."

"Get out, you dissembler. You care nothing for this man. You just want to mock me."

Father Nathanael came forward, looking over the head of Father Pious and addressing Elder Woodard directly. "Now is not a good time. Father Andrew needs rest."

"I understand," Elder Woodard said. "I just wanted to offer some explanation concerning his great-niece."

"The audacity," Father Pious hissed. "You strangle a young girl's soul and then you come to explain it?"

"Be quiet, Pious," Father Andrew snapped. "You know nothing about it."

"Oh, don't I? Everyone knows that your great-niece has been going to their meetings. Her heresy is not a secret."

"Get out!" Andrew said through clenched teeth. He wished he were twenty years younger so he could bodily throw Father Pious from the room. "Father Nathanael, would you please follow him out?"

"Of course," Father Nathanael said, taking Father Pious gently by the arm. "Shall we go and see if the floors need sweeping?"

"What? What's this? You cannot tell me what to do. I am senior to you!" Father Pious spluttered.

"Yes, but I am stronger." He headed Pious towards the door, and Elder Woodard followed.

"Wait, Elder!" Andrew said sharply. Elder Woodard turned. "I do have some words for you, sir. Come and sit down."

Elder Woodard moved to sit in the chair opposite the priest. The side of his face was healing, but still carried the evidence of the beating he'd received. Father Andrew studied him for several moments. He had met the man when he hosted the missionaries for dinner at the monastery, but he had been reserved, choosing to spend his time observing. Albertina had spoken of the man from England in glowing terms—of his storytelling, his humor, and his brilliance. All Andrew saw was a fox. A wounded fox, but a fox all the same.

Andrew leaned forward. "I am sorry that you have been hurt."

"Thank you for that kindness."

"Do you mind my speaking to you in French?" Andrew asked.

"No, of course not. I love the French language."

"Do not try to flatter me, young man."

"I wouldn't think of it. I mean what I say."

Andrew's pique was somewhat blunted by the man's straightforward manner. "Very well, then we can speak to the point."

"I find it best," Elder Woodard replied.

"So you speak French. And how many other languages?"

"Several."

"And you think yourself brilliant?"

"I think myself fortunate. I thank the Lord daily for my abilities."

Andrew grunted. He remembered his raucous youth, when pride in his abilities and accomplishments made him boastful and uncouth. "How old are you?"

"I am nearing thirty."

"That is young. I have seen more than eighty winters and

summers." Elder Woodard nodded, but did not speak. "At this age of my life," Andrew continued, "I do not want conflict and sorrow."

"Of course not. No one wishes that."

"But that is what you have laid at my doorstep. That is what you have brought into my nephew Rene's home. Look at what happened the other night. Look what you brought to the door of the inn."

"I am aware—"

Father Andrew cut him short. "I am sorry for your injuries, but do you think I will accept you bringing peril to my family? Do you think you can preach falsehoods to an impressionable girl like our Albertina and not be held accountable?"

"Falsehoods?" Elder Woodard asked calmly. "You have listened to our words . . . to the words of Elder Snow."

"Words that an impressionable girl like our Albertina cannot untangle from her feelings."

Elder Woodard chose his words carefully. "Perhaps you are right, though I find her very bright."

"Bright is not the issue. Being able to decipher what is true from what is false—that is the issue."

Elder Woodard tamped down his irritation and spoke softly. "Father Andrew, there was a time when our words seemed of great interest to you, and now you accuse us of preaching falsehoods?"

Andrew was about to respond, but he stopped. He had read *The Voice of Joseph* pamphlet and been intrigued by much of the narrative. The story of Joseph Smith's vision moved him to tears, but he could not give away his anger and disbelief. He was fighting for the safety of his family, the soul of his great-niece, and the foundation of his faith. "Your preaching has caused strife in the community. There are rumors that Joseph Smith copied the words of your Book of Mormon from someone else, that he stole people's money, and encouraged mob violence against the authority of the states and even the United States government. What do you say to that?"

Elder Woodard's head was bowed. He took a breath and looked

up into Father Andrew's face. "I would say that martyrdom for himself and a brother he loved dearly was certainly a high price to pay for deception." He took another breath to calm his emotions. "I did not have the privilege of knowing the Prophet Joseph Smith, but I was taught the gospel by many who did know him, and to a man they testified that he was a good person. Elder Snow was a personal friend and has a depth of feeling for the man, and for the miraculous things he accomplished in his short lifetime. Do you find Elder Snow a man to be easily misled?"

Andrew dismissed the question with a grunt. "Even the best of men can be deceived, Elder Woodard." He quickly changed to a different issue that was vexing him. "It is also rumored that once a person joins your church they are expected to immigrate to the desolation of Salt Lake City, where your new prophet, Brigham Young, will rule over them as a tyrant and a would-be king."

Elder Woodard paused. "May I ask you a question?"

"Of course."

"Are you afraid?"

"What?"

"Are you afraid?"

How had the man thought to ask *that* question? How had he known that it was indeed fear that prompted his vitriol against the Mormon preaching? Fear that his own turning to the Lord had not been inspired by heaven. Fear that his years of prayers and service were without consequence. Fear that his Albertina would join with the Mormons and turn her back on her family—and him. Fear that she would leave them. He fought to keep the anguish out of his voice when he answered. "Why would you ask me that question?"

"I have only been a member of this church for a short time, and I assure you, Father Andrew, that when the doctrine was first preached to me I felt the fire of testimony and the chill of fear. Had my life in the Lord been a fraud up to that point? Had my prayers never reached God's ear? Had I been walking all that time in a dark underground tunnel, never realizing that above me was a beautiful meadow filled with flowers?"

Andrew felt the press of tears at the back of his throat and he swallowed several times to stop the emotion. "And how did you answer that fear?"

"I laid my fears out in front of the missionaries who were instructing me. They assured me that the Lord loved me and was aware of every prayer, every kindness, and every act of service. That I was God's child and He knew my heart, and that none of my righteous sacrifices had gone unnoticed. They also assured me that God holds close all those who honor Him."

"Then why the need for a different faith? Do we not have all that we need in the religions of the day?"

"Do the scriptures say, one Lord, one faith, one baptism? I grant that there is truth in all faiths, but what of the fulness of truth?"

"And the Mormons have the fulness of truth?"

Elder Woodard reached into his satchel and brought out his Bible. He turned to the Old Testament and began reading. "Behold, I will send you Elijah the prophet before the coming of the great and dreadful day of the Lord; and he shall turn the heart of the fathers to the children, and the heart of the children to their fathers, lest I come and smite the earth with a curse." He lowered the book. "This is the doctrine that took me from fear to rejoicing. The doctrine preached to me by the missionaries was one of eternal sealing. Just as the apostles of Christ's church had been promised that those things that they bound on earth would be bound in heaven, the restoration of priesthood keys and powers assured the same eternal bonds."

Andrew's heart was beating fast. "What are you saying?"

"With the return of priesthood power, the promises of Malachi would be realized. The hearts of the fathers and the children would turn to each other in a desire for eternal families. Family is the purpose of the earth and the promise of heaven—families bound together by sacred temple ordinances."

Andrew sat forward. "Families bound together in heaven? Temple ordinances? What temples? Do the Mormon people have temples?"

"There was a temple built in Nauvoo, Illinois, and the Prophet Joseph was given all the temple ordinances. Many sealings were performed before the Prophet was murdered and the Saints were driven out of the state by mobs."

Father Andrew was silent for a long time, and Elder Woodard did not intrude on his ponderings.

"And the temple?"

Elder Woodard shook his head. "It was taken over by the infidels and destroyed."

Tears leaked from the corners of Andrew's eyes. "I am sorry. I am sorry to hear that. So the power to seal families is lost?"

"No. The power remains with the Quorum of the Twelve Apostles," Elder Woodard said, leaning forward in his chair. "And one of the first things Brigham Young did when they reached the Salt Lake Valley was to walk to a certain spot, plant his cane in the ground, and declare that on that spot they would build a temple to the Most High God." Elder Woodard paused to steady his emotions. "And I believe that there will come a time when many temples will be built—many temples around the world."

Father Andrew studied Elder Woodard's face. "Families together in heaven?"

"Yes."

The library door opened and Father Nathanael came into the room. He moved to Father Andrew's side. "Are you all right?"

"Yes, yes," Andrew said, quickly wiping the wetness from the corners of his eyes. He was upset that his conversation with Elder Woodard had been interrupted, but he couldn't make that known. He was still angry and sorrowing, but a ray of sunlight was glimmering at the corner of his understanding.

Father Nathanael looked at Elder Woodard. "It is time for our prayers."

"Of course. Then I'll be going."

"Elder Woodard?" Father Andrew said softly.

"Yes?"

"Come again."

Elder Woodard smiled. "I will when I can. I am moving out of the inn. I'm going to live with the Malan family, and it's a bit farther away."

"Are you leaving because of the trouble?" Andrew questioned.

"Yes. I admire the Guy family, and I do not want there to be contention. But I'm also going because I was invited. There is much interest in the gospel message in that part of the valley, so I will go where I am needed." He walked over and took Father Andrew's hand. "Albertina will not be attending any more meetings. I stand firmly with Rene and Francesca regarding this. I hope that brings you some peace."

Father Andrew gave a slight nod, and Elder Woodard turned and walked away. Father Nathanael escorted him to the door and then returned.

"There is time before prayers for a little supper," he said. "Shall I bring you something?"

"Yes, I would like that."

"Are you sure you are all right? You look tired."

"I have much on my mind—much to ponder. Nothing to worry about."

After Father Nathanael left, Father Andrew closed his eyes and let his mind drift through his life. *Home.* Somehow home was always the resting place. His mother was making barley and vegetable soup and his father was giving corn to the geese. He and his brother, Tristan, were chasing will-o'-the-wisp fluff in the warm sunshine, and from somewhere in the side pasture the old donkey was braying. Albertina came chasing Pauline and Joseph through the meadow, the sound of their laughter filling the scene with delight. Home. Family. Father Andrew's heart settled and he slept.

NOTE

Sacred temple sealing ordinances and keys had been restored to the Prophet Joseph Smith in 1836 in the Kirtland Temple. Moses came to restore the keys of the gathering of Israel, Elias to restore the blessings that were conferred upon Abraham, and Elijah to restore the sealing power of the priesthood to bless both the living and the dead.

CHAPTER TWENTY-EIGHT

Prassuit

February 27, 1851

Elder Woodard looked up from his writing to the snow falling outside his bedroom window. He smiled. Not really a bedroom—he had a small cot and table in amongst the household stores. He didn't mind. The Malan family were cheerful and accommodating and filled with the spirit of the work. Since Elder Snow's departure for London, Elder Woodard's days had been filled with hiking, visiting, and preaching, wondrous days that fixed his testimony as he saw the light and power of the gospel change people's lives. Young Stephen Malan often accompanied him on his travels, helping with the mountain dialects and standing up to the harsh persecution of some of the Waldensian pastors. He actually thought the boy found pleasure in voicing his new-found truths and sparring with the older men.

Elder Woodard rubbed his hands together to warm them. Wood was a scarce commodity, so the house was often cold. Most of the time he wore his mittens, but that was not a possibility when writing a letter. He cupped his hands around his mouth and blew warm air into them, then picked up the letter to look over what he'd written.

Prassuit, Piedmont, Italy
February 27, 1851

Dear Elder Snow:

I write to you from the home of John and Pauline Malan. They took me in upon my departure from the inn. There were several reasons for leaving the inn, none of which shadows the Guy family in an unfavorable light. Indeed, the gracious care of Rene and Francesca made the departure difficult. There is no need for you to ponder on this decision. We will discuss the particulars when you again return to the beautiful valleys of the Piedmont. Be assured that all is well, and that the work is moving on.

I am happy to inform you that the brethren and sisters in Italy are all well, and send their salutations to you, with the request that you will also salute the churches in England for them.

On the twenty-fourth of February, two young men, John Daniel Malan Jr. and David Pons, presented themselves for baptism. It rained and snowed alternately, and the atmosphere was so dense that we could not see distinctly a little way ahead. But as we descended towards the Angrogna River, a singular scene was presented: the clouds were suddenly rent asunder, as if they had been a sheet of paper, and the side of Mount Brigham was visible, in the moment, from the top to the bottom.

I exclaimed, "The veil over Italy has burst," and yet, at the instant, I knew not what I was saying. I stood paralyzed with the magnificent views that opened on every side, then with a prayer to Israel's God, we entered the stream.

In the evening a congregation assembled, and I commenced preaching; but the devil entered into some who had been resisting the truth, and I saw that he had got a firm hold, and my words seemed to be wasted on the assembly, through the presence of such a deadening and defiling influence. I therefore stopped short, and sat down, after intimating that everybody might go where they liked. By this means I got rid of the chaff while the good grain remained. I then commenced preaching, and the power of God rested upon us. Many a tear rolled down those weather-beaten faces. The next day I baptized ten persons—the rest of the Malan family and a relative, Francis Combe. That evening, after their confirmations, the Spirit of God was made manifest and a joyous feeling filled the room. Sister Pauline Malan spoke in tongues and translated.

The people here are not the rich and noble, but you shall judge their spirit by their own language, as they have each given me a line to send to their foreign brethren. As follows:

May we meet when the earth is renovated.

Pray for a young sister who wishes to grow in grace.

Absent in body, but united in spirit.

Hallelujah, for the Lord has remembered His people.

If we do not meet in these bodies, may we embrace each other in the resurrection. (This brother is sixty-two years old.)

In the midst of weakness I hope for strength.

Pray for a poor brother.

May we be crowned with glory when the world is judged.

The other brothers and sisters send the following:

We thank our Heavenly Father that we have begun to walk in the pathway of a new and endless life.

Brother Malan, who you know is a firm believer in The Voice of Joseph, I have advanced as an elder.

The work moves on apace. I often travel to the Cardon home to continue my preaching there. Madeleine Cardon is stalwart in her faith and helps me in the work of translating for some of the older Waldenese from the high mountains. The Beus family is one of the strongest in the faith, and I believe they will soon apply for baptism. The Pons and Bertoch families are very interested in the message, but several members cling to their religious traditions. They are worried of offending.

Elder Woodard lowered the letter and looked again out the small window. The snow was falling more thickly now; big, soft flakes drifted past the glass. He thought back to his early days of listening to the message of the gospel and how he'd fretted over the thought of leaving the Church of England. He well understood the difficulty of the decision. He found his place in the letter and continued reading.

You will find it interesting that Albertina Guy, who attended several meetings with her friend Madeleine Cardon, has now been absent for many weeks. Hers is a difficult situation. I see what the gospel means to her, but I also understand the deep affection she carries for her family, especially her great-uncle. The old priest and I had a talk a month ago, as he was upset about his great-niece's interest in our message. The Spirit prompted that I should preach to him of eternal sealing, and I think he found solace in that doctrine. I find him the most interesting of fellows.

How goes the work of translation? Many here have voiced interest in the message of the Book of Mormon, and long to evaluate it for themselves. I so admire their constant reading of the Bible. They truly are a people prepared.

I think of you in the streets of London and I hear the call of home.

Elder Woodard stopped reading. He mustn't let thoughts of his dear wife and two enchanting children pull his mind and heart away from the work he was called to do. He also must not envy Elder Stenhouse, who now had his wife and little girl in the mission field with him in Switzerland. Discipleship was not easy. Elder Woodard warmed his hands again and picked up the pen to finish the letter.

Remember me to Sister Woodard, and all friends whom you see in your travels.

I have heard from Elder Toronto in Sicily. He indicates that the work with his family is not going as he'd hoped. He will continue on for a few months and then return to us in the summer. I will be grateful for his help, as all kinds of calumny and petty persecution are brought into use here. The devil is not idle.

Yours in the new and everlasting covenant,

Elder Jabez Woodard

Elder Woodard waved the parchment in the air to dry the last of the ink, folded the missive, and put it into an envelope. He had made the decision not to tell Elder Snow about the attack at the inn, or of several other incidents of harassment and physical intimidation. Why worry him about something over which he had no control? Jabez moved to put on his winter coat, hat, and mittens. If he hurried, there was time for him to hike into Torre Pellice and post the letter for the outgoing mail. He also thought it would be a grand idea to take a bottle of the Malans' walnut oil to the inn and visit briefly with the Guy family. He missed Rene and Francesca. He missed Joseph's grown-up antics, and Albertina's inquisitive spirit.

He left a note on the table for the Malan family explaining that he would not be at the house for supper. He placed the letter to Elder Snow securely in his inner coat pocket, and ventured out into the snowy afternoon.

NOTES

The letter is an actual one from Elder Woodard in Italy to Elder Snow in London, with only a few sentences added for story flow.

Records of the baptisms concerning the Malan family indicate that John Daniel Malan Jr. was the first to be baptized. Elder Woodard's letter indicates a second young man but does not give a name. I chose David Pons to be the second individual. The Pons family was very interested in the missionary preaching at this time, so their son seemed a viable candidate.

Chapter Twenty-Nine

Salt Lake City

May 12, 1851

Eliza placed a bouquet of wildflowers on Charlotte Snow's grave and pulled a few errant weeds from around the headstone. It did not seem possible that the young woman was gone. Eliza could still hear her laughter and envision her hanging laundry. At those moments of disbelief, Eliza would think about Charlotte's visionary appearance to Sarah Ann announcing that she dwelt in a beautiful place. *It is heaven because we are there with the ones we love*, Eliza thought. She laid out the lap quilt, sat down, and took a letter from her skirt pocket.

"What a beautiful day, my dear sister," Eliza said, speaking to Charlotte as if she were present. "Perhaps as beautiful a day as one can expect in a fallen world. The temperature is mild, the sky is blue, and there is still a cap of snow on the tops of the mountain. I know you liked the snow, so that is why I tell you." Eliza took off her bonnet and let the cool breeze blow through her hair. She knew it was unsuitable behavior, as a lady always wore a bonnet when out in public, but there were no other visitors in the cemetery that day, so she felt the need for propriety could be set aside.

It was nice to be outdoors. The winter months after Charlotte's death seemed intensely bleak, and it was agreeable to see the trees greening as life renewed. Eliza took a deep breath of the fragrant spring air and took the letter from the envelope. "Since there is no one near to overhear my recital, I will read to you openly, dear Charlotte. It is a letter from our Lorenzo—from London of all places! Come, shall we discover what carried him from the fascination of Italy? You are welcome to sit with me on the blanket." Eliza grinned. "Hmm. When I get back to the house, I will have to have a discussion with President Young on the subject of the rights and limitations of those who have departed." She cleared her throat and read.

London, England
April 3, 1851
My dear sister Eliza,

I know that seven months have come and gone in the Valley of the Great Salt Lake without word from me, but it has been a sorrow to think on home and the passing of my dear Charlotte. As my mind contemplated the filial scenes, there was forever a sad vacancy—a sad vacancy that shadowed the beacon light. I therefore found it easier to spend my days in work and service, and the Lord has blessed me with bounteous opportunities for both.

I have now been in England a little over three months, and a short sojourn in this land has served to bind more closely those feelings of interest with the Saints in the British Isles. The mission fares well under the wise and prudent presidency of F. D. Richards. The many interesting and useful publications he has issued, together with the enlarged and much improved edition of the hymns used by the Saints, in addition to his other labors, furnish a true testimony of his indefatigable zeal and enterprising spirit. I wish to follow his example.

By letter from Father Andrew, and introduction from President Richards, I have secured the services of a retired Oxford professor who is working on the translation of the Book of Mormon into Italian. I have felt for many months the urging of the Spirit concerning this enterprise. It is of vital importance,

Eliza, for I believe, like many of us, the Italian faithful will be drawn to the restored gospel of Christ because of the power of the Book of Mormon.

It was this urgency that propelled me to travel in winter and leave the pleasant valleys of the Piedmont. As I took my departure, much kindly feeling was manifested towards me from those Waldensian faithful who have found interest in the gospel. With the pamphlets The Voice of Joseph and The Ancient Gospel Restored in my trunk, pockets, and hat, I crossed the Alps in the midst of a snowstorm, scarcely knowing whether I was heading toward England or Greece. It is one thing to read of traveling over the backbone of Europe in the depth of winter, but doing it is quite different.

Eliza lowered the letter and glanced over at Charlotte's headstone. "I can see him with his hat full of pamphlets, pushing on through a blizzard, can't you?" she said with a chuckle. Her thoughts turned towards scenes of days growing up with her brother in Mantua, Ohio, and of Lorenzo's mental and physical tenacity when confronted with a difficult task. Those qualities served him well as he tied himself to a new church that struggled to stand against prejudice and persecution. Such strength of character had served them both well. As Eliza found her place in the letter, she prayed for those in Italy who were seeking for the truth, as they would surely face the same challenges. "So, shall we see how he conquers the mountain?"

As we approached the towering Alps, there came a heavy snowstorm, which made our journey very gloomy, dreary, and altogether disagreeable. We commenced the ascent of Mount Cenis, and though but one passenger beside myself saw proper to venture over the mountain, it was found that ten horses were barely sufficient to carry us forward through the drifting snow. The deep snow rendered it very dangerous making our way up the narrow road and short turnings. One stumble or the least unlucky toss of our vehicle would, at very many points of our path, have plunged us a thousand feet down rocky precipices.

Eliza put her hand on her heart. "Thank you, brother, but I do not think we need to hear every detail of your adventurous life." She rattled the paper in protest, and read on.

We descended the mountain with much more ease to our horses, and more comfort to ourselves; and I felt thankful that my passage over those rocky steeps was completed.

"Amen," Eliza said, without taking her eyes from the paper.

My time in England has been spent visiting conferences, meeting with the brethren, and preaching, as well as supervising the printing of more pamphlets and the work of translation. I keep myself busy, but must confess that I miss the growing flock of Saints in the valleys of the Piedmont. Elder Woodard, whom I left in charge, now informs me that there are nearly thirty members, with dozens more interested. He has raised up a branch of the Church under circumstances that would have paralyzed the efforts of anyone not in possession of the most unshaken confidence in the power of the Lord. In Italy we publish books and pamphlets at the risk of coming in collision with the Catholic Church and, thereby, the government. We cannot sell Bibles or books of scripture, and we are not permitted to preach in public. At every step we find ourselves far off from the religious liberty enjoyed in England, but in spite of every obstacle, we have disposed of nearly all we have printed, and the gospel message reaches the ears of the earnest seeker within the walls of the humble cottage.

The Waldenese were the first to receive the gospel, but by the press and exertions of the elders, it will be rolled forth beyond their mountain regions.

"It is a miracle, Charlotte," Eliza said, looking up. "Twenty years ago, the Church had six members. Now there are thousands." Eliza's mind caught an image of Joseph Smith preaching to her family, and her heart chilled. *The mobs conspired to ruin the Church by killing the Prophet and driving us from our homes*, she thought with ire. *Yet here we are. Here, in this rugged mountain valley, and in many countries of the world.* She took her watch from her pocket to check the time. "Oh, my! We need to finish. I have chores to do and I am sure you have heavenly work of some sort to accomplish." She found her place and read.

> *When I was called to Italy on my mission, President Young instructed that should I be inspired to expand the field of labor, then I must follow the prompting. Well, respecting the progress of the mission, I have undertaken prospects for the future, and I feel the work should open in the countries of Asia. Elder Willis I have appointed to the Calcutta mission. Elder Findlay is now on his way to Bombay. Elder Obray I have appointed to Malta, while Elder Stenhouse presides in Switzerland, and Elder Woodard in Italy. Having set in operation those missions, I turn my thoughts to the far distant fields of labor. I contemplate shortly undertaking a mission requiring all my energies—extending over nations, continents, islands, seas, oceans, and empires.*

Eliza sighed, and wiped a tear from the corner of her eye. "I do not think he will be returning to us soon, Charlotte. Oh, how we will miss him, but it seems he has devoted his life to the service of God, and there is nothing to be done about it." She shaded her eyes and looked up towards the mountains. "I will pray for you, my dear brother." The words of the letter were blurred by tears as she read on.

> *When finished with my work here in England, I will take my departure to Switzerland to check on the advancement of the mission, and then back to stay a time with the Saints in Italy. I will stay as long as the Lord directs, and then off to all the*

casualties of sea and land that must be encountered. To assist me in this enterprise, deeply do I feel to call for your prayers, dear sister. I have often relied on your spiritual strength to fortify my resolve. How comforting it is to know that my family is in the embrace of your kindness and fortitude. They will also be receiving the news of my plans to extend the boundaries of the mission, and thereby time away from those dearest to my soul. Please assure them of my love, especially my little ones. I miss hearing the sounds of their infant prattle.

I testify that the Lord is aware of us. Be well.

I remain forever,

Your loving brother,

Lorenzo.

Eliza stood and stretched her back. She folded the letter and walked nearer to Charlotte's headstone. "Well, that is that. It would seem your husband and my brother does not do things by half measures."

A young sister came into the cemetery, and in a moment, Eliza could see that it was Eleanor Jones, a Welsh girl who had made a promise to Joseph Toronto before his departure for Italy. Eleanor was moving in her direction and carrying a posy of flowers.

"Hello!" Eleanor called, waving the bouquet. "I was just bringin' flowers to Sister Snow's grave."

"How kind," Eliza said as she drew near. She put the letter into its envelope and slipped it into her pocket.

"Been here havin' a chat, have ya?" Eleanor said, as she reached Eliza's side.

Eliza smiled at the young woman's Welsh accent and outgoing manner. She liked that Eleanor did not treat her with anxious deference, as did many of the Saints. Her background in the Church might be notable, but in Eliza's mind, not subject for awe. "We *have* been having a chat," she answered amiably. "I had a letter from Elder Snow and came to share it."

"That is a glory. How's he doin'?"

"Well, he is in London supervising the Italian translation of the Book of Mormon."

Eleanor's eyes grew wide. "My, my, my. The word is goin' out to all the world, then?"

"It would seem so."

Eleanor laid her small bunch of flowers on the grave. "There ya are, my friend Charlotte. I'm sure ya have better flowers in heaven, but 'tis the best I can do."

"She cherished your friendship, you know," Eliza offered.

"Aye, I know it," Eleanor said with a crooked grin. "We kept each other movin' forward on the trek across—I with my stories, her with her kindness." She patted the headstone and turned to face Eliza. "Uh . . . I was wonderin' if Elder Snow had anything to say about Elder Toronto? If you don't mind my askin'? It's just that I don't get word as Joseph doesn't know his letters."

"Of course, my dear! I should have thought. I've only received a few letters from Elder Snow, but most contain news of your Joseph."

The young woman brightened. "Is that a fact?"

"It is. If you'll come by the house later this afternoon, I'll share all the news with you."

"Oh, Sister Snow, that would be heather on the hillside."

Eliza smiled at the very Welsh expression. "I'm sure you've heard that he traveled to southern Italy to preach to his family."

"I have not!"

"Oh, dear. I think perhaps you should come with me now, and we'll fill in the whole story of your Mr. Toronto," Eliza said picking up her blanket.

"That *would* be a joy." The two women started off together. "And I'll tell you one thing for sure," Eleanor said, a tone of conviction in her voice.

"And what is that?"

"When Elder Toronto returns home, I'll surely be teachin' him his letters."

Eliza laughed. "I am sure you are equal to the task, Miss Jones. More than equal."

NOTES

The story of Elder Snow's treacherous trip over the Alps was taken from his journal.

Elder Snow was in London from January 1851 to February 1852, attending to the translation of the Book of Mormon.

Switzerland, Malta, Bombay, and Calcutta were missions opened under the direction of Elder Lorenzo Snow.

Eleanor Jones and Elder Joseph Toronto were introduced by the Prophet Brigham Young upon Joseph's arrival home from his mission to Italy. I found her such an interesting character, I decided to bring her into the story earlier.

Chapter Thirty

Torre Pellice

July 10, 1851

The three friends sat in the shade of the garden wall. The wall, tall as a man and speckled with lichen, retained the coolness of the night in its smooth stones. That blessing would last a few more hours until the midmorning sun began to bake the countryside.

"It's good to be up early in the summertime," John Malan said with a yawn.

"Up early?" Jean Cardon replied. "You are still sleeping."

"And so am I," Father Andrew grumbled. "So stop talking or you'll wake me."

John Malan protested. "I just meant it was good to be up in the cool of the morning. Later it will be dreadful."

"Humph," Andrew grunted.

"At least we're not them," Jean Cardon said, pointing.

Andrew opened his eyes a slit to see the younger priests working in the garden. "I put in my years doing that," he said.

"You? You, the man of learning and letters?" Jean Cardon teased, sitting forward. "Never."

"I did, you old fool. You saw me in the past."

"In the old days," John Malan chimed in. "The old old days."

Andrew opened his eyes and gave his friends a malicious grin.

"Yes, that's right, and you two were with me in the old old days. We have been friends since Noah boarded the ark."

The three friends laughed.

After a time, Jean Cardon sobered. "The years went by too quickly." His companions nodded. "I remember when I was teaching my young sons how to build houses and plant crops."

John Malan sighed. "And to take care of the milk cows."

"Time runs swifter than any river," Andrew said.

"Perhaps things will be different on the other side," John Malan said, his voice sounding hopeful.

Jean Cardon let out an exasperated breath of air. "Of course things will be different. It will be heaven."

"But what will we do?" John persisted. "Will we work? Will we eat? Will we tell each other stories?"

"Will I hear the sweet singing of my Madeleine?" Jean Cardon broke in.

"Yes, what of that?" John said. "What of that? Will all my family be near me, or will they be scattered to the wind?"

Father Andrew's mind went to his discussion with Elder Woodard and the wonder of eternal sealing, but it was not his doctrine to share. "Our minds are finite, my friends. We cannot comprehend eternity or the mansions of heaven. The scriptures tell us that all tears will be dried, so I think it will be a place of peace and happiness."

Some of the tension left John Malan's face. "Thank you for that." He sighed. "You're right. You're right, of course. Eye hath not seen nor ear heard nor hath it entered into the heart of man the things that God hath prepared for them that love Him."

"My son Philippe and his family have been listening to the preaching of the Mormon missionaries," Jean Cardon said.

Yes, and my Albertina with them, Andrew thought, vexation causing him to pound his walking stick on the ground.

"What's troubling you, friend?" Jean Cardon asked.

"It's just that we've had a difficult time convincing Albertina that she must not attend any more of their meetings."

"Well, you know that my John and his family have joined with them," John Malan said with a little shake of his head. "Turned their back on their faith. Baptized." John took a deep breath. "I do not understand it. The Waldensian synod wanted him to be an elder in our church, and he said no, and now he is an elder in the Mormon Church? I do not understand."

Jean put his hand on his friend's shoulder. "I do not understand it myself, but Philippe says they bring back the light of the ancient church."

"But the Waldenese have always felt that we are the light of the ancient church," John countered.

"Wait! Wait now!" Father Andrew said firmly. "I think *we* have something to do with the apostle Peter, if my mind serves me."

John Malan chuckled. "If your mind serves you? Well, that *is* the question, isn't it?"

Jean Cardon smiled broadly and collapsed back against the cool stone wall. "Ah! It is too pleasant a morning for worries and troubles. I say we let God figure it out."

"Probably a good idea," John Malan agreed. "He is smarter than we are, anyway."

"He is, indeed," Andrew said. His tone and features softened, but not the argument in his mind. He closed his eyes and images swam into his head: Albertina reading from the Bible, Father Pious throwing the ancient parchment into the fire, the weathered faces of his Waldensian friends, he and his fellow priests chanting morning prayers.

"Father Andrew! Father Andrew!"

It was the grating, nasal voice of Father Pious, and Andrew shuddered.

"Ah, here comes the Northern Star," John Malan quipped.

"John Malan!" Jean Cardon scolded. "You will not get into heaven."

John gave him a crooked grin. "I think I will let God figure that out."

Jean Cardon squinted at the approaching figure, and then over to Father Andrew. "Be ready," he counseled. "He has tragedy written on his face."

Andrew grunted. "Bah! That gnat cannot trouble me. Remember that I watched the guillotine drop."

Breathless, Father Pious reached their side. "Father . . . Father . . ."

"Take a breath," Andrew offered petulantly.

Father Pious gulped air and glared at him. "Your nephew . . . is . . . here."

"Yes?"

"Yes."

"So why the running and the yelling? Unseemly behavior for a priest."

Father Pious stood straighter and slowed his breathing. "He has come to fetch . . . ah . . . collect you. I overheard him talking with Father Nathanael, so I ran ahead to tell you. Something about your great-niece"—he paused—"and baptism."

Andrew stiffened. "Baptism?"

Father Pious was gratified to see the color drain from Father Andrew's face. Andrew struggled to stand and Jean Cardon supported his arm.

"I must go. I must go," Andrew gasped, stumbling forward.

"Here! See here!" John Malan said, pushing against his cane and standing. "You cannot just go off on your own."

Father Pious stepped forward, reaching out for the old priest's arm. Andrew pulled it away. "No! I do not wish to walk with you. It was your great pleasure to run ahead and give me this news, wasn't it?"

Father Pious gave him an innocent look. "You do not wish my help?"

"I do not."

"We will help you," Jean Cardon said, standing.

"The lame leading the lame," Pious said under his breath.

The three companions had only trudged a few steps when Andrew caught sight of Rene and Father Nathanael at the edge of the garden. "Thank you, thank you, my friends, but we are saved. Sturdier hands are coming."

Andrew glanced around to give Father Pious a dismissive look, but the man had disappeared.

"I'm sorry I had to bring the donkey cart," Rene said as they bounced along the rutted road, "but it was the easiest to ready."

"Never mind," Andrew grunted, gripping the side of the cart with one hand and bracing himself against his nephew to lessen the jostling. His old bones ached and the sun stabbed at the top of his head. Rene did not speak again, and Andrew was glad of it. He was trying to formulate his thoughts, but they were schoolboys on the final day of school. He tried closing his eyes to organize his thinking, but that only made him nauseated.

Soon Rene turned the donkey onto the track to the inn and slowed their pace. Andrew shaded his eyes and saw Joseph sitting on the ground under the chestnut tree. When the boy heard the sound of the cart, he jumped up, but did not leave the cooling shade. Rene pulled the cart into it, and Joseph rushed to his great-uncle's side. His face was streaked with tears and dirt.

"Oh, Uncle, everyone is yelling and yelling."

"Yes, yes, my boy. Be still," Andrew instructed, trying to calm the spinning of his head.

"Joseph, get back!" Rene barked. "Let me get Uncle out of the cart."

Rene swung his arm around Andrew's back and took his hand, helping him slowly down. Andrew gritted his teeth as his feet hit the hard earth. His left leg was numb, and he was just gaining his balance when Francesca rushed from the inn.

"Oh! Thank heavens! Thank heavens you've come! We cannot talk sense into her. She will not listen to a thing!"

"Francesca, give him a chance to breathe."

"Oh, yes. Yes, of course. I will bring him some water." She ran back into the inn without waiting for comment.

"I want to sit in the garden," Andrew said weakly. He did not want the closed heat of the indoors. He needed air and cooling shade.

"But Uncle—"

"I will sit in the big wooden chair—the one with arms."

"It is not very comfortable."

"Tchet. I have slept on the hard ground."

"Yes, but that was many years ago."

"Do you want my help or not?"

"Yes, of course."

"Then take me to the garden. And ask Albertina to bring my water and a pillow for my back."

Rene did as he was told, helping Andrew into the chair, and leaving to give Albertina her instructions. When his father was gone, Joseph timidly approached his great-uncle.

"Why is everyone so mad?"

Andrew patted the boy's hand. "They are not mad, they are frightened."

"Frightened? Father is frightened?"

"Yes."

"Why?"

"Because he does not know what will happen tomorrow."

"I don't understand."

"It is all right, my dear little fellow. You don't need to understand."

Joseph laid his head on his great-uncle's shoulder, and Andrew hummed him a simple children's song. When he saw Albertina come around the corner of the inn, he sat straighter. "Now, Joseph, you must leave me so Albertina and I can have a talk."

Joseph looked into his eyes. "Do not scold her. Do not scold my Albi."

"No, I won't. You go and wash your face."

"Yes, Uncle." Joseph started off for the inn, his head down, his shoulders slumped. When he passed by his sister and she placed a gentle hand on the top of his head, he burst into tears and ran.

Albertina came silently to her great-uncle's side, handing him the cup of water and taking the pillow from the crook of her arm. "Behind you?"

"Yes."

She placed it and stood back. "You wanted to see me?"

Andrew shaded his eyes and looked up into her sullen face. "Sit down, please."

"I'd rather stand."

"Please sit so your old uncle doesn't get a crick in his neck." She sat, but did not speak. Andrew sipped his water, waiting for wisdom and for his heart to calm its beating. "It is warm today."

"They brought you here to talk to me about the weather?"

Andrew was shaken by her tone. "No . . . I—" He forced his mind to still. "No. They brought me here because you are breaking their hearts."

Albertina sat back, a stunned look on her face.

He knew the words were harsher than she deserved, but he would not take them back. "You must honor your parents, Albertina. It is one of the commandments."

"I have always honored my parents! And you! And God! How can you say that to me? I have always kept my place, especially after Pauline died. I always made sure I made Mother happy."

"Calm down. Calm down, my girl."

She stood. "I am not doing any of this to make them sad. I am doing this because I am brave."

"What?"

"You told me that I was brave—brave for asking questions and for seeking knowledge. Do you remember when you told me that?"

"I—"

"You said that I wasn't to be afraid of the answers."

Andrew's mind was spinning. "Well, I—"

She began pacing. "For months now I have been seeking, and learning, and praying."

He was losing his grasp of the conversation. He motioned with his hand for her to sit down—the movement was making him sick. "Please, Albertina—"

"And everything I learn feels right to me."

"Albertina Marianella Guy!" he bellowed. "Sit down!"

She turned abruptly, her eyes wide, her face flushed. "I . . . I'm sorry." She sat.

Andrew had spent his strength on the shout, and sat struggling to catch his breath.

"Uncle?"

He held up his hand to stop her talking, his fingers moving to rub the pain from his temple. Andrew's mind drifted away from the shade of the tree and the face of his great-niece. He thought about his first quill pen, his mother catching the white goose. The distraction of memories lessened his pain, and he groaned in relief.

"Uncle?"

"What?" Andrew came back to the moment.

"Are you finished talking to me?"

Andrew frowned. "No. Not at all."

"Then why the silence?"

"I . . . I was thinking about my mother."

"Your mother?"

"Yes. I was thinking about her. She was catching the white goose."

Albertina sat forward in her chair. "Uncle, are you well?"

The softer tone in her voice made him sigh. "Yes, I am well." He gathered his thoughts. "I am just worried about you. We are all worried about you—this decision to join with the Mormons. This is not a wise choice."

Albertina's defensiveness returned. "I am not a child."

"No, you are not. So you must take everything into consideration."

"I have."

"Have you? You will be giving up a faith that has existed for nearly two thousand years—the faith that is the foundation of your life and heritage. And for what? An unproven American church less than thirty years old?"

"But you said you admired many of their teachings."

"Yes. But philosophies come and go."

"I do not think this is a philosophy, Uncle. I feel they have truths from Christ's ancient Church."

"Their interpretation of the Bible."

"No. The Prophet Joseph—"

"And what will you do if the missionaries and their Waldensian converts leave for America? What will you do then? Will you leave your grieving family to go with them?"

She faltered. "No. No . . . I won't leave."

"You do not seem sure of your answer."

Albertina looked at the ground. "There will be members who stay here. There will be missionaries," she said slowly.

"What are you not telling me?"

"Nothing, Uncle. Nothing."

The ache in his head made him surly and his response brusque. "You must not join with them, Albertina. You must stay true to the church. It is your only hope of salvation. You must confess your sins and pay penance for disobedience to your parents."

"Uncle, please. Won't you listen to me? Won't you listen to what I've been learning at these meetings? I have seen miracles. *You* have seen miracles! We would not have our little Joseph but for the priesthood blessing of the Mormon missionaries."

His hands began to shake. "Enough, Albertina."

"You were there! You heard the words of the blessing and you saw life come back into Joseph's body. Do they not have some truth to tell?"

A sharp pain shot up the back of his head, and Andrew groaned and slumped forward.

Albertina jumped out of her seat. "Uncle!" She ran to catch him as he tumbled out of his chair. "Uncle! Uncle!" She held him in her arms. "Help! Help me! Papa! Papa! Help me! Please! Please, old bear, stay. Stay with me!"

A gray stillness was pulling him away. "Do not leave . . . me," he slurred.

She rocked him back and forth. "I won't. I won't. I'm sorry. I'm sorry. I'm sorry. You have to stay. I'm sorry." Albertina screamed out again for help, but she could already feel her great-uncle's body going limp in her arms.

CHAPTER THIRTY-ONE

Torre Pellice

July 13, 1851

The library storeroom smelled of old parchment and ink. Andrew stood with his eyes closed, breathing in deeply the familiar smell, his mind and fingers imagining the feel of a quill pen and the soft brush of vellum. He sighed.

"The power of parchment," spoke a mellow voice.

Andrew smiled and turned. "Yes, the feeling is still with me."

"Of course."

"But I was only a trickster, a copier, a scribbler. Never anything original like your creation. 'We hold these truths to be self-evident' . . . I was a young boy, but those words went through me like fire."

"Ah, but do you imagine that I did not copy the thoughts of others— that I did not read the words of great thinkers? What would I have done without brilliant words printed out from your scribblings—yours and others like you?"

Andrew bowed his head. "That is kind."

"That is truth. Shall we walk?"

"I would like that."

"Where would you like to go?"

"Up over Mount Cenis? Perhaps I can walk to my home in Lyon."

"Whatever suits you."

Andrew walked. "Tchet! This is not so difficult. I remember these trails and these cliffs. And that waterfall? I bathed in that waterfall." He drew in a deep breath and felt the water beating against his young skin. "A great weight has lifted."

"Freedom," his companion said.

"Yes! Freedom!" Andrew's mind drifted to their first meeting in the library in Paris. He, his uncle, the tall statesman, and a thousand books. Andrew wanted to talk to him about that day, but the weather had turned cold and the sky spoke of rain. "I need to find my father," Andrew said anxiously. He looked across the amber field and saw him scything hay. "I need to help him. Why have I been so long from home?"

The dark sky pressed against his head, blurring his vision and stripping the strength from his arms and legs. A church bell rang far away in the valley, and with each clanging sound, heaviness overwhelmed him. He stumbled and fell. Someone held his hand and squeezed his fingers.

"Father Andrew."

It was a pinprick of sound.

"Father?"

Rumbling and heaviness.

Andrew tried to find the sound, but his body would not move. Where was his father? He wanted to be with him, but he could not see in the dark.

"Open your eyes."

Andrew frowned.

"Open your eyes, honored one."

The dark pressed him to the ground. *What is this weight that holds me?* Panic tore at the edge of his reason. Someone was squeezing his fingers while a low voice commanded him to open his eyes. He did. Smudges of gray and white swam in front of his vision. He breathed and the panic lessened.

"His eyes are open."

Movement near him. Pressure on his arm. "Uncle?"

Rene? The name stayed trapped in his head. A thickening in his throat stopped any sound from moving to his lips. He tried to blink to clear his vision, but even his eyelids betrayed him. The panic returned.

"Look at his eyes. He's frightened." Francesca's voice.

"Can we sit him up slightly?" Rene's voice.

"I think it should be all right." Father Nathanael's voice.

"Be calm, Uncle. We're going to help you."

Hands grasped his upper arms, and he was pulled slightly higher onto pillows. Air rushed into his lungs and the fear receded. He tried to thank them, but all that escaped his body was a muffled groan.

Weeping. From far away came the sound of a young woman weeping.

I want to go back to sleep. I must go back to sleep. Andrew closed his eyes and returned to the field and his father.

"You must let them pray for him."

"I will not."

"At least let them see him. Elder Woodard has been asking for days, and Elder Toronto has just returned from southern Italy. They both want to see him."

"No. Only family."

"Father Nathanael is here."

"Father Nathanael attends him."

"Papa, you know what they did for Joseph."

"That . . . that was just . . . he was getting better on his own."

"What? How can you say that? He would have died."

Andrew groaned.

Rene's answer stopped midsentence. "Ah!" He glared at his daughter. "Quiet your voice. You've woken him."

Albertina rushed from the hallway to her uncle's side. "Uncle," she whispered, touching his face. "Uncle?"

"Leave him be. Get back to your chores."

Andrew opened his eyes. "No."

Father Nathanael came into the room at that moment. "Did he speak again?"

"He did," Rene said stepping to the bedside.

Father Nathanael joined him. "The doctor said he was getting stronger."

"He is! He is getting stronger," Albertina replied, a desperate hopefulness in her tone.

"Lower your voice!" Rene snapped.

"Uph," Andrew said.

Father Nathanael looked at Rene. "Did he say *up*?"

"He did," Albertina answered. "He wants to sit up."

"Move back," Rene said, brushing her aside. He and Father Nathanael gently lifted Andrew higher onto the pillows.

Andrew gritted his teeth as they lifted, feeling the heaviness of his arms and legs. He wanted to talk to his caregivers, but was afraid the attempt would be met with sympathy instead of comprehension. It was frustrating. The words formulated in his brain, but often refused to make the journey to his mouth.

Albertina edged her way closer, and Rene turned.

"Get back to your work now."

"I want to sit with him."

"Later. Father Nathanael will look after him. There's work to be done."

"It's always later."

"Do not argue with me."

Albertina began to protest, then instead pressed her lips together and reluctantly turned towards the doorway.

Andrew's fingers lifted a few inches off the coverlet. "W—waith."

The three stared at him, and Father Nathanael moved closer.

"What is it you want?'

Andrew's finger pointed at Albertina, and then tapped several times on the coverlet.

"You want her to stay?"

Several more taps.

Rene's body stiffened, and there were several moments of tense silence before he turned to her. "Do not upset him."

Albertina hung her head. "No. No, I won't."

As Father Nathanael moved the wooden chair closer to the bed, Rene gave him instructions.

"Do not let her stay long. Send her out to her chores in a few minutes. And if she begins to agitate him, send her out immediately and let me know."

"Yes, Monsieur."

Rene moved out of the room, giving his daughter a final stern look. Albertina stood unmoving until Father Nathanael stepped forward and took her by the elbow.

"He wants you to be near him. That is a good thing."

Albertina let him lead her forward to the chair. "Father Nathanael?"

"Yes?"

"Will he get well?"

"I believe he will, Mademoiselle Guy. He seems to get stronger every day, don't you think?" She nodded, and he smiled at her. "Besides, you have surrounded him with so many prayers that I do not think death can find its way to him." He patted the back of the chair. "Now, sit and keep him company. I will be nearby, reading, if you need me."

"I promise not to upset him."

"Of course you won't."

Albertina edged her way quietly into the chair. She glanced at her uncle's face and found that he was looking directly at her. She pressed her lips together to stop the flow of tears, but it did not help. She laid her head on the bed by her uncle's hand and gave in to her emotion. After a time she felt her uncle's fingers clumsily stroking her hair. She sat up and took his hand. "I'm sorry, Uncle. Sorry. This is my fault."

"No." The word was soft, but clear. It made Albertina gasp and choke on some of her tears.

"It was. It was my fault, my headstrong anger. I'm so sorry."

He frowned at her. "No."

She noticed that the right side of his face showed the emotion clearly, but there was also a tinge of expression on the left side as well. It was a good sign. "Father and Mother are so angry with me. They don't say it, but they know it was my fault." She dried some of her tears on her handkerchief. "Can you ever forgive me?"

"Confession?"

The word came slowly and was slightly slurred, but its unexpected advent made Albertina and Father Nathanael start. "Father Nathanael, did you hear?"

"I did. Praise God, a long word!" He pressed his open Bible to his chest. "I knew your presence would be good for him, Albertina."

Albertina's joyful expression moderated into thoughtfulness as she turned back to her uncle. "There . . . there *is* something I must tell you—something I've been keeping secret."

He laid his fingers on the back of her hand. "No need."

"There is a need," she said softly. "I want my heart to be free of this."

He patted her hand. "Go on."

"You remember the music competition in Pinerolo?"

A slight smile. "You won."

"Yes. Madeleine Cardon and I won." She shifted in her seat. "At that time I had been listening to the missionaries and I was praying about what I should do." She hesitated and took a breath. "I promised the Lord that if I won, I would be baptized . . . and . . ." she struggled with the words. "And I would use my part of the money to go to America, if my friend Madeleine went."

A look of fear crossed over Andrew's face.

"But I'm not going!" she said quickly. "I will never go! Never." She looked straight into his eyes. "I promise, old bear. I will stay here and take care of you. I've made up my mind, so don't worry. I will always be here with you and Mother and Father."

"And with me, Albi?"

Albertina turned quickly and saw her brother at the door. "Yes, Joseph, especially with you." He ran to her and she took him in her arms. "I need to stay and make sure you keep out of trouble."

"I don't get into trouble," he said indignantly. Albertina laughed and Andrew smiled. "Look! Uncle is better!"

"Yes, he is better, but we must let him rest. Give him a little pat on the hand and then run along."

Joseph leaned over and laid his cheek on his great-uncle's hand. "Get all better."

"Good boy."

Joseph stood quickly. "He talked!"

"Yes, he talked. Now, off you go."

Joseph cupped his hands around his mouth and leaned towards his uncle. "I will come back again to talk to you," he whispered.

"Good."

Joseph beamed at his uncle as though he had just performed a feat of magic. "I will tell Mother you are better!" He turned and ran from the room.

"Water," Andrew said.

Albertina reached over immediately and fetched the metal cup from the nightstand. "Here." She helped him to drink. She wiped his face with a cloth when he was finished.

"My cup."

"Yes. Father Nathanael brought it from the monastery."

"How long?"

Guilt colored Albertina's face and she lowered her head. "Nearly a week."

He struggled to formulate the words. "Look at me." She looked up. "Not your fault."

"But—"

"I am better."

"I am glad that you are better," Albertina said, taking his hand. "And you must promise to stay with us."

"For now."

"For always."

He pointed at her. "You?"

"Yes, there is nothing that could take me away from you."

"True."

The word in Father Andrew's mind had been *truth*, but it had altered when it came from his mouth. Would the power of truth someday pull her away from him to a distant place? Andrew pushed the impression from his mind, as thinking of it dropped sadness into his chest. For now, his sweet songbird was staying. His fear took a step back. He gave Albertina's hand a slight squeeze. "Song?"

"I'll try," she said. "There may be too many tears."

"Try."

She nodded, and after taking time to calm her emotions, she began singing a simple hymn of gladness.

Andrew closed his eyes and felt his burdens lift. His thoughts turned to gratitude. *Thank you, Christ Jesus. Thank you for my Albertina. May she never leave me.* A twinge of conscience pestered him. Perhaps for selfishness he was bending the Lord's purpose, but surrounded by the tender comfort of the song, Andrew knew that he would not change his prayer.

CHAPTER THIRTY-TWO

The Cardon Borgata, Angrogna Valley

September 6, 1851

"They had taken away their guns against the laws of America. The godless Colonel Pitcher forced the Mormon men of Jackson County to surrender their arms, promising that the weapons of the violent mob would suffer the same consequence."

"The Mormon men didn't give them up, did they?" Stephen Malan called out.

Madeleine and Albertina turned to look at him, both desiring the same information, but too shy to ask.

Elder Woodard looked around at the young people seated together under the chestnut tree. Their faces held the memory of the slaughter and atrocities perpetrated against their own people, and Elder Woodard knew they wanted an answer of defiance. It was an answer he could not give them. "Trusting Colonel Pitcher's word, they surrendered their guns."

"No! No! That was their mistake!" several young men yelled. "Those guns were their defense!"

"What happened to them?"

"What did the mob do?"

Elder Woodard prayed for guidance. He'd wanted this time with the Waldensian youth to teach them of the similar sufferings that the

Latter-day Saints experienced because of their witness for the truth. He had not anticipated how deeply the story of persecution would affect them, and how they would long for the details of the injustice. Elder Woodard reasoned that if they were going to align themselves with the Mormon faithful, they had to know the history.

"I have been a member for two years," he said, sitting on the ground with them. "And when I was investigating the Church and learning the history, I remember being horrified at what the Mormon people suffered. They came up against bigotry and violence for trying to live their faith."

"We understand violence," Madeleine said solemnly.

"Yes, you do," Elder Woodard answered.

"So what happened?" Stephen Malan pressed.

"The mob, who had *not* had their guns taken away, went on a rampage. They were determined to drive the Saints from Jackson County. The mills, stores, and homes of the Mormons were destroyed—ransacked and burned. Some two hundred homes in one area were burned to the ground. The people were dragged from their houses and beaten, the women and children terrorized. Twelve hundred people were driven out."

Madeleine and Albertina moved closer together and took each other's hands.

"One group of a hundred and fifty women and children were forced out of their homes in the middle of the night. They walked thirty miles across a prairie in the month of November. The rough ground was thinly crusted with sleet." Elder Woodard's voice broke with emotion. "I've heard several brethren testify that you could easily follow their trail by the blood that flowed from their lacerated feet."

Madeleine's heart jumped. *Bloody footprints in the snow?* It was her dream. Her stomach churned with anger and revulsion.

The group was silent, and Elder Woodard felt the Spirit guiding his thoughts in a new direction. "You are young, but many of you may have to face persecution if you join with this church."

"Many of us have already had persecution, Elder Woodard," Stephen Malan said. "Just like you and the other missionaries, we have been humiliated and threatened. Some of us have even been knocked about."

"Perhaps it has always been the way of things," Madeleine said sadly.

Elder Woodard nodded. "Perhaps." He studied the morose faces. "But the fire of adversity makes the strongest Saints. Look at Elder Snow and Elder Toronto."

"What about Elder Toronto?" the man himself said as he ducked under a low-hanging branch of the chestnut tree.

Elder Woodard stood and took Elder Toronto by the hand. "I was just saying that adversity has made you strong."

"Well, adversity—and herding cattle on the open range."

Elder Woodard laughed. "That's right. Brigham Young appointed you to be the cattle manager."

"Do you really know the prophet Brigham Young?" Stephen Malan asked.

"I do. I lived with his family when we first came into the valley."

"And you believe him to be a prophet?"

"I *know* him to be a prophet. It was revelation that had him leading the Saints after the death of Joseph."

"And did you know the Prophet Joseph Smith?"

Elder Toronto shook his head. "No. I arrived a year after he'd been killed, he and Hyrum. But I knew their mother well. Sister Lucy Smith. Tiny woman." He held up his hand to his chest. "Only came up to about here." He smiled with the group. "But she was mighty in character and testimony. Even after she lost her boys she did not turn back."

"A lesson for all of us," Elder Woodard said.

"Is your meeting done, Brother Woodard? Because Sister Cardon sent me to bring you all to supper."

Madeleine Cardon jumped to her feet and grabbed Albertina's hand. "Oh, no!"

"Are you all right?" Brother Woodard asked.

Madeleine was moving off, dragging Albertina with her. "Fine. Fine. I just forgot that we were supposed to help my mother serve!"

The girls ran.

"She won't be very angry with us, will she?" Albertina asked. "I mean, we did help her bake thirty loaves of bread this morning."

The soup and bread had been served, the kitchen cleaned, and most of the people who had gathered for the re-union were on their way home. Albertina and Madeleine, now freed from their chores, hiked the trails and wandered the hillsides around the Cardons' home. A slight breeze tousled their hair and played at the hems of their skirts. It had been a good day, and Albertina pondered many things as they hiked: the stories Elder Woodard shared, the image of Lucy Smith, and thoughts of Elder Toronto herding cattle across the American wilderness. What would it be like to hike for a thousand miles? She glanced at the sun lowering toward the western mountains.

"How far are we going?" she called to Madeleine, who was outpacing her on the trail.

Madeleine stopped. "I thought we'd go to the waterfall."

Albertina hesitated. "I need to be starting for home soon."

"It's still light until late."

"Mother wants me home before nightfall. She doesn't like me on the trail in the dark."

"There will be a moon tonight—besides, I hike the trails at night all the time."

"But you are Waldenese, aren't you? I think your ancestors were taught to climb by the mountain sheep."

Madeleine started off. "We'll just go to the stream, then."

Within a short time they came to an enchanting spot where a stand of pine trees surrounded a bend in the stream. The water tumbled over a shelf of rock into a shallow pool.

"Ah, this is lovely," Albertina sighed as she knelt to get a drink of water. She sat down on a flat rock near the edge of the stream, patting her face with the droplets on her hands.

"Put your feet in," Madeleine said.

"It's cold," Albertina answered.

"Not *that* cold."

Albertina watched as Madeleine removed her boots and stockings. "But I—"

"It will feel good," Madeleine coaxed. "Aren't you warm from hiking?"

Her skin did feel sticky, and after watching her friend slide her feet into the clear water, Albertina quickly followed her example, but while Madeleine walked around in the pool, Albertina dabbled her toes at the edge. She was enchanted by the flecks of sunlight playing on the water and the soft trill of birdsong.

"It will be hard to leave this," Madeleine said.

She spoke so softly that Albertina wasn't sure she'd heard all the words. "Did you say *leave this*?" Her friend did not answer. "Madeleine? What do you mean?"

Madeleine made ripples in the water with her feet. "I knew I would have to talk about this sometime."

"About what?" Albertina's heart was racing. "About what? Are you leaving?"

"I heard Father and Mother talking the other day. There is a group of members who are thinking of going to America—to Salt Lake City. When we join the Church, we will go with them."

"When are they going?"

"A year or so. We will need time to prepare."

Albertina was stunned. "That . . . that's not possible. You have your family here—for generations . . . and your father's work . . . and your property. And none of your family has joined the Church. Maybe you won't join."

Madeleine came over and sat next to her. "My sweet friend, I have told you my dream about the coming of the evangelists and the message they bring. You know that my dream says we will join with this church and travel to a new country for the truth."

"But you haven't joined! Maybe it's not right. Maybe that's why you're waiting. Because you have questions."

"We are waiting for Elder Snow to return with the Book of Mormon so we can read its words. When we have done that, we will join." She took Albertina's hand. "The gospel they teach is true." She looked straight into her friend's face. "You know it's true, Albertina."

"You could join and stay here. Your family would be a great strength to the Church here in the Piedmont."

Madeleine shook her head. "We will go." She looked out to the hillside, the first tinges of autumn coloring the edges of the leaves. "You could come with us."

Albertina gasped. "I can't! You know I can't! I have to take care of my uncle."

"But he is doing much better, isn't he? He was out sitting in the garden the last time I visited you."

"Yes, but he is still fragile. I have to help him with his memory, and doing his daily tasks."

"And . . . you promised him you wouldn't leave."

Albertina began crying. "Yes, I promised. I promised. I won't leave him or my family. I can't."

"And you will not join the Church."

"No."

"Albertina—"

"No, I won't! Don't you understand? I would be giving up *everything*."

Madeleine took her hand. "I do understand. I do understand, my dear friend. Do you think it will be easy to leave everything we've ever known, our beautiful mountains, our lives, and our Waldensian faith? Where are we going? To an unknown wilderness." She stood and walked back into the water. "An unknown wilderness."

"Then why would you go?"

Madeleine took a deep breath. "Remember the story Elder Woodard told of the women and children walking over the snow-crusted ground? Their feet bloody from the walking?"

"Yes."

"Years ago I had a dream about those women and children. A nightmare about bloody footprints in the snow. When Elder Woodard told the story, I knew it was true. I knew those women had taken their children and fled into the wilderness." Madeleine closed her eyes and shook her head. "Why didn't they give up? Why didn't they just go back to their old lives where they had comfort and security?" Madeleine took a step forward. "Because they knew it was true. A light had been placed in their hearts, Albertina—a light that would never go out. So no matter what they were asked to go through or give up, they would do it. They would not go back."

Albertina stood slowly, picking up her boots and socks. Her voice, when it came, was low and pointed. "I have to go home now." She wiped the tears away with the sleeve of her dress. "I know why you're saying these things, Madeleine. I know what you're asking me to do, but I can't."

"Albertina—"

"No. Please do not ask me again, Madeleine. I understand that you must stay with your family, but so must I. I must honor my father and my mother." She walked out of the shade of the trees and into the grassy meadow. She saw the sun sinking toward the mountaintop and hurried her pace. She longed to turn around and call out words of affection, but things had changed between her and her childhood friend, and Albertina did not know the new words of closeness. She set her face towards home and did not turn back.

NOTES

The scenes of violence against the Latter-day Saint people in Jackson County and many other places where the Saints resided are well documented in journals, newspaper reports, and other chronicles.

The Borgata Cardon, the ancestral home of Philippe Cardon, sits high in the mountains above San Secondo. At some point Philippe Cardon moved his family down the mountain nearer to the village of San Secondo. I have placed the home as having closer access to the Angrogna Valley and the town of Torre Pellice to accommodate the friendship between Madeleine and Albertina and the Cardon family's interaction with the Mormon missionaries who were located in Torre Pellice.

CHAPTER THIRTY-THREE

London, England

December 10, 1851

My Dear and Highly Regarded Sister,

As I pen these words to you, another year draws to a close, and though the time seems fleeting I have endeavored to fill it with the earnestness of my calling. The translation of the Book of Mormon into the Italian language is complete, and a hundred books have thus far been printed. Several dozen I have sent to Elder Woodard to distribute among the Saints in the Piedmont for their instruction. He reports that several more of the Waldenese have joined with the branch in the Angrogna Valley, and even though there is persecution, the Saints remain steadfast in their commitment to the restored Church.

A spirit of inquiry is abroad in Italy, Eliza, and this mission has been attended with much solicitude. Many have felt that labors bestowed in Italy would prove futile and unavailing—that doctrines of present revelation would not be able to obtain credence with the people. But we endeavor to establish the Church of Jesus Christ upon the most substantial basis—the rock of revelation, and I believe the veil over Italy has begun to burst. The Alpine hills have commenced to reverberate the tidings of salvation and the gift of the Holy Ghost to those who have wandered long in darkness. I look with wonder upon the road in which the Lord has led me since I came to this land. From the first day I trod the Italian soil, there has been a chain of circumstances, which has not sprung by chance, but from the wise arrangements of Him who ruleth in the kingdoms of men.

How lovely to contemplate that at some future time the fulness of the gospel ordinances may be the reward of those who embrace our message. In thoughts of temple blessings, my heart is drawn to the experiences of the Kirtland Temple. There we had the gift of prophecy, the gift of tongues, the interpretation of tongues, and visions. We heard the singing of heavenly choirs, and saw wonderful manifestations of the healing power through the administrations of the elders. The sick were healed, the deaf made to hear, the blind to see, and the lame to walk. It was plainly manifest that a sacred and divine influence—a spiritual atmosphere—pervaded that holy edifice.

And now, I extend my memory to the temple in Nauvoo, where thousands of resolute Saints received their sacred ordinances, though evil mobs threatened their very existence. How venerated is the house of the Lord to the Saints of God, my dear sister? Think how we in the valley will rejoice when a temple is again raised in our midst. Then think how those in the far-flung reaches of the world who accept the gospel will long for the clarity of the temple. This is why we labor. This is why Elder Toronto, Elder Woodard, Elder Stenhouse, and I sacrifice for the precious souls of our brothers and sisters.

Elder Stenhouse reports from Geneva that many have shown an interest in the gospel message, and declares that the pamphlet _The Voice of Joseph_ is receiving genuine inquiry. I will leave England soon, having accomplished the Lord's requested task, and sojourn for a brief time in Switzerland to evaluate conditions. Then I will once again ascend the forbidding Alpine mountains in order to return to the cherished people of the Piedmont valleys. You may well find it amusing that I vowed never again to cross those rugged heights in the grip of winter, *but I will not delay my return for more clement weather. I am fixed in my course of spreading the truth of the gospel to the world, for I know it to be the primitive Christian faith restored, the ancient gospel brought back again. I know that though you and I may not be present, Eliza, the Church is here in the last dispensation to usher in the Millennium.*

Thank you for the watchful care extended to my family. Whenever I receive a letter from my little band of Saints, they refer to your consideration. I have a difficult time expressing what comfort this affords me, one who longs to be with my precious darlings and to be responsible for their safekeeping.

I pray that the Lord's Spirit will attend your endeavors.

I remain, as always, your very affectionate brother,

L. Snow

NOTE

With a few minor changes, this is an actual letter written by Lorenzo to his sister that was included in his autobiography.

Chapter Thirty-Four

Angrogna Valley

January 2, 1852

An outsider—that is what Albertina Guy knew herself to be. An outsider. The cold that swept across the Angrogna River was mirrored in her feelings. She stood at the side of the river watching the water run beneath the slivered sheets of ice clinging to the bank. While others of the company chatted in lowered voices, she stood in silence, ruminating about her early-morning argument with her father.

"Why are you going to this baptism if you are not going to be baptized?"

"Madeleine is being baptized, and she is my friend."

"A friend whom you haven't seen for months."

"I have been busy with Uncle."

"I thought you were going to mind your mother's and my wishes."

"I have minded you. For months I have not been to their meetings."

"Then I don't see why you should want to be a part of this ceremony."

"Madeleine is my friend. This day is important to her, and I'm going to be there."

"Albertina, I—"

"No, Father, I'm going."

The wind stopped blowing and the sun came from behind a bank of clouds, giving a brief respite from the chill to those waiting to enter the water for baptism. Albertina opened her eyes to find Madeleine shivering at her side.

"Will you hold my coat for me when I go in?" Madeleine asked.

"Of course."

Madeleine reached down and took her friend's gloved hand. "I am glad you came."

"Ah! I can feel your cold hand through my glove. Where are your mittens?"

"In the pocket of my coat. I can't wear them into the water."

"No, but you can wear them now. Put them on! Put them on! No wonder you're shivering."

Madeleine pulled the mittens from her pockets and put them on. "I think I'm nervous, too."

"About your decision?"

"No. Our decision is right. I just wonder what comes after this day."

Philippe Cardon came to stand beside his daughter, slipping his arm around her shoulder and giving her a hug. "Well, my girl, your dream is coming true."

"Yes."

"Are you feeling all right?"

"Yes. Nervous."

"Perhaps it is the thought of putting your feet in that cold water."

She smiled up at him. "We are pioneers now. Should we be worried about a little cold water?"

"That's my girl." He looked over at Albertina. "You are a true friend to come out on such a cold day, Mademoiselle Guy."

"It is an important day."

"Yes. Yes, it is."

Elder Snow drew near, standing with his back to the water and addressing the group. "The weather dictates that my comments be brief."

The people smiled as they gathered closer to hear his words.

"I am grateful that I have returned from England in time to be here with you. I am grateful that many of you have been able to read the Book of Mormon in Italian. I am grateful for your faith in the gospel, and your desire to take upon you this holy ordinance, for it surely is the gateway into eternal life. John, in his revelation, chapter fourteen, verse six, having seen and spoken of the wandering of the church into darkness, speaks of the restoration of the gospel: 'I saw another angel flying in the midst of heaven, having the everlasting gospel to preach unto them that dwell on the earth.' It is evident that prophecy was to be fulfilled at some time previous to our Savior's second advent. I now bear testimony, having the highest assurance by revelation from God, that this prophecy has already been fulfilled, that an angel from God has visited man in these last days and restored that which has long been lost, even the priesthood, the keys of the kingdom, the fulness of the everlasting gospel."

Albertina was surprised when Madeleine leaned over to her and whispered, "It is my dream—my dream of the everlasting gospel."

Elder Snow smiled as he looked into the face of Madeleine Cardon, and then to her parents. "You have been a people prepared with visions and dreams, and the Lord is pleased that even though you have had to leave precious traditions and face persecution, you have been true to those promptings and stand now at the waters of baptism."

Albertina took her friend's hand. She glanced around at the waiting believers, noting that Madeleine's entire family was joining the Church—all except her older sister Ann, whose husband refused her any association with the faith. Movement from Elder Snow caught Albertina's attention. He was motioning for John Malan to step forward.

"I have called upon President Malan, as your branch president, to perform the baptisms, while Elders Woodard, Toronto, and I will act as witnesses. After the baptisms, we will adjourn to the Cardons' home, where they may change and get warm prior to their confirmations. President Malan, would you please take Sister Cardon into the water?"

Elder Malan reached out his hand for Madeleine's mother. The girls huddled closer together and stepped nearer the river's edge, watching the two move carefully out into the deepest part of the frigid water. When they were nearly waist deep, Brother Malan stopped and instructed Sister Cardon to take his wrist. He then raised his other arm to the square, and, in a voice loud enough for all on the bank to hear, he called her by name and proclaimed that, having been commissioned of Jesus Christ, he baptized her in the name of the Father, and the Son, and the Holy Ghost. He put his hand on her back and buried her in the water.

Just as Sister Cardon disappeared under the surface, Albertina Guy inched her foot forward and put the toe of her boot into the water.

NOTE

It is historically accurate that Brother John Malan was the branch president at the time of the Cardons' baptism and performed that sacred ordinance for the Cardon family. Records indicate that Philippe and Marie Cardon were baptized January 2, 1852, followed later that year by other family members. Other records indicate that Philippe Cardon was baptized June of 1851. For the sake of story cohesion, I chose to place all the baptisms together.

CHAPTER THIRTY-FIVE

Torre Pellice

February 10, 1852

"The first thought of the day?"

"God."

"The first act of the day?"

"Prayer."

"The first thought?"

"God."

"The first act?"

"Prayer."

"Hold up three fingers."

"Albertina."

"Do as you're told."

Father Andrew glared at his great-niece.

"Do it, or I won't let you go to morning prayers."

"You would keep me from the first act of the day?"

"Do not be petulant."

"Oh, ho! That is a big word."

"I learned it from your behavior. Now, three fingers."

Andrew condescended.

"Now six."

He obliged.

"Now two."

"You are a tyrant."

"Two."

His two fingers shot forward as if to poke her in the eyes.

"Wait now! Just for that you don't get any breakfast."

"Tchet! That is no loss. Nothing tastes good anymore."

"Such a pity. Mother sent country bread with plum jam."

Andrew sat straighter. "Plum jam? I would agree to walk an extra twenty steps for your mother's plum jam."

"Actually, I made it."

"What's that?"

"Don't look so surprised. I help with most of the cooking now."

"Getting ready for a home of your own?"

Albertina gave her great-uncle a cautionary look. "I think you are talking too much today."

Andrew chuckled. "All I'm saying is that you're not a girl anymore, adventuring in the mountains with your friend Madeleine. Your life has gone in a different direction."

"That is the way of things."

"Where has she been, by the way?"

"Who?"

"Madeleine Cardon. We still have not finished reading *The Count of Monte Cristo*."

"That was a long time ago."

"So?"

"She and I have both been busy with other things."

"Yes—taking care of me, for one," Andrew growled, sitting back in his chair. "I have been wasting too much of your time."

Albertina sat forward and took both of her uncle's hands. "Stop growling, old bear. There is nothing I'd rather be doing."

He gave her a serious look. "Well, that is a sad statement."

She stood to put another log on the fire. "So you don't like my company?"

"I love your company, but at eighteen you should be off with your friends or spending time with a beau."

"A beau? I didn't know matchmaking was part of your priestly calling." She gazed into the fire. "I am content where I am."

The room grew quiet except for the snap of the burning log.

Andrew thought back to eighteen and his time in Paris with his uncle Jacques: the girls in their pale, empire silk gowns, their hats festooned with pastel ribbons and bows, the glazed pastries, and the late-night carriage rides. He wandered the halls of the grand libraries, running his hand along the backs of leathered books, and saw again the great statesman, tall and elegant. How far away the sculpted gardens of Versailles and the lavish salons of Venice? How many winters had come and gone—how many summers? He felt a light touch on the back of his hand, and looked up into Albertina's lovely face.

"Drifting?" she asked.

He sighed. "Back to when I was your age—I remember the blood of eighteen. You may not think so, but I do. The blood so restless and insatiable. I have lived my life, Albertina, and I am content where I am, but I do not think the same is true for you."

Albertina set his writing desk across his legs and tapped the parchment. "Let's continue with your exercises."

He held the small desk out to her. "No. And this time I will not let you bully me."

"Uncle—"

"Sit down, please."

"But I—"

"Please."

She took the writing desk and placed it on one of the library tables. Reluctantly she went back to the chair and sat. "Father Nathanael will be in soon."

"This I know. We will talk until then."

"There is nothing to talk about."

"Albertina, I have known you all your life—tears, happiness, struggles." She opened her mouth to respond, but he went on. "And though you may not have shared every worry, I have read it in your face." She lowered her head. "For the past several months you have been unhappy, and though you mask it with gentleness and work, I see it there."

"I have been worried about you."

"Yes, and I thank you for that, but I think you are unhappy because you have broken a promise to the Lord."

"What?"

"You told me of the promise, remember? After the singing competition in Pinerolo."

Albertina labored to find the words. "I . . . that . . . that was just my will for the moment. Like you said, I hadn't thought it through. It was foolishness to think of joining another church and of leaving you. I could never do that."

"May I tell you a story?" She gave a slight nod. "After I watched the guillotine drop on Danton's neck, I doubted the road I was on. It was a dark time. I wandered the streets of Paris searching for purpose, for answers. The only answers that come from the streets are of the streets. Do you understand this?"

"I think so."

"For years the world called my name. For years I opened my hands to the gold and my heart to the praise, but I was not happy. The darkness followed me wherever I went. By the time I stumbled into the cathedral at Lyon, I was a wretched man."

"Uncle—"

"Without question, a wretched man. That day, as I gave up my pride and my sins to God, a light came into my heart, at first a small flame like the light from a candle." He placed his hand over his heart. "And then it grew to encompass every part of me. It was a feeling I could not deny." He leaned forward. "I think you have felt a similar light, my dear one."

Albertina studied his face. "I have."

"Then you must be true to your feelings."

"But you said—"

"I was wrong."

"But Mother and Father—"

"You must honor them. You must honor their wishes. But there will come a time when you must do as the Lord directs."

The library door opened and Father Nathanael came in, followed by Elder Snow. Albertina turned in her seat and gasped when she recognized the apostle.

"Well, this is a timely meeting," Andrew said.

"Are you finished with your exercises?" Father Nathanael asked as he drew near. "I do not mean to interrupt you, but Monsieur Snow has come for a visit, and it is time for prayers and breakfast."

"It is no interruption," Andrew said. "You have rescued me from my punisher." He reached out his hand and Lorenzo took it. "Elder Snow, welcome. Please sit down."

"I cannot stay for a visit. Perhaps another time. We are on our way to preach in Pinerolo." He opened his satchel and brought out a book. "I wanted to stop and offer you one of the Italian copies of the Book of Mormon."

Andrew looked at the book and then to Elder Snow's face. A half grin printed itself onto his mouth as he reached for the book. "Ah, so here it is. Here it is. You realize that when you publish and distribute this book, you risk coming in collision with the government?"

Lorenzo grinned back. "We are aware."

"Did you want me to check the translation?"

"No. This time you may read for pure pleasure and enlightenment."

Andrew laughed. "You are a shrewd man, Elder Snow, giving a man of letters a book with an intriguing history."

"I was counting on your curiosity."

"Well, you will have to come again and we will discuss it."

"If there is time. It seems that the Lord is calling me to other places."

"You're leaving us?" Albertina exclaimed. "When? Where are you going?"

"Elder Woodard and I will leave for Malta in a month or less."

"Malta? Elder Woodard too?"

"Yes, Mademoiselle Guy. We would stay in this glorious land if we could, but the gospel must be preached to the world and the world is a very large place." He opened his satchel and brought out another book. "A book for you as well."

She reached for it slowly. "Really?" He nodded. "Thank you, Elder Snow."

"You are welcome. And now I must be on my way." He hesitated. "I testify that you hold in your hands a sacred book, a second testimony of our Lord Jesus Christ." He looked directly at Father Andrew. "I testify that it was translated by the gift and power of God. Read it carefully, read it prayerfully, and you will know of its truth."

"Albertina and I have always been seekers."

"That is what I hear," Lorenzo said, taking a step back. "I *would* like to visit again before I leave, if that is acceptable."

"It is expected, Elder Snow. Expected."

Albertina moved quickly forward. "May I walk with you for a time, Elder Snow? I have questions."

"Of course, Mademoiselle Guy. I love your questions." He waited as Albertina picked up her coat and went to say good-bye to her great-uncle.

She took his hand and looked fondly into his face. "Old bear." She leaned over and whispered in his ear. "I see the light shining in your face." She straightened. "A big breakfast for him today, Father Nathanael."

"Bread and plum jam!" Andrew said happily.

"Yes, you worked hard this morning." She kissed his forehead and moved off with Elder Snow. "I will see you tomorrow!" she called back.

"Can I not have a day of rest?"

"You may rest on Sunday."

"Cruel taskmaster," he grumbled.

"If she is such a cruel taskmaster," Father Nathanael questioned, "then why are you smiling?"

"Never mind! Never mind!" Andrew blustered. "Get me up. I need to go to the water closet, and then to breakfast."

"And then to prayers," Father Nathanael corrected, reaching down to lift him from the chair.

"Of course, to prayers. Prayers first," Andrew grunted as he stood. "The first thought of the day—God. The first act of the day—prayer."

Father Nathanael put Andrew's shawl around his shoulders, and took his arm, waiting for the old priest to begin moving. "You are getting stronger every day."

"Tchet! Soon you will be telling me that when summer comes I will be hiking over Mount Cenis." He started forward with determination.

"It wouldn't surprise me, honored one. It wouldn't surprise me in the least."

CHAPTER THIRTY-SIX

Torre Pellice

My dear sister Eliza, February 20, 1852,

Today I will bid farewell to the valleys of the Piedmont and the people who have come to fill such a large part of my heart. It will be difficult to leave them, but many are looking forward in a year or two to travel to Zion, where we will rejoice together in the fellowship of the gospel. We have not been permitted to preach in public or to distribute our pamphlets or Italian copies of the Book of Mormon, yet we have few left in our possession, and there are nearly one hundred converts to the Church. Italy is not silent under the shackles of spiritual despotism. Many noble sentiments and liberal ideas have been spread through the country by the speeches of honest-hearted men in Parliament who have called loudly for religious freedom, and we trust they will not always call in vain.

Several Waldensian pastors have attempted to stop the work of salvation with slander, threats, and even physical violence, but the message of the gospel has gone forth and has been heard and embraced by many.

I know, dear sister, that the Book of Mormon will lend its powerful aid in building up the Church. After many anxieties with regard to that work, it was no small pleasure to find it welcomed by the Saints in Italy as a heavenly treasure, and the translation so highly approved.

The Waldenese were the first to receive the gospel, but by the press and the exertions of the elders, it will be rolled forth beyond their mountain regions. At this season they are surrounded with snow from three to six feet deep, and in many instances all communication is cut off between the villages. Our labors in such countries will be eminently blessed when we can have persons in the priesthood who are not under the same disadvantages and liabilities as foreign elders—and such are rising up here. The Saints embrace the manifestations of the Spirit, and there are many reports of dreams, visions, and healings.

Luckily this winter has been mild, and there is only a skiff of snow, so Elder Woodard and I will be traveling by coach to Genoa—indeed, our time of departure is near, so I must be brief. While Elder Toronto will remain in the Piedmont, Elder Woodard and I will be traveling to Malta, where I will stay for a time and then, as circumstances permit, I shall be moving forward to other realms. From whence my next communication will proceed, I cannot say—perhaps from Malta, or the crumbling monuments of ruined Egypt, or the burning climes of India.

I pray that the Lord may always be with you and with my treasured family. Hold my little ones in your arms and whisper my name in their ears. I must go on with work so my heart does not break in the thinking of them.

I remain, as ever, your affectionate brother,

Lorenzo

Lorenzo perused the letter quickly, blew on it to dry, and placed it in its envelope. He looked out at the lightly falling snow. "Thank you, Father. *Grazie per tutto.*" He put on his coat, grabbed his bags, and went out to say good-bye to his friends.

The wind blew Elder Snow's hat across the courtyard and he ran to secure it. He shoved it back on his head and returned to the gathering of friends and Saints. "Why is it I always seem to be traveling in the winter?"

"Because, my friend," Colonel Beckwith offered, "if you tried to leave us at any other time, the beauty of this place would keep you here."

"That is true," Lorenzo said with a nod. "So true. The Piedmont in the spring is a place of enchantment."

"Then I wish for spring always," Madeleine Cardon said. There were mummers of assent throughout the group.

"I agree with my daughter," Philippe Cardon added. "Perhaps you should stay and see what the spring is like, and then, if you don't care for it, you can leave."

Lorenzo chuckled. "That is a sly trick." He looked around at all the dear faces who were part of the miracle of the Piedmont and felt tears press at the back of his throat. He struggled to gain control of his voice. "Thank you. Thank you for your friendship and love." He looked at his traveling companion. "At this time Malta calls us, but I promise to send Brother Woodard back to you when I embark for other lands of antiquity." Elder Snow put his hand on John Malan's shoulder, marveling at the strength of the man and the small band of Saints for whom he was shepherd. "Elder Woodard and I have been awed by your faith—your willingness to try the word of the Lord, your willingness to stand against persecution." He coughed to clear the huskiness from his voice. "I would stay with you always if I could, but the Lord has called us to other places. And at the end of the journey I am anxious to see the faces of my dear family." He coughed again. "Now, we have left the mission to our brother in the gospel Elder Toronto, and the branch in the loving care of President John Malan." Lorenzo turned to face him. "Brother Malan, we have such confidence in you. Thank you for your able service."

"Thank you for the gospel of Christ," he returned. "We will work hard and prepare ourselves to come to Zion."

Lorenzo nodded. "We will keep track of your progress." He moved over to Colonel Beckwith, picking up Nellie as he went. The dog rode in his arms as if a little king, which made Lorenzo laugh. He shook the colonel's hand with vigor. "Colonel, your influence has been a great help to us in this work. Thank you. We esteem you highly, and I know that your name will be spoken of with love among the Waldenese— and the world—for generations to come."

"I can easily say the same for you, Elder Snow. But thank you for that. And thank you for putting up with this little mongrel over the years." Nellie barked and Colonel Beckwith shushed him as Lorenzo handed him over. "Perhaps you will return to the mountains someday."

"Perhaps," Lorenzo returned. He went next to Madeleine Cardon. "And here is our little sister of vision, who dreamed of the coming of the three missionaries. What a day that was when we met you in the meadow."

"A day of wonder," Madeleine said.

"Wonder indeed," Lorenzo said, smiling. "And can you see that time of departing for you and your family?"

Tears welled in Madeleine's eyes. "It's not far off," she said quietly. "As my dream said. We will leave our homes and travel across the wilderness to a place where we will gather with you and the Saints."

"That will be a happy day," he said.

"A glorious reunion," Madeleine answered.

Elder Snow turned his face to the woman standing next to Madeleine. "Albertina Guy. We are so grateful to you and your family for the care and hospitality you gave us when we first arrived in Torre Pellice."

"Amen," Elder Woodard said as he came to Elder Snow's side. "We saw your family a few weeks ago, but please tell them again of our affection."

"I will."

"And please remind dear little Joseph that I will be sending him some things from America," Elder Snow added.

"He is not likely to forget."

Lorenzo laughed. "No, he's not."

Albertina reached into the deep pockets of her coat and brought out two scrolls of parchment. "My great-uncle wanted me to give these to you." The elders took them with great deference. "He wrote out something special for each of you. For you, Elder Snow, the Declaration of Independence, and for you, Elder Woodard, your Magna Carta." She smiled at the stunned looks on the elders' faces. "He did them in Italian so you will be able to practice the beautiful language."

Elder Woodard shook his head. "This is a treasure. A true treasure."

The press of tears at the back of Lorenzo's throat increased. "Please, tell him we are honored by his gift. He is one of the most remarkable men I have ever met."

"I'll tell him."

Lorenzo nodded. "Good. Good." He took a breath to calm his emotions, and turned his full attention to Albertina. "Before I leave, I wish to promise you something."

"Yes?"

"Put your trust in the Lord, Albertina. You may not be able to see the way as yet, but the Lord knows all. Trust in Him, continue to honor your parents and your great-uncle, and the time will come when hearts will be softened. Do you understand this?" She nodded. "Good." He looked around at the gathering—taking in each precious face. "Until we meet again, my friends." There followed a chorus of well-wishes as the two missionaries made their way to the coach and the rest followed.

Albertina and Madeleine lagged behind, each feeling the sting of parting acutely, and not wishing to be part of the larger emotion. They waved from a distance as the coach pulled away.

"At least you will see him again," Albertina said, wiping the tears from her face.

"Remember what Elder Snow said, Albertina."

"What?"

"You may not be able to see the way as yet, but the Lord knows all." Albertina nodded. "And now," Madeleine continued, "I think we should go to see your great-uncle, sit in the warm library, and tell him all about the parting and what the elders said and how much they loved his gift to them."

"Yes, that's a wonderful idea," Albertina agreed. "And perhaps he'll give us bread and currant jam."

The two friends began walking quickly towards the monastery.

"And perhaps there's another book to read!" Madeleine said excitedly.

"There is always another book to read!" Albertina called out into the snowy morning. "Always another book!"

NOTE

The major part of the letter Elder Snow wrote to Eliza are the actual words taken from his journal.

EPILOGUE

Torre Pellice

February 8, 1854

Albertina Guy and Madeleine Cardon stood inside the Waldensian temple, looking at the simple wooden plaque with its depiction of a lighted candle and seven stars. *Lux Lucent in Tenebris.* "The light which shineth in darkness." Albertina glanced up and noted the pale winter sunlight casting a faint glow on the high windows. Her fingers ached and her breath came out in white puffs.

"I thought I would be married here," Madeleine said.

"Really?" Albertina questioned, looking over at her friend. "I pictured you in the high valley with wildflowers in your hair."

"Oh, that would have been lovely," Madeleine answered, loneliness and loss creeping into her voice.

Albertina took her hand. "Don't worry, you will find a wonderful man in the wilderness of America."

"Do you think?"

"Of course. Perhaps one of the sons of Brigham Young."

"Don't tease me."

"I'm not. All you will have to do is sing to them and they will fall at your feet."

Madeleine decided to change the subject. "It's hard to believe that Elder Snow left nearly two years ago, isn't it?"

"It is," Albertina replied.

"And now the first group of Waldenese are following," Madeleine said, taking Albertina's hand. "Well, the first group of Waldenese plus one brave friend."

The door to the temple opened and Philippe Cardon stepped inside. "It's time, girls." The two swallowed down sadness and anxiety and followed him out.

After the dimness of the church, the brighter outside light made them squint, and it was several moments before Albertina's eyes adjusted and she could see people milling about the three sleighs. Colonel Beckwith was helping the men load the last of the luggage as Nellie cavorted at their feet. The women were making sure their families were nearby and that the quilts and blankets were sufficient for the journey. John Malan Senior leaned on his cane and watched his son organize the assembly while Jean Cardon called out to Madeleine when she emerged from the church.

"Oh! My grandfather is here!" Madeleine said. She let go of Albertina's hand and hurried to embrace her loved one.

Albertina walked to her mother and father. She noted that her brother, Joseph, stood stoically at his father's side, focusing on the movements of the horse teams, and refusing to glance in her direction. Albertina searched for the one face that would bring her some reassurance, but he was not present.

"He is old, Albertina. He will not be here," her father said, as if reading her thoughts.

"I know." She turned to her family. "I am glad you came," she said. "I know this has not been easy." She tenderly ruffled Joseph's hair and he swatted at her hand. "For any of you."

"You are a woman now," her father said. "You will make your own choices." The words should have been comforting, but Albertina found no solace in his disappointed tone.

"But you promised you wouldn't go. You promised all of us," Joseph protested.

Albertina had tried to prepare her emotions for the bitter sorrow she knew this day would bring, but the look on Joseph's face wounded her heart. She knelt down in front of him and he avoided her eyes. "Look at me, dear one. Please." Finally he looked at her, holding on to his irritability as a protection. "I am grown now, and I must find my own way in life," she began. "And though it is very hard, I must go where the Lord directs me." She tied his scarf more snugly around his neck. "That does not mean that I will forget you or lose connection with you."

"But you will. You are going far away."

"Yes, but I will write to you and send you things, and perhaps I will come back to visit—or you could come to America to see me."

"Do not give him false hope," Francesca said.

Albertina stood. "We do not know what's in store for any of us."

"No, we do not. But I doubt that America holds any part of our future."

"Can we not keep our hearts open?" Albertina pleaded. Her mother did not answer. "Mother?"

The voice of John Malan lifted above the noise and chaos. "Everyone? Everyone, please gather to me for instruction and prayer."

"She is forsaking us," Joseph said as she walked away.

Albertina crossed her arms in front of her and felt the sting of tears at the back of her eyes. When she reached the group she maneuvered her way to Madeleine.

"Everything is loaded," Madeleine whispered. "We will soon be on our way."

Albertina noted the excitement in her voice and felt a twinge of jealousy. *Of course she's excited*, she thought. *She will have her entire family with her.*

President Malan waited for the murmur of voices to quiet. "Today is not only a momentous day but a day of reflection. Why did the Mormon missionaries come into the valleys of the Waldenese? Why did their message bring such clarity concerning the primitive church?

And why did our hearts respond with such favor to their words? Like the beloved mountains around us, we are firmly planted in the restored gospel, and as testimony to that faith, today the first group of converts will leave for Zion: the Cardon family, the Pons family, and the Bertoch family. And with them will go the courageous Albertina Guy." Several in the company reached out and laid a hand briefly on her shoulder, but instead of the gesture fortifying her conviction, Albertina felt a chill of apprehension. She was glad when President Malan began speaking again. "I will give you instruction and then we will have a prayer. You have your course set from here to Turino, then over Mount Cenis, and finally to Geneva, Switzerland, where you will be met by Elder Stenhouse. He will accompany you to Liverpool, where you will meet up with Elder Woodard. He has been in England for a time and will meet you in the port city for the express purpose to help with preparations and language. He will then travel with you to New Orleans, America." The members of the company shared looks of relief.

Madeleine squeezed Albertina's arm. "See, I told you the Church would not leave us stranded. How marvelous to see them all again."

Several others of the company were talking and President Malan waited for quiet. "When you get to America, Elder Woodard will see you safely secured on one of the Church's wagon trains moving west, and when you reach the valley of the Saints, Elder Toronto and perhaps Elder Snow will be there to give you welcome."

A cheer went up from the normally restrained Waldensian members, and Madeleine and Albertina joined the commotion. Albertina worried that she was caught up in the excitement and the adventure. *Had she thought enough about the unforeseen consequences of her decision?* She watched as President Malan furtively wiped tears away with a large pocket handkerchief. She could tell they were tears of joy, not sadness. The man was confident in the choices he had made, and Albertina vowed to imitate his emotions. He raised his hand for quiet.

"Hopefully in less than a year another group will leave from here to join you in Zion. My family and I hope to be in that company."

Another cheer rent the cold winter air and President Malan wiped away more tears. "Now, we will have the Pons and Bertoch families in one sleigh and the Cardon family with Mademoiselle Guy in the other. The third, of course, is for your trunks and parcels. As soon as I have finished saying the prayer you will have only a few minutes for good-byes before the sleighs depart. Our prayers and our love go with you."

Albertina's courage was crumbling. Her stomach hurt and she couldn't stop shivering. This decision was foolish. Perhaps she would never see her family again. Perhaps she would die on the crossing and they would mourn her all their lives. And what about the old bear? Tears that Albertina had pushed away for weeks coursed down her cheeks. She could not concentrate on the prayer or the solace and protection it was meant to give. All she knew was that she was not going to get into the sleigh. She was not going to cross an ocean and thousands of miles of wilderness. She was not going to leave the safety of her mountain home. Suddenly she heard a chorus of muffled amens and knew the prayer had ended. She opened her eyes and turned quickly so Madeleine would not be able to read the decision on her face. She looked up and encountered black cassocks.

"Father Nathanael! Uncle!" The tears started again and she went to take her great-uncle in her arms. He was so frail that she hugged him with little pressure. "What are you doing here?"

"I came to see you off."

She turned on Father Nathanael. "But he is not well enough."

"He threatened to come by himself."

"Uncle—"

"Hush now. I do not think you have time to scold me."

"I do . . . because I'm not going."

"What do you mean, not going?"

"I have changed my mind."

"Albertina Marianella Guy," he said tenderly. "I have come out into the cold to say good-bye."

"No, Uncle. No good-byes. I need more time. I have not thought this through."

"My dear one, you have been thinking this through for years. What is it? Are you not brave enough?"

"I . . . I am brave, but . . ."

Andrew shuffled forward and took her hands. "When you go to America, my Albertina, I know that I will not see you again in this life."

"Uncle, please don't."

"I am nearly eighty-seven. I will not see you again. But I am brave—I am brave enough to let you go. I know you must go. You must. We believe in the Lord and we believe in heaven, isn't that right?" She nodded. He reached out trembling fingers and brushed away a tear. "And we know that your heart and my heart are connected." She gave him a miserable look and he smiled at her. "Yes?"

"Yes."

"Then all is well. And now I believe you must go and do what you promised the Lord."

"But I *am* afraid, old bear. I am."

"Of course. You are wise to be afraid. Do you not think I was afraid the first time I crossed the mighty Alps to find my new life in these valleys? Of course I was. But I'd set my sights and I just kept walking. You will do the same, because you are brave and faithful."

"Not as brave as you."

"Braver." Albertina began weeping. "'Trust in the Lord with all thine heart and lean not unto thine own understanding. In all thy ways acknowledge Him and He shall direct thy paths.'"

Rene and Francesca came to stand beside Andrew, and Albertina attempted to dry her tears on her mittens.

"What?" Andrew scolded. "Did you forget to bring your hankie?" He turned to his niece. "Francesca?"

Francesca brought a hankie from her pocket and handed it to Albertina. "It has embroidery of the mountain flowers."

286

Albertina rushed into her mother's arms, and Rene and Joseph joined in the embrace.

"I promise that I will see you again," Albertina vowed. "I promise."

"We will hold you to that," Rene answered, his voice rough with emotion.

"It is time to depart!" President Malan called out.

Albertina stepped back. "I have to go. I love you." Her words were clipped to keep away from sentiment. "You have always been a good boy, Joseph. Continue on."

"I will, Albi."

As the Waldensian Saints moved to the carriages they sang their hymn of the mountain. *"For the strength of the hills we bless thee, our God, our fathers' God . . ."*

Albertina went to her uncle. "I love you, old bear."

He nodded. "One favor?" She waited. "Sing to us as you go."

"I . . . I'll try." Tentatively she began singing as she backed away, joining her voice to that of her traveling companions. *"We are watchers of a beacon whose light must never die; we are guardians of an altar 'midst the silence of the sky."* She was to the sleigh and about to step in when she heard her uncle's feeble voice call out to her. She turned and saw him shuffling forward, Father Nathanael doing his best to keep him from slipping on the snowy ground. Albertina rushed back to him. "Uncle, what are you doing?"

There was a look of urgency on his face. "Leave me for a moment," he instructed Father Nathanael. "I will be fine." He held onto Albertina's arms for stability.

"Uncle, I have to go."

"I know. I know, dear one. But there is one more thing. One more very important thing. Come here. Come here." She moved close and he put his forehead onto hers. "When you arrive in Salt Lake City and are taught the lesson of temple sealing . . ." His voice broke and he began weeping.

"Yes, old bear. What is it?"

With a quavering voice full of longing he said, "Remember me."

"Remember you?" She kissed his forehead. "I will always remember you. Always."

"Albertina, hurry!" Madeleine called.

Father Nathanael stepped forward and took Father Andrew by the arm. "The Lord bless you," Albertina said. She turned and ran for the sleigh. She climbed into the back seat. She and Madeleine knelt facing backward so they could wave good-bye to their friends and family.

As the sleigh pulled away, Andrew kept moving after it until it pulled around a bend and disappeared from sight. He stood staring at its last visible spot until his two friends came up beside him.

"The Lord keep them," Jean Cardon said in a hushed voice.

"The Lord keep them," Andrew repeated.

The three stood in silence for a long while staring down the deserted, snow-covered road. Finally, John Malan spoke.

"Will you be with me next year when *my* family departs?"

"If we are alive," Father Andrew said.

"Yes, perhaps we should see if we make it to spring," Jean Cardon added with a chuckle.

"I cannot wait for the warmth of spring," John Malan said, missing the joking undertone of his friend's words. He went on wistfully with his own thoughts. "It will be good to sit in the garden by our favorite wall."

"And share stories," Jean Cardon added.

"But for now," Andrew said, "it is home and a cozy fire. My old bones are cracking."

"Yes, we must be off for home too." John Malan said, looking around for his family. "Ah, come on, old friend. I see them over talking to Colonel Beckwith." The two companions started on their way.

"Would you like assistance?" Father Nathanael asked.

"The Lord bless you, Father Nathanael, but here come some of our young, strong nephews to help us."

Father Andrew watched as his friends were escorted into the

safety of their families. He knew it was senseless to look for Rene and Francesca, because he had seen them take Joseph's hands and leave the square as soon as the sleighs had started. He would talk to them later; now he knew their hearts could bear no word of comfort or reassurance. He felt the same. *Lord, grant me the strength to accept the things I cannot change.*

"Let's get you to the warmth of the library, shall we?"

"Yes. Yes," Andrew heartily agreed. "And then prayer, and then food."

"I think the kitchen has made apple cake," Father Nathanael informed him.

"Apple cake? I like apple cake," Andrew said, shuffling forward. He thought back to his birthday when he had been given the white quill from his father and the ink from his uncle Jacques. On that day his mother had baked apple cake. His foot slipped and he held tightly to Father Nathanael's arm. "Tell me a truth," he said when they were safely on their way.

"A truth?" Father Nathanael asked, looking sideways at his charge. Andrew nodded. Father Nathanael took his time answering. "I will tell you two truths."

Andrew smiled. "Good. One cannot have enough truth."

Father Nathanael patted his hand. "Your Albertina will do well in her new life, and . . . your heart will mend."

After a long pause, Andrew nodded his acceptance. "Thank you."

The priests reached the cobbled road to the monastery. "Stumble stone," Father Nathanael warned.

"Tchet! I have been over this road a thousand times. I have climbed mountains, you know."

"Yes, I know, honored one. You have climbed many mountains. That is why I am so fond of you. So very fond."

AUTHOR'S ENDNOTE

Lorenzo Snow was called back to Salt Lake City in the spring of 1852. He left Malta, never to complete his travels to India and the other mission areas eastward. He arrived home July 30, 1852. Lorenzo Snow would go on to settle Brigham City, complete another mission in the Sandwich Islands (Hawaii), serve in the state legislature, and become the fifth prophet of The Church of Jesus Christ of Latter-day Saints in 1898 when he was eighty-four years old. President Snow passed away October 10, 1901.

The first group of Waldensian Saints left Torre Pellice on February 19, 1854. They sailed from Liverpool, England, with some four hundred other European converts on the ship *John M. Wood*. The company arrived in New Orleans on May 2, 1854. The group then traveled by steamboat to Saint Louis, where they were placed in quarantine because of an outbreak of cholera in that city. Many of the company fell ill and many died. Eventually the sickness abated and the quarantine was lifted. The Cardon family, along with the Pons and Bertoch families, reached the Salt Lake Valley on October 29, 1854, and were greeted by Joseph Toronto.

Madeleine Marie Cardon was twenty-one years old when she

traveled with her family to America, reaching the Salt Lake Valley in October of 1854. She married Charles Guild on February 19, 1855, and they settled at Marriott's Landing in Ogden. She and Charles had eleven children. Eventually the family moved to Piedmont, Wyoming, where Madeleine lived out the rest of her life. She died July 21, 1914, and is buried in Piedmont.

Following is a list of surnames of the Waldensian families who immigrated to Zion between 1854 and 1860: Bertoch, Beus, Bonnet, Bosois, Brodero, Cardon, Chatelain, Gardiol, Gaydou, Gaudin, Jouve, Justet, Lazald, Malan, Pons, Rivoire, Rochon, Roman, Rostan, and Stalle. Emigrating in the 1890s were the Avondet, Combe, and Long families. The majority of the Piedmont Saints settled in Utah in and around Ogden, Logan, and Lehi. They also settled in parts of Wyoming, establishing the town of Piedmont. Of the seventy-two Waldenese who immigrated (mostly from twelve original families), their descendants now number in the tens of thousands. A large number are faithful members of The Church of Jesus Christ of Latter-day Saints. They honor the rich heritage left them by their faithful Waldensian ancestors.

Some original Waldensian converts returned to the Piedmont to encourage family members and former neighbors to immigrate to Utah. Many of those who came did not convert to Mormonism but associated with Protestant congregations in the valley. This second wave of immigration continued for about three decades, from 1879–1910, bringing an additional eighty-eight emigrants.

In the late 1850s, the proselyting efforts in Italy began to decline, and the mission became part of the Swiss Mission. In 1862, proselyting work in Italy ended completely. Unification of Italy occurred in 1861, which caused political, cultural, and economic instability. This, along with opposition from the Roman Catholic Church, prevented LDS missionaries from returning. Then came two World Wars and the Great Depression between them. Benito Mussolini came to power in Italy in 1922, setting himself up as a fascist dictator. He established the Lateran Accords of 1939. One of the edicts contained therein reconfirmed Roman Catholicism as the official religion of the State. This edict curtailed non-Catholic religions. After World War II, restrictions began to loosen, and in the mid-1960s, sporadic missionary work in Italy became more structured as the Italian Mission was made a zone of the Swiss Mission with more than forty elders and two sister missionaries working in twenty Italian cities. Their success prompted a reopening of the Italian Mission on August 2, 1966. On November 10, 1966, Elder Ezra Taft Benson held a dedicatory prayer service in Torre Pellice and rededicated the land of Italy for the preaching of the gospel. The small gathering of Church officials and missionaries stood on Mount Brigham near the spot where Lorenzo Snow had stood 116 years earlier. By December of 1966, there were 116 missionaries working in thirty-five cities. Over the years, many of the descendants of the original Waldensian Saints (often unaware of their Waldensian ancestry) have been called to serve missions to Italy.

In 1967, there were sixty-six members of the Church in Italy. At the end of 2016, the Church's official records showed Church membership at 26,550, with two missions, ten stakes, and 101 congregations.

The Church of Jesus Christ of Latter-day Saints was officially recognized as a religion by the Italian government July 30, 2012.

During the October 2008 general conference, President Thomas S. Monson announced that a temple would be built in Rome, Italy. Ground was broken October 23, 2010.

Acknowledgments

Thanks go out to the many individuals who shared family research concerning their Waldensian ancestors along with family histories and stories. Allyson Clayton for information on the Malan family; Craig Cardon for information on the Cardon family; and Sue Hall for information on the Beus family. A warm thank you to Becky Cardon Smith for including us in the 2014 Cardon family reunion trip to Piedmont, Italy. To walk those valley trails and wander the fields around the Cardon Borgata was bliss. Gratitude to Jana Erickson for encouraging me at every step, and to the stellar team at Deseret Book for their proficiency.

Un ringraziamento sincero to Daniele and Norma Salerno for their friendship and their masterful translation of this work into Italian.

Grazie mille!

BIBLIOGRAPHY

ARTICLES AND WEBSITES

Burrup, Jay G., comp. "First Missionaries to Italy. Excerpts from Letters written by Elders Lorenzo Snow & Jabez Woodard." *Italy Milan Mission Online*; available at www.mission.net.

Christianson, James R. "Early Missionary Work in Italy and Switzerland." *Ensign*, August 1982, 35–46.

Crockett, David R. "History of the Church in Italy." Bella Sion > General History; available at www.bellasion.org.

"History of Italy." Available at www.historyworld.net.

"History of Torre Pellice." Available at www.torrepellice.com.

"John Charles Beckwith." Available at www.whoislog.info and www.find-a -book.com.

"Pope Francis asks Waldensian Christians to forgive the Church," *Catholic Herald*, 22 June 2015; available at http://www.catholicherald.co.uk /news/2015/06/22/pope-francis-asks-waldensian-christians-to-forgive -the-church/; accessed 21 August 2017.

"Waldensian History." Available at www.chiesavaldese.org.

"Waldenses Way of Life." Available at www.wayoflife.org.database/waldenses .htm.

BOOKS

Anderson, Vicki Jo. *The Other Eminent Men of Wilford Woodruff*. Malta, ID: Nelson Book, 2000.

Beus, H. Lynn, with Charlotte Gunnell. *Whence & Whither: Origins and Descendants of Michael and Marianne Beus*. N.p., 1984.

Derr, Jill Mulvay, and Karen Lynn Davidson, compilers and editors. *Eliza R.*

Snow: The Complete Poetry. Provo, UT: Brigham Young University Press and Salt Lake City: University of Utah Press, 2015.

Gibbons, Francis M. *Lorenzo Snow: Spiritual Giant, Prophet of God.* Salt Lake City: Deseret Book, 1982.

Museum of Waldensian Women Guide. Torre Pellice, Italy: Centro Culturale Valdese, 2002.

Museums and Sites of Memory of the Waldensian Valleys. Torre Pellice, Italy: Centro Culturale Valdese, 2002.

Nibley, Preston. *The Presidents of the Church.* Salt Lake City: Deseret Book, 1941.

Smith, Eliza R. Snow. *Biography and Family Record of Lorenzo Snow.* Salt Lake City: Deseret News, 1884.

Snow, Lorenzo. *The Italian Mission.* London: W. Aubrey, 1851.

Toronto, James A., Eric R. Dursteler, and Michael W. Homer. *Mormons in the Piazza: History of the Latter-day Saints in Italy.* Provo, UT: Brigham Young University Press and Salt Lake City: Deseret Book, 2017.

Tourn, Giorgio. *The Waldensian Valleys.* Torino, Italy: Claudiana, 2005.

Waldensian Museum Guide, Torre Pellice. Torre Pellice, Italy: Centro Culturale Valdese, 2002.

FAMILY HISTORIES

Farley, Madeline Malan. "Autobiographical Sketch of Madeline Malan Farley." Typescript. LDS Church History Library, Salt Lake City.

Knighton, James Barker, Lisa Knighton Delap, and J. Malan Heslop, comps. *Malan Book of Remembrance, Vol. 1, no. 2.* Typescript. LDS Church History Library, Salt Lake City.

Malan, Alan P. "John Daniel Malan: Conversion," *The Malan Monitor* (A publication of the John Daniel Malan Family Organization): Summer 1991.

Malan, Stephen. *Autobiography and Family History.* Unpublished. LDS Church History Library, Salt Lake City.

Tippets, Susan Thomas, comp. *An Autobiography of Marie Madeline-Cardon Guild.* LDS Church History Library, Salt Lake City.

Toronto Family Organization, The. *Joseph Toronto (Giuseppe Efisio Taranto).* Compiled in commemoration of Joseph's 167th birthday, June 25, 1983. Alan F. Toronto, chairman; Maria T. Moody, genealogist; James A. Toronto, historian.